THE
LAY
OF
STARSTONE
TOWER

NOBILITAS OFFICIUM
FIDES AETERNA

THE Lay OF STARSTONE TOWER

The Glory Road

Book Two

CASEY COOPER

Publishing Services provided by Paper Raven Books LLC
Printed in the United States of America

First Printing, 2025

ISBN (Paperback) 978-1-966512-03-5
ISBN (Hardback) 978-1-966512-04-2

Dedicated to:

Rachel Aaron

and

David Brin

Whose work in Fantasy and Science Fiction
helped keep my dreams alive.

CONTENTS

Part One

Artos at the Crystal Tower

N
WHERE THE EAGLES LEFT THEM
LAKE OF THE SETTING SUN
SWAN'S NEST X
RAINBOW VALLEY
TOWER OF THE MAGIC MAN X
TO THE KINGS VALLEY
ALFHIEM X
FIVE MILES
MAP BY INKARNATE

CHAPTER ONE:

ARTOS ALONE

1

HUNTER HORNETS

ARTOS

9/22/1971 ar

5:00 p.m.

Artos looked around the clearing, an uneasy feeling in his gut. Just moments ago, the air had been alive with the normal bird calls and the rustling of the wind blowing through the autumn foliage. Now, a brooding silence had descended on the forest. The wind still stirred the reddish-brown leaves of the oak trees that surrounded the clearing, but the birds had fallen silent.

He took a deep breath and forced himself to relax. He closed his eyes and turned to his inner sight, probing the forest in front of him for anything out of place, anything out of the ordinary.

There! Ahead, still a short distance away, was the distinct feeling of anger. Something was hunting, and the malice he detected brought a shiver to his spine.

Summoning his crysword into his right hand, he felt the familiar weight and grip, offering him a sense of comfort. Standing in the center of the clearing, he felt vulnerable and quickly scanned his surroundings for a strategic spot to defend himself.

The old forest trees were all huge, some of the trunks being over eight feet in diameter. The scrub between the trees was taller than Artos, making visibility more than a few yards outside the clearing all but impossible.

Artos backed up into a space between two of the smaller giants and continued to scan the surrounding woods, keeping his inner focus on the things hunting him. They weren't men. He was sure of that. *Not dogs either,* he thought to himself. The emotions felt alien, unfamiliar, unlike anything he had ever encountered before.

Using the mental probing techniques Donel had taught him, he tried to determine how many enemies he faced. He didn't have much range. He knew they had to be within a couple dozen yards for him to detect them at all. There were three of them, not too distant, probably almost to the far edge of the clearing, and there was another group, also of three, further away. That was all he could locate, but that was enough—too much really. How could he defeat three foes at once, much less double that amount?

He needed a plan! Suddenly, he could hear a humming noise from across the clearing. No, not a humming, a buzzing like the sound of a disturbed bee's nest.

Bursting from the brush on the opposite side of the clearing came three black-and-gold hornets, each at least eight inches long. Buzzing belligerently, the formation came to a halt, hovering in midair and slowly turned, the three creatures moving in perfect unison, surveying the empty clearing.

Artos froze, hoping the creatures would fail to notice his motionless form, but to no avail. The creatures stopped turning, their formation aimed at where he stood between the two oak trunks. Then, with the angry buzzing increasing, they shot forward directly at him.

Artos instantly realized his mistake. By positioning himself between the two trees, he had protected his left side, but had very little room to maneuver his crysword. He swung the sword up before him defensively as the hunter hornets streaked to attack.

The three hornets crossed the small clearing in a matter of seconds. The lead hunter twisted its body as it approached, so its stinger aimed directly at his face.

Artos swung his crysword in a short stroke and felt the razor-sharp blade cleave the nasty thing in twain. He felt a burst of triumph, but his joy was short-lived as the remaining hornets, following close behind the leader, each scored a direct hit to his exposed sword arm.

The pain was excruciating, and the sword flew from his hand as he lost all feeling in his fingers. The two remaining hornets pulled away from his arm and hovered before him. Without thinking, he summoned the sword back into the grasp of his left hand and made a desperate swing at the creatures.

His uncle Bretton had made all the brothers spend countless hours using their swords with either of their hands, and the practice served Artos in this moment of need. The crysword sliced through each of the two monsters in one smooth stroke.

Where are the others? he thought to himself as he looked wildly around the small clearing. *I need to move away from this clearing so they can't come at me so quickly.* He moved to his left, walking around the clearing in the general direction he knew the other hunters had been moments before.

Artos held his crysword at the ready as he slipped from behind one tree trunk to another, the pain in his right arm making him break out in a cold sweat. Leaning against the rough oak bark, he listened for the faint buzzing of the flying hunters he knew were seeking him. He should use his mind to pinpoint them, he knew, but he needed a few moments' rest before he could concentrate.

He took a moment to thank his deceased uncle. If not for Duke Bretton's relentless training, he wouldn't have been able to summon his sword instantly to his other hand. He would never have struck down the remaining hunters. They would have each scored another sting.

Then he heard the buzzing sound again. It came from somewhere before him. His right hand was numb, but shooting pains flooded his right arm from his wrist to shoulder as he pushed himself upright again. He bore two large, red welts from their stings now and knew he couldn't take another.

The buzzing sounds grew louder. They must be almost upon him! There were only three of them left. The buzzing sound stopped, and a faint scraping sound alerted him. The hunters had landed on the tree, crawling around the trunk to attack! He opened his thoughts to pinpoint their locations. One was coming from the right and another from the left. Where was the third?

He stepped to the left, choosing to attack the one on his sword side while frantically probing to locate the last hunter. The six-inch-long black and gold striped body of the hunter hornet appeared. Artos sliced it cleanly in two, then quickly took a step back and waited for the second to appear. Before it came into view, something landed on his shoulder, and Donel's voice sounded in his ear.

"That's three, Art. You lose."

There was the third hornet, perched on his left shoulder.

"It's dinnertime, so I took pity on you. But I could have

stung. Denar would have never spared me the third sting."

The trees faded away, replaced by the training chamber wall-screens glowing with their faint blue light. The bodies of the dead hunters melted away just as they had after the first exercises.

"But then, my master would never have gone from beginning exercises directly to an advanced one, either. You did very well, considering." The hunter on his shoulder vanished.

Artos chuckled ruefully. "I think you cheated, Donel. The last hunter wasn't buzzing."

As the screens went inert, Donel emerged from the control room. He walked up to Art and began applying almas to the welts on his right arm. The pain and swelling quickly dissipated.

"I set only four of the six to buzz on that exercise, Art. The second one you hit, the first to sting you, hadn't buzzed. You must be more aware of your surroundings. I felt your probe, but you only probed before you, where you heard the buzzing. The direction you expected them to attack from. An enemy will seldom be so polite as to inform you of their location. How does that feel now?"

Artos flexed his arm. "Better, thanks. I'll be ready for another round after dinner."

"That's the spirit. I'll take it a little easier on you next time. I'll try a more intermediate setting. I really should have used it for the last match, but you did so well with the first two, I wanted to make it a challenge."

"I think you succeeded."

*

With only the two of them at the large table, Artos thought he had never felt so alone as he did now. "How long do you think it will take Bort and Angel to persuade the West Wind to give us a guide, Donel?"

"I really don't know … not long, I would think. Bort and whoever Andune should choose to send should be back here within a few days. It may be longer—four or five, perhaps. However, from the tone of Andune's letter, he may not allow Angel to return. I expect he may send Bort back with the guide and no one else. Andune knows where the Crystal Tower stands. He sent people here once or twice when Angel was being taught."

"But he has to let Angel go. She leads the daughters."

Donel just shook his head, took a bite of his venison steak, chewed, and swallowed before answering. "The giant Raven watching the Rainbow Valley will give Andune pause. He is not without skill with the quanti. He may have sensed the Abomination. When we met, when he was deciding if I would be the proper teacher for Angel, he told me he believed one of them may have murdered Stephanie, her mother. He may decide that he wants his daughter where he can see she is in no danger."

"But what about the Daughters? Angel told me he was using them to watch that part of the valley."

"I do not know Andune's mind, Art. He may tell them all to go home now and post his own men to watch the western part of Rainbow Valley. The raven has changed the situation."

"That would be terrible. Do they even have homes anymore?"

At that moment, Liv entered the commons and sat down a few feet from the table. Sitting as she was, her head was at the same height as the two diners. Artos was amused to see that she turned her head and watched whoever was speaking, just as if she was following the conversation, which, as he considered, she probably was. For although she was a Mist Cat, she was a very intelligent being.

"The human families that farmed the Valley now reside in a remote dale to the north, in a tiny village called Cedars. I think it's pretty crowded. Only seven or eight families dwelt there originally. Now there are more than double. It may even have been a reason Andune assigned the daughters to keep watch from the Nest—fewer mouths to strain the resources at Cedars. Angel told me the valley folk all hoped to return and start their farms again next spring. With that raven patrolling, I don't see that happening. I think it depends on you now."

Donel smiled at Liv and tossed her a bite of his steak, which she caught neatly and swallowed.

"On me? What do you mean?"

"The Abominations want to find you and your brothers. You, above all else, you are the symbol of everything they wish to destroy. That harpy that wounded you was likely being mind-controlled by Anndr, the Raven's master. The legends say he is the most adept at regalos of the mind. He is most certainly seeking you. The raptor saw four likely subjects, and Tirinvo told him he sent you away to safety. They know I am here, and Andune is in Alfhiem. Two havens where you might hide. Both places have shields to cloak you and your brothers. They will divide their attention between us until they find you. It is fortunate he does not have any of your minds patterned."

"What do you mean?"

"To someone who is skilled, every mind has a distinct pattern. All three of you have powerful auras. The auras of House deDraconis. I knew you were Dragonbloods as soon as you entered."

"That means Bort and Cari are in danger! How could you send them out with that thing flying around above the Valley?"

"To detect your auras, he would need to be much closer. A few yards away, at least. If he had your patterns, he might find you from further away. Not miles and miles, but within a few hundred yards, perhaps. He is looking for you, there is no doubt, and if he thinks he sees you, then he will come closer to detect your aura. Both Bort and Cari will stay on the forest trails. I discussed this with Angel and Joy. They won't allow your brothers to be exposed to his sight. The sooner Cari is removed from the Valley, the safer he should be. Bort will be safe in Alfhiem. Liv knows the scent of them, and she has not detected it near the Crystal Tower for several years. She and her brood are watching over us. I think the Raven and its rider will keep watching the Valley until you give it a reason to go elsewhere."

Artos looked at the Mist Cat again and she gazed back at him solemnly and he felt she was agreeing with Donel's words.

"But we are going through the mountains to keep the Abominations from detecting us. From following us."

"When you return to Castle Draconis, they will converge on you. I think Tomung will try to unite them all again. We know that at least two of them were involved in freeing him from your trophy wall. I think when you strike at the Abomination, who we know was at Castle Draconis, the one who will have freed

Tomung, then the rest will converge there as well. Tomung will summon them, I think."

"How long will it take Tomung to be whole once more?"

"I do not know, but it will take some time. This is another reason you must act with haste."

"What more do you know of these creatures and their regalos, Donel?"

"Very little, I'm afraid. Just the myths and legends. As I have said, Tomung is the leader. Legend states his lieutenant is named Mohattri. That one is cloaked in mystery. The legends say nothing more. Anndr has mind regalos and the reputation of being a master craftsman. He is most likely the source of the black crystal. Creating crystal is a feat that no one besides the crystal-masters of Fairinhorst, the disciples of Angellar, are known to possess. He is the most adept at mind control, which makes him undoubtedly the most dangerous. Of the other two, Babich and Kargyn," Donel shrugged, "the tales say they are little more than ravening beasts, totally enslaved to the will of Tomung. For three hundred years, they have been free of his direct control. Who knows how things will stand once he is whole again? But they are all masters of deceit and users of illusion. Creatures dark of heart, totally evil and, of course, shapeshifters."

"You could see Duke's crysword at the castle. Can you see Bort's and Cari's too?"

Donel gazed at Art for a moment and then nodded. "Of course. You are missing them, aren't you?"

Artos shrugged. "I've always had them around. At home, we'd always be together for meals and most of our classes. Occasionally, one or another would be away. Bort was gone with Uncle Brett a lot, sometimes for weeks. Duka and I spent some time at House deDarrellyel last year, but now there's only me and you, and I just feel empty, like something is missing." Artos realized how that sounded and glanced up at Donel. "I don't mean that you aren't good company …"

"I understand, Art," said Donel. "The Glory Road can be very lonely. I had three brothers, too. They are all long gone now, of course. Allison was the king. He was your great-great-great-grandfather. My other brothers were Baeddan and Caerwyn. I missed them all when they finished their classes at Starstone Tower. We all went there together at first, but only Caerwyn and I stayed there after the first term. Later, when Caer went home, I was lonely, but Denar was there, and other students were coming and going. Daimion deDraconis was still alive then and the keeper of this tower. His brother Charales was alive then, too. He was the Loremaster of deDraconis and Caer's teacher after he left Starstone. They were both quite old. But you don't wish to hear ancient history. You want me to go find Bort and Cari on the screens so you can see them and reassure yourself they're safe. We'll do that after dinner."

"I don't mean to seem childish, Donel. It would be nice to see them, though. I am the eldest, and for all Bort saying we are his duty to protect …"

"I understand. It is the king's duty to watch over all his own. And Bort and Cari are your brothers." Donel sighed. "I wish I could show you, Duka. I hope the Angellar has good news for Cari."

Chapter Two:

The Blue Flame

2

THE FLAME
REVEALED

ARTOS

7:00 p.m.

AFTER DINNER, they went to the upper level of the tower. Using the large screen, Donel located Carimus, who was helping Susi wash the dinner dishes at the Swan's Nest. Next, they located Bortis, striding in the dim twilight of evening across a huge lily pad and some colored rocks as he went under the boughs of an enormous thousand-year oak tree. As Artos watched, a Fairborn woman he didn't know wrapped a cloth over Bort's eyes and bound it in a knot at the back of his head. Angel and Kae then led him away, and the picture went blank.

"They made good time. It is over fifty miles from the spires to Alfhiem. Angel must have set a hard pace. We found Bort just in time," said Donel. "A few minutes later and I wouldn't have been able to scry him. Andune's home is safe from prying eyes and minds."

"Alfhiem is beneath that tree somewhere?"

"I assume so. I never traveled there. Since Duke Bretton

never located Andune's stronghold, it must be well hidden. Tirinvo told me that Andune has well over one hundred people living there. Many Fairborn felt Farnir should not have removed Andune from the succession. Some followed him from Fairinlan.

"Of course, many more thought the king did the correct thing, and some thought he didn't go far enough. When Andune married Stephanie, some among the Fairborn thought Farnir should have totally disowned his firstborn, not merely remove him from the succession. Many Fairborn have a deep dislike of our people. Tirinvo will try to change that when he is king, but I'm afraid too many of our people feel the same way about the Fairborn. It is a sad thing when two free people cannot respect each other for who they are." Donel sighed. "But enough. The world will go as it will, not as we will it. I have something else to show you. Where you must go in Starstone Tower."

At that moment, a chime rang out, different from any Artos had heard before. Donel looked dumbfounded and leaned back in surprise. Artos looked all around to see if any of the screens had activated. On the screen where the prophecy had appeared before, there were now large words: NOT YET. COME TO ME. BOTH OF YOU.

"Are you sure?" Donel spoke softly into the air. "This is not Duka."

Some words faded away, but the COME TO ME remained.

Donel took a deep breath and gazed at Artos appraisingly, and then slowly nodded.

"Who is writing those words? Who are you speaking to?"

"It is the heart of the tower itself—The Blue Flame."

"The Blue Flame? Who is that?" Artos looked at Donel.

Donel arose and began walking out of the room. "I really

can't explain. I don't understand exactly myself. Denar didn't know when I asked him to explain it to me. Perhaps no keeper here has ever known. Come with me."

What is going on? Artos thought to himself as he followed.

On leaving the screen room, Donel turned to his right and faced the blank place in the wall. But this time, Donel didn't reach out and touch anything. He simply waited. With a slight tremor, a section of the wall slid up into the ceiling, revealing an empty hall running to the west, ten feet wide and twenty feet long. Donel glanced at Artos, then walked across the room and stopped before the wall at the other end. As Artos walked along with him, he felt the tremor repeat. He looked back. The door had returned to its original position.

"I wondered if there was another room here."

Donel nodded as they stood waiting. "Except for here and my cellars, I believe you have now been everywhere in the tower. Since Denar's death, no one has been in these rooms besides me." After a moment, the wall in front of them slid up into the ceiling. The new room opened up to the south, totally empty except for a round, gray dais a few inches tall in the center of the room. There were no screens, and except for a large mirror on the eastern side, the walls were just the bare blue crystal of the tower. The mirror was twenty feet wide and ran from the floor to the ceiling. The dais stood before the mirror, matching its width. The room was dimly lit with a soft glow coming from everywhere and yet nowhere at all. Neither he nor Donel cast a shadow, yet the room was far from dark. *Now what?* thought Artos, *there's nothing here.*

The door slid shut behind him as they walked up to the dais. Faint markings appeared on the top surface. A five-pointed star with a circle in the center was all he could make out.

Donel stepped up on the dais, walked to the center of the circle, and faced the mirror. When he did, the pattern on the floor glowed. Between each point of the star was another smaller circle, and within each circle was a design, a twisted star. The center circle where Donel stood held a larger copy of the same device.

"Stand in one of the circles, Art." Donel pointed to the smaller one, to the left of where he was standing.

As soon as Artos stepped into the smaller circle, there was a loud crackling sound, and bolts of lightning flickered into being, completely covering the front of the mirror with a multitude of horizontal bands.

"What is this?" Artos asked, flinching back from the sudden crackling bolts of lightning that swept across the surface of the huge mirror, not more than six feet from where he stood. He felt the hair on his arms bristle with the static charge.

"I'm not sure it has a name. Denar called it the inner circle. I always thought that more of a description than an actual name. This is where the keeper of the Tower and the Blue Flame meet. Relax and wait. I do not know why we were summoned here. The Flame will address us when it is ready and not sooner. I am surprised. Denar had instructed me to never reveal the Flame's existence to anyone except my successor. I expected to show this to Duka, no one else."

Artos felt uneasy as he stood watching and waiting. Being this close to so much energy was unnerving, yet Donel stood unflinching, gazing at the mirror with no alarm. After a few moments, the lightning faded away, and the surface of the mirror changed. What was a mirror became a transparent window looking into another space beyond. It was another room with barren crystal walls, dominated by a pillar of blue flame—a pillar at least ten feet across, which ran from the blue crystal floor to the ceiling—a throbbing, flickering column of cold blue fire surrounded by an array of white lightning that flickered all around. There was no apparent source of fuel for either the flame or the lightning. Both flowed from floor to ceiling, leaving no sign of burning or even scorch marks. The window changed back into a mirror, and Artos stood looking at their reflections.

Then, before he could question Donel, the surface became foggy. Their images faded and were replaced by a familiar scene. It appeared to be the Hall of Mirrors in Castle Draconis, looking from the rear of the room as if from the room's doorway, across from the screens. A person was seated at the oaken table in the room's center with their back to them. Two of the House screens were active, that of House deAnson and House deHerndar. Each House screen had someone pictured, but the features of the persons were obscured. Both had hoods drawn over their heads, and their faces were hidden in the shadows. There was no clue who was at Castle Draconis, either. The figure appeared to be small and slightly built, wearing neutral gray clothing.

The scene faded away, and the mirror returned. The door slid open. With a crackling sound, the lightning bolts reappeared before the mirror like horizontal bars.

Donel turned and stepped out of the central circle, and the lightning faded away as quickly as it had appeared. "It seems we are finished here, Art."

"But … but what was that? What did it mean? Let's go back to your screens and listen in to what they are doing!" Artos stepped off the dais and hurried toward the entrance room.

"What did you see?" Donel followed behind him.

"The Hall of Mirrors! The people there … three of them, I

mean, one person there and two more on the screens! Didn't you see it?"

"No, I saw something very different, Art. The Crystal Mirror is not like other screens. We can check, but I doubt we will see anything. The mirror was probably showing you something that has already happened or possibly might happen, although I suspect it was a scene that has already occurred."

They reentered Donel's screen room, and Donel sat down and studied the gems on the tables flanking the chair. "There is no ongoing communication from Castle Draconis, nor anywhere else that I can detect."

"But what did it mean? Who was using the screens? Who were those people?"

"Indeed, those are the questions. I wish I knew the answers. But I know this—the Flame wanted you to see it. Now please tell me exactly what you saw. Were the people you saw moving and talking? Arguing perhaps?"

"No, nothing like that at all. In fact, it was more like a picture, I guess," Artos shrugged. "No one was moving or anything."

"Which screens had people? Which Houses?"

"It was House deAnson and House deHerndar. Of that, I am sure." Artos described the vision in more detail.

Donel looked grave. "We suspected that both those Houses are up to no good. I think the Flame was showing you it is true. They may be involved in treason, but the problem we now have is whether it is the entirety of both Houses, or just one or two people within them. It will need to be proven beyond any doubt. If you were to call out an entire House for treason before the Great Council and you have no proof, the more conservative will believe you are not ready to rule without guidance, and a second House would only make it worse."

"But House deYung rebelled, and they were destroyed!" protested Artos.

"It was different. Count Thomas Yung led a revolt against all the other Houses and was revealed as being the Abomination, Tomung. This hides in the shadows at deAnson and deHerndar. But if you lay a charge of treason against the two Houses, it might split the entire Great Council and plunge all of Veda into a civil war. If you have proof that someone in those Houses is plotting treason, the rest of the Council will join with you against them, along with any within those Houses who may still be loyal to Veda, and remove the rotten apples."

"But what if it is the entire Family? Both Families? What then?" Donel shook his head and looked grave.

"I think, Art, we must hope some in each House are still loyal, or at least …" he trailed off.

"At least what?" Artos clenched his fists in frustration.

"I hate to even consider it. But evil people are seldom loyal, to each other or to supposed allies, and if you were to prove, say, that Count Anson was plotting treason, then his son or nephew might declare with you in order to secure their place as head of the Family, throw the Count to the wolves, and take his place."

"That would be better than a civil war, but I see the problem. It wouldn't solve the issue, only postpone it. I guess." Artos sighed and shook his head.

"The way things stand now, each House swears their loyalty to Veda, to King and Crown. But there is no means to be sure what is in their hearts. I'm not sure there is any easy solution to this. You are going to have to consider this after they crown you with the Dragon Crown and you sit upon the Dragon Throne. I am sure your father was very uneasy, considering the manner of his ascension. Your grandfather's hunting accident, his early death, were disturbing, to say the least."

Artos thought for a moment. "We could ask every Count to take the loyalty test at Castle Draconis."

"I fear you would not find many on the Great Council willing to accept that. I know it would offend the pride of more than one of the Counts. Those who are loyal would feel slighted by your lack of trust. Those who feel some doubts as to your ability to rule would probably fail the test, even if they were not disloyal. Would you ask your grandfather to prove himself? And if you excused him, who would you enrage by asking them to accept being tested?"

"I suppose you are right, but what can I do?"

"I fear you are not the first, nor will you be the last to have that worry. But our House has ruled Veda for nearly two thousand years, and it has not failed yet. I will teach you the spell to force a person to speak only what they believe to be truth, but it requires you actually being able to touch them to deliver."

Artos nodded. "Donel, what is that … that thing … that blue fire beyond the mirror?"

Surprise apparent on his face, Donel turned to look at Artos. "You saw the Blue Flame?"

"Yes." Artos explained the vision. "You didn't see the fire?"

"No, I have, but today I saw a scene from my past, long ago, a time before I was the Keeper of the Keys. Apparently, the flame felt there was some reason to show itself to you. Perhaps it relates to the prophecy. I don't know. But you asked about the Flame. I only know what Denar told me as was passed down from each keeper here to his successor. The Blue Flame is the heart, mind, and spirit of the tower and comes from a time long lost in the past. I believe it is something held over from the First Age of Man. I have questioned it concerning its origins, but it has never chosen to give me a reply. I know it can show many things from the past, if it chooses to. It often chooses not to answer at all or to give answers that seem to bear no relation to the question asked. It does not have to bring you before the Mirror to impart information. In fact, it usually does not. I have had far more interaction with the flame sitting right here, or in my dreams, than standing before the Mirror. That was why I was so surprised it summoned you, though I suppose you find it much harder to dismiss when shown in this manner."

"My dreams? That is not something that makes me feel comfortable. If it can enter my dreams, what else can it do?" Artos looked at Donel, feeling uncomfortable.

"Here within the Crystal Tower, I suspect it could do a great deal, and yet, perhaps very little at all."

"What do you mean? You talk in riddles."

"What is real, Art? You depend upon your senses to tell you, and yet in the training room today you stood in a forest, did you not?"

"A projection. If I had been using my mind-shield, there would have been no forest."

"Remember, Art, what I told you. An illusion can kill you. The hunter hornets did not really exist, but the stings they gave you were real. Were they not? Remember, the stings did not fade away with the rest of the illusion. You believed you were stung, and thus the welts were real."

"Yes … but …"

"Remember what Veryan told us in his story about that poor guardsman?"

"Yes, he threw himself off the battlements."

"No. I meant the other guard. One fell to his death, but the other, the one Varyan carried back inside. He was dead, too. The Abomination filled his mind with so much terror that his heart burst. But that is not my point. Art, we live in the world that our senses tell us surrounds us, but we use quanti-magic to control many things. Have you ever seen a quanti?"

Artos shook his head.

"Nor have I, but I know the quanti exist. I use the magic every day. As do you. Does a blind man know color? Can a deaf man know the joy of music?"

"You still speak in riddles. I don't understand what you are trying to tell me."

"When you are cloaked within your mind-shield, you are protected from projections, free from mind speech, and beyond the reach of the Flame to reach into your mind. So if you are within your shield, you are cut off from the Flame."

Donel held his hands before him, steepled his fingers, and sat staring at them.

"When you arrived, you told me of waking up on Duka's birthday morning from a nightmare."

"Yes." Artos nodded. "Duke and I both had bad dreams that night, but what does that have to do with anything?"

"I didn't tell you then, Art, but I too awoke that morning from a nightmare. A dream of death, doom, and destruction."

"I think our dreams were a warning," said Artos. "A foreshadowing of what was to come that night. But I had other things to think about. It was Duke's birthday, and I forgot about it very soon."

"I think the Blue Flame wanted us to share that dream."

"But ... we were at Castle Draconis, and that's miles and miles away."

"It's less than sixty miles in a straight line through the stone of the mountains. Double that, or more by the roads, but the quanti aren't affected by distance or troubled by obstruction. They taught you that you can never be separated from your crysword, did they not? You can summon it to your hand, no matter how far away."

"Well, yes … But isn't that different? I'm attuned to my sword. I had never met you, never even dreamed you were still alive." Artos felt puzzled. His uncle's training had never even hinted of such things.

"We are of the same blood. That is an attunement of sorts. The realm of the quanti does not follow the same natural laws as the world in which we live. They are connected in ways we cannot conceive. We have lost so much knowledge through the ages. The masters at Starstone Tower didn't begin recording lessons until about eight hundred years ago. I think some of them were worried that even then we were losing some of the abilities which had been commonplace in earlier days. I showed you some of the recordings I have found of the earliest days; there may be more that the Blue Flame has not revealed to me. If there are more recordings of those things, then we have lost the means to access them except what the Flame chooses to reveal. I suspect the Blue Flame hides things from me it believes I do not need to know. I have asked many questions throughout the years I have been Keymaster. Some knowledge is freely shared, and some is not."

"How? I mean, do you just go stand in front of that mirror and ask?"

"I have done that, or I have just trained my thoughts at the Flame sitting here, or anywhere within the tower." Donel made a rueful chuckle. "Sometimes I ask a question, and an answer comes to me within a dream that night. Or the night after. Or a month later, or a year … or never. Sometimes it sends me dreams of things I didn't ask, at least not knowingly. I had some other dreams in the weeks leading up to that day. Nicer dreams. I dreamed your father sent you and your brothers to be taught the ways of the quanti. All four of you."

"But Father didn't send us, at least not directly, and all four of us didn't come. Duke is lost. He might be … he could be …" Artos faltered to a stop and took a deep breath.

"No, Art, I think Cari is right. He would know if Duka was dead. You would know as well, I think. But, as of now, he is lost to us, though I hope the Angellar can help Cari."

Artos furrowed his brow and tilted his head. "I guess I don't understand. Were the dreams foreseeing? Isn't to foresee glimpsing the future?"

Donel shrugged, then sighed again. "I sometimes think I understand very little about the quanti, Art. The Angellar is the greatest seer known. She was going to give me lessons, but with Denar's death, we never began. Apparently, she did not foresee that event. I know the past has already happened and does not change. If I ask, the Blue Flame will sometimes show me scenes from the past, but not always. Sometimes the visions of the past I have asked to see are not those the Flame shows me. I cannot explain why. But with the realm of the quanti, when we foresee, we only see that which might be. Something as small as stubbing your toe in the morning could cause a very different future than one you foresaw earlier."

"So you are telling me I should not trust a foreseeing?"

Donel shook his head. "I am not telling you to disbelieve it, merely not to have total faith it will occur as you expect. Remember to question and verify as much as you can.

Sometimes you will have to trust your instincts. The Glory Road is not an easy road to walk, but when fate sets your feet upon that path, you can only strive to do your best. That is all anyone can do."

"I have been meaning to show you Starstone. I was preparing to do so when the Flame interrupted me. If I can, that is. There has been something peculiar happening with my scrying there."

"What do you mean?" Artos thought he saw a shadow of worry flicker across Donel's face.

"I have been meaning to do this for the last few days, but until today there has been some problem, and I wasn't sure why. I need to show you where you have to go within Starstone Tower, but I was unable to scry within. I'm not sure what caused the problem, but when I attempted earlier today, they seem to have disappeared. The tower is ancient, one of the first redoubts built during the Quantum Wars. Its defenses may have been triggered. Perhaps a wandering hunter attempted to enter. Someone with no regalos."

"How would that make a difference?"

"The qulan field surrounding the tower is not the same as the one at Castle Draconis or the one here. The doors can only be opened by someone with at least a regalo of minor strength, although once the doors are opened, anyone can enter the building. There are places in Starstone which are quanti-locked, and you cannot scry within those areas, but over the last few days, the entire tower was blocked. That shouldn't have been, but it was open this morning. There are places which have fields which bar all but certain bloodlines, though the majority of the tower was open to all students, even those who were not of the Noble Houses."

"Until of late, I haven't had cause to view the school in years ... decades or longer. It has been abandoned for so long, and it only made me sad to look at places that I remember bustling with students and activity. Maybe bustling is too strong a word, but when I was a student there, and later when I taught, there were always people moving about, and now ..." Donel sighed. "Now it is an empty shell. It makes me feel sad to look within."

"We will change that," promised Artos. "I will reopen the school there, and we will have classes there once again."

"It is a lovely thought, Art. But who will be the teachers? The priests who train quanti used in the Sky Church schools are not inclined to teach anything different from what they have been taught, and they know so little. I'm sure the druids would be willing to help, but again, their teachings are not what the school was designed to teach."

"But you have said there are recorded lessons—wouldn't those help?"

"Perhaps, but how many people do you think will be willing to learn from a disembodied voice that couldn't answer questions? Someone has to know enough to explain when someone doesn't understand. Tell me, Art. How much of what you have learned could you teach someone else? Say Duka came here tomorrow, and I was unable to teach him?"

"Not much, I guess. Probably nothing at all. I'm not sure I would know the right words to say, even though you have spoken them to me."

"And I have but given you a thimbleful of what I plan to teach you after you have reclaimed your throne. And I must confess—it will not be easy, for without a successor I cannot teach you anywhere except here. You will find, once you are king, you will not have much free time to spend here away from your duties. I had always pictured having enough time to train Duka along with the rest of you. I did not foresee the untimely death of King Aaron. My visions were of a different future. One that would have allowed me to begin your training here, and then when Duka was ready to spell me to spend some time with you, perhaps at Starstone Tower, Castle Draconis, or even at the palace at Phoenix."

"I still don't understand foreseeing at all. How could you be right about a few things but so wrong about others?"

"The teachers at Fairinhorst were just beginning my lessons on foreseeing when I was called back here. If I had spent more time there than the few months I had, perhaps I would have had a better grasp on how to find the right vision of the future among the myriad visions that exist. I think the Blue Flame has tried to guide my dreams, but I feel perhaps I saw the future I wanted to see, rather than what was the most likely to happen. I know Kae spent three years there, and she left after what many Fairborn would consider a very brief time."

"So Cari will be there for years? You should have told me ... I don't think I would have agreed to that."

"I do not think she would expect him to stay overly long. I doubt I would have spent an entire year there, although I really do not know. Few humans have spent time there at all. I know some of House deSpryngdal have received training there. Denar didn't, nor Daimion before him, I think ... although I do not really know. I only met my great-uncle occasionally and never for extended times. I was summoned by Varyan, the bard, who said the Angellar directed him to bring me before her."

"Oh, funny, I had pictured you were summoned like Cari was. Words appearing on a screen."

"No, I was at Castle Draconis for the Summer Solstice ceremony when Varyan and Prince Meldien came to visit King Alexavier. Varyan took me aside, delivered the invitation, and presented me with my rune bracelet. I was eager to go, but Denar did not want to lose his successor for any amount of time. Daimion had died the winter before, and being Warden was chafing on him. His true love was Starstone Tower and teaching there. He and Lord Daimion differed there. Daimion had enjoyed life as the keeper here. Denar found it stifling. He really didn't wish to put me in charge of the school for the few decades he was forced to remain here. I think perhaps he was afraid I might learn more from the Angellar and be disinclined to become the Keeper here, wishing to pass on the knowledge I had gained. He told me he thought we could share the duty, and he would stay on as head of the school instead of presenting me with that title. It was a year of death. King Aregis died early that spring, and my brother, King Allison, reigned for only six months when he died. And his young son, Alex, became king before his twenty-third year. "

"Only six months—I never heard that. What happened?"

Donel looked sad. "It was another accidental death. He was trampled by horses—his own and that of our brother, Baeddan. They were out riding in the valley with their guards when one of them suggested a race. Both were avid horsemen, which was not a joy Caer or I shared. Al was winning the race, though Bae was close on his heels when something spooked their horses. Al was thrown, and Bae rode right over him while trying to bring his own under control. Al's own horse had already struck him as he lay in the dirt, and then Bae's finished him ... probably. By the time the guards reached them, it was too late. Al was gone." Donel shook his head. "It still saddens me, though it has been over three hundred years."

Artos thought back to the time his own horse had thrown him. *I thought it was pretty bad when I broke my wrist.* His stomach clenched tight at the thought of being trampled.

"After Alex was crowned, Bae was marshal for less than a year. He resigned in favor of Bethel and withdrew from living at the castle. He came and spent some time here with me that next summer. I feel he never healed. He was haunted by the thought he was the cause of Allison's death. He died young, barely fifty years of age. His family disappeared shortly after his death."

Artos nodded. "I know how Bort would react if he thought he had accidentally killed me." He let out a sigh. "He would never forgive himself."

Donel straightened up and looked into Artos's eyes. "Since the death of your father, I have begun to wonder about Allison's death. Was it an unfortunate accident or something more sinister? Three out of the last five high kings have died young. Your grandfather's incident with the vine-crawler and my brother's death both may have been accidents, but your father's demise was murder most foul and the more I think on it, the more I wonder about the others. All three who died young were reformers or wished to be. Alexavier certainly was not, and Arlond was responsible for the end of the schools of wizardry."

"You don't think Alexavior was involved somehow, do you?" Artos was shocked by the thought.

"No." Donel shook his head. "Alex was not evil. Arrogant? Yes, and overly filled with a sense of his own importance, but not evil. But I doubt he was perceived as more than a useful step to the Abominations. They thought he would be easy to dislodge from the throne, thus Tomung's rebellion. He spoiled that by beheading the fiend. If only he had the wisdom to finish the job. Who knows how much of his actions and those of Arlond's may have been done under the influence of the Abomination Alex foolishly brought into Castle Draconis?" Donel let out a long sigh.

"But we have strayed far from our topic. You need to know where you are going when you get to Starstone and how to gain the entrance to Castle Draconis from there. I can show you where to go on the screen up to a certain point, but then you must enter the warded part of the tower. I cannot show you anything beyond that. My memories are from three hundred years past, but they will have to serve as a guide in the rooms beyond.

"What do you know about the Blasted Heath, Art?"

"It was laid waste when the Great Houses destroyed the holdings of House deYung," said Art, confused by the abrupt change of subject. "Wasn't it?"

"It was," said Donel. "Did your father tell you anything about the destruction?"

"Father? No, our tutor Elaer taught us history, although I believe Uncle Cameron gave us the lesson about the destruction of Blachaas in his lessons on the politics of Veda."

"Aaron should have spoken to you about this, although I can guess that he couldn't. He didn't know the story. Attios didn't instruct him because his father, Arlond, didn't deem it important enough to pass on. I told you the wizard's colleges were allowed to fade away under his reign. Alexavier and Arlond thought that magic should be taught in the Church rather than by wizards."

"Yes, something I still think we can remedy somehow."

"I told you Alex wanted me to leave my stewardship of this tower and return to help in the war against Tomung. I explained why this was impossible, but had Denar not been slain, I would have been placed in charge here, and Denar would have gone to Starstone to use the forbidden weapon there. Then the Blasted Heath would still be Blacheath and be lush and green."

"Forbidden weapon?" Artos crinkled his brow.

"Starstone Tower was not built to be a college of quantimagic. It was the first of the strongholds hidden in the Mountains of Myst, built to combat the Three. It was originally an armory. They developed weapons there and then took them to other strongholds to use against Demigoran. However, he inevitably smashed those citadels. Blachaas, Darylhelm, and Castle Draconis were the only ones that weren't destroyed before they trapped Demigoran in the Hellesgate."

"You mean Daryelhaas?"

"No. Daryelhaas was built after the Reckoning. Darylhelm is on the plateau in the Darrelwood. I don't think any of the other Great Houses ever go there. The Darrell refers to it as his hunting lodge."

"Oh yes! I have seen it from a distance. It stands on the edge of the plateau. I remember asking what it was when I visited the Darrel a few summers back. He said it wasn't used much."

"House deDarrellyel hides their secrets in plain sight." Donel smiled.

"As I was saying, The Starstone Tower was where the quantimasters developed their weapons to use against the Three. After Demigoran was trapped, they turned their attention to Tiameng, and she fled to the far north. My personal belief is she was not driven off by the weapons as much as the fear of being trapped like Demigoran, so she retreated to wait until she knew more. It is said she was trapped somewhere in the cold north, but if she is imprisoned there, it was in the

Reckoning's aftermath, not by any action of our forefathers."

Donel swiveled his control chair to face the large screen that covered the eastern wall of the screen room and placed his hand upon the gems in the side table. A view of the King's Valley appeared dimly in the light of the full moon, as if seen from a bird flying high above through the night sky.

"The mist in the mountains always makes viewing a very questionable task, but I can key in on Castle Draconis and then proceed north across the loch and be sure to find Starstone Tower."

The bird's-eye view narrowed in on the castle of Artos's family, and he saw the shadowy remains of his family's crushed airship. With the sight, he felt a renewed surge of grief and anger.

"Because I could not go," continued Donel, "and with Denar dead, Alex sent my brother Caerwyn to Starstone to use what weapons he could find there against the Abominations. Caer could not make his way to the hidden armory chamber at first. He contacted me from the Hall of Mirrors at Starstone and asked for advice. I gave him what help I could over the screens, unfortunately."

"The vision on the screen moved past the Eyrie and started across the waters of Loch O'Wrens, delving into the fog that masked the northern part of the loch.

Artos felt confused. "Why, unfortunately?"

Donel sighed. "Because he succeeded. Caer's regalos were primarily green, those of nature and nurture. Most of the weapons at Starstone Tower were created for use by those strong in the red regalos, those of the body, of the warrior. Moreover, the Starstone, the weapon the tower came to be named after, had been created to destroy Tiameng. By the time Caer gained access to the armory, the Abominations had all fled except for Tomung. I thought Caer might find something there to destroy what was left of him, but Alex had other ideas. He instructed Caer to see if anything in the armory might be used at a distance to destroy Blachaas. I was not consulted. Alex should have secured Blachaas, cleansed it of whatever foul magics might have remained, and named a successor to House deYung. Instead, he chose to make a display of his power, to destroy their stronghold and extinguish the line—or so he thought. I am not so sure. Caer discovered the Starstone. He directed it against Blachaas. Or rather, he *tried*. He was so inaccurate, his misfire turned the park into a wasteland. He finally controlled the weapon and directed it against the stronghold of Tomung, but he was never the same man after that day."

Artos's eyes widened in horror. "This is what you are sending me to find? I want to reclaim Castle Draconis. Not destroy it."

"No. The Starstone was shattered by Caerwyn shortly after he finished razing Blachaas. He saw what he had done to the heath and vowed it would never be used in such a way again. Alex was furious. He had hoped that once Caer had mastered the weapon, he could use it to hunt down the Abominations where they had fled into the Beastlands to the east. Control of such a weapon would have given Alex far too much power, I'm afraid. There is no telling what else he might have chosen for a target.

The vision left the waters of the loch and slowly moved across the rocky far shore. Artos found his attention was torn between listening to Donel's words and watching the fog swirl as the scene moved across the stoney ground.

"While I was thinking about the sealed tower, I was

reminded of something. There may be something still in the armory you can use against the Abominations. Caer told me there were other weapons locked away, there in the tower's top chambers. I think he would have destroyed them all had he any strength left, but the backlash from the Starstone weakened him. He left the topmost chambers of the tower. Later, when he had recovered his strength, he found he could not reenter the topmost chamber. He could not pass the shields. My belief is that he did not try too hard to return there. It was not a place of victory for my brother, but a reminder of bitter, wasteful destruction.

Suddenly, the side of the massive tower appeared in view, and the vision picked up speed, following the wall around a corner and then another until it came upon a large set of double doors with no handle or ornamentation except a square of blue crystal where a handle would normally be found. The vision stopped its movement and waited at the door.

"My brother was greatly upset by what he had done. I believe Caer had lost so much of himself that he was unable to train Cameron correctly in much of what he should have. His guilt at so horrifically destroying so much of The Mother's beauty made it impossible for him to focus on his Nature regalos, so Cameron was never properly instructed in them and was deficient with them. I believe this is why the Sky Sect has been so favored during his time as head of the Church of the Four. He did not receive proper training in the nature regalos because Caer could not pass them on to him." Donel shook his head, a sad expression on his face. "Caer and I spoke little after the destruction. I could tell his deed haunted him. It is a guilt I share with him, but he bore the brunt. I invited him to visit me here. I was hoping to assuage his guilt, but he would not come."

"But he didn't mean to destroy the heath. It was not a deliberate action. Surely you told him so!"

"I did, Art. But King Alexavier praised him for it, even as he cursed him for destroying the weapon, which probably only made the wound deeper. Caer was both a Druid and a Sky Priest. That part of him which was a Druid burned with shame. Praise for what he considered unnecessary destruction wounded him deeply."

"So what kind of weapon am I looking for, then? What do I need that would be better than my crysword?" Artos felt a surge of excitement. A weapon from the ancient quantimasters! A marvel from ages past; surely it would be something amazing and powerful.

"The quantimasters of old feared the Abominations that served Demigoran. They were familiar with them, something which I am not. I believe they created a weapon the Abominations would be powerless against, or maybe specific weapons to use against each of them. I am not really sure."

"You're not sure? What do you mean? You have examined them, haven't you?"

"No, Art, I was never in the Starstone Chamber. The last person to enter there before Caer was Daimion, and he told Denar some things about it, which he passed on to me. Denar never had a reason to seek out the hidden chamber. The Starstone was created to use against Tiameng, but she was gone and Yeenaghou as well. It was over a thousand years before we knew the Abominations were still among us. Tomung's rebellion revealed our folly."

Artos slumped a little as he felt his excitement lessen. "So you haven't even been to the place these weapons might be?"

"No, Art. I am sorry, I have never been into the armory itself.

But I have been in the sealed tower many times. The armory is in the topmost chamber. Your goal is Starstone Tower's Hall of Mirrors, which appears to be the uppermost chamber, but is in reality directly below the armory. Denar had told me of its existence and how to access it, but I never found the time. I planned on exploring the tower fully when I was installed as the dean there. Something which never happened due to Denar's murder and my having to take his place here. This is something you may seek in that spire of the tower. There might be weapons which may aid you in destroying the Abominations within Castle Draconis, but they are not as important as you regaining entrance to the Castle itself."

"Starstone's Hall of Mirrors? Like the one in Castle Draconis?"

"Exactly. You see, besides being a room for communication, the Hall of Mirrors was also a means of quick transport between Castle Draconis and Starstone Tower."

"So we could have gone there any time? Why didn't we know this?"

"That the gate even existed was not common knowledge. After Denar's death, only I had the knowledge and the means to open the gate. Only those with the proper regalo can access it, and only with the proper training. Caer didn't have the proper regalo. No one at Starstone could open the Gate from Draconis for him. None of the remaining instructors could enter the sealed tower. He had to make the trip to the tower by physical means. By road, it is thirty miles between the castle and the tower, though they are less than two miles apart across Loch O' Wrens."

"What is the needed regalo to open this gate?"

"Ansuz, the same that is used for mind-speech. Bort has it,

as does Angel. I suspect Seth does as well, although I haven't tested him. Kae and Jaek do not, so they will be able to travel through the gate, but not open it."

"I understand, we can … wait … Ansuz? That's not one of my regalos, either. You showed me mine: Mannaz, Skjebne, Algiz, Tiu, and Sig." Art looked at Donel in confusion. "So it will have to be Bort. Have you trained him to open it?"

"No, Art, remember, Skjebne and Sig will allow you to use any of the regalos. That is one of the things I will be training your mind for in our private sessions. I will use hypnosis to make that gift easily accessible to you."

Art looked at Donel, then nodded. "I guess there really isn't any choice, is there? I can't get into the Castle except through the gate or by flying."

"Well, you could go down below the basements of Starstone and find the river passage and follow it to the Castle. But no one has used the route for a very long time. I don't know exactly where it comes out at Castle Draconis. I never knew of its existence until Denar told me about it when he was preparing me to take over as dean of the school."

"I see. I wonder if Father even knew of it. Well, no matter, I should be able to open the Gate, and then we all can travel through to the Hall of Mirrors at Castle Draconis."

"That is correct. Now let me show you where you shall be going. This is the front door to the tower. Indeed, except for the hidden passageway below that leads to Castle Draconis, this is the only door."

"Why are there no doors? Are there windows?"

"Every dormitory and private room has windows, but they are very unusual windows. They do not open and are not visible from the outside. There are no openings except this door, but all the personal rooms have widows, even rooms, that do not have outside walls. My first room, shared with Caer, was deep inside the tower, yet we had a window that overlooked the loch. When the quantimasters built the tower, it seems they felt everyone should have a room with a view. The classrooms and other rooms, such as the dining hall or the kitchens, were only lit with everlights, but all bedrooms had windows. They are screens, of course, but they are permanently set as windows with very specific views. I'm sure every student, at one time or another, tried to bend them to their will, to look into the other rooms, but to no avail."

"Why would someone want to look into another person's room? Just to see if they're home?"

Donel chuckled. "Art, there were students of both genders attending classes. Can't you think of any other reasons a person might want to look into another's room?"

"Oh. But … but that wouldn't be right."

"Not everyone would feel that way," said Donel with a slight smile. "In truth, I don't think the quantimasters who raised the tower had future students in mind. I rather think it was a privacy issue more than policing peeping-toms."

Donel reached down and touched a button on the right onyx control panel, and their view approached the massive door and then moved right through the door. For a sudden blank moment, sparks of light filled the screen, and then the view returned. They were now looking into a vast, dusty room lined with many doors on each side. Donel did a quick pan of the room. There was dust everywhere. Three balconies, also lined with doors, rose above the floor on each side. A stairway on each side of the entrance provided access to the upper reaches. An everlight strip ran down the center of the ceiling, providing light for the immense room.

"What was that? Those sparks?"

"Hmnn? Oh, the static? That was our passing through the tower's qulan field, that's all."

"You mentioned that before. How will we get in if there is no one to invite us?"

"I'm sorry, I tend to forget. One of the early lessons I would normally have given any of my students details the various types of qulan fields. It is just another thing we hurried past because our time is short. The field that surrounds Castle Draconis and the one here require an invitation to pass through. Some fields do not stop physical entry at all, but do block mental forces. The wards of Alfhiem are of this nature. That is why Bort was shielded from our scrying. The qulan field of Starstone Tower prevents those without regalos from opening the doors. What they referred to in some histories as 'the mindblind.' The level of training did not matter, but someone without gifts could never open them. The outer qulan field at Fairinhorst is similar to this, though somewhat different. Cari will find when he enters the outer boundaries of Fairinhorst it is always spring within, and there are birds and butterflies abounding the year-round."

Artos nodded as their ghostly presence moved to the far end of the hall and passed through the door there into a room dominated by a magnificent spiral stairway which wound upwards. What looked to be huge windows were set high on the walls, each featuring a different scene showing some large buildings. Donel focused their view on one window in particular—Castle Draconis, as if he were standing in the King's Valley gazing up at his home.

"Those look like windows," said Artos, "but they can't be.

They show broad daylight rather than nighttime."

"You are correct. These screens look like windows, but they are memorials. They show the redoubts where weapons were used against Demigoran before he destroyed them—one after another, until only three remained. Now the only original fortresses left are Castle Draconis and Darylhelm."

Donel returned their vision back to floor level. They circled the stair and proceeded to another door on the far side of the room.

"This is as far as we can scry into the tower. Past that far door is the stairway that leads upwards to the armory and the tower's Hall of Mirrors. Another qulan field, one that prevents scrying, protects this door. Our bloodline is one of three, with access to the rooms beyond. Anyone of the bloodline of House deEagledon or House dePenrodyn can also open this door."

"Why those three and not the other Families?"

"That question's answer is lost within the mists of history, Art. I asked it too. Neither Denar nor Daimion could answer me for certain. You remember what I told you about the time before the Reckoning?"

Artos nodded.

"House Draconis was not always the First House. In the war against the Three, House Eagledon was the First House, with Draconis and Penrodyn behind them. Then came the other five Houses. It was after the Reckoning that House Draconis became the First House, much to the dismay of House Eagledon. In legend, the rebellion against Austin was led by elders of Eagledon, along with a few others. After the Sky spoke and those elders disposed, the Houses fell in behind our House."

The view moved closer to the door and then stopped.

"When you go through this door, Art, you will be in the

Armory proper. The rest of the tower was converted to a quanti school, but this tower was left unchanged. There is really nothing to see there anymore except at the very topmost levels. The rooms on the bottom floors are all empty. The limited access made them unhandy for storage, and what they were used for originally is unknown. In the center of the room, there is a narrow spiral staircase. It looks dangerous, for there are no railings, just a set of stairs winding upward. There are two floors above, and on each floor, a walkway leads from the stairs. The Hall of Mirrors is on what seems to be the highest floor. Several other conference rooms flank it. They, too, were empty and unused in my day. It isn't as dangerous as it looks. An invisible wall wraps around the stairs with openings at the landings.

"Invisible wall?' asked Artos, turning his attention from the screen to gaze at Donel. "How can something solid be invisible?"

"It's the magic of the quanti," Donel shrugged with a smile. "Is an invisible wall any stranger than the walls and floor of the Winding Way—a hard wall with a yielding floor with nothing to mark where one stops and the other starts? I thought the Hall of Mirrors was on the top floor when I was an instructor there. Only after I became the head instructor did Denar tell me of the hidden floor above. I planned to go up there, but something always seemed to keep me away. There wasn't any feeling I needed to. I had thought I would be the head instructor for many years. Then I received the summons to Fairinhorst, and, well ..." Donel trailed off.

"So we go into the Armory part of the tower and climb the stairs to the top floor, and the Hall of Mirrors is there? Then what?"

"In the center of the room, there is a desk like in Castle Draconis. Sit in the chair there, place your hand on the small screen set in the desk's surface, call the Rune Ansuz to the forefront of your mind, and think of Castle Draconis. The gate will appear in the wall to your left, but before you do this, go to the Armory on the hidden floor above. A hidden stairway accesses the floor above. It is very disconcerting. It only forms when you summon it forth. It is invisible but solid. The stair that leads up from the floor seems to end at the landing to the Hall of Mirrors, but if you stop at the top, picture Raido in your mind, and think of the Armory, the stairs will form which continue up one more flight. Only after you reach the top will you see the room that's above. I can tell you nothing more about it. I told Caer the same things I have told you, and he was able to access the room, so you should be able to as well."

"At the top of the stair, I just concentrate on the Armory, and an invisible stair will allow me to go up to the hidden room."

"I wish I could tell you more about the Armory, Art. But I cannot. I would not spend a great deal of time there if I were you. If the other weapon or weapons are not easily recognized, I would proceed to Castle Draconis and use the new things I have taught you and Bort to defeat the foes within the Castle. I wish I could scry fully within Castle Draconis to tell you how many Beastmen remain there and where the Abominations are, but except for the Hall of Mirrors and scrying Duka's sword, the Castle is masked. The same qulan field that keeps enemies out prevents friends from looking in."

"I know. Do you think Bort could use any weapons we find there in the Armory? Or wouldn't it be safe?"

"No. You have the regalos to use them. At least, I have trained you as best I could, not knowing what they are. I have not even tried to train Bort's mind to use anything except his own gifts. It is probably best that no one, except you, touches anything in the Armory. I will use hypnosis to plant triggers for the regalos I think you could use there, but you will have to trust your own instincts when you find the weapons. If your mind warns you, do not force yourself to use anything. As I said, I do not even know what remains, except that Caer told me there were more weapons. Things he wanted to go back and destroy."

"I understand. Time will be of the essence, so I shall look for the weapons and only choose one if it feels right to me."

"That will be best, Art. Life is full of things we might have done, things we should have done, and things we should not have done, but did anyway. There is no use regretting past choices, but it doesn't stop us from doing so. It is a part of being human. Is there anything else you can think of that you wish to know?"

The vision of the door disappeared from the screen.

"Nothing occurs to me now. I will probably think of things three days upon the trail, but now my head is full of what you have told me and everything you have taught me over the last few days. Everything is all jumbled together in my mind."

"You will be guided safely to Starstone; of that, I am sure. I have learned the pattern of you and Bort's minds. I will check in on you from time to time, but there is nothing more I can do. If we only had more time." Donel sighed. "I keep hoping Duka finds a way to summon his crysword. I would much rather see him than his sword hanging in an empty room in the castle."

Artos nodded. "Would you scry into the Hall of Mirrors? I would like to see where the gate opens, if I can."

Donel nodded. "That is easy enough to do. Both The Darrell

and Maria keep track of any use of the screens. They look into the room at random moments, but as yet, neither of them has caught anyone using the screens there, as in your vision. I think if they used them, as you were shown, it was a one-time communication. I do not know how knowledgeable anyone from the Houses is about the uses of the screens. But I fear some Abominations may understand them a great deal. If they were hidden at House Yung over the ages before the rebellion, they are probably far more knowledgeable than anyone else in the world. Including me."

Donel touched a control. Suddenly, the Hall of Mirrors was visible on the large screen. Once again, Art was looking into the room as if standing in the entrance, with the control chair and the oaken desk in front of him with the wall of screens beyond.

The view moved forward until it was as if they were floating in the air over the desk and then slowly turned to the left.

"Wait! Go back."

Donel turned to look at Artos and then back to the screen. The view slowly rotated back to the view of the House screens. "What is it, Art? What did you see? Something on one of the screens?"

"No. The block on the table! The crysharp that was there is gone!"

"Oh, that." Donel chuckled. "There was no reason for me to keep my crysword in the trophy block any longer. It was handy for spying on the room and not leaving any clue. If I had looked into the room as we are doing now, when Cameron was using the screens, he could have detected me." The view focused in on the gems inset in the oaken table on either side of the small screen set in the table. One was glowing. "At least I used to think that. Now I am not so sure. I believe I overestimated how skilled your great-uncle was. Caer could have detected me without a doubt. That was why I left the sword there, in the glass. Alexavier thought I was blocked from the room because he had the screen that we used to talk with painted over with black lead paint. Also, he thought he had my crysword imprisoned in the leaded glass. I saw no reason to dissuade him from thinking so. I have the sword in my room below now. One moment." Donel closed his eyes, and the blue crysharp appeared in the clear trophy block. "You see?"

"Can anyone who owns a crysword change its nature like that? You move it around so freely. I tried to move my sword from its sheath to the table in my room and was unable to do anything except summon it to my hand."

"Bort asked me the same question a few days ago. Yes, but it would take more time than we have right now. I have taught you the mindset you need to make your sword be charged with lightning and for Bort to make his blade flame. If we had another few weeks, I would teach you both how to cast bolts of your element at your foes."

Artos smiled a sad smile. "I remember saying something to Father about wishing I had a crysharp. It seems like it was years ago, not the weeks it has been. He told me I wouldn't have the time to learn such a skill."

"Art, you have so much potential. Aaron had no idea how much. I believe if you wish to learn something, you will find a way." Donel sighed. "But right now, your path along the Glory Road has much to keep you busy."

Artos nodded. "Where will the gate appear?"

The view on the screen changed again. Now it showed the oaken table from the right side and the western wall of the room, showing the infinite view of a mirror reflecting another mirror.

"The gate will open up there. It will appear a square of bluish light. Come through prepared for battle. There may be something awaiting you. I wish there was time to teach you the skills of using the control panels, so you could view the room before entering, but there just isn't enough time. Just remember when you and Bort enter, the Hall might not be empty."

Artos nodded grimly.

"Now, let me begin to teach your mind to use Ansuz. Let us go to the training chamber. I will give you the first session tonight."

Artos followed Donel back to the testing chamber and entered when Donel opened the door. Within a few moments, Donel had activated the screens. A red dot appeared on the screen before him. As before, Donel spoke, and Art watched and listened. Suddenly, Donel was back at the open door of the room. Liv was waiting with him now, studying him with her amber eyes.

"Have you finished? It never feels like you did anything." Just as he spoke, there was a strange feeling in his mind, almost like being in two places at once. Liv looked up at Donel and then walked away.

"Liv tells me she can feel your mind, Art. You now have access to Ansuz. I have put the use of the gate controls into your mind when you are in the Hall of Mirrors. Trust in yourself. If we had more time, I would train you in the complete use of the screen controls, but that will have to wait for another time. For now, opening the gate will have to suffice."

"I… I think I felt her thoughts, just for a second."

"Very likely you did. The other Daughters should arrive here sometime after noon tomorrow, and I will need to spend some time testing them and begin training them to Mindshield. I will set up some exercises for you while I am testing the girls. You will not be neglected just because I must test them. Time is essential. Of that, I am sure you agree."

Art nodded, then gave a prodigious yawn.

"It is getting late," said Donel as he stood up from his chair. "I think it is past time we both should be sleeping."

3

DREAMS

ARTOS

11:30 p.m.

ARTOS KNEW HE WAS DREAMING, but there was something important just ahead. Whatever it was, he knew he had to find it. So he walked through the pine forest, snow crunching under his moccasins, looking all around him as he went. The fog-shrouded forest was quiet except for the sounds of his footsteps. Not a bird called out, the pine boughs silent beneath a white coverlet of snow. He was leading the way. Bort was behind him with the others, but he was all alone out in front. A clearing in the pines opened before him, and he glanced out from the trees. He was looking down into a valley. The fog had blown aside, revealing a village laid out below him. He crouched down and watched. Was this their destination or some place to avoid? He waited for someone from the village to show themselves so he would know.

Suddenly, a cry rang out behind him. Beastmen were attacking!

Instantly, his sword was in his hand, and he and Bort stood side by side, fending off a swarm of the monsters. Angel was next to some Fairborn, one holding a sword and the other shooting arrow after arrow into the horde, charging at them through the trees.

A roar to his other side alerted him. A large black bear entered the field, swatting the Beastmen left and right. It must hate them too. Maybe they were stealing its food, Artos thought. Or maybe everyone hates Beastmen, even bears.

The fighting was more and more unbalanced. For every Beastmen Artos struck down, two more would take their place. Was there no end to their numbers? He fought on. Soon they would be overwhelmed, but what could they do?

Wait! He knew! He could give up the quest and wake up!

Suddenly, he was upright in his bed, his crysword clutched tightly in his hand. He was breathing in ragged gulps and sweating profusely as he looked around, expecting to see the others from his dream, but he was alone in his bedroom at the Crystal Tower. That was strange. *All that talk of dreaming tonight must have stuck with me and gotten into my dreams*, he thought. *I don't think I need to talk to Donel about this one. It's just me worrying about our journey to the tower.*

He stared at his crysword. *I wonder if I can connect to Bort or Cari through my sword? Well, probably not Bort. He's behind the West Wind's wards at Alfhiem, but Cari should be sleeping at the nest. Maybe I can see him?*

Artos lay back down, still holding his crysword in his hand. He made sure he thought the edges were nicely rounded and the point dull, and then he concentrated on his younger brother and the room they had stayed in at the Swan's Nest. But to no avail. Soon, his eyes were closing of their own accord. Chuckling, he put the sword back into its scabbard and rehung it on the bedpost. He closed his eyes.

He was running through the forest, leading his pack. They had flushed out a young buck away from the thickets, running it down. He was the smallest of them, but the giant black wolves running with him all feared him. And rightly so. He was the strongest, even if he was the smallest. They all knew it and followed his guidance.

The giant red deer was panicking now. It knew the pack was closing in for the kill. A black wolf was running on either side of it, snapping at its sides. There was no escape. They were forcing it to run directly to where he was waiting. The young buck burst into his view, and he leaped up and tore at its throat. The sweet, hot blood gushed as the deer tried to wheel away in panic!

Artos sat back up with a shout. "What kind of dream was that?" he asked the empty room. His heart was beating wildly, and he was drenched with sweat. "I think I might want to ask Donel about that one. It felt … real. Not like a dream at all."

It took a long time for sleep to recapture him that night. The only thought that brought him any peace was the fact that at least Cari was going away from danger.

Part Two

Bortis at Alfhiem

Chapter Three:

Alfhiem

4

ALFHIEM ARRIVAL

BORTIS

9/22/1971 ar

12:00 p.m.

ANGEL SET A MUCH FASTER PACE for the return trip to the Nest than what they had used on their trek to the Crystal Tower. Fortunately, most of this journey was downhill. She called it the scout's hike, but Bortis knew it from his journeys with his Uncle Brett as a forced march. They would jog one hundred steps, then walk another hundred, then repeat. They reached the Nest by noon.

Bortis followed Angel into the dining room at the Nest, where two Fairborn awaited them—a woman with a smirk and a man with a scowl. They stared at him without uttering a single word. Well, that suited him just fine. *Arrogant, aren't they?* he thought. *Just like Uncle Brett said.* He decided to ignore them as well. Angel addressed them as Kateeri and Bachar, then had a heated discussion. Angel addressed them in Espro, so he didn't follow the conversation, but Angel seemed to disturb the two somewhat, and soon Kae and Joy entered the conversation as well. Bortis sat motionless, trying hard not to fidget and to keep his expression neutral. He was determined not to let these two strangers see how anxious he felt about being Art's ambassador. As if it were their business, anyway. The strangers gave in to her. Bortis grinned to himself. Angel was used to getting her way, and for once, it didn't annoy him. Kae and Joy then left.

Angel sat silently for a few minutes, then called for Susi and asked her to bring Bortis and her some of her rabbit jerky. They had barely finished their sticks when Kae was back with her pack, and they set out for the West Wind's camp.

It had been a silent thirty-mile hike. Art understood a little of the Fairborn tongue, but it was just gibberish to him. The two Fairborn escorting them spoke a few quiet words to each other during the trip, but little to Angel or Kae, and nothing to him. He might have been a pack mule or a dog as far as the attention they gave him. That suited him just fine. *Arrogant elitists.*

7:00 p.m.

As they neared the end of their journey, dusk enveloped the mountains, and the twilight made the path hard for Bortis to follow. He was forced to watch his step carefully lest he trip over dimly seen roots or other obstacles as they hurried. He seemed to be the only one of the group bothered by this, and he struggled along as best he could, vowing to himself he would not be the one who forced Angel to slow her pace.

An enormous thousand-year oak dominated the north end of the valley. They finally reached a clearing with a small lake. A stream wound its way back through the valley. The trail skirted the lake's edge and offered a good view of the gigantic tree.

I bet they set their camp between the roots of that monster; he thought. *That has to be one of the biggest oak trees I have ever seen. I wonder how they protect themselves from falling acorns? They must be the size of a house.* He envisioned a village with huts made from fallen acorns and chuckled to himself.

The path led to an enormous log that straddled the far end of the lake. It was hollow, with their path leading inside.

Angel stopped and waited for him to join her. "The log is a trap," she said softly when he drew up beside her. "The trail leads to it at both ends, but in the middle, there are spots that, if stepped upon, will sound alarms to my father's men. When this happens, hidden doors will spring shut and trap the unwary. The true path is on the far side. There are rocks of different colors. The first is hidden under lily pads. Beyond the pads, the rocks are different colors. Don't step on the blue or green ones. Red, orange, and yellow are all safe." She took a few hurried steps, caught up with Kae, and exchanged a few hushed words.

How am I supposed to tell the colors? he thought to himself. *Doesn't she realize I can't see in the dark like they can?*

At the mouth of the hollow log, their Fairborn escorts stopped and turned to wait for all to catch up.

"By tradition, we leave the path here and cross the river beyond the log. You may follow us, or take the path through if you prefer not to get your feet damp." Bachar finally deigned to address him, and in Common no less. He gestured at the path through the log.

Bortis shook his head. "I'll follow you. Wet feet don't bother me."

Bachar's eyes flicked to Angel for a moment, but his face

remained expressionless. "As you like." He gestured to his partner. "Kateeri will lead. I will cross last."

The Fairborn woman led the way, trailed by Angel and then Kae. Bortis followed, determined to step where Kae stepped.

The pool on the lee side of the huge log was still and covered with many lily pads. Some of the round leaves were nearly ten feet across. A few floated alongside the bank near the log. To Bortis's relief, all the stones glowed with phosphorescence—some blue, some green, others orange, red, and yellow.

Without appearing to pay much attention, Kateeri walked onto the first large pad and crossed it. From there, she nimbly leaped to another. Beyond, a number of rocks of different hues were laid out like a path across the pool, next to the huge fallen log. Angel, Kae, and Bortis followed along behind the Fairborn woman. Bortis watched closely to make sure he chose the same stepping stones Kae did. Several times, she bypassed an easy step for a more difficult one, always stepping on rocks that glowed orange, red, or yellow.

On reaching the far side, Bortis glanced around for the Fairborn village, but there was nothing but barren ground with some smaller oaks struggling to survive in the shade of the gigantic thousand-year tree.

"This is as far as you may come with your eyes uncovered," said Kateeri, pulling a cloth from her belt. "No one who is an outsider may see the entrance to Alfhiem."

Before Bortis could protest, Angel added, "I'm sorry, Bort. I should have warned you about that, but it slipped my mind. This is my father's mandate for all outsiders. I'll help guide your steps." He glanced at her sharply, but the look on her face indicated she was truly sorry about her admission. Determined not to make a fuss, he simply nodded his head and let the

Fairborn woman cover his eyes.

The woman wound the cloth in an expert manner. He couldn't see anything around the edges. Angel took hold of his right arm, and another hand grasped his left. "We'll warn you when there are steps," came Kae's voice.

They led him forward across the smooth ground for a long way. Bortis heard creaking, and Kae said, "There are three steps up, right in front of you."

Bortis shuffled his feet slowly until he felt the first. He carefully ascended. He was led forward again, on what felt like a hardwood floor. The creaking noise repeated and ended with a soft thump and a click. A fresh floral scent filled the air, warmer than the evening air of the Valley. *Well,* he thought, *I guess I have entered the stronghold of the West Wind.*

Angel, Kae, and two guides exchanged welcoming-sounding words with some other speakers. As far as he could tell, the voices were not hostile. Bortis wasn't completely reassured. He would have liked to have looked upon the speakers. A door opened, and he was turned and guided a few steps to the right, where he was released, and his blindfold removed.

"Make yourself comfortable here and rest, Bort," said Angel. "I'll have some food sent. There's a basin and some towels on the side table. I'll find my father. He may send for you this evening or wait until tomorrow. I don't know. We've missed the dinner hour. When Father is here, he usually only eats two meals, one just after sunrise and the other in the late afternoon, so afterwards he can watch the sunset and the moon rise. Please wait here until I return or Father sends someone for you. He won't take it kindly if you wander around." Angel, Kae, and Bachar left the room. The door shut behind them with a solid thump.

Bortis noted the circular room was paneled in dark wood; there were no windows. Six everlights shaped like candles were spaced around the walls. The floor was polished wood of a lighter color, and there were three curved couches spaced around the room against the wall. There was a brightly colored oval rug before each one. Each couch was flanked by a pair of end tables. To his right was a small table with several towels of various sizes and a basin of steaming water. Between it and the door were a pair of wooden pegs, there to hang his jacket on. Bortis felt a pang of homesickness. *This could be a guest chamber back home*, he thought as he removed his jacket and hung it on the peg. He followed by removing his shirt and proceeded to wash up.

I don't know why, but it just feels like someone is watching me, he thought to himself as he looked around the chamber uneasily.

Thirty minutes later, he was sitting on the couch to the left of the door when it opened. Kae entered the room along with another Fairborn woman carrying a tray with several covered dishes.

"Andune will wait until morning to meet with you, Bort. He has another guest whom he is meeting with this evening. Rest here and eat. Later, he will send Nykia to escort you to a guest room where you may sleep tonight." Nykia gave him a polite nod.

Bortis jumped to his feet, and returned the nod, and reached out to take the tray. "Uh ... thank you. I'll be ready. Um ... could I ask you something?"

"Of course, Bort." Kae smiled and arched a brow.

"Just where are we? I expected to be in a hut in the El... err Fairborn village. But this doesn't feel like a hut."

"Ahh ... Well, I think I can safely say you are not in a hut;

you are correct in that, but more I should leave for Andune. He is touchy about such things, like our privacy. I would simply say to you to wait and ask him yourself on the morrow. I'm sorry. Is there anything else?"

Bortis nodded. "No, I can be patient and question him if I think of anything else." He set the tray down on the couch and sat beside it.

"Excuse me," said Nykia. "Let me show you." She picked up the tray and deftly maneuvered her fingers along the sides. Legs released on the underside, and she placed the tray over his lap. "I shall return in a little while to escort you to your sleeping chamber."

"Thanks," said Bortis, feeling somewhat foolish.

"I shall see you tomorrow, Bort," said Kae, and the two Fairborn women left the room.

Bortis ate his meal of greens and porridge. Though unlike the meals he was used to back home, the grains with bits of meat were savory and quite filling. Just as he placed the spoon in the empty bowl and removed the tray from his lap, the door opened, and Nykia entered. He creased his brow. Was the timing simply a coincidence, or was someone spying on him? He assumed the latter, though as far as his casual surveillance of the room could tell, there were no obvious spyholes in the walls or door.

He took another quick glance around the room, but nothing revealed itself.

Nykia interrupted his thoughts. "Have you finished?" she asked.

Bortis nodded.

"I will take you to your sleeping room, then. Leave the tray. Someone will get it later."

Bortis followed her out into the hallway, grabbing his jacket off the peg on the way. The hall ran about thirty feet and ended with a blank wall.

That's odd, he thought. *I know we came in down there, but there's no door.*

The hall was paneled in the same dark wood as the room he had just quit, and the floor was an intricate parquet. Nykia had turned right, and he trailed her down the hallway, past other doors and through several intersections. At the end of the hall was a grand stairway sweeping up in a spiral to the left.

What is this place? he thought. *By the sky! We're inside the thousand-year oak tree. It must be.*

After climbing a good way, the stair opened to a landing with a hall running off in two directions, with another spiral staircase on the opposite side. Nykia led him across to the other stair, and they continued up. As they climbed, a pair of Fairborn passed them going down, wearing leather armor similar to his own. Bortis felt their scrutiny, but they didn't look hostile and passed by without a word.

"Guards, going on duty?" he asked.

"I beg your pardon?" asked Nykia.

"I asked if those men we passed were guards."

"Oh. No, those are hunters getting ready to go on a night hunt. The giant hares come out at night this time of year. Or they might be going frogging, although I imagine they are going for hare. There are usually more men if they are going after a frog. More dangerous, you understand."

"Frogs are more dangerous than hares?"

"Well, yes. Of course. A giant hare doesn't try to eat the hunter. A giant frog might."

"Oh. Are there frogs in the pond outside?"

"Probably not the giant kind. You need to go all the way to the Lake of the Setting Sun for those to be common, but there could be. They warn us to be wary at night around the pond on the downstream side of the fallen tree."

They reached another landing, but this time, instead of proceeding up the stairs, Nykia turned to the right and walked down the hall. Bortis thought he heard singing coming from the other direction, but it was faint, as if behind closed doors. She walked to a door and opened it. Inside was another smaller spiral staircase going up.

Soon they reached another landing, with a narrow hall leading away from the stairs. Standing one on each side of the doorway were a pair of Fairborn in bright chain mail and helms of silver with azure trim.

Nykia turned to the one on the left. "Which room is intended for Prince Bortis?"

"The second room on the left is prepared for the prince. I will show him the way, thank you." He nodded to Nykia, and she smiled and nodded back.

"Thank you. Sleep well, Prince Bortis. I, or someone else, shall come in the morning to bring you your breakfast. After which you can expect to be summoned to Prince Andune for an audience." Nykia nodded to him and turned and went back down the stairs.

"This way, if you please." The guard walked down the hall, stopping before the second door on the left. There were six doors on the left-hand side of the hall to only three on the right, and the doors on the left had a fancier trim. The guard opened the door. "There is a push panel beside the door. It will sound a bell. Push it should you desire something in the night. A servant will attend as soon as possible." He stepped aside and motioned Bortis inside.

Bortis stepped into the room, and the guard closed the door behind him. It shut with a click, suspiciously like a lock bolt sliding home. Bortis closed his eyes and stood silently for a moment. Once more, he felt the prickly sensation of eyes watching him. He opened his eyes and looked around the room. It was comfortable looking, he admitted. Again, there were no noticeable spyholes that he could discern. The bed was canopied with curtains at the end and the sides, all drawn back at the moment. A small table with two chairs stood to the right of the bed, with a comfortable armchair beyond. Also on the right side of the room were two doors. The one on the left opened to a small walk-in closet. He hung up his jacket where it looked rather lonely, he thought, with nothing else hanging within. The door on the right led to a washroom, complete with a sink and shower. Thick, dark green towels hung invitingly on racks, and a matching bathrobe hung on a hook beside the door.

"Now that's interesting. I wonder how they get plumbing inside a tree?" He tried the sink. It was indeed running water, and the temperature was quanti-controlled, just like he was used to. "They must have a quanti-controlled cistern, just like we had at Castle Draconis. Interesting."

How often had the West Wind laughed inside his treehouse while Uncle Brett searched around the Rainbow Valley? Looking for his nemesis in vain. He felt a momentary twinge of anger, but then sighed. It wasn't the Fairborn who had murdered his father and uncles. He was here to ask a boon of Andune, not to rehash old grievances. From what he had been told the ill feeling of his uncle toward the Fairborn was as much caused by his own actions as anything. He thought for a moment of Elaine deEagledon, his brother's intended bride, and for a moment felt he understood his uncle's pain. His own emotions would not override his duty. He vowed to himself, *I will not let my feelings for Elaine come between me and Art, like what happened with Father and Uncle Brett.*

Bortis took a shower and donned the thick green robe. He tested the armchair and determined it was indeed comfortable. After a few moments, he walked over to his jacket hanging in the closet and, from a hidden pocket inside, pulled out his piccolo. He sat back in the comfortable chair, pushed the thoughts of Elaine from his mind, and played a lively tune until he felt ready to sleep.

Chapter Four:

The West Wind

5

BADHRON BUI
DAGR-NAEG NAST

BORTIS

9/23/1971 ar

6:00 a.m.

Bortis awoke to the sound of a melodious voice calling his name. "Prince Bortis? Are you ready to break your fast?"

He sat up, his crysword appearing in his clenched fist, disoriented, confused by the curtains surrounding his bed. Then he remembered. He was in Alfhiem, and today he would meet with his uncle's nemesis, Andune, the West Wind.

"Who's there?" he asked.

"I am Joanar, and I have a tray with your breakfast, Ser Bortis."

"Okay, ah … thanks, just set it on the table. I'll get right to it."

"As you wish. I was told to inform you Prince Andune will summon you in two hours."

Bortis heard plates being set on the table, then the door shutting. He climbed out from beneath the feather comforter, pushed back the curtain, climbed out of the soft bed, and looked to his clothes. They were on the armchair where he had left them, but where he had tossed them carelessly upon the seat, they were neatly folded. While he slept, they had been cleaned and mended. The small rip in his left shirt sleeve had been neatly stitched, and the fabric smelled like lavender.

He looked around the room, shrugged, and said, "Thank you." He got dressed and went to examine the breakfast left for him.

The table had been set for one with a dark green wooden plate with a glazed surface. In the center of the table was a silver-lidded pan and a steaming carafe which smelled of fresh coffee. The silver lid of the pan had a wooden handle that matched the plate. Lifting the lid, the smell of eggs and ham assaulted his nose. Steaming hot! He transferred a generous amount to the plate and dug in.

Shortly after he pushed his chair back from the table, there was a knock on the door, and a mail-clad Fairborn stepped into the room.

"Prince Andune is holding his morning audience. I was sent to escort you to the great hall."

Bortis nodded and followed the guard into the hallway and on through the tree.

After descending one level, the guard led him through several halls and up another large stairway into a great hollow within the heart of the thousand-year oak—Andune's Great Hall.

How different it was from the Great Hall of Castle Draconis. Instead of gray stone walls and floors with mounted trophies hung behind the king's dais, here the walls were polished wood with planters of bright, colorful flowers adorning the spaces between the everlights and occasional wooden carved statues.

The air within the hall was fresh and cool, the floral scent more noticeable than ever. It was very different from Castle Draconis, where the quanti kept the air from growing stale, but tended to remove scents rather than enhance them.

A few dozen Fairborn stood in loose groups around the room. The Fairborn prince, clad in black silk, sat on an intricately carved wooden throne at the far end of the room. An empty throne sat on the left side. Near the thrones were more of the Fairborn, some in the silver and azure chainmail of guards and some in silken finery that rivaled the finest attire of the Noble Houses Bortis was accustomed to. As Bortis approached, he was shocked to see Andune had a scar on his face near his left eye—in the exact spot as the scar his uncle had sported.

Bortis had always judged the Fairborn race through the words of his Uncle Brett. Where others saw them as a beautiful, graceful people, he saw them as arrogant, elitist snobs. Now, he was to meet with them and ask for aid for his brother's cause— to be his brother's voice.

This is going to be difficult, he thought. *Just how do you ask for help from someone you know considers you an inferior? Groveling is not in my nature. Should I demand help? Would that work? Can I act humble and not give away my true feelings? I doubt it.* He felt the disdain in Andune's eyes as he drew near the throne.

"Well met. I bring you greetings from my brother Artos, High King of Veda," said Bortis, with a nod, deciding to hide behind formality. He expected a response in kind. He did not expect the peal of hearty laughter he received.

"I must have missed the news. When was your brother's coronation, exactly?" asked Andune in a voice dripping with disdain. "Did the Great Houses have a convocation and invite none of my family? Who placed the Dragon Crown upon his brow exactly?" The Fairborn prince was not sneering, but looked very close to it.

"I ... I am afraid that I may have spoken in haste." Bortis felt his face growing warm as he flushed. "Yes, my brother Artos has not yet taken his place on the Dragon Throne, but that is what I am here for. Donel has told me that Artos is the pretender to the throne and not yet the actual king, but he shall be. That is why he sent me here to speak with you. He would have me ask a boon of you in the name of the friendship between our houses. I have here a scroll he prepared for me."

Bortis pulled the scroll Artos had written and stepped forward to hand it to the Fairborn prince, but before he could approach the throne, a guard intercepted him and held out his hand.

Bortis took a deep breath, then placed the scroll in the guard's hand. The guard did not offer it to the Fairborn prince as Bortis expected but handed it to a silver-haired Fairborn in silken robes of forest green, who held it in one hand and slowly waved his other hand above it as he studied it intently.

"There is no sign of poison or magic, my lord."

Bortis bit back a furious retort and breathed in a slow, cleansing breath.

Andune did not reach for the scroll, as Bortis expected. Instead, he continued to gaze at him with an amused expression. "You are to be Duke Bretton's replacement, I presume?" he asked. "You bear the red crysword?"

"Yes." Bortis nodded.

The Fairborn prince's face grew taut, and his penetrating gaze bore into Bortis. "A cousin of mine died for you. Did you know that?" There was no amusement in the Fairborn's voice now.

"Yes. The Bard Veryan gave us the sad news a few days ago. I am sorry that Prince Tirinvo's liegeman, Taur, was killed by the Abomination. The same Abomination that killed my father, my great-uncle, and my Uncle Brett. We plan on avenging their deaths, all of their deaths."

"I see … and just how do you plan on doing that? I understand that the foul creature chased you from your castle and killed your retainers. Do you plan on storming the castle and slaying the Orch there?"

"No, not at first, at least. Donel has a plan. We go first to Starstone Tower. That is what I am here to ask of you. We need a guide to lead us through the mountains. Donel thinks we should avoid the King's Valley."

"Nénarambal Tirion, eh?" said Andune. "Just what hope does Donel think you will find there? The quanti-school has been abandoned for centuries."

"I don't know. He has a plan. He is working with Artos on that. They sent me here to ask for your help. He told me to be sure you understood I am not requesting strength of arms from you. Merely someone to guide us to Starstone through the mountains." Bortis held his breath.

"I see, just a guide. Well, that is a simple question to answer … No." The Fairborn prince gave a small sardonic smile. "Was there anything else?"

Feeling his face flush, Bortis bit back his first response. "Why?"

"Because I choose not to. That should be a sufficient answer. However, I can see you are not inclined to accept it as such, so I will elaborate. I decline to send any of my people to guide you and your brother on a fool's errand to what will surely be your demise."

Bortis clenched his teeth, holding back the biting retort he wanted to deliver to the smug Fairborn prince. He knew his face gave away his anger. He could feel the hot flush on his cheeks.

"May I speak, Hir Andune?" came a voice from behind Bortis. A Fairborn man stepped forward. A man he had seen before. It was Jaek. Brother of the slain Taur.

"Jaek, my Selarquyono. What would you say?" said Andune. "If you have a feud with this man, I cannot grant you this. Not here."

Jaek stepped forward and bowed to the Fairborn prince. Bortis chided himself. *I forgot to bow. This man is a Fairborn prince. He expects formality, and I just stepped up and started talking. No wonder he's mad.*

"You misunderstand, Hir," said Jaek. "I was offering to be a guide for the task the young lord is asking. I am not familiar with the lands, but I have traveled through parts of these mountains, as you know well. If you could spare another who knows the lands to the north, I would accompany them." Bortis looked at Jaek in surprise. He had not expected this; surely this would help sway the Fairborn prince.

"You? This man's family is responsible for the death of your brother—my cousin Taur. I would not think you would be one to offer them assistance."

"The Sauraonna who killed Taur was not there on behalf of the deDraconis family, but there to slay them. I do not lay his death at their feet, Hir Andune."

"To reach the Nénarambal Tirion, you would need to cross the lands of the House deEagledon," said Andune. "As you well know, I have vowed I will not set foot there, nor send any of mine into those lands. No, I will send no one of mine on that fool's journey."

Bortis couldn't hold back any longer. "Are you afraid? The mighty West Wind?" he burst out in anger.

Andune's jaw clenched, and he stood up slowly, but before he could answer, a Fairborn man stepped out from the group near the throne. "Ni challarge tye, orqui!"

"Hold!" cried Jaek. "Don't let this get so out of hand, Hir Andune. This Hir doesn't mean offense. He is young and foolish, but he does not mean to insult you."

Bortis kicked himself mentally. He was here to speak for his brother; he had started off poorly, and it had gone downhill from there. He bowed his head as he reined in his emotions. "I … I am sorry, Lord Andune. I spoke in haste … wrongly and without thought."

"Yes, thoughtless words and hasty actions are a trait I have learned to expect from those of your House. Your Uncle Bretton's words show in your speech. He attacked me with his crysword and left the scar I wear to this day. Had I not been a quicker man, I would surely have been slain by his attack, and our people might have gone to war because of his thoughtlessness." Andune sat back on his throne. "I returned the favor, as I am sure you well know. Wounds made by such weapons never truly disappear."

Andune rubbed his fingers across the scar on his brow. "Your words of apology do not ring true. I will allow Bergan's challenge in defense of my honor. Prince Bortis, you can accept the challenge or forever be branded a coward. What is your choice?" Andune folded his arms, his sardonic smile once again on his face.

"My Lord, this is not seemly," said Jaek. "The young Hir has come to you as a supplicant. He is young and not familiar with—"

"I have made my decision, Jaek Ka`Naurf!" interrupted Andune. "Let the prince answer the challenge. Badhron bui dagr-Naeg nast. Accept or refuse! What say you, Bortis deDraconis? Do you accept the Dala Ath Emar?"

"I don't understand the words, but I am no coward!" cried Bortis, feeling his face flush again. He took a step toward Andune.

Jaek jumped in front of him, grabbed his arms, and pushed him back a step. Cries of anger rang out from the crowd.

"My Lord! He is not threatening you!" he shouted. To Bortis, he said urgently, "Do not make any aggressive moves towards the prince, or you are a dead man. There are archers watching from above who will slay you if you take a step nearer to Lord Andune!"

Bortis relented, and Jaek pushed him back. Several of the Fairborn near the prince had drawn their blades. "I don't understand," he said helplessly, feeling his anger drain away to be replaced with confusion.

"You accused Prince Andune of weakness with your foolish words," said Jaek. "One of his court, Bergan Na`Silarne`, has challenged you to a duel of honor. The Badhron bui dagr-Naeg nast. That is a non-lethal duel with naeg-nast—pain sticks. I tried to get Lord Andune to dismiss it as an error on your part. He has refused. You must accept now or be branded as a coward."

"I did not mean to offend anyone," said Bortis, looking at Andune. "But I will accept the challenge. I do not understand your ways. What do I need to do?"

The angry murmuring of the crowd died away.

Another Fairborn stepped up beside the first. "I offer myself as Tatya otorno to Bergan."

Bergan answered, "I accept."

Andune looked around at the gathering. "Will anyone stand for the human as his second?"

Jaek looked back at Andune. "I offer myself as Tatya otorno to Bortis."

Andune shook his head. "Why am I not surprised?" He stared at Bortis, waiting.

Everything was going too far too fast for Bortis to understand what was happening, but he realized he needed to answer. "I accept."

"As the person challenged, you have the right to set the time. Right now, perhaps?" asked Andune with the half-smile Bortis was coming to detest.

Jaek answered before Bortis could digest the question. "As Bortis' otorno, I set the time at moonrise this evening. Who will you name as Gwanur to the challenge?"

"I think I shall claim that duty as my own if neither party objects?" replied the Fairborn Prince.

"I accept," said Bergan.

"I accept for Hir Bortis," said Jaek. He took Bortis by the arm and pulled him away.

Things were moving too fast to digest. A guard in silver and azure approached them, but at a word from Jaek, he nodded and let them proceed unaccompanied.

"We shall go to where Andune has quartered me to discuss this, Bortis," said Jaek. "I fear you have not made a good impression with the Prince, but perhaps something may be salvaged yet. But I warn you—you must learn to curb your tongue and quickly."

"Art never should have trusted me with this task," said Bortis, shaking his head. "I'm not good at courtly manners—

courtly speeches. I'm a warrior, not a diplomat."

"Lord Andune respects strength at arms, Bortis. He has fought with bandits and Beastmen for more years than you have been alive. I warn you, though, he will not respect you if you put on a poor showing with the naeg-nast."

Jaek led Bortis through several passages and stairways until they came at last to an ornate door with vines and trees carved on its surface.

"The Prince has seen fit to give me rooms as fitting for his cousin, though when Taur and I served as his liegeman back in Fairinlan, our quarters were not as commodious," said Jaek, stopping before the door.

The rooms Andune had assigned to Jaek were far grander than the room where Bortis had spent the night. It was a suite, in fact, for they had entered a sitting room complete with a comfortable couch grouped with several armchairs covered with plush gray velvet. There was a side table upon which was a large bowl of red apples and russet pears. A trio of closed doors lay at the ends of the room, two to the left and one to the right.

"Which weapons are you most familiar with?" asked Jaek. "You will be given the choice of size. You may choose any of four lengths: dagger, short sword, longsword, or the staff. I would suggest you do not choose a dagger or a staff. Bergan is skilled with all four, but he is a master with the staff and very skillful with the dagger. If you choose dagger, Bergan is sure to suggest a nauta hollen hend contest, and you certainly do not wish that, and he will imply you are cowardly if you refuse."

"I don't know those words. I don't speak any Espero," said Bortis heatedly, wringing his hands in frustration. "I was trained in dagger fighting with one or two daggers, short sword, rapier, longsword, hand-and-a-half sword, and great sword.

With quarterstaff as well. I was the best shot with a longbow and, though I would never admit it to his face, second best with the crossbow to Carimus. I can use a sling, but I am far from an expert with one. But at least I'm not likely to brain someone standing behind me, unlike Carimus. What does nauta hollen hend mean?" He threw out his hands and shook his head, trying to control his emotions. Remembering his uncle's lessons, he took a deep breath and tried to clear his thoughts. Pushing the thought that he had already failed in his mission to the back of his mind, he tried to focus on his immediate problem, a duel he must fight to protect his honor and the honor of his House.

"Nauta hollen hend is a duel where your left arms are strapped together in a leather cuff and your eyes are blindfolded."

"Oh ... You're right. I don't want to try that."

Smiling grimly, Jaek nodded. "I had guessed you did not speak our language. That was a part of why I wanted to delay the duel until this evening. I think it might take you some time to learn the proper form to address Prince Andune when he calls the duel to begin. You could do it in the common tongue, but as I believe you are trying to win Lord Andune's favor. The proper form will be a good first step. Do you agree?"

"I ... I guess. You would know better than I. I ... I want to thank you. I don't know why you are helping me, but I am grateful. I truly am." Bortis realized it was true, even as he spoke the words. He was grateful that Jaek would choose to help him.

"Prince Tirinvo told me how your brother Duka has disappeared. I know how it feels to lose a brother." The Fairborn shrugged, a sad expression on his face. "And it seemed you needed a friend."

Speechless, Bortis merely nodded back. The enormity of Jaek's words suddenly struck him. Just how many friends did he truly have? Other than Artos, he wasn't sure. Oh, he loved his brothers, but could he truly say he was friends with Carimus and Duka? Had he ever given them a chance to be friends? Ellis deEagledon was a friend, wasn't he? They joked around; surely that was friendship, wasn't it? And Elaine? No, he pushed the thoughts of Ellis's sister from his mind, not wanting to think of his brother's chosen fiancée.

"Let us practice the opening salute," said Jaek, drawing his attention. "Lord Andune will walk to the center of the circle and say the ritual opening. 'Nohor ncas brin quintare`, man indóme ocerato?' That means 'Honor has been questioned, who will answer?' We will stand outside the circle, opposite Bergan and his Tatya otorno. As the challenged, you will be expected to answer first. This is what you must do—hold up your naeg-nast and then say, 'Ni termáre an mime nohor' followed by 'Ni paime nohmage ana tye, Hir Andune.' It means 'I stand for my honor, I pay homage to you, Lord Andune'. Do not enter the circle until he has signaled that it is time to begin. Do you understand?"

"It will take me some time to memorize all those words, but I think so." Bortis vowed to himself he wouldn't let Art down. Not again. He would learn the words and win the duel. At least he would do his best to win the duel. "What happens if I lose?"

"The same thing that happens if you win—nothing. This is only a matter of honor, Bortis. You said foolish words and insulted Prince Andune. You called him a coward, which he is most assuredly not. You spoke words of apology, but honor has not been satisfied, thus the duel. No matter who wins or who loses, the matter of honor will be settled, and your ill words and misguided actions forgotten. Only if you had refused would there have been any onus upon you."

"So, the outcome doesn't matter?"

"Not if you show bravery and fight well, with honor. Those are the important qualities. Now use your crysword, as we have nothing else handy, and let us practice. Let us use this design on the carpet as the line of the circle. Stand next to me and salute the chair as if it were Prince Andune."

Bortis took a deep, cleansing breath, stood next to the Fairborn, held out his left hand, and called his crysword.

"Wait! Are you left-handed?" asked Jaek.

"Yes, but Uncle Brett trained me to fight with either hand. He said a battle wouldn't halt if you couldn't use one of your arms."

"This may be to your advantage, Bortis. All the Fairborn are naturally right-handed, unlike humans. I am sure Bergan has fought left-handed foes before, but not near as often as those who are right-handed. Hmm … Anyway, you must not salute with your left hand. Use your right."

"Okay, I'll use my right hand to salute and to begin the duel as well. Then, if the time presents itself, I shall switch and perhaps catch him by surprise. Ah … Just what are the rules for the duel? And what is a naeg-nast, anyway? A practice sword?"

Jaek shook his head. "The words mean 'pain-stick.' What do humans use when they fight a duel?"

"That's right, you said pain-sticks before, but I don't know what that means." Bortis thought for a moment. "We rarely duel anymore. Uncle Brett told me they were more common a hundred years ago. The choice of weapon was up to the person challenged, and it would be decided before the duel what the conditions were to be. It could be as simple as the first to draw blood was the winner, or it could be to the death."

Jaek shook his head. "A death duel is forbidden by our law. Even a blood feud is not fought to the death, but only to the first blood shed. A pain-stick is a much more civilized way to conduct an affair of honor. There is a small tree called sae-sangwa. It is harmless in its natural state, growing in the wild. But the flesh of the tree beneath the bark, when fresh, extrudes a sap that is very distressing to flesh. The touch leaves a painful welt. It burns. A naeg-nast is a wand of sae-sangwa with the bark freshly removed except for a small amount left for a grip. The name pain-stick is very apt."

"The rules are simple. Although Prince Andune can introduce changes, it would be unlikely for him to do so. You each will go into the circle without a shirt. You can only strike with the naeg-nast; no kicks or blows with your other fist, your knees, or any other part of your body. However, you can use your other hand to push your foe away. The areas allowed to be struck are between your belt and your neck, including your arms. Any hits below the belt or to the neck and above are fouls. Three fouls are considered a loss. If the naeg-nast is dropped to the ground, that is a loss. If either party is unable to continue, as decided by the Gwanur, who is Lord Andune, of course, that too is a loss. Once the duel has begun, to leave the circle is a loss. And of course, either party can concede at any time."

Bortis nodded. "What about magic?"

"Neither party is allowed to use magic on the other. No illusions or spells to slow down an opponent."

"What about on yourself?"

"I think the wands are so light that casting strength upon yourself or using the light-blade spell would not give you an advantage. You could use lightness upon yourself, but that could be disastrous. You could leap around easily, but your opponent could use it to hurl you from the circle. Lord Andune may forbid any quanti use, but the normal rules only forbid using it upon your opponent."

Bortis nodded. "I think we better start practicing those words. I shall need practice to say them right." He switched his sword to his right hand and copied Jaek's motion and his words.

Jaek was a patient teacher, and although Bortis was not fond of school, he had an excellent memory. After many repetitions, he could repeat the phrases without disgracing himself.

"Do you know anything about Bergan's capabilities as a fighter, Jaek? Does he have any tricks or feints that you know of?"

Jaek's brow furrowed slightly. "I'm afraid I do not. I knew him slightly, but that was twenty years ago. As I said, I know he is skilled with knife fighting and with the quarterstaff. I know that his personal philosophy aligns with that of our King Farnir rather than Prince Tirinvo regarding humans." Jaek shook his head and frowned. "Which is undoubtedly the reason behind his challenge. I do not think Prince Andune would have had more than angry words for you in return for your ill-chosen ones. But Bergan saw it as a way to curry our Lord's favor. Since the death of Lady Stephanie, Lord Andune has moved closer to his father's thoughts in that regard."

"His father's thoughts? What do you mean?" Bortis began doing some stretching exercises as his uncle had taught him to do before any strenuous training.

Jaek took a pear from the fruit bowl and sliced it into quarters, discarding the seeds from the interior. "King Farnir has always felt that Humans and Fairborn were better apart than in proximity. His belief was bolstered when your uncle foolishly attacked Prince Andune at the Ball in Phoenix all those years ago. Then, when Andune wed the Lady Stephanie against his father's direct command, it worsened the situation. Bergan believes humans are lesser beings, only slightly better than the Beastmen. It is a prejudice more widely felt back in Fairinlan than here. Did you know there were three Fairborn families farming alongside the humans in the Rainbow Valley when the raiders came?"

"I didn't. I rode through this valley two summers past with my uncle, but we only visited a couple of farms. I never saw any Fairborn there."

"Kaerin Arastina and her sister Joycel had a small vineyard there before their farm was destroyed by raiders, along with two other Fairborn families. All burnt completely to the last shed. They wisely kept away from your uncle, no doubt. But back to the business before us. It is my duty to inspect the naegnast and choose your weapon for the duel. Shall I pick one equal to a short sword?" asked Jaek.

"Yes, and I shall start the duel right-handed and then, if I see an opportunity, switch to my left and hope it confuses Bergan."

Jaek nodded. "Remember, victory in the duel is not as important as fighting well and with honor. Switching hands would not be a dishonorable tactic, but I would not count on any confusion lasting too long. Bergan is no novice to fighting. He *is* proud. If he were to act dishonorably to win the fight, it would be a victory of sorts for you. Now let us practice the opening again."

Chapter Five:

The Duel

6

THE FOUL

BORTIS

6:00 p.m.

BORTIS STOOD AT THE EDGE of the thirty-foot diameter circle, the corin dala rind, mentally repeating the Espero phrases he had been taught. A sizable crowd gathered in the Great Hall, and he felt his chest prickle with beads of sweat. The hushed voices of the spectators murmured loudly in his ears. The everlights around the hall were dimmed, and flaming torches were set at each of the cardinal points around the circle. Fragrant smoke smelling of sage and pitch mixed in his nostrils and added to the surreal scene. The flickering torches cast dancing shadows, like something from a dream or a nightmare.

Prince Andune was sitting on his throne with Angel seated on his left. Bortis nodded to her, but she only stared back, her face stern, with just a touch of pity in her eyes.

I guess she thinks I was stupid, he thought. *Well, I can't blame her. I was.*

His opponent had yet to make an appearance.

Bortis whispered to Jaek. "What happens if he doesn't show up? Do I win?"

"He will be here. Lord Andune's seneschal will ring a chime three minutes before the duel is due to start. If he were to fail to make an appearance within four minutes of the chime, they would declare you the winner, but that won't happen. Bergan has fought duels before. He is trying to unnerve you."

A soft chime sounded in the hall, and voices fell silent in expectation. Prince Andune rose from his throne and walked to the center of the circle.

As if by magic, Bergan stepped up to the opposite side of the circle and stared insolently at Bortis.

"As I said," Jaek muttered.

The Fairborn prince stopped near a small circle in the center of the corin dala rind.

"Nohor ncas brin quintare, man indóme ocerato?" said Andune, looking at Bortis with his sardonic smile.

Bortis raised his right hand with the naeg-nast and said slowly but as clearly as he could, "Ni termáre an mime nohor. Ni paime nohmage ana tye, héru Andune."

The Fairborn prince arched a brow at the use of Espro, then nodded at Bortis with what he thought might have been a sliver of respect. Andune turned to Bergan, who repeated the salute.

"We are here to settle an affair of honor with the Badhron bui dagr-Naeg nast," said Andune, switching to the common tongue. "As the challenged party, Prince deDraconis has chosen sinta ecet naeg-nast. Are both parties ready and able to proceed?"

Jaek assented and was echoed by Bergan's second.

The Fairborn prince repeated the rules. "Does either party have any questions?"

Bortis shook his head. Jaek answered, "The challenged does not!"

Bergan's second responded, "The challenger does not!"

Andune walked back to his throne and seated himself. "Let the Badhron bui dagr begin!"

Immediately after his words, the chime sounded, and Bortis advanced into the dueling circle. He strode to the edge of the smaller inner circle, as Jaek had instructed him. *This is it*, he thought, *my chance to make it right and maybe win Andune's aid for Art.*

Bergan swaggered to his place opposite Bortis across the inner circle. He waited for Bergan to hold out his naeg-nast first. Jaek had told him he would probably hold it low, showing his lack of respect. He surprised Bortis by holding it high above his head. Bortis reached out with his naeg-nast and touched it to that of his opponent.

Holding his naeg-nast against his opponent's weapon seemed to last forever. The second chime rang out, and Bergan struck quickly, not at Bortis's body as he was expecting, but with a lightning-quick strike against his right hand—the one holding his naeg-nast.

The pain was excruciating. A welt appeared on the back of his right hand. His fingers went numb, and the wand flew from his hand. Instinctively, he reached out with his other hand and grasped the wand in midair before it could fall to the ground. He jumped back and waved the pain-stick before him defensively. If his right hand hadn't hurt so badly, he would have laughed at the disappointment flashing across the face of his opponent, who had thought he had secured a quick victory.

The disappointment quickly fled, however. Bergan took a step back. "Do you wish to concede now, or shall we continue, orqui?" he sneered.

Bortis felt his face grow warm, a sure sign of his anger, but he couldn't give in to rage. Rage was not a warrior's friend. It was as if he could hear his uncle's words when Brett would score a painful hit against him. "Focus! No anger, concentrate on the objective!" His uncle may have had his faults, both as a teacher and a person, but he was a born warrior and he had done his best to teach Bortis the way of the warrior.

He pushed his anger to the back of his mind. He thought to make some witty comeback concerning elves, but his thoughts flew to Jaek—he was a Fairborn, and he had done his best to help Bortis prepare for this duel. No, he would not lower himself to the level of Bergan and stoop to taunts and insults.

He circled to his left, swung the pain-stick in tight, looping swirls, and made feints and jabs. The back of his right hand burned as if someone had branded it with a red-hot iron, but the feeling was returning. He could flex his fingers now, as he and the Fairborn circled around the center of the dueling ring.

Bergan feinted, then followed up with a pair of slashing attacks Bortis defended against with ease. He then answered with a quick jab of his own, scoring a poke against Bergan's upper arm. Bergan leaped back with a growl. A small red welt appeared on Bergan's upper arm.

Bergan scowled and attacked with a flurry of slashing attacks Bortis was hard-pressed to evade. However, Bergan's muscle memory was failing him because Bortis's parries were not coming from the accustomed angles. Bortis parried again and scored with a quick riposte, leaving a large welt across Bergan's chest.

Bergan grunted in pain and surprise, then assailed Bortis with another flurry of rapid attacks, which he easily dodged.

Bortis silently thanked his Uncle Brett once again as he deflected a series of rapid, slashing attacks. His quick riposte scored another jab to Bergan's ribs, and Bergan answered with a feint aimed at Bortis's legs. Although such a strike was illegal, Bortis instinctively brought his guard down to block. Before he could recover, Bergan answered with a slash that scored a hit upon Bortis's right cheek.

Tears filled his eyes, and he almost dropped his pain-stick. He wiped at his eyes with his right wrist, trying to clear his sight as he swung the naeg-nast wildly.

"FOUL!" came Jaek's loud cry, echoing around the hall. A loud gong reverberated.

"Stand down!" came an imperious cry from Prince Andune, and he strode into the circle, glaring at Bergan.

"It was an accident, my Lord. The Orqui bent forward just as I made an attack toward his chest," said Bergan.

"Liar!" Jaek stepped up to Bortis's side and pulled his hand away from his face. "He missed your eyes, thank Mother Veda."

"Healers! Bring almas!" cried out Andune.

"I am right here, my Lord!" said a familiar voice. Kae already had a small jar open, and covered her fingertip with a glob of the rosy salve. "It will help with the sting, Bort." She wiped the aromatic substance gently upon the welt.

The pain receded, and Bortis wiped his eyes again, his vision clearing.

"It was an accident, Lord Andune. I can't help if the human is clumsy," said Bergan.

Jaek turned to Bergan. "Ni challarge tye."

Bergan snapped his head to glare at Jaek. "You challenge me because I accidentally hit a clumsy human? Are you mad? I refuse!"

"No, I do not call challenge for Prince Bortis's sake, but for the honor of Lord Andune. You have lied to his face. Twice! You feinted a foul to his legs, and when he reacted, you struck his face with deliberate malice."

Bergan's face grew pale at the sting of Jaek's words, and he licked his lips. "My Lord … I … I ask your forgiveness. In the heat of battle, I acted without thinking, but … but …"

"Do you accept the challenge, Bergan?" asked Andune. "I am afraid you have gone from defending my honor to attacking it, and Jaek is my cousin and my former rúatan hrondo tíri. I know well how he defends my honor. What say you?"

Bergan's face had the look of a trapped animal. He licked his lips as he looked around. "I accept, but under protest!"

Andune peered around at the gathering. "Who will be Jaek's Tatya otorno?" Several Fairborn stepped forward. Jaek pointed to one who bowed in return. "Who will stand with Bergan? Will you, Tomo?" Andune glanced at the Fairborn who was acting as Bergan's second.

"I do not offer myself as Tatya otorno for Bergan in this matter. If this challenge was not underway, I would withdraw as his second now. It was a dishonorable attack he made against the human."

"Nevertheless, as no one seems to offer themselves for this role, I will ask you to stand with him for the challenge with my cousin," said Andune.

Tomo bowed. "As you will, my Lord."

Prince Andune looked back at the couriers, still standing by his throne. "Quawl Istar, I appoint you Gwanur to the challenge."

A white-haired Fairborn bowed in return. "As you would, my Lord."

Andune looked back at Bortis. "Are you ready to continue?"

Bortis grinned. "Of course." Again, he thought he saw an approving gleam in the Fairborn Prince's eyes.

Andune walked to his throne. Kae and Jaek retreated to stand outside the circle. Bortis looked at Bergan and smiled sweetly. "Shall we dance?"

"Begin again upon the chime," called Andune. Within seconds, the chime rang out.

Bortis flexed the fingers of his right hand. It no longer hurt nearly as badly. The welt on the back was an ugly red, but he judged he could use the hand again if needed.

With his left hand holding the naeg-nast before him, he advanced a few steps toward Bergan, a confident smile on his face. The Fairborn sneered at his approach.

"Let's finish this, Orqui trash. You don't stand a chance against a real fighter, and you know it."

If Bergan tried another foul, he would be disappointed. He would not use quanti-magic against the Fairborn, but he decided casting a protection upon himself wasn't forbidden now that Bergan had feinted one foul and committed another. Donel had told him he didn't need to be holding his crysword to cast a shield. He pictured the rune Eihwaz in his mind and envisioned himself surrounded by invisible armor.

Bergan sprang forward with a series of slashing attacks aimed at his midsection. Bortis parried and attempted a riposte, but Bergan had learned a little from his earlier attacks, and he counter-riposted with a solid hit to Bortis's left arm. Bortis felt the blow, but there was no sudden flash of pain. His shield was working!

He jumped back as if he felt the agony, furiously conceiving a way to end the fight quickly. He was almost at the edge of the circle, which gave him an idea.

Letting his arm hang down as if it pained him, he pointed the naeg-nast to the ground. He took another step back, as close to the edge as he dared.

Smiling with triumph, Bergan charged at him, leading with another barrage of slashing attacks. Bortis let him land a solid blow against his ribs, and he pretended to have trouble holding his naeg-nast steady with his left hand.

Bergan swung another slash, and Bortis smoothly moved to his left, grabbed Bergan by his right wrist, and gave a hard pull. The naeg-nast hit his ribs with a solid blow, but Bergan, aided by Bortis's powerful tug, went past his target. His left foot came down outside the circle.

Bortis turned his back on his opponent and walked away. The gong rang out, but he heard Bergan's footsteps as the Fairborn ignored the sound and advanced to attack his exposed back.

"STOP!" shouted Andune, now on his feet. "BERGAN! DAR!"

Bergan stopped and looked at the Fairborn Prince in confusion. "Did he concede?"

"No. You stepped out of the circle. I declare Prince Bortis the victor," replied the prince.

"But the Orqui pulled my arm!" Bergan cried out. "I think he cast magic!"

Andune strode into the circle. "Prince Bortis, did you use magic to pull Bergan from the circle?"

Bortis shook his head. "No, I just grabbed his arm and helped him step out."

Andune peered closely at Bortis's chest. "Did you use magic upon yourself?"

Bortis hesitated a moment, then nodded. "I cast a shielding upon myself in case he tried another foul. Did I break a rule?"

Andune thought for a moment, then shook his head. "Had I known you were capable of casting such a spell, I would have forbidden it. But I did not. You have won the challenge fairly. Healers, attend to the duelists," said Andune, and he walked back to his throne.

Kae rushed to Bortis's side, treating each welt with the soothing balm. Another Fairborn stepped up to Bergan and began attending to him as well.

After Kae had administered the soothing almas to the welts upon his body, Bortis stood before Andune's throne. When he caught Andune's eye, he bowed and waited.

Andune looked down from the dais. "May I ask you a question, Prince Bortis?"

"Of course, Lord Andune."

"If you were capable of casting the shield upon yourself, why did you wait until after Bergan scored hits upon you? Were you trying to trick him and then use your shield as an advantage?"

"No, I didn't plan on using the shield at all. Only after his dishonorable acts, his strike to my face, did I decide I would not stain my honor by using the shield against him. I remembered your words, and you only prohibited using magic against the opponent."

Andune stared at him for a long moment, as if weighing his words, and then nodded. "So I am correct then in assuming if he had not fouled you, you would not have cast the spell."

"Yes, Lord Andune."

Andune nodded again. "Has Donel taught you the Truth Spell?"

"No, I have heard of such a spell in stories, but Donel has only taught me shielding, the Mindshield, and trueseeing. He has told me he plans to teach me more upon my return to the Crystal Tower. But it is a matter of time. We do not have much, and he plans to spend most of it with Artos, teaching him that which he needs to know. What more he plans to teach me, he did not say."

"The Truth Spell is very helpful to a leader, whether he be king or war leader. I would suggest you ask him to teach you—time permitting, of course."

Bortis nodded, confused.

"When my cousin Jaek called out Bergan for lying, I cast the spell. When he lied a second time, it was clear to me. I am glad you did not lie to me, Prince Bortis."

"What? Oh … you mean about what spells I cast?"

"No, about your intentions. You are correct—your honor is unstained. Unlike Bergan, who I think will feel the wrath of my cousin for his unsavory tricks against you and for lying to me about it."

"I hope Jaek will beat him! He deserves a few welts!" said Bortis wholeheartedly.

"My cousin is one of the best swordsmen in all of Fairinlan. Bergan is nowhere near his skill with a blade."

"What if he chooses to duel with quarterstaves? Or blind with a dagger? Jaek said Bergan has skill with those."

Once more, Andune smiled his half-smile. "I predict Bergan will pick sicil naeg-nast and will refuse a blind fight if Jaek suggests it. The dagger-sized wands leave the smallest welts. I was surprised that you chose the sinta ecet."

"That was my doing, Lord Andune," said Jaek, stepping up and bowing. "I told him Bergan's strengths and asked him which weapon he was most comfortable fighting with. He said he would fight with any, but the short sword was what he was most used to."

Andune nodded. "When is the duel, and what weapon did Bergan choose?"

"Amrún anor tomorrow, and as you predicted, he chose sicil naeg-nast."

"So soon? I am surprised," said Andune.

"That was Tomo's doing, I believe. I heard him tell Bergan he was leaving to go back to Fairinlan tomorrow at midday, and if Bergan wanted him to stand with him, it would have to be early tomorrow."

"Sunrise tomorrow it is then. I imagine you would like to witness this duel, Prince Bortis?"

"Very much, Lord Andune, if I may?" said Bortis.

"Congratulations, Bort," said Angel, who had sat silently beside her father during the conversation. "When do you plan on returning to the Crystal Tower?"

"I think I should go as soon as possible. Tomorrow, I guess. After the duel, of course. Will that be okay with you?"

"Oh, I will not be setting out with you. Kae will be your guide back to the Magic Man's tower."

Bortis blinked. All of their prior conversations had led him to believe that Angel was planning on returning. He was about to ask when something in her eyes made him stop.

"I see. Well, I know Kae knows the way." Clearing his throat, he turned back to the Fairborn prince. "Have you changed your mind, Lord Andune? Will you give us a guide?"

The Fairborn Prince shook his head. "When my wife was murdered some years ago, I swore I would never enter the deEagledon demesne again nor send any of my people there as long as her brother rules. They stole her birthright, Prince Bortis. I promised her I would do no harm to her Family, but when she died, I swore I would never set foot there to help the usurper. That is true for my people as well. I am sorry, but I will not break that vow."

Bortis's heart sunk. He had let Artos down.

"Lord Andune, I still intend to go with the two brothers," said Jaek. "You are not sending me. I go of my own free will. I go to avenge my brother. There is a blood debt I wish to settle."

"I will not forbid you a blood debt. Taur was my cousin as well. But I will allow no others of my people to go with them. That includes you, Kaerin Arastina."

Kae had come up and was standing nearby. "I hear your words, Lord Andune," said the Fairborn healer, bowing to the prince.

"Prince Bortis, I would speak with my cousin now, in private. Kae, would you escort the prince back to his quarters?"

"I will be happy to do so, Lord Andune," she answered. "I believe more almas might be needed on Bortis's wounds before he sleeps, so I shall attend to that as well." She took Bortis's arm and led him from the Great Hall.

Chapter Six:

Failure

7

SETH
DEDARRELLYEL

BORTIS

9/23/1971 ar

5:00 a.m.

Once again, Bortis awoke to the sound of knocking.

"Prince Bortis? Kaerin said you wished to be awakened in time to eat your breakfast before the Badhron bui dagr. It is on your table. Kaerin should arrive within the hour to escort you to the Great Hall."

"Thank you," he called out and waited until he heard the soft click of the door before throwing back the curtain and climbing from the bed. A sick feeling filled his stomach. He had let down Art. No guide would help them reach Starstone Tower. Jaek was going to join their enterprise, but Jaek himself had said he was not familiar with the places they would need to traverse to reach the ancient magic college. Bortis's inability to secure a guide had probably added weeks to the journey. Weeks they didn't have if Donel's assessment of the situation was correct.

Perhaps things in his world were not quite the way he had thought they were. He had thought about it a great deal on the

99

trip from the Crystal Tower to Alfhiem. The burnt-out remains of the farmstead they had passed between Swan's Nest and the Great Tree had shaken him a little. Angel had said it belonged to Cat and Susi's family. What convinced him it was more than just a raid by bandits was the destruction of the orchard and the chicken yard. Bandits rarely destroyed the things their victims used to make money. They would mark who had means of income and return at a later date to rob them again. At least that was what Uncle Brett had told him, and it made sense to Bortis. Who would kill the chicken that laid diamond eggs?

He would have liked to have asked Kaerin some questions, but on their trip back to his room last eve after the duel, she had cut him off, shaking her head. She told him they must wait until they left Alfhiem to discuss matters. She wouldn't even say why; she simply refused to talk. It was probably the presence of the guard escorting them, but it was frustrating.

Breakfast smelled good. Though his stomach felt a little queasy, it was far from enough to spoil his appetite. He quickly dressed and sat down at his table.

He was only halfway through his meal when there was a knock at the door. *That's odd,* he thought. *Usually they don't come until right after I've finished.* "Enter!" he called out and continued to eat.

It was Kae. "I'm a little early. You have time to finish your meal. I brought some almas with me if you are still sore."

He shook his head. "The welts are gone. Your balm is very good."

"Yes, I will make certain to give you and Artos a supply to take with you on your journey to Nénarambal Tirion. I believe Jaek carries a supply as well. I need to wash my hands. May I avail myself of your washroom?"

"Uh … sure. Feel free." Bortis finished his ham, took the last gulp of coffee, and pushed back from the table.

Kae was only gone a moment and came back to stand near the exit of the room. When Bortis began walking towards the door, she met his eye and flashed a quick glance at the door to the washroom.

"Let me wash up, and we can head out to watch Jaek tattoo Bergan."

She nodded. "We have time. Sunrise is at least twenty minutes away. Take your time."

Bortis entered the washroom. The edge of a piece of paper poked out from beneath the bar of fragrant green soap. He picked up the soap with his left hand as he waved his right over the faucet to start the flow of warm water. Glancing at the note, he pretended to examine the soap. Printed in a graceful hand was: 'This room is probably safe, but your room has ears and eyes. Keep your questions until we have left Alfhiem. Wet this paper.' He held the note under the warm stream of water as he washed his hands. The note dissolved and washed away with the suds.

Silently, he walked to the great hall. He and Kae went side by side with the ever-present guard following a few steps behind.

The Great Hall's everlights were once again dimmed, and torches outlined the thirty-foot circle of the Badhron bui dagr-Naeg nast. If anything, even more spectators were present than the evening before. The crowd parted for him and Kae, and they joined Jaek, already waiting at the circle's edge with his second. Bergan waited on the other side. No last-second entrance this time. This amused Bortis.

Jaek turned. "Good morning, Prince Bortis. I trust you slept well after your exercise of last evening?"

Bortis nodded. "I did, thank you."

"I shall be ready to join you on our trek back to the Crystal Tower. It will be good to see the Earl again."

"The Earl? … Oh, you mean Donel. I guess if Prince Tirinvo and he are friends, of course you must know him. I hadn't even thought about it."

"Oh yes. Taur and I used to join in the singing with Prince Tirinvo when Lord Varyan and Lord Donel would play their crysharps together."

"I know he has a blue crysword, but I didn't realize he has a crysharp as well."

Jaek chuckled. "If you saw his sword, then you saw the harp. They are one and the same."

Bortis's jaw dropped in amazement. "I didn't know he could do that." He thought back to the Bard's tale of the events at the Eyrie. "I remember the Bard made his harp into a bow. Can anyone do such things? Uncle Cam told us that those were just tales."

"I do not know. But Prince Tirinvo could also change his crysword to a bow, so I would think with training, any wielder of a crysword could. You would need to ask Lord Donel."

"I will do that."

Further conversation was cut off as Prince Andune walked into the corin dala rind and spoke the opening words of the ritual. Kae and Bortis stood next to Jaek's second as the duel began.

The outcome was short and anticlimactic—three quick flurries of blows after a few steps and feints, mostly by Jaek. Then Bergan conceded. He had two welts upon his chest and another upon the wrist with which he had held his naeg-nast.

Jaek was unmarked. Directly after the blow to his wrist, Bergan dropped his pain-stick and conceded.

Jaek's Tatya otorno, a dark-haired Fairborn who introduced himself as Naidro, chuckled. "Less than two minutes. The fool knew he was outclassed. He got out as soon as he felt he wouldn't look like a total coward."

Jaek bowed to Andune, then made his way over to Bortis. "I shall go ready my pack and join you within a half an hour and we may depart."

Bortis bowed to the Fairborn. "That was quick work. I wish he had been braver, so you could have given him a few more welts."

"His kind are bullies. They seldom learn. He might even try to pick another quarrel with you to make himself feel better. Watch yourself." Jaek nodded, and he and his second walked off. Bortis looked around to catch Kae's eye to signal he was ready to return to his room. She was standing near Andune's throne, speaking quietly with Angel. He made his way to join her when Andune called out to him.

"Prince Bortis! A word with you before you depart."

He stepped up to a few yards before the throne and bowed. A person stood next to the throne wearing the robes of a druid, his cowl drawn closely around his face to hide his features in the shadow.

"I have received some packages that need to be delivered to Hir Donel," said Andune, nodding at the druid beside the throne. "I would ask that you escort the bearer of these to the Crystal Tower, as it seems my usual method of delivering them has been temporarily discommoded."

"I can do that," said Bortis, examining the druid. "No problem."

"Thank you." Andune turned to speak in Espro with the Fairborn standing beside the throne.

The druid nodded, still hidden in his cowl, picked up a large pack which he slung over his shoulder, and stepped up beside Bortis.

Feeling dismissed, Bortis looked to see Angel had disappeared and Kae was awaiting him.

"Shall we be on our way, Prince Bortis? By the time we swing past your room, get your pack, and make our way to the door, Jaek should be prepared for us. Lord Andune has chosen to let you leave without restricting your sight. This is something he has done for all the Daughters of the Wind, but only a few other humans from Rainbow Valley. I think you made a good impression on him."

"Not good enough, I'm afraid." Bortis sighed. "I'm going to have to tell Art I failed. We will have to make our way to Starstone Tower unguided."

Irritatingly, Kae seemed to be trying not to smile.

The trip back to the entrance of Alfhiem took little time. They arrived there on the heels of Jaek, who was carrying one pack upon his back and another in his hands. The druid had remained silent as he followed them, first to Bortis's room and then to the entrance. This suited Bortis. He didn't feel like talking anyway. He was trying to decide how to tell Art that he had failed miserably.

"Thank you, Mel," said Kae as she took the pack from him.

Jaek smiled warmly at Kae. "My pleasure, Melba."

"Melba?" asked Bortis. "Is that your middle name, Kae?"

"Oh, no!" The Fairborn woman smiled and then, to Bortis's astonishment, she held her pack in one hand and pulled Jaek close to give him a quick kiss on the cheek.

"Mel and Melba are terms of endearment in our tongue."

Jaek looked at Bortis and gave a quick nod. "If you are ready, shall we proceed?"

Bortis nodded and followed Jaek as he walked to the end of the hall. Upon reaching the blank wall, the Fairborn spoke a word softly in Espro, and the wall before him split open with the creaking sound Bortis had heard when he had entered Alfhiem. Jaek and Kae led the way, with Bortis and the druid following behind. Moments after they stepped down the three steps, the creaking sound repeated. When Bortis looked back, the steps had vanished within the bark of the majestic tree. After a few strides, Bortis realized he could not discern where the entrance was located. The hard ground left no tracks, and the bark at the base of the thousand-year oak showed no sign that an entrance existed.

The group made their way to the stepping stones the party had taken when they first approached Andune's hidden stronghold. They crossed the lily pads, then followed the track to the east, and when the path divided, they followed the track to the north, back toward Swan's Nest.

They had walked for most of half an hour when they reached the burnt-out remains of the farmstead that had been home to Cat and Susi. Kae paused. "We are past Andune's sentries, Bortis. If you have questions, I think I can safely answer them now."

"Well, the only question I had was about Angel. I thought she was going back to the Crystal Tower with us. I guess I could have just asked you back there." He gestured behind him toward the gigantic tree they were leaving behind.

"I think that was best not raised in Alfhiem, Bortis. Because you see, I couldn't have answered you. At least not truthfully, and I prefer to always be truthful."

"What? I don't understand."

Kaerin smiled at his confusion. "Why did you think she wouldn't be returning to Donel's home?"

"Because she said so. You were right there. Weren't you?"

"I said I wouldn't be setting out with you, Bort," said a familiar voice. "Not that I wouldn't be going back."

Bortis spun around to see Angel walk up behind him.

"Well met," said the scout with a smile at his obvious confusion.

"It will displease Lord Andune that you have followed us, Angel," said Jaek, frowning at Andune's daughter. "He will send people after you. He will know where you have gone." He looked at Kae with a quirked brow, but the Fairborn woman only smiled back and shrugged.

"Undoubtedly," Angel replied. "But not for a few days. I told him I was fasting. So if I am not present for dinner tonight or breakfast tomorrow, he will think nothing of it. Perhaps longer. Then, when they go into my rooms, they will find the note I have left for him. In it, I told him I was returning to be with the Daughters."

The druid, silent up to this point, let out a hearty laugh. He pushed back the hood from his head and nodded to Bortis. His features were familiar.

"Seth! Seth deDarrellyel. I didn't know you were a druid.

You weren't wearing robes when you came to Castle Draconis last Midsummer with Count Glendon."

Seth was seven or eight years older than Bortis, but had been to the castle many times and knew the brothers well. "Both my sister Brandi and I are druids, Bort. My father knows how your Uncle Bretton felt about The Mother's Church, and he suggested it was better to go visiting your castle in regular garb rather than get into an argument about the relative merits of the two sects. I believe your Uncle Cameron knew I was of The Green Bough, but he said nothing."

"Uncle Brett preferred the Sky sect, but to be truthful, he wasn't really a religious person at all. He just thought the Sky Knights were a better choice for a man than being a druid, or even a priest, for that matter, because they weren't afraid to fight."

"Yes, I know. The Darrell said Duke Bretton thought we druids were all tree huggers. Not every man chooses a sword as his weapon." Seth smiled, reached into his robe, and pulled out a slender green rod about a foot long and an inch in girth. He shook his hand, and the rod grew into a staff a full six feet long. The staff appeared to be a plain wooden staff, but it had to be far more. "My preference is the quarterstaff. Like my father and brother Yoshua."

"Is The Darrell a druid too?"

"No, only my sister and me. But we all have crystaffs. Except Brandi prefers her crysickle."

Seth looked at Angel and shook his head. "You are as bad as Brandi. She would often say something sure to be misconstrued in order to get her own way."

"Brandi and I both understand our fathers. Yours at least is not as hard to manage as mine is." Angel started walking along the trail toward Swan's Nest.

"I might argue that point. Prince Andune can be stubborn, but in a temper, I think he might fall behind The Darrell."

Angel looked doubtful, and Seth was quick to add, "Andune has a temper, it is true, but he is ice to my father's fire."

Angel laughed. "It is true he does not rant and shout. But his icy glare makes people wish they were not the object of his scrutiny."

Seth examined Bortis as he fell in beside him. "Is something bothering you, Prince Bortis? You have been quiet on our journey, yet I seem to recall you were always somewhat of a boisterous brother. Artos and Duka were the silent, introspective ones."

Bortis sighed. "I have failed in my mission for Artos. It galls me, though I knew I was the wrong person to send to ask for the help of The West Wind. But they wouldn't listen."

"I see. In what way have you disappointed Prince Artos? Perhaps it may be remedied in some manner?" After Bortis explained, Seth said, "I see, and yet he asked you to escort me to the Crystal Tower, did he not?"

"Yeah. He said there are some things to be delivered to Donel."

"Yes, I have a package from the Countess Spryngdal. Then I will be free to go about my business. I attend to many of the smaller settlements scattered through the Mountains of Myst. There are several which have no priests or druids of their own, and so I go from one to another doing The Mother's will. I was thinking it might be time to wander up into the deEagledon demesne and see if any were in need of my services. I had mentioned this to Andune two nights past when I first arrived at Alfhiem."

Bortis's jaw dropped open. "Then ... then he knew you could guide us!" He turned to Angel. "Did you realize?"

"I did not discuss your mission with my father. I thought it better that I showed no interest. He is worried about the giant raven." She shook her head. "He knows an Abomination rides it, and he wants to keep me safe. I should have told Cat not to inform him about the harpy attacking me. That was what made him call me to Alfhiem more than anything else."

"You are all he has left of your mother, Angel," said Kae. "It is natural he would want to keep you from harm's way."

Jaek nodded in agreement. "Andune has lost a wife, and now a cousin, to this affair. He does not wish to lose his daughter as well."

"I remember you said your mother died, Angel," said Bortis. "Was she killed by a harpy too?"

"A few years ago, she was visiting some friends in the valley. A band of Beastmen attacked and murdered her and her two guards. Not far from here, in fact. It was the first time a band of them had made a raid into the valley in years, decades. My father admitted to me he believed there was an Abomination involved as well. He never told me that before. They followed the band back into the mountains to the south. My father said they caught up with them about twenty miles from the Valley. They killed the Beastmen, but something escaped. It took the form of a wolf and fled deep into the mountains. They lost its track in a valley far from here, where it disappeared into an area that has many giant wolves. My father still hunts that beast."

Bortis felt a chill. "You mean where we sent Cari? There's an Abomination who hides among the wolves?"

"My little sister knows the trail to the Fairborn lands, Bort. They won't stray from that path. Andune keeps a good watch upon it," said Kae. "It may well be the same Abomination that's now patrolling on the giant Raven."

"I hope so," replied Bortis. "It's good to know that Cari, at least, is going away from danger instead of running right into it. Let's get going. If we hurry, we can be back at the Crystal Tower yet tonight."

Part Three

Carimus's Journey

N
THE MOUNTAINS OF MYST
WOLFE
LAKE DETH
|TEN MILES|
FAIRINHORST
MAPS BY INKARNATE
HIDDEN VALE

Chapter Seven:

The Trek South

8

WOLVES AND...

CARIMUS

9/24/1971 ar

9:30 a.m.

"RUN, CARI! RUN!" panted Vix.

The four companions raced down the path, all of them breathing in panting gasps. A wolf's howling cry shattered the air.

Rachel, leading the flight, stumbled and nearly fell, causing the group behind her to slow. "We can't keep this up much longer!" cried Vix as she caught up to Carimus. He nodded numbly, with no wind to spare for words, his breath coming in jagged gasps.

"That fir ahead," cried Joy. "Climb it!"

"We'll be trapped!" protested Vix.

"No! See the branch of that other tree? Go. Trust me," replied the Fairborn, last in the line.

Carimus was too tired to object. When Rachel started climbing, he was right behind her. He was running on pure adrenaline now and would soon be completely spent. He heard

Vix climbing behind him, and his vision was filled with the form of Rachel ahead of him.

Suddenly, the path up the tree was blocked—an enormous branch from a thousand-year pine lay alongside the trunk of the fir. Rachel had moved to the left side of the trunk ahead of him, and he followed her. She reached out from the large branch she was standing on and pulled him over to join her.

The branch was slightly rounded, but was so large that Carimus could collapse upon it with no danger of falling off. He lay there panting as Vix, and then Joy, joined Rachel upon the rough surface.

"We can't stay here, Cari," said Joy. "Catch your breath, and then we must keep moving."

Nodding, he drew a long, ragged breath. His wind was returning. But he just wanted to lie there and take a nap. He was so tired.

"Where can we go?" he gasped. "We're trapped up here, aren't we?"

The howls of the wolves on their trail turned to frustrated yips and growls. The wolves had reached the fir tree.

"There's eight … no, nine of them!" said Vix, who peered over the edge of the branch at the pack below.

The branch they were on disappeared into the fog in both directions. The boles of more of the gigantic trees were scattered around him. Between the thick foliage and the habitual fog, it was impossible to see very far in any direction.

"How far have we come?" Carimus asked as he gradually stopped panting.

"Almost twenty miles from the valley," answered Joy. "Four miles since the wolves came upon us."

"I didn't expect to find giant wolves on this trail," said

Rachel. "When we came this way last year, you told me Andune's scouts patrolled this path."

"I didn't expect them either," said Joy. "I never heard of giant wolves coming this far down from the high reaches. It's abnormal."

All three daughters looked at Carimus.

"I fear someone, or something, is looking for you, Cari," said Joy. Vix nodded glumly.

"How could they?" asked Rachel. The tall, blond girl shook her head. "It has to be bad luck, that's all."

More howls echoed in the distance.

"More wolves." Carimus felt a quiver in his voice. The sounds were terrifying.

"That settles it!" said Vix. "This isn't natural. We gotta get out of here."

"We must move silently along this branch, and we may leave them at the base of the tree we climbed," said Joy.

"We'll be leaving the trail, though," said Carimus. "How will you know where to go if we lose the trail? We'll be lost in the mist."

Joy, studying the branch they were perched on, put her finger to her lips and led them down the branch.

It was easy to walk on. It only got larger, and soon they neared the junction with the tree. Carimus followed Joy, with the other two following behind. He tried to model his stride after that of the Fairborn girl ahead of him, although he could hear the slight scuff each time his feet came down on the rough bark. Joy and the others all moved as noiselessly as cats.

By the time they reached the tree, the branch was at least thirty feet wide, where it joined the trunk. How would they ever get down from here? There were other branches, but none were close by or small enough to be of any use in climbing to the ground, anyway.

Once Joy reached the trunk, she put her fingers to her lips and motioned Carimus to come close.

"Be very, very quiet," she whispered in his ear. He nodded. When Vix and Rachel joined them, she leaned close to Vix and whispered a few words to her. Vix silently slipped out of her pack, reached inside, and took a coil of the spider-silk rope. She efficiently tied a loop around her waist and passed the rest of the coil to Rachel, who nodded and held the rope ready.

Vix went to her hands and knees and crawled toward the edge of the branch, with Rachel keeping the rope free but playing it out behind the crawling girl.

Joy joined Rachel and wrapped an arm around her, feeding the rope that tethered Vix.

Slowly and carefully, Carimus sat down on the branch with his back against the gigantic tree. He felt he should offer to help; he felt so useless. But he was so tired. Just how had they gotten into this mess anyway? What would Bort do if he were here? He would know what to do. He wouldn't be afraid of wolves. He thought back upon their parting. Was it just two days ago?

9/22/1971 ar

11:00 a.m.

The trip back to the Nest differed from their trip to the Crystal Tower. Instead of the steady walk used on their trip into the mountains, they jogged, walking off and on the entire way. Plus, he was burdened, carrying two packs—one stuffed inside the other—and wearing his new one, the one gifted to him by Donel, heavy with a spider-silk tent, sleeping bag, and all the supplies he would need on this trek. Bortis was wearing a new pack as well, but his was much lighter, carrying only a few sticks of elk jerky. Except for a dry canteen, the pack Bortis was carrying was empty. Carimus had asked Bortis to carry the other packs rather than make him carry them along with the load on his back, but Bortis had refused, telling him he should consider it training for his trip to Fairinhorst. Bortis now treated Donel with more respect than he had at first, but he was still very bossy as far as his little brother was concerned, as if he were trying to step into the role of their Uncle Brett. Oh well, he had promised Susi he would bring her pack back, and Artos needed someone to return his borrowed one as well.

At the last ridge, Angel motioned for them to wait while she crested the edge on her hands and knees. She carefully surveyed the landscape below before signaling for the others to join her.

"No sign of the Crow. Everyone keep alert. If you spot it, give a whistle and freeze." She turned and began the trek down the last slope. At the bottom, she changed their marching order.

"Alright, here's the plan: Joy and I will take Bort to the nest, and I'll meet with whoever Father has sent to nursemaid me back to Alfhiem. Vix and Rach, you wait at the west watch post until you see the all-clear. That will mean we have left, and the three of you can go to the Nest. Whoever Father sent might want to wait until tomorrow, but I'll insist we go right away. I'll take Kae with me and Bort. Joy will wait for you three, and you can leave early tomorrow morning. Joy knows where Father's sentries will be posted, so avoid them and get as far from the Valley as you can before you make camp."

Vix nodded. "Safe journeys, Angel. We'll be back as soon as we can. Before the winter snows make the mountains too treacherous for travel."

Angel nodded, then hugged Vix and Rachel. To Carimus's surprise, she smiled and hugged him as well. "Safe journeys."

Joy gave them each a smile, then followed Angel.

Bortis turned to Carimus. "Stay out of trouble, Squirt. Find out if the seer knows where Duke is hiding and then come back and let us know, okay?"

"I will, Bort. Remember now, you are Art's voice. Be nice … for once. Okay?"

"Hey, I'm always nice, and I'll punch anyone in the nose who says I'm not!" Bortis smiled, but doubt shone in his eyes as he turned and followed Joy and Angel.

When they reached the spot where the trail branched, Angel looked back at Vix and nodded. Vix put her hand on Carimus' shoulder, and the three of them stopped and waited as the others walked out of view.

"Come this way." Vix softly left the path and proceeded through the brush until she stopped near the base of a tall fir tree. "There's a watch post up here. You can climb up if you like or wait here with Rach. Be as quiet as you can. We don't know who's listening." She slipped off her pack, leaned it against the base of the tree, and started to climb.

Carimus was winded from the long hike. He was tempted to rest, but after setting aside the packs he was carrying and removing the pack he was wearing, he followed Vix up the tree.

It was a long climb, and Carimus was wishing he had stayed below when he finally reached Vix's perch. She was sitting comfortably on a small wooden platform nestled between two sturdy branches. Trying not to pant, he turned around and sat down, looking out at the Rainbow Valley. His eyes widened as he took in the beauty of the multicolored autumn foliage. They sat above the tops of the nearby trees.

Before he could say a word, Vix covered his mouth with her hand and pointed into the sky. There, floating above the Valley, circled three large birds. Carimus recognized them as harpy eagles, just like the enslaved bird that had tried to attack Angel and wounded his brother. A chill ran down his spine.

"They must have been down at the southern end of the Valley when we came down the slopes. Good luck for us," whispered Vix. "Those birds must be why the West Wind is so upset. He would know it's not natural."

Carimus nodded. "How will we keep them from seeing us when we set out tomorrow?" he whispered.

"Don't worry about that. The path to Alfhiem is through the woods, under thick cover. The trail south is through a pine forest all the way we want to go. I think. I've never been south of Alfhiem myself, but I have seen the trail. We should be okay."

"I can see the Nest's oak grove." He pointed to where the reddish-brown leaves of the autumn oak trees stood out from the verdant foliage of the surrounding evergreens and the gaudy hues of the rainbow birch. "But I don't see the paths anywhere. How will we know when Angel and Bort have gone?"

Vix smiled. "We have our ways, Cari. Just watch the oak trees and tell me if you glimpse anything."

"I see the oak trees. But what else should I watch for?" Carimus felt a little irritated. Everyone was always telling him he would see and never what he was looking for. He switched his gaze back and forth between the eagles and the grove of trees. The horrid birds kept circling high above the

Valley. The leaves on the oak trees danced in the breeze, but otherwise, nothing attracted his attention. Despite being tired, he stubbornly kept staring at the circling birds and then the oak trees a couple of miles away.

After thirty minutes, he wondered whether he would die of boredom or fall asleep first. Vix didn't talk. Every time he asked her a question, she kept her answers terse or simply said, "Don't know." So he just kept silent and watched, idly fingering the silver tiles on his bracelet that the bard Varyan had called the runes of Fairinhorst.

Suddenly, a flash caught his eye, coming from the oak grove. It was so sudden he wasn't sure he even saw it until Vix stirred. "That was the signal. Did you see?"

"I saw a flash … there it is again!" Sure enough, three quick flickers repeated near the top of one of the oak trees.

"That was it. Let's climb down. We have a lookout post at the top of the tree where Oswald perches when he visits. We use a mirror to send flashes. Three is the 'all's well' signal. If there was trouble, it would be one flash, then a pause, then five quick flashes, and then one flash once again. Then, after a break, it would repeat. We send the signals three times. If we don't show up in twenty minutes or so, they will repeat them in a half hour."

"What do you do if there's no sun? Or at night?"

"We have other ways, but we don't have time for that now, Cari. Come on, follow me." Vix swung over the edge of the platform and made her way down to where Rachel was waiting below.

Carimus trailed as quickly as he could, but Vix already had her pack and was waiting with an impatient look on her face. As he adjusted his pack on his shoulders, she set off at a rapid pace. He grabbed the empty packs and followed.

When they reached the oak grove, Vix made a hooting call. A girl peered down at them and lowered the spider silk ladder. Vix quickly swarmed up, and Carimus stood helplessly waiting with the pack within a pack in his hands.

"Vix will drop the rope for those, Cari," said Rach. "Give them to me."

Carimus nodded in thanks, glad to be rid of it, finally.

Rach used her free hand to steady the rope, and he climbed up. Once he reached the top, he turned to the girl who had lowered the ladder.

"Hello, I'm Carimus."

She brushed a lock of black hair from her face and regarded him solemnly. "I'm Sherri. Joy is waiting for you in the dining hall." She pointed toward the large hut where they had eaten their meals.

Over their late lunch, Carimus learned the Daughters were very worried. It seemed Andune wasn't going to let Angel return from Alfhiem, but Joy relayed Angel's instructions and told them to go to the Crystal Tower and wait there while she, Vixen, and Rachel took Carimus to Fairinhorst. Cat seemed skeptical, but Suzi cheered up at the thought of meeting Liv.

9/23/1971 ar

5:00 a.m.

They set out from the Nest before sunrise and followed a well-used track south through the forest of aspen, rainbow birch, and mountain pine. When they passed the ruins of a farmstead,

Vix told him it had belonged to the family of Cat and Susi. Blackened stumps marked where the apple orchard had been burnt. No wonder Cat was so bitter, he thought. Shortly beyond the ruins, Joy left the group to scout ahead. After a brief wait, Vix told him to follow close behind her, and Rach would watch the rear. She warned him not to speak again until they knew they were far beyond Andune's sentries. He walked between the two girls, stopped when they stopped, and started again when they did, and so made his way out of the Rainbow Valley and into the mountains. They soon left the trail and set off through the trees and underbrush. The girls kept shushing him whenever he stepped on a stick or made a rustling sound in the dried leaves. He thought he was moving quietly, but try as he might, he still made more noise than any of the three scouts.

They made their camp in a small clearing Joy had located, and he collapsed, weary from the long day's hike.

"I'm sorry, Cari," said Vix. "We can't make a fire here. We're still too close to Andune's sentries."

"Do you want help with your tent?" asked Joy as she unrolled her sleeping bag nearby.

All three of the girls were just putting down their sleeping bags. "You're not putting up your tents?"

"No," Joy answered. "I have some weather sense, and there's no rain nearby. Our sleeping bags will keep us warm enough. We have all slept under the stars before. Although, I guess we won't be seeing any here. With the fog so thick here in the mountains, we probably won't see the sky until we reach the shores of Lake Deth, and maybe not even then."

"I'll just eat some jerky and go to sleep. I don't need a tent either. It's not as cold as I thought it would be." He unrolled his sleeping bag, sat atop it, and opened his pack, rummaging around for his rations.

The next thing he knew, Joy was shaking him awake. "I think you will be more comfortable, Cari, if you take off your moccasins and get into your bag rather than sleeping on top of it."

To his embarrassment, he realized he had fallen asleep with a half-eaten piece of venison in his hand. He finished the stick, unlaced his boots, and pulled off his jacket.

"Use your pack as a pillow, Cari," suggested Vix. "And take your mocs right in with you. Then they'll be warm when you slip them on in the morning."

Carimus tried, but the pack was too thick to be comfortable. He ended up with his moccasins rolled up in his jacket under his head and his pack right beside it. The last thing he remembered was the soft sound of the girls deciding who would keep first watch. He should offer to take a turn, but fell asleep with the words half-formed in his mind.

The next thing he knew, Joy was shaking his shoulder.

"My turn to keep watch?" he muttered sleepily.

"No, roll up your bag and get ready. We'll eat our rations as we march. We need to get moving."

All three girls had their sleeping bags rolled and were munching sticks of venison. The early morning air was brisk when he opened his sleeping bag. He pulled on his jacket and laced up his boots.

He had some stiffness in his legs, but it didn't take long to work out, and soon they were back on the trail and hurrying along. Joy went a little way ahead of the others to watch for any travelers who might be traveling toward Alfhiem. Vix warned him that Andune probably had patrols out, and Joy would spot them before they detected the rest of the party as long as he kept as quiet as possible. He might have felt some resentment, but Vix and Rachel didn't talk either. He walked between them and tried to place his feet as quietly as the two girls.

They made good time that day. Carimus was weary and his legs were sore when evening came. Joy guided the group off the trail and to the shelter made by a fallen thousand-year pine. The tree, struck by lightning many years before, had split into two parts, each falling in their own direction. Joy led them to a spot where the trunk crashed down over a large fir, destroying the smaller tree, but still held off the ground for a dozen yards, making a natural shelter for them to camp in.

Carimus noticed the circle of stones. Joy had led them to a spot other travelers had used before. "Aren't you worried that someone else might choose to camp here tonight?" he asked.

"I think we are safe enough," Joy replied. "Kae showed me this place. We have camped here before, and no one else has ever joined us."

"I remember. We stopped here when I journeyed with you," said Rachel. "We had it to ourselves then."

"Do you think we can make a fire tonight? Now that we've stopped moving, it's getting chilly," said Carimus.

"I think it would be safe enough," said Joy. "We are at least fifteen miles from the Valley now. We go mostly east for a while now. We left the watershed of Rainbow Valley and are in Lake Deth's. Sometime tomorrow morning, we'll reach the White River. We follow that to the lake, then we go south again. The cliffs are the last hard bits. The trails are good, but they are pretty steep. From first fall to second is about a mile, then three or four to third fall to Elpeler. After the cliffs, it's an easy trail all the way to Tarcitime and on to the Hidden Vale. We'll camp tomorrow above the first falls and then sleep at Pogue the next night."

"Pogue?" asked Carimus. "But you said Elpeler."

"Elpeler and Pogue are twin villages. Elpeler is above the falls, Pogue is below. We'll make our way down the last cliff and be ready to spend the night."

A wolf howled, a mournful cry far in the distance.

"Is that a wolf?" asked Carimus. "Are they dangerous here?"

"Andune's patrols keep the trails fairly safe, Cari," said Joy. "Don't let it trouble you."

"Oh! I'm not worried. I just never heard one before. I know there are coyotes in the Kings valley and some giant foxes. Even a few bears, I think. But not wolves."

"Wolves stay clear of Andune's patrols. They know to fear our kind. Just like they avoid the King's Valley," said Joy. "Wolves are smart. They know there are safer animals to hunt than men."

Vix and Rachel had gathered some dry deadfall. When Vix prepared to strike a spark with her flint and steel, Carimus stopped her. He thrust his crysword into the tinder, causing it to burst into flame.

He offered to take a turn at watch that night, but wasn't upset when Joy thanked him. He admitted the girls knew the night sounds and he didn't, so it would be better if they divided the watches among themselves.

He crawled into his sleeping bag and fell into a deep sleep shortly after.

9/24/1971 ar

5:00 a.m.

"Cari! Cari! Wake up! Hurry!" Someone shook his shoulder, and he looked up into the worried face of Vix.

"What's wrong?" he asked.

Before she could answer, the howl of a wolf was followed closely by two others, much louder than the cries they had heard the night before.

"That's a hunting pack! And they are getting closer. Get your boots on! Hurry!"

Carimus quickly laced on his moccasins, pulled on his jacket, and stuffed his sleeping bag into his pack. There were many more howls, and they were getting closer!

The four quickly made their way back to the trail and stared down it at a fast trot.

"They're hunting, alright! I hope it's not us!" said Joy.

But it soon became apparent that they were. The baleful howls stayed close behind them as they ran down the trail for their lives.

10:00 a.m.

Carimus awoke with a start. He had fallen asleep and was confused for a few moments. He had dreamed swans were taking flight around him. Vix was back, and the three girls had clustered around him.

"We can't climb down here. The main pack is still surrounding the fir, but they have outliers patrolling," whispered Vix. "What we can do, though, is go higher. There is a glory vine higher up the tree, and we can use it to cross to another tree and scale down a few miles away."

"What's a glory vine?" Carimus asked. "How can we climb this tree? It's huge, and the nearest branches are way up there."

"A glory vine lives on other plants. It has huge purple flowers. When it's in bloom, they open and close with the light. It grows from tree to tree and can run for miles and miles," answered Joy. "As to how, we climb up using the cracks in the bark. It's hard to see the vine through the fog, Cari, but it's only about another fifty feet up."

He gazed up into the ever-present fog where Joy was pointing and thought he could make out something.

"Did you ever do any rock climbing, Cari?" asked Vix.

He shook his head. "No."

"Too bad. This is something like rock climbing," said Vix.

"Only a lot dirtier," added Rachel.

"The cracks in the bark are dirty and sticky but climbable," said Joy. "We'll rope ourselves together. I'll go first to find the easiest path. We'll put you between Vix and Rach. All you have to do is watch Vix and use the handholds she does. Think you can do it?"

"I can try. If you think there's no other way, what choice do we have?"

In the distance came the howl of another wolf and with it, another sound. It almost sounded like someone was laughing. Not a cheerful laugh, though, more hysterical than joyful.

"What is that?" he asked.

The three girls gazed at each other, shaking their heads.

"Nothing I ever heard before," said Joy. "And I don't think I want to find out."

They climbed to their feet and tied themselves together. Joy went first with a stretch of rope between her and Vix, then a shorter gap between each of the other three.

If the circumstances were different, Carimus might have enjoyed the climb. As it was, with the strange laughing sound repeating and getting nearer, and with the various howls of the wolves, it was more terror than fun.

They reached the place where the vine ran next to the trunk of their thousand-year pine. Smaller tendrils extended from the enormous vine to anchor it to their tree, making it effortless to cross over. Carimus was relieved. *I wish Bort could see me now. Even he'd have to admit it is pretty brave to walk on vines from tree to tree a hundred feet up in the air.*

However, just as they reached the top of the vine, a strange rasping voice from somewhere below them rang out.

"I sense you there in the trees. You cannot escape. Give me the dragon-spawn, and I'll let the rest of you live. If you don't … well, my wolves are hungry." Strange yipping laughter rang out.

"Mind-shields!" said Joy urgently.

Cari shivered despite himself as he closed his eyes and pictured himself surrounded by a suit of golden armor, remembering his lessons with Donel.

Joy tugged at his arm. With a finger to her lips, she led the group across the vine away from the thousand-year pine. Cari lost track of where the trail had been, but he thought they were heading north. He didn't dare drop his shield to use his direction sense though, and followed Joy.

"You can't escape!" the voice cried, but it was further away. That voice gave him goosebumps. *Who is that? Is it the Abomination who was riding the Crow? Has he tracked us somehow?* He shivered again at the thought as he remembered the creature the bard had shown them—the beast that murdered his father and Uncle Cameron.

The new surface they were traveling on was much more slippery than the rough bark of the tree limb, and their pace was slowed, but they hurried as safely as possible. Carimus worried they were going to lose their way, traveling away from the trail, but he didn't see any other course for them to follow.

As they hurried cautiously along the smooth surface of the large vine, Carimus smelled water. Joy whispered to Vix, and she quietly answered. "There's no help for it. At least it will slow down the wolves."

"What will?" whispered Carimus.

"We're crossing the White River, the primary source of Lake Deth. The trail is on the south side. We are crossing to the north," whispered Vix back.

"What does that mean? Is there a way to cross back?"

"I don't know. I've never been this way. Rach has once—but they traveled on the trail. We will have to wait and see. Maybe Joy knows."

The vine soon wrapped around another thousand-year tree, a huge smooth-barked aspen. Though they looked carefully, there was no good way to travel from the vine to the new tree to climb down. Worse yet, the vine wrapped once around the trunk and went under itself, then off in a new direction.

Joy called a halt, and Carimus sat down to lean against the trunk as the girls conferred.

"No choice, really," said Vix. "I'm the lightest. You can lower me on the rope to where the vine comes out from under. It's only a dozen feet down, and I can cut grips for half of that. Then where it curves under, it will only be about six feet to the other vine."

"Who was that calling at us?" asked Carimus. "Do you think the Crow rider followed us?"

Joy sighed. "I don't know for sure. But I can guess. It's probably an Abomination, Cari. But probably a different one. Kae told me that when the Beastmen murdered Angel's mother, Andune thought an Abomination was involved—one that could take the shape of a wolf."

"What was that horrible laughing sound?"

"I don't know. I've never heard anything like it before. We need to keep going. Whatever it was, it's still too close to us. Everyone, keep up your mind-shields. Hopefully, we have thrown it off our track."

Soon, they reached the new stretch of vine running off in a new direction. They roped together again and set off through the fog. The scene was unreal to Carimus. It seemed to him they must be hopelessly lost, and he felt himself beginning to despair. *We'll never find Duke like this,* he thought. They walked through gray nothingness on a green vine that disappeared shortly before them and behind as well. Several times, the branches of other giant trees appeared above or below them, but none were close enough for them to transfer to.

"How far have we come? It seems like miles and miles," said Carimus.

"That's because it is," said Joy. "We have come at least five miles along this vine. We need to find a way to the ground."

After a short time, the fog lessened. Regular evergreen trees intermixed with the thousand-year giants, but none were close enough to allow an escape from the vine.

"I don't understand why this vine isn't sagging," said Joy. "The tops of trees must support it underneath, ones we can't see."

"That's probably it," answered Vix. "The tops of the other trees seem to be all around our height. But look, the vine goes over a branch of that thousand-year pine up ahead. Maybe we can climb down there. It's another tree with rough bark."

As they approached the thousand-year giant, Carimus saw the fog wasn't really clearing away. They were climbing above it. Or rather, the ground must have been falling away beneath them. It was still thick below them. He couldn't see the ground, but ahead and to the right, where the fog was thinning away, he could make out the edge of a large lake.

Before he could ask, Joy pointed. "Lake Deth, and we're coming up on the wrong side. We need to find a way down, and soon."

Just then, the strange laughing cry sounded behind them, not far off. In the distance, the howling of wolves answered.

"Oh, no!" said Joy softly, looking along the vine ahead of them.

Vix stopped examining the branch beneath the vine and craned to look around Joy, then back at the branch supporting the vine. "We have to get off! Now!" She pulled her dagger and swiped at the spider-silk rope that held her to Carimus, severing it instantly. She did the same to the rope that connected him to Joy. "Jump onto the branch, Cari. Follow me. Hurry!" She jumped off the smooth green vine and landed sprawling on the rough bark of the wide branch below.

"What's the matter? What's going on?" he asked plaintively.

Joy pointed along the vine in the direction they had been

going. Something emerged out of the foliage, where the vine ran across the next tree branch. "It's a vine crawler! Jump, Cari! Jump!"

The creature was massive, with a grayish-green body about the same size as the vine. It moved along on eight short legs that gripped the vine securely with wicked claws. It moved with the same motion a caterpillar makes on a flower stem. It was the same kind of monster that had killed his grandfather. He stared at the lumbering behemoth, frozen in terror.

Rachel had already jumped down to join Vix. Both girls were frantically motioning him to leap down and join them. The vine crawler was moving much faster than anything with that bulk should be able to, the vine trembling from its body moving in his direction. He shook off his terror, turned, and jumped down to the branch ten feet below. Both girls grabbed him as he sprawled on his hands and knees. Joy followed, landing lightly beside them.

"We're trapped," said Vix. "We can't climb to the ground before it gets here! What do we do?"

The maniac laughing behind them sounded again. Louder! Whatever was chasing them must have followed their path on the vine and was getting closer fast.

Joy crouched down against the vine where it ran across the branch, pulling Carimus after her. The branch they stood on was almost twenty feet wide, and the ten-foot-diameter vine rested on it, leaving a small space underneath the curve. "Under here, quickly. Don't move. No noise."

Vix and Rachel joined them as the pounding thump of the massive vine crawler grew closer and closer.

The laughing cry repeated, getting louder, approaching from the direction they had come from. It had to be coming out of the fog any instant now.

They huddled against the base of the vine, feeling it shudder under the massive pounding as the vine crawler neared the branch they were hiding on. *THUMP, Thump, THUMP, Thump.* Closer and closer. It had to be nearly atop their hiding place. *THUMP, Thump, THUMP, Thump.* The vine compressed as the enormous creature paused directly over their hiding place. It was right above them. Carimus held his breath, hoping it would keep moving.

The maniacal laugh sounded again, then suddenly changed to a startled yip. There was a whistling, puffing sound above them and an answering shriek of rage and pain from the laughing cry. The cry changed to an anguished dwindling scream, followed by a distant thump far below. Carimus smelled the odor of rotten eggs and almost gagged at the stench.

They felt the vine shake and quiver as the creature on the vine above them twisted. It was leaving the vine and moving directly over them onto the branch where they huddled. Carimus was paralyzed with fear. Its claws gripped the rough bark of the gigantic tree branch as it moved to the trunk and headed down towards the ground below.

They waited silently until the scrabbling sounds of the creature faded away. Joy climbed to her feet. "Quickly, before it returns, we have to get out of here. Back on the vine—back the way we came!" She spoke softly but urgently, and they all moved quickly to rope themselves together again.

They scrabbled onto the vine and started back the way they came, but quickly realized going back was not an option. Forty feet away, a smoking pool of some noxious substance covered the vine. The breeze blew a small amount of smoke in their direction, and they gagged and choked from the acrid smell of rotting eggs. The pool bubbled and hissed, eating away the huge vine.

"We can't cross that; crawlers spit venom," whispered Joy. "It's acidic. It would burn through the soles of our moccasins. We'll have to keep going the way we were and hope there's no more where that thing came from." She put her finger to her lips to signal the need to remain silent and led the group back in the direction they had been heading.

They reached the gigantic tree where the vine crawler had appeared. On the other side, the vine sloped downwards towards another immense tree, not too distant. They were descending into the valley of Lake Deth.

"Come on, we'll try to climb down over there." Joy pointed. "Be careful. It will be easy to slip on this part. There are some regular trees close to that big pine. We should be able to get back to the ground there."

Carimus noted she murmured quietly, as if she feared the creature might still be able to locate them somehow. He refrained from asking the questions that most concerned him now. Where were they? And how would they find their way back to the trail?

It was a slow and treacherous walk down to their destination. If the top of the vine hadn't been perfectly dry, Carimus doubted they could have traversed it. The rips from the vine crawler's claws bled a milky fluid that ran down the sides, but the top remained dry. As it was, the slight slope made them walk slowly and carefully, even though Carimus's heart's most desire was to run as fast as possible from the monster that had passed so close to him.

They reached the next tree and climbed down onto the wide branch that supported the glory vine. As Joy had foreseen, a tall regular fir grew near enough to make a transfer over to it rather easy. From there, it was simple enough to climb down to the ground. This brought them back into the fog, but it was not as thick as what they had passed through earlier.

"We'll make our way toward the lake," said Joy softly. "We can decide from there what looks to be our best route."

"Does anyone live by the lake?" whispered Vix. "Some fishermen, maybe?"

"I don't know," replied Joy, "but I don't think so. I don't think anyone lives up above the second falls. We won't find any Fairborn until we are near Elpeler. That's a good five miles from the lake, at the top of the third falls."

"Why not?" Carimus stretched. It was good not to be tied together anymore, he thought. He looked around uneasily, listening for the sound of the vine crawler.

"Lake Deth has an evil reputation. People disappear. Kae told me frogs and turtles are common in some places."

"So? Frogs and turtles live around Dragon Loch."

"You don't have these kinds, Cari. Giant frogs eat people. And a giant snapper is the match for a dozen hunters."

"Giant frogs? Turtles too?" He looked around uneasily.

"We're still a mile or so from the water. Don't worry. Well, don't let your guard down. There are still wolves and other creatures to watch out for." All three of the girls had their bows in hand, with arrows notched to the strings. "Hopefully, we've had our bad luck for today."

Chapter Eight:

The Shores of Deth

9

ABOMINATION

CARIMUS

5:30 p.m.

A SHORT WALK and they were out of the fog, but as the fog diminished, the brush thickened—soon they were hard-pressed to walk in any kind of straight line toward the lake. Rest breaks became more and more frequent until Joy declared it was time to make camp for the day and plan their path forward. After a brief look around, they decided to camp in a small grove of four scrub pines surrounded by the thick underbrush.

Carimus dropped his pack to the ground and sat on it wearily. "Where are we now?"

"We are somewhere north of the White River," said Joy. "Or maybe even the west end of Lake Deth. I'm not sure. We'll figure it out in the morning. Tomorrow we'll go straight south till we get to the water. The White is wide where it joins Deth. Half a mile or so. When we get to the shore, we can try to figure out how to get back on the right side."

A wolf howled far in the distance, and everyone peered

around uneasily.

"It's still a long way off," said Vix. "Let's hope they stay that way."

As if in answer, the wolf howled again, answered by a second howl and, shortly after, a third.

"They're still hunting us," said Rachel. "If they find our scent, they will be right back on us again! What do we do?"

Listening intently, Joy motioned for everyone to keep still. "Sound plays funny tricks in the fog. I thought the first howls were south of us, but those sounded from a completely different direction. Either there is more than one pack, or they have split up to track us. I think they're still on the other side of the river, southwest of us. The White wouldn't be healthy for them to swim. Just like it wouldn't be for us. Kae told me it has pike, big ones. Like thirty feet long. Not a lot of them, just enough to keep the frog population down."

"How will we get across, then?" asked Carimus.

Joy didn't answer. She just shook her head, obviously worried.

"I don't think we should risk a fire tonight," said Vix. "We have nothing to cook anyway, and the wood around here is all pretty green. I haven't seen any dead wood."

"Me either," said Rachel. "I've been keeping an eye out. The scrub pine would burn, but it's not good firewood, and the brush doesn't have much that's dead that I've seen."

"I'm going over to that fir over there and climb up for a look around," said Vix. "Before it gets too dark. I might see something that will give us a clue which way to go."

"Okay," said Joy. "Cari and I will rest here and have a bite to eat."

Vix and Rachel walked toward the lone fir tree about fifty

yards to the south, disappearing from view in the thick scrub that was the most common underbrush around—thick bushes of a kind Carimus was unfamiliar with. They were some kind of evergreen, had pale green leaves, and grew anywhere from three feet high to huge bushes over ten feet tall and thirty feet across. They were impossible to push through, so their path wound along the path of least resistance. After a few minutes passed, he saw movement in the branches—Vix climbing upwards on the fir.

Carimus had eaten two of the sticks of elk venison by the time the two girls returned.

"Anything interesting?" asked Joy.

Vix looked at Carimus and then shook her head. "I think I could see where the river joins the lake. It's about a half mile south of us. The lake gets narrower down there. No sign of any way to cross. No traces of people. There's an island about a mile to the southeast and another, bigger one east of there. It all looks wild."

Carimus unrolled his sleeping bag and unlaced his moccasins. He rolled them up in his jacket to use as a pillow and crawled into his sleeping bag. The girls all grew quiet as Vix and Rachel ate their dinner jerky. Carimus was exhausted. His legs hurt from a day of climbing trees and running far more than he was used to. They almost ached too much for him to sleep—he tossed and turned a few times, trying to find a comfortable spot on the hard ground. He was just beginning to doze when he thought he heard Vix say, "No, it's too dangerous!" But when he tried to ask what, sleep overcame him.

Carimus then slipped into a dream—he was a swan flying high over the land looking for something.

The howls woke him suddenly, and he sat up in fright. Were

the wolves upon them again? In the light of the waning moon, Vix stood nearby.

"It's alright, Cari. It's a wolf alright and on this side of the river. But it's not getting closer. I think it's hunting in the mountains to the north of us. Go back to sleep. We're watching, and we'll wake you if it gets closer."

"OK," he said, and laid back down, rolling over on his side. He could just make out the sleeping form of one of the other girls in the dim moonlight.

He wondered who it was as he dropped off sleepily. And shouldn't there be two others sleeping?

9/25/1971 ar
8:30 a.m.

When he awoke, the world was shrouded in fog again; he sat up and looked around confused. Joy nodded to him. "Mind-shield, Cari." He quickly protected himself once again.

"We didn't wake you up, Cari. The fog rolled in from the lake a few hours ago, and we decided we would let it burn off before we started again. It's already a little thinner than it was. I'm guessing it will be gone in another hour or so."

"In the meantime, we need to discuss what we are going to do," said Vix. "It seems we have two choices. We can hike through the wilderness to the east and try to go around Lake Deth. Then we would get to the falls on the wrong side of the Falling River. We'd have three cliffs to scale down with no trails and be on the wrong side of the river from the villages. It's probably fifteen miles around the lake and another five to the bottom of the cliffs across from Pogue."

"That doesn't sound good," said Carimus as he rubbed his aching calves. He didn't ache nearly as much as he thought he would. His legs must be getting stronger.

"No, but the other choice is to go west and hope to find some way across the White River. If nothing else, we could probably find our way back to the vine we crossed on. That's over five miles of backtracking. But the wolves were howling back that way all night and we might go right back to them."

"What about that thing with the horrible laugh? What do you think happened to it?"

"My guess is the vine crawler sprayed it with acid, and it fell or jumped off the vine. If it was an Abomination, that probably wouldn't have killed it, but the vine crawler went after it. My hope is that it's in the crawler's belly. But we still have the wolves to consider when we get across the river."

"We can't just go south and cross the river here?" he asked as he laced up his moccasins. He reached into his pack and pulled out a stick of venison jerky and began to devour it ravenously.

"I told you about that last night, Cari. Half a mile wide and thirty-foot-long pike in the water. I wouldn't even feel comfortable in a small boat crossing the river, and we don't have a boat."

"I don't know—what do you think is our best route, then?"

Joy sighed, but before she could answer, they heard something pushing through the brush. On all sides. They were surrounded!

A figure lurched out of the fog. It was tall, with the head of a snarling, misshapen wolf on the body of a gaunt man. It was wearing tattered rags, its features scarred with fresh burns and oozing sores. As they stared in horror, it glared down at them, reared back its hideous head, and howled. No, not a howl, the horrible yipping cry that had dogged their steps the day before. A cry like maniacal laughter—the laughter of a madman. It wasn't alone. Four giant black wolves the size of horses moved closer, encircling them. They snarled and bared their huge white teeth.

"You should have listened to me, you fools!" said the creature in a raspy voice. "The dragon-spawn is mine, but the three of you will fill the bellies of my companions. Poor little dragon gets to watch his friends torn to pieces and eaten alive."

The four jumped to their feet and stood back-to-back. Carimus had his crysword in hand, and the girls pulled their daggers.

The creature snarled, "A little sport, eh?" Its hideous laughter rang out once again.

It was answered by another howl, loud and close by. The four black wolves stopped snarling and looked around uneasily.

The beast-headed creature snarled, then shouted, "Kill them quick, my friends, all but the boy!"

The new howl repeated, and the black wolves whined uneasily. The fog swirled, and footsteps approached, crackling through the brush. *What now?* thought Cari in despair. The black wolves stirred and backed up a few steps, turning to look to the north. The wolf on that side moved quickly out of the way as the footsteps grew louder.

Another beast-headed creature walked into view. He wasn't as tall as the first, and his head was that of a wolf, though not misshapen, like the first monster. A wolfhead Beastman, thought Cari. He shrank back, pressing against the girl behind him.

"You are in my lands, Kargyn." It spoke quietly but

confidently.

"KILL HIM!" shrieked the first creature, and the black wolves growled half-heartedly.

The second creature made a loud, snarling sound. Carimus flinched, and the four black wolves all turned tail and slunk away, whining.

"Get out of my lands, Kargyn," said the second creature.

"Tomung demands the man-child—give him to me!" said the first. "Then I'll go. You can have the rest!"

"No. They are in my lands, and they all belong to me." Suddenly, the creature grew even bigger, and long black talons extended from his hands. "Do ye wish to challenge me, Kargyn?" it growled.

Another Abomination, Carimus thought in despair. *Maybe they'll fight and we can run!*

"You will hear of this, Wolfe! You will pay!" shrieked the creature called Kargyn, and it turned and disappeared from sight.

"Run, ye yellow-bellied hyena! I catch ye on my side of the river again, and I will strip yer hide, hang it on a tree, and send ya back to your den whimpering. RUN, COWARD!"

The creature called Wolfe turned to look at the four of them standing huddled together.

"Hmm ... Interesting." He sniffed the air as he shrank back to his original size. "What have we here? A Fairborn lass, two human girls, and a young dragon-blood. Interesting indeed. And not all is as it seems, eh?"

Joy, Vix, and Carimus all spoke at once.

"Who are you?" asked Joy.

"What do you want with us?" asked Vix.

"Abomination," whispered Cari.

The creature looked at each of them appraisingly. "Put up your weapons. I'm not some mangy hyena-spawn to bluster and snarl." He turned and gave a growling sound, and two gray wolves walked from the fog to flank him. Normal wolves. They were not young. White fur trimmed their muzzles and more white grizzle showed in the gray of their hides. They sat flanking him, and he studied them a moment, then looked back up.

"Kargyn and his pack are still running west. Some of my pack be trailing them and watching. Nipping at their heels when they start to slow." He laughed, but it was not a cheerful laugh. Carimus felt himself shiver again.

"Now what am I to do with ye?" He eyed their weapons, which were still in their hands. "If I wanted ye dead, those little toys wouldn't stop me. Put them AWAY."

No one moved, and he looked at each of them once again. "Mind-shields, eh? Very nice. But not very polite to threaten the man who just saved yer lives. Kargyn's wolves would have pulled ye down. Ye would have bloodied them a bit, eh? But they'd a killed ye none the less."

Carimus pointed his crysword at the creature. "What do you want with us?" He felt his voice quiver. "Go away!"

The creature studied the sword with interest. "A green sword. Ye'd be the third son then, eh? Where are ye brothers then? Who's your father? Arlond, is it?"

"Yes, I carry a green sword. I will be the head of the Church. We will hunt your kind down and destroy them. Aaron was my father. Attios was my grandfather. Arlond was his father, my great-grandfather. Your kind murdered my father, and a vine-crawler killed Attios many years ago."

The creature shook his head. "So many years, so many of

the dragon kings, both flying quickly by. They come and then they're gone." He looked down at his hands and shook his head. "I make ye uncomfortable like this, don't I?"

He took a breath and then began to change—the wolf head dissolved in upon itself, the snout dwindling, the wolf's fang shrinking, and the fur on his body changing color and texture. Suddenly, a blond-headed man stood before them, wearing a silver-gray coat and under it a white shirt and blue pants.

"Is that more to yer liking, lad?" He looked down at himself. "I don't remember the last time I took this likeness. My pack prefers the other. Well ... it's what they be used to, anyway."

"You're an Abomination!" said Carimus once again. Vix tried to shush him, but he ignored her. "One of your kind murdered my father and my uncles! We are going to make you all pay!" He felt his body trembling, but with fear or anger, he wasn't sure.

"Abomination is it? Hmm, I suppose in a way ye are right, but if ye mean one of the five, then no. Yeenaghou, Tiameng, even Demigoran tried to convince me to work for them, to join the ranks of their minions, but I told them all to go to hell! I am no man's minion. Thomas Wolfe was in the army once, never again. I am a free man!" His eyes burned as he stared into Carimus's face. "I am not one of them."

"Thank you for driving off that horrible creature," said Joy. "But why should we trust you? Leave us alone. Go your way and we'll go ours. Take your two wolves and go."

"Yer not free to go. Ye are in my lands, in my hand." He looked at Joy. "Two wolves? I'm disappointed in ye, lass. Ye are a Fairborn." He looked down at the elderly wolf on his right side. The wolf leaned his head back and gave a howling cry.

All around them, the cry was repeated many times. They

were surrounded again!

"Now the question be, what should I do with ye?" Wolfe shook his head. "These lands are mine. It were your own family, dragon-blood, that deeded it to me, and mine it be. It's not a big grand kingdom, mind ye! But I don't need a lot. Starting where the White River springs out of that hole in the mountain, everything east of there that be north of the river, all away around the Lake Deth to the first cliff. The mountain peaks are the line to the north and to the east."

"My uncle Cameron was Loremaster for the House of deDraconis, and he was teaching me to take his place. He taught me geography, and he never mentioned you or any kingdom here," said Carimus, his voice cracking again. "He taught me that Abominations were evil—before they murdered him."

Vix reached out and tugged at his shoulder, but he ignored her and kept glaring at the man before him. His sword shook, no matter how hard he tried to hold it still.

"Cari," she hissed. "Look around us. Now!"

Carimus obeyed, irritated that she was tugging at him. The fog was lifting. Between the small pine grove and the thick underbrush, there was a circle of gray wolves, at least thirty of them, all sitting and watching the drama playing out in the grove.

"Now I think ye best be telling me why ye be trespassing. I think my friends would prefer ye do it after ye put away those little knives and that pretty green crysword."

"Why should we make it easy for you to kill us?" Carimus couldn't keep his voice from wavering. "I'd rather die with my sword in my hand. I won't go down without a fight!"

"Why die at all, lad?" said Wolfe. "Ye be the only one here who keeps suggesting it."

"Rúatan-ráca," said Joy suddenly. "That's you, isn't it? The man-wolf?"

Wolfe looked surprised and nodded. "Tis been many a year since anyone called me that, but yes. The Fairborn do remember me, eh?"

"Put your sword away, Cari." Joy slipped her dagger into its sheath. "Remember what Donel said—not all shapeshifters are evil."

"Do it, Cari!" whispered Vix as she sheathed her dagger. Rachel followed suit.

Unsure what to do, Carimus lowered the point of his sword, certain that as soon as he did, the wolves would spring to attack, or maybe the man would change back to a wolf and do it himself. The wolves just watched, tongues hanging out, and eyes glittering as the shadows disappeared and the fog burned away.

Wolfe sniffed a few times as if his wolf nature was too ingrained, and chuckled. "Lad, if ye think shapeshifters are evil, why—"

"What do you want from us?" interrupted Joy.

Wolfe looked at Joy shrewdly. "Ha! So that's the way of it, eh?" He glanced back and forth between Joy and Vix and then Rach and Carimus, then chuckled again.

"We need to cross the river," said Vix. "We have to take Cari to Fairinhorst."

"Fairinhorst? Why would ye be taking a dragon-blood to the Lady, I wonder? You, I could understand to be going there," he said, looking at Joy. "Or maybe her." He pointed at Vix.

"The Angellar sent for me!" said Carimus. He sheathed his sword and then nervously rubbed his hands together, the silver runic bangles of his bracelet tinkling softly in the grove's stillness.

"Did she now? Now that be interesting. Then I would be

guessing ye best be going to see her then." Wolfe looked over at the wolves surrounding the grove, and two of the wolves jumped up and rushed away. "But not just yet, lad, not just yet. My den … err … my home is a short walk. Come with me and we'll be talking about how ye are goin' to be getting back on yer path. Come on. Yer safe enough, fer now."

Wolfe walked a few steps to the north, looked back, and arched a brow. The wolves to that side of the grove stood up and moved to the side, leaving a path between the animals. The only path between the animals, Carimus noted.

"I think we should go with him, Cari," said Joy softly. "The Fairborn tell stories about the man-wolf. They don't portray him as evil, but speak of him as a symbol of living free."

"He might be able to set us on the shortest path," added Vix. "He might know of a trail down the cliffs on the east side of the lake. It could save us time, and I, for one, don't want to go back where that Kargyn creature might find us again." Rachel nodded in agreement.

"I don't trust him!" whispered Carimus, and then looked around. "But what choice do we have?"

"None, laddie," chuckled Wolfe, who also seemed to have keen ears. "None at all." He waved his hand, inviting them to walk with him.

Carimus looked at his companions, still unsure. Joy and Vix both nodded, and Rachel only shrugged, as if agreeing that their choices were limited.

"Where are you taking us? How far is it?" asked Carimus.

"I told you, lad. We be goin' to my home and there we will be having a bit of a talk, and I have decided to give you a spot of supper. After that … well, we'll be deciding that when the time comes. It's not far."

Carimus gave up and fell in beside Rachel as Joy and Vix led the way, following the man called Wolfe back to the North. The wolf pack kept pace, like some canine honor guard, spread out in a half-circle beside and behind them.

They followed him about a mile to a thousand-year pine with a gap in the bark between two enormous roots. Wolfe ducked into the gap, and the four companions followed. A large space within the giant tree featured several openings high above, which cast a dim light in the hollow. Toward one side was a ring of sooty stones with a spit made from two wooden Ys with a metal bar laid across the top. A pile of firewood was stacked neatly just beyond it. Sitting next to the ring of stones were two wolves, and lying at their feet were the bodies of two hares.

Only the two older wolves, which had flanked Wolfe earlier, had entered the hollow. The space inside of the tree was large, and Carimus couldn't see much except in the center where the light was brightest, but a pile of dried grasses was off to one side. Otherwise, the space was empty except for the fire ring, the woodpile, the two wolves, and their hares.

Wolfe looked at the two wolves. Although he didn't say a word, they both stood up and fawned at his feet, like trained dogs receiving praise from their master. They then ran from the hollow.

"I'm sorry I don't be having any furniture, but I don't usually be having guests either. If I could trouble ye to make up a cook fire, I'll prepare these coneys fer roasting. I assume ye'll be wanting them cooked, eh?"

He looked at Carimus, but before he could stammer out an answer, Wolfe burst out laughing. "I know ye do, lad. I be funnin' you. Old habits die hard. I still prefer cooking my meat."

He took the bodies of the hare aside and, though Carimus never saw a knife, he quickly skinned and gutted the pair of them. After spitting the bodies, he leaned the skewer against the woodpile to wait for Vix's fire to burn down to coals. He took the hides and placed them away from the fire-circle. The two elderly wolves cleaned up the remains with noisy slurps. What little remained Wolfe carried outside.

"Who is he, Joy?" demanded Carimus. "You seem to know about him."

"Just legends, Cari. I've heard legends, but they never told where he lived or what he is exactly."

"He's an Abomination. He admitted it."

"My name is Tom Wolfe, Cari. I already told ye that. What more need ye to know than what I already said to ye?" Wolfe was back, and although he was yards away, he seemed to have heard what they said.

"Why have you taken us prisoner? What do you want?" Carimus tried to speak to the man as he imagined Artos would have, but he couldn't keep the fear out of his voice.

"I be thinkin' ye be my guests, lad, not my prisoners. Yer friends made up my mind for me. If ye be traveling to see Angel, who be I to stand in yer way?"

"The Angellar," corrected Cari. "Angel is visiting the West Wind, then taking Bort back to Donel."

Wolfe tilted his head to the side and looked at him with confusion. He arched an eyebrow at Joy. "Do ye know what he is talking about?"

"Angel Andunsuruessa, the daughter of Prince Andune Naurfindl, who is called by some the West Wind, is who Cari is speaking of. Bort is his brother and Donel, their great-great-uncle. Who is the Angel you refer to?"

Wolfe hesitated a moment. "She is long dead. I meant the Angellar, of course." He shook his head. "I have many years of memories, and sometimes they get confused, that's all. Now, ye be knowin' my name. I know he is a dragon-blood named Cari, with a brother named Bort, but maybe ye all should be telling me yer names and the rest of yer story, like why that hyena-spawn Kargyn be chasing ye." He looked at the fire, which was burning merrily, and bent over it. Carimus gasped. Wolfe didn't use a poker, but just reached in and twitched the burning logs around with his bare hands. He took the spit with the brace of hares and set them over the fire to cook. "Well?"

Carimus stared at Wolfe's hands, unharmed by the fire. Vix poked him in the ribs.

"It's your story, Cari." She looked back at Wolfe. "I'm Sarah, but everyone calls me Vix. That's my friend Rachel, and she's Joycel."

"Pleased to meet ye, Rachel, Joycel, and Vixen," said Wolfe, and chuckled as if he found something amusing. He sat down near the fire and looked at them expectantly.

"Just Joy."

Carimus wondered if Vix was going to correct him as well, but she poked him again.

"Well ..." he began. "It all started on the equinox. That's my brother Duke's birthday ..."

5:00 p.m.

"Then you appeared out of the fog … and you know what happened next."

Wolfe listened quietly, only stirring to rotate the spit, where the hares were roasting and giving off a heavenly smell.

"That be quite a tale, lad. I still wonder what the Angellar can tell ye about yer lost brother, though. The storm ye be talking of never made it o'er the mountains this far south, so I doubt yer brother would be at Fairinhorst. Even so, she be a seer, so maybe she is just calling ye to tell ye where he be." He shook his head and shrugged. "You can stay the night here, and I'll set you on yer way in the morning." He looked at the roast hare. "Dinner's ready. I don't have any plates or fancy silverware, though …"

"We have our camp gear," said Vix, and they all rummaged through their packs to get what they needed for their first hot meal since breakfast back at the nest. Carimus thought the roast hare was one of the most delicious meals he had ever eaten, even though there was nothing to go with it and naught but water to wash it down.

Dusk was falling. It would soon be night again. *We need to be going*, he thought, *but it's almost dark, and it sure felt good to rest for a while.*

"I guess I talked all day. I didn't realize how long it took to tell all that. It's only been ten days since Duke's birthday."

"Our legs needed the break, Cari," said Joy. "We've been doing a lot of marching, running, and climbing the last two days."

Wolfe had been staring off into space, but he suddenly stirred. "Kargyn and his brutes have just gone behind the falls at the river source. He be off my lands now, and I have no means or desire to trace his steps. His kind don't need to rest or sleep, but his wolves do, and he's too big a coward to go on alone. Those four aren't his only wolves. If he has others awaiting him, it won't be long before he be back on the south side of the White. He'll probably go to that place where ye crossed the river on the vine and set guards there. No telling if he waits there himself or if he comes further east. Ye have yer mind-shields, but can ye keep them up when yer sleeping?"

Joy sighed. "I can, but none of the others are able. Donel didn't know there might be an Abomination in the mountains south of Rainbow Valley, or he would have spent the extra time teaching Cari how to keep his mind shielded when he sleeps. But then he'd still be training him. That isn't something you can learn in a couple of days."

"It's probably my fault," said Carimus miserably. "I should have been shielding from the time we left the Nest, from the Crystal Tower even. I just wanted Donel to track us on his screen, so he could tell Artie where we were. That way, he'd know I was safe. He didn't want us to split up."

"If Donel had thought that thing would find us, Cari, he would have never let you go," said Joy. "You know that." Rachel and Vix nodded in agreement.

"So you think that thing knows where we are now?" asked Rachel with a slight shudder.

"He might, when you three fall asleep," said Joy.

"No, he won't have a clue," cut in Wolfe. "Yer as safe here as in the Crystal Cave an fer the same reasons."

"You have a qulan field? Here? Around this tree?" asked

Carimus, his voice full of doubt.

"No, nothing that fancy, but my den is warded. Even if ye drop yer shield right now, Kargyn would never feel yer thoughts, never touch yer mind, patterned or not, no matter how hard he try."

"Well, that's good news, at least," said Joy. "But we're still on the wrong side of the White River, and we still have to figure out how to get back on the trail south to Elpeler."

"Too bad ye can't all turn into birds an' fly across the river," said Wolfe.

"No, we can't," replied Joy icily. Carimus thought she looked angry at the silly joke.

"Well, I can help ye there, I think," said Wolfe.

"You have a boat?" asked Carimus. "But what about the pike?"

"A boat? Hmm ... Well, something like that. Don't ye worry about the pike. If any try to bother us ... well, they be good eating, but they won't bother us. You'll see."

Chapter Nine:

To Cross the River

10

I DON'T SEE YOUR BOAT

CARIMUS

9/26/1971 ar

7:30 a.m.

WHEN CARIMUS OPENED HIS EYES to a dim, dusky light, the hollow inside the enormous tree was still pleasantly warm from the fire of the night before. A hint of smoke still lingered in the air. Carimus suddenly remembered their host and sat up hurriedly. It was hard to see into the dark recesses around the edge of the room, but it just felt empty. Neither Wolfe nor his two grizzled companions shared the space with them.

He quickly pulled his moccasins out from his rolled-up jacket he had used again as his pillow and started lacing them up.

As soon as he finished, he slipped over toward the nearest sleeping girl on his hands and knees. Her red hair revealed it was Vix, but before he could reach her, she opened her eyes and sat up.

"What's wrong, Cari?" she asked, quickly alert and looking around the spacious hollow.

"He's gone. Quick, we can escape now," he whispered.

Joy raised her head. "He told me he would go out early to look around, Cari. He'll be back soon to show us the way south." She pointed at the fire circle. "There's still some roasted hare. Have some breakfast."

"We don't need to escape," said Vix. "We're not his prisoners, remember?"

"I don't trust him. He's a shapeshifter! They can't help it. They are just naturally evil."

"If I had a pillow, Cari, I'd throw it at you!" came the sleepy voice of Rachel. "I was having a pleasant dream until you woke me up."

"Cari, some men are bandits… does that make all men evil because some are?" asked Joy.

"Of course not. But that's not the same thing. My Uncle Cameron was a wise man, a good man, and he wouldn't tell me shapeshifters were evil without reason. He wouldn't."

"But he might have been wrong. Don't you think Donel is a good man? He's your uncle too. He told you that this wasn't true."

"I know, but he lives all alone and away from the real world. He could be the one who's wrong."

"Cari, I'm sorry, but your uncle Cameron was incorrect." Joy looked like she was ready to continue the argument. At that moment, a large gray wolf loped into the hollow, followed shortly by the two grizzled wolves, Wolfe's companions.

Carimus gasped, and his crysword was in his hand. Before he could even stand up, the wolf reared up on its hind legs, and its form flowed back into the shape of Wolfe.

"Did I startle ye now, lad? Ye seem to be a bit jumpy, but ye can relax. The fog's burning off, and in a little while ye can all set off back on your journey," said Wolfe. "There's still some hare left fer yer breakfast. There's a spring on the way if ye need to refill yer canteens. Get up, sleepyheads. The lad seems to be the only one who wants to be a-going."

Wolfe was correct. By the time they'd eaten a quick meal of cold hare, the fog was lifting off the land, and the sun was trying to break through the autumn clouds.

As they walked south from the hollow giant tree, Wolfe seemed to be in an excellent mood—he kept humming bits of unfamiliar melodies and occasionally whistling bird calls in answer to the birds they heard as they walked along.

Shortly, the ground grew marsh-like. It filled the air with a smell of dead, rotting plants. Reeds, ferns, and giant cattails replaced the thick brush, and shortly the smell of water grew more prevalent. Soon, they were stepping from one tuft of solid ground to another. Wolfe, however, just splashed through, ignoring the wetness through which he trudged. His wolf companions kept up with him, but the others were hard-pressed to match their pace.

"Slow down!" protested Carimus. "You may not mind getting soaked, but we do! We have a long way to go, and we don't want to be marching in wet boots."

Wolfe turned around and chuckled at Carimus's distress. "Then take 'em off, lad. Been many a year since I bothered with shoes of any kind." Although Wolfe wore trousers, a shirt and a jacket, his feet were quite bare.

Wolfe continued to lead the way, but he slowed down and picked a path that wasn't as full of pools and puddles.

Eventually, they came to a drier, grassy bank. Wolfe walked out onto a lone rock in the river. The rock was enormous and gnarled with many large bumps as tall as Carimus's waist.

Carimus followed and stood looking across the river. Wolfe's two companions sat down on the bank and looked as though they were settling in for a wait.

"So this is the White River?" asked Carimus. "How do you figure we are supposed to cross it? It looks like it's easily a half mile wide, and I don't see your boat."

"I never said I had a boat, lad. Ajax has agreed to take ye across. That's what I was seeing to this morning."

Carimus looked around. "Well, where is he? Is he late?" Joy and Vix stared at him, shocked. He looked around hastily to find the danger he had somehow missed.

"He's not late, lad. He's right here," said Wolfe, smiling as he tapped his head. "I be talking with him right now, mind to mind."

"Where? Is he invisible or something?" Something about the broad smile on his face made him uneasy. He looked around again.

"Come along, lassies, it's safe," said Wolfe. "It's not polite to keep him waiting now, is it? Not when he agreed to carry us across the river and all."

"What are you talking about?" said Carimus.

"Look down, Cari," said Joy in a strange, small voice.

Carimus noticed the roughness of the rock formed a pattern, a bunch of large diamond shapes. The bumps were each neatly aligned in rows. It reminded him of something he'd seen before, but what?

"Are ye coming, or not?" chuckled Wolfe.

It dawned on Carimus where he had seen that kind of pattern before. Before he could decide whether to run, Wolfe clamped a firm hand on his shoulder. Vix and Rachel stepped up next to him. Vix seemed fearful, but Rach still appeared as if she were trying to figure out the joke. Joy finally came after them as well, and she promptly sat down.

"That be a good idea, lass. Ye should probably all sit down. Ajax might sway a bit as he gets moving," said Wolfe.

Wolfe's hand pushed him down to a sitting position as Vix and Rachel followed suit.

Suddenly, the rock moved! An enormous head rose from the water before them. Carimus gulped. They were sitting on the back of a giant snapping turtle! Its shell was at least twenty-five feet across and thirty feet long. They rocked from side to side as the turtle stood up, and waves washed away from them. The turtle walked into the deeper water. Then they glided across the river as the giant began to swim.

"If there were any pikes about, I'd bet they all decided they had better places to be," said Wolfe. "Don't ye think, lad?"

Carimus just sat in silent shock. Soon the other bank drew near, and the turtle settled down and stopped.

"I thought … I mean … I was told that mind speech wasn't possible with insects, amphibians, and reptiles," said Joy in a subdued voice.

"Hmm … I'm not sure I want to be informing Ajax. He might stop talking with me." Wolfe chuckled. "Ye can all get off now. I think yer trail be off that way someplace." He waved his hand airily, gesturing to the south and southwest. "I wouldn't be dawdling. Kargyn could be here today if he didn't decide to wait where ye crossed the river before. Ye aren't on my lands now. Be off with you. Shoo! Ajax wants to go frogging. Best to let him, eh?"

Carimus quickly got to his feet and hurriedly scrambled up the bank, eager to get away from both the turtle and from Wolfe. The three Daughters of the Wind were right behind him.

When they turned around, Wolfe and his steed were already heading back across the river. He didn't look back.

"Do you still think he was evil, Cari?" asked Vix.

"I … I don't know … maybe," he sighed. "Probably not, I guess, but …"

"But what?" asked Joy.

"I just don't know."

"Let's get going," said Joy. "We're probably three or four miles to the cliffs and the first falls. We want to get to Pogue tonight and that's another five miles with three cliffs to climb down. But the trails aren't too difficult. Let's go."

Part Four

The Crystal Tower Redux

Chapter Ten:

Reunited

11

NEW CLOTHES

ARTOS

9/24/1971 ar

7:00 p.m.

DUSK WAS FALLING AT THE CRYSTAL TOWER when Bortis returned with his four companions. With the four daughters having come the previous day and the addition of Jaek and Seth, accommodations were strained. The six Daughters of the Wind occupied the dorm while Bortis reclaimed his room. Jaek and Kae went to what had been Carimus's room. Seth declined the offer of a bed, saying he would take his rest outside and commune with The Mother. Artos thought this was strange, but Donel just nodded as if it was what he expected, so he shrugged it off.

After dinner that night, Donel took Artos, Bortis, and Angel to the upper reaches of the tower to check on the whereabouts of Carimus and his three companions. The dusk made for poor visibility, but they were glad to see them camping in a pine grove. Carimus was in his sleeping bag, snoring, while Vix and Rachel sat on theirs, having a conversation. Joy was nowhere

167

to be seen, but a sleeping bag was rolled out for her next to Rachel's.

"Joy may be off hunting," said Angel. "They don't have a fire, though. Perhaps she is gathering herbs. If she saw a good patch, she would certainly collect some. Can you tell where they are camped?"

Donel tried adjusting the view, but the failing light made it impossible to see. When he attempted to return to the first scene, the darkness had deepened, leaving only vague shapes visible. "It's too dark. We were lucky we looked in on them when we did. I'll try to do so again a little earlier tomorrow. Hopefully, they will be at Elpeler in a day or two at most. From there, it is a well-traveled trail to Tarcitime and on to the hidden vale and Fairinhorst. Cari should be there by this time next week."

"I'll be happier when we know Cari is off the road," said Artos. "At least we know they're safe. It was good to see Seth again. He was not the guide I expected you to return with. I never suspected that Count Glenden had a druid in the family."

"I imagine every family has their own little secrets they aren't willing to share with the world," said Angel.

"Which reminds me," said Donel. "I opened the package Ser Seth brought with him. Had he known the contents, he might have made his load lighter."

Donel led the brothers back down to the commons. Angel went to tell the other Daughters that Joy, Vix, and Rachel were fine and well underway to Fairinhorst. Donel then went to fetch their gift from the Countess Spryngdal.

As soon as they were alone, Artos turned to Bortis. "Now, while we're alone for a minute, tell me your impression of Andune."

"Well, at first, I thought he was pretty … um … aloof and

obnoxious, I guess. I think he was testing me. I know he and Uncle Brett didn't like each other. He wanted to see how much like Uncle Brett I was, but I think we came to an understanding. He said he wouldn't allow any of his people to go to the lands of the deEagledons, but that was because he felt they cheated his wife, Lady Stephanie, of her rightful inheritance. When Jaek said he was going because of a blood-debt against the enemy, he didn't protest at all, and he sent Seth with us. I thought about this the entire trip back here—he could have just given me the packages, but he asked me to bring Seth here, knowing that Seth would be the guide we needed. Though he never said as much. I think he wanted to help us."

Artos nodded, thinking about how much his brother had changed his views about the Fairborn. *He has changed for the better*, he thought, but before he could respond, Donel walked back into the room carrying a bundle of black items, a complete suit of clothing for each of them. Donel chuckled. "You could have worn your new clothes, Bort, instead of letting Seth carry them here."

"New clothes?" asked Artos.

"Silken frippery?" said Bortis in a slightly scornful tone. "I think my old leather is better gear for the road ahead of us."

"The clothes of House deSpryngdal are not all silk shirts and dancing gowns, Bort," said Donel. "The gear she has sent with Seth is spider-silk. It's true. But do not think it unfit for mountain travel. She does not sell this cloth in the markets or use it to pay tribute to the crown as she does with other silks. It is light but very strong. There is quantimagic woven into the cloth. It will keep you warm when the temperature is cold, and it blends in with your surroundings nicely. It protects the wearer. It is not exactly armor, but it is close. I know the Fairborn have their own versions of this, and Seth's robes are spider-silk as well." He looked at Angel, who nodded to affirm this was true.

The pant legs ended in stockings, and the shirts came with hoods to be pulled close around the wearer's head. There was also a light jacket and a pair of skintight gloves for each of the brothers.

Bortis held the jacket before him with doubt on his face. "This is supposed to keep us warm in the mountains, in the autumn chill when we're crossing the high passes? And the color—I like black, but we'll stand out in the snow like a lump of coal on a white blanket."

"Wait until you have seen it in action before you judge. Jaek's traveling gear is Fairborn made, but it is very similar. Angel's as well. The quanti-magic woven into these is mind activated." Donel walked over to one of the blue crystal walls of the commons; his black robe stood in harsh contrast to the light blue crystal. He pulled the hood up over his head and faded from sight. He blended perfectly with the wall. His outline was faint and blurry. The brothers stared in amazement. Donel pushed the hood back from his head and his robe turned back to its normal black. "Go change into those and come back. Wearing them will help you bond with them. Tomorrow, I will give you your first lesson on controlling your new clothes."

The two brothers exchanged a glance and then nodded to Donel as they hurried off to change into their new gear. They returned to find Seth and Donel exchanging a few words. When they entered, the druid gave them a friendly smile, nodded approvingly at their new outfits, then walked to the hall that led out of the tower.

"Shouldn't we find him somewhere to sleep inside?" said Artos. "The nights are getting chill here in the mountains.

I expect to see snow any day now when I look out in the morning."

"He would find it stifling," replied Donel. "Druids train to become one with nature, to make themselves at home with the elements. I would wager that when he is at home in Daryelhaas, he sleeps in a room with the windows open wide. Even in the heart of winter. If we had time, I could train the both of you to sleep comfortably in a snowdrift, and one day I will. But not now. For this trip, you will have to make do with the tents and sleeping bags I have on hand. They will keep you comfortable. You both have been born with exceptional regalos, but we only have time for you to be trained in a few. Enough to keep you alive to complete your mission to Starstone Tower. Then to reclaim Castle Draconis and your destinies."

"Andune told me I should ask you to train me in using the Truth Spell," said Bortis.

Donel sighed and shook his head. "He is right, of course. Although the Truth Spell may not be necessary for either of you on your trip to Starstone, it may be vital for the first time you meet members of the other Great Houses. There are two ways the truth spell may be cast. With the first, the caster can tell when a person lies from the aura that surrounds them—an aura only the caster can see. In the other, which requires the caster to touch the person being tested, it makes them physically unable to utter something they know is untrue. I will teach you both each version of the spell. It is related to trueseeing."

"It will take the best part of another week just to give you the minimum of what I feel you will need. I would rather it were double that, but people will wonder where you are all too soon. Marie is watching the screens for me, as is The Darrel, and so far, there has been no alarm about your family not arriving in Phoenix. The deEagledons probably arrived at Eagleton today, or will tomorrow, and the dePenrodyns should be in Kent by Sevenday. They undoubtedly believe your Family is following close behind. In another week, people will notice the king is absent. You must be on your way soon."

"What do you think will happen when the Council learns Father has been murdered?" Artos asked, voicing the concern that had troubled him ever since he learned of possible traitors within some of the Noble Houses.

"I think that will depend on how they receive the news. It would be best if you announced it. Declare from the Hall of Mirrors at Castle Draconis how you have slain the murderers and reclaimed your crown and throne. I know we suspect some will already know, but they dare not reveal that knowledge, lest they show they have ties to those who killed King Aaron and the others. No, if there are traitors on or near the Council, they will have to act as shocked as anyone at the news. Unfortunately, the Truth Spell does not work through the screens in either form, only in person."

"I have been putting a good deal of thought into this, and I have conferred with Count Glendon and Countess Maria. After you secure Castle Draconis and recall what troops you still have at the Gatehouse to garrison the Castle, Count Glendon has offered to use his airship to take you to Phoenix for the Winter Solstice. With the Beastmen and Abominations destroyed, you can leave your cousin, Captain Jarid derDraconis, in charge of the castle, go to Phoenix, and call for a Grand Concourse at the Solstice. There you can be officially crowned as the High King of Veda, and Bort declared your Duke Grand Marshal of the realm. Then you can use the Truth Spell when you meet with the Grand Council in person. Of course, if it is known you have the ability to cast it, the people who need to hide their thoughts may not attend. Which will, of course, in itself, speak volumes.

The fewer who know you have that ability, the better."

"Will the Countess Spryngdal travel with us as well?" asked Artos.

"No, but Marie will stand for you at the Grand Concourse through the screens. It is as much as you can expect, Art. She is an old lady, though you wouldn't know it to look at her on the screen. She has not left Zanadar since before your father was born. Her Voice may attend the Concourse, however. That, in itself, will raise a few eyebrows. I don't think her Voice has attended a Concourse in decades, though Sprynfield is not really that far away from the twin cities of Eagleton and Phoenix."

"What about Squirt?" asked Bortis.

"Carimus should wait until he finishes his schooling with the Angellar at Fairinhorst. There is really no good way or enough time for him to return to Phoenix. I have sent word to Stanley, and I believe he will back us. Count Glendon seemed fairly certain, anyway. Ser Aubrie is traveling to Kent with your grandfather, Count Estel. Until we confer, we won't know for certain, but I trust Stanley. If King Artos declares the Canon and the Cantor as Regents for Carimus, it will suffice, for a time, anyway. This will probably be enough to secure the backing of Ser Pietro Neubre.

"I believe it will convince your grandfather to back you if you present the council with Castle Draconis under your control, and of course Count Stephan will not wish to look as though he would undermine his own future son-in-law."

Artos grimaced. "I'm still not sure I'm happy to have my marriage arranged for me. Elaine is a nice girl, and we have known each other since we were children, but ..." He trailed off.

"You're crazy, Art," said Bortis. "Elaine is a beautiful woman." He cleared his throat. "You said you would show us how you blended in with the wall, Donel. I have been trying to make them change color, but nothing happens."

"It's really very similar to how you bonded with your crysword, Bort. I suggest you keep them close to you when you sleep tonight. Next to you on the bed or under your pillows. Put them on again in the morning, and I will make that the first lesson in the morning. I think you also will find that combining your shield with these outfits will make your shielding easier. I said they are not quite armor, but with your shields, they are very much like it. I think we should call it an evening and plan on a rigorous training session tomorrow."

"We'll be ready," said Bortis with a yawn as Artos nodded, "and I am ready to sleep now. I'm about dead on my feet."

Artos remembered his nightmare. He still hadn't discussed it with Donel. He shrugged to himself and decided that it really wasn't important. He would seem very childish to admit that a dream had scared him to the point he awoke in a cold sweat. After all, it didn't recur, so it had to be his worries about the upcoming trip, that was all. Surely that was it.

"Good night, Donel. I have a feeling the next few days are going to be busy." He and Bortis went off to find their beds.

CHAPTER ELEVEN:

PREPARATIONS

12

SURPRISE ADDITIONS

ARTOS

9/25/1971 ar

FOR THE NEXT WEEK, the training chamber would be for Artos and Bortis exclusively until they were ready to start their trip to Starstone Tower. Furthermore, Donel would have no time to devote to the training of the Daughters until after the brothers set forth. Seeing that the greater share of the venison, which had been procured over the previous week had gone to trail supplies for Carimus's journey and the upcoming trip of Artos and Bortis, he suggested more hunting might be in order. The Daughters were more than willing. Jaek, Seth, and Liv were also included in the hunting parties. The first day passed quietly. The hunting party secured another giant elk, and Artos and Bortis spent the day practicing using their shielding skills and learning the Truth Spell.

As Donel had promised, he and the two brothers returned to the upper level before dusk to check on the progress of the group on their way to Fairinhorst. This was not a successful endeavor.

5:00 p.m.

"They must be using their Mindshields as they travel," said Donel. "I cannot locate them this evening. I'll scry for them after dinner. When Cari was asleep last night, I located him easily enough. Joy is the only one of the four with the training to hold a Mindshield while asleep. We may not see them very well if they choose to have no fire again. But we will have to take what we can get, I suppose."

After dinner, Donel, along with Angel and the two brothers, checked the screens again. Jaek and Kae went for a walk, and Seth entertained the other Daughters in the library with tales of his travels in the mountains. To their dismay, they could not discover Cari's whereabouts at all. Both brothers found it very hard to sleep.

9/26/1971 ar
6:30 a.m.

After a restless night, the brothers awoke early and found Donel in the room of screens sitting in his chair, seemingly asleep.

When Artos approached, however, he opened his eyes and shook his head.

"Still no sign of them. I have been using the eyes of an eagle to search the area for signs of them this morning, but I have had no luck yet. With so much mist and tree cover, people traveling the trails are almost impossible to spot from the air."

"What can we do?" asked Bortis. "I knew we shouldn't have sent him off alone!"

"He's not alone, Bort. We can't do anything except keep trying to locate them, and I shall. But the two of you need to attend to your training. Let us have breakfast, and I shall set up some exercises with the hunter hornets for you in the training hall. Then I will continue to search for them. Now that it is daylight, there will be more birds and animals about. If I get extremely lucky, I will find some eyes that will see them."

"I feel so helpless," confessed Artos. "First Duka and now Cari—isn't there anything we can do to help?"

"I understand, Art, but Veda's fate is being determined. Black hearts will rejoice if you cannot recover your throne, Art. You and Bort must attend to your duties."

"Cari is our duty!" said Bortis. "How can we attend to an entire country if we can't even protect our little brothers?"

"So what would you do, Bort? Rush off to find him somewhere, fifty miles away, in a place you don't know?" replied Donel.

"He's right, Bort." Artos sighed. "We can't do anything …"

"Yes, you can!" said Donel. "You can do your duty. You are Dragonbloods! You need to remember that! Today will be a very hard day for you to think about your training. I will not give you simple exercises to assuage your guilty consciences. The Glory Road isn't easy, but it is the road you now walk."

11:00 a.m.

Both Artos and Bortis found it a very trying morning. Donel asked Kae to watch over their training and to apply almas as needed. She found they needed it far too often. Then, an hour before the scheduled break for lunch, Donel interrupted them after an exercise.

"I have located them. They are fine and should be to Elpeler this afternoon and then Pogue this evening." Donel was smiling as he delivered the news. "They are traveling with their minds shielded, but I saw through the eyes of a cliff swallow and found them going down the trail by First Falls."

"Can you show us?" asked Artos.

"No, I didn't have them on the screens. I was in the swallow's mind. But tonight, we will locate them in the inn at Pogue and you will see for yourselves. Now, back to your training. It's still an hour until lunch."

The rest of the day was much better for both brothers.

6:00 p.m.

At dinner on Firstday, six days before they planned to set out on their journey, Jaek made an announcement. Observing Fairborn custom, he and Kae declared they were Feanauta, soul bound, husband and wife. They formalized the bond by Jaek giving Kae a ring and by her renaming herself no longer to be Kaerin

Arastina, but Kaerin Ka'Naurf.

There were many congratulations to the couple and some tears from the Daughters. Donel retreated to his wine cellar and returned with four bottles of Vhert for the celebration. After a round of toasting, Angel surprised everyone.

"I suppose you will now join us on the trek to Nénarambal Tirion?" asked Angel with a smile.

"That is my plan, little sister," replied Kae.

"Us?" asked Jaek, a look of concern on his face.

"But you can't," said Bortis at the same moment.

"Why would you say that, Bort?" asked Kae.

"I was standing right there when the West Wind specifically said you were not to come," said Bortis.

"Think back upon his words, Bort. Héru Andune proclaimed Kaerin Arastina was not to accompany you, did he not?" asked Kae.

"That's what I just said!" replied Bortis.

"But I am no longer Kaerin Arastina. I am Kae Ka'Naurf. I am subject to his laws, it is true, but I am bound as Feanauta to Jaek, and we will not be separated. We have discussed it, and he has agreed. I shall accompany Héru Artos. Providing Art has no objection."

"That is true," said Jaek. "However, I know my Lord Andune would greatly oppose the idea of you joining us. Surely you know this, Heri Angel. Your father has decreed that none of his people are to enter the lands of the deEagledon. It is a matter of the dishonor the House has shown your mother. You know this well."

Angel's face clouded. "What is my name, Jaek Ka'Naurf? By law, although I am Andune's daughter, I do not have his name. I am called Angel Andunsuruessa. Angel, Andune's daughter.

But that is not my name. I am Angel deEagledon, daughter of Stephanie deEagledon, who should have been the Countess Eagledon. And my father has no right to keep me away from my family lands."

Jaek looked helplessly at Donel, who shrugged and said, "She is correct, Jaek, although the fault is not Andune's, but his father Farnir's for refusing to accept his son's wife officially under Fairborn law."

"Farnir could not declare Lady Stephanie Feanauta Nuin Sanye to Andune," protested Jaek. "It would have caused an uproar among the people of Fairinlan, such as the world had never seen. Perhaps as much as provoking a civil war by those who hold humans with disdain. It would have put their children in the line of the royal succession. As much as it shames me to say it, some would never have accepted a half-human in the royal line."

"The only person who can rightfully exclude me from this journey is you, Art." Angel looked at him levelly. "Do you forbid me to accompany you?"

Artos was under scrutiny from every person in the room.

"I ... I would welcome your company, Angel—" began Artos, knowing it was true. Angel was someone whose company he enjoyed, but he also wondered if it was partly because she was forbidden fruit.

"Good, that's settled then!" interrupted Angel, giving him a warm smile. He smiled back, but a little voice in his head asked him if his future wife would approve, and he felt some guilt.

"Perhaps this is not wise, Art," said Seth.

"It is most unwise," agreed Jaek. "Do you really wish to cause a split between yourself and Hir Andune in this manner? Think of his rage against you and your House if something were to happen to his daughter, his only child. You would not want—"

"Art will be The High King of Veda," interrupted Bortis. "Unless Andune really wishes to become an outlaw, he will have to accept that Angel is of age and can make her own decisions."

"Your uncle falsely declared him an outlaw already. Have you forgotten?" asked Jaek with some heat.

"I have addressed that," said Artos. "The letter Bort delivered to him told him I realized my Uncle Bretton had declared him Outlaw wrongly, and I officially declared it was void. My very first official decree. I did it as Crown Prince Artos Draconis, son of Aaron Draconis, Pretender to the Dragon Throne. I sealed it with this." Art held up his right hand and displayed the signet ring on his hand with the sign of the dragon.

"Nothing is going to happen to me!" snapped Angel. She looked around. "It doesn't matter. I am going with you and Art, Jaek. Are you thinking of stopping me? Are you going to run home to my father telling tales?"

"I should do just that, but you know what would come about. We would return here, and you and your father would have a terrible row and you would defy him. Then he would be so angry he might disown you." Jaek shook his head. "You two are too much alike. You are both stubborn with heads of ambal when you are set to do something. No, all I can do is try to keep you safe."

"I am perfectly capable of minding my own safety, cousin!" Angel looked around. "I am so sorry, Kae. I did not mean to cause a scene on this night of your happiness."

"You are your mother's daughter, little sister," said Kae. "I could wish you had not upset my husband, but I would never try to persuade you to not do something you feel you must do. However, I would ask that you think long and hard about this course of action. If it is truly something you feel in your heart, then you must do what you must do. Just as I would have asked your mother." Kae smiled, and then she and Angel hugged. Jaek just sighed and shook his head, but said nothing more.

Artos saw his uncle was regarding him thoughtfully, but before he could speak, Donel shook his head and mouthed, *Later.* So he merely nodded back.

When the Vhert was gone and everyone retired for the evening, Artos tarried to speak with Donel.

"Do you think I am doing the wrong thing, allowing Angel to come with us?"

Donel tilted his head to the side and regarded Artos for a long moment. "What do you think, Art?"

"I see right on both sides of the argument. Prince Andune wants to protect his child. I understand how important that is. But Angel is an adult and has the right to make her own decisions as a deEagledon."

"If you were traveling to Eagleroost and seeking aid there, I would agree with you one hundred percent. You will travel through the deEagledon demesne and might meet with those who dwell there. But they will not recognize any claim to the Family on the word of some unknown half-Fairborn girl. It would assuredly cause more problems than it would solve, if either of you were to announce her as such."

"Then you think I should have told her she should not come?"

"I think it was your decision to make. Angel is a capable young woman. She is a skilled woodsman and tracker. As you know, she is a superb archer and was gifted with a crysbow, something worth taking into account. Jaek knows how angry Lord Andune will be and how serious a matter it would become were something dire to happen to her. You have not met him, but then neither has he met you. I would say in this ... you may be allowing your heart to decide and not your head. That is something only you can judge."

Artos shook his head, then sighed. "The word Jaek used—ambal, is that something forbidden?"

Donel laughed. "No, Art. Ambal means stone. Jaek said that both Andune and his daughter have heads of rock."

"Oh! I guess I have to agree, at least about Angel. She is a very stubborn woman."

Chapter Twelve:

Unwelcome Guests

13

KATEERI AND BACHAR AGAIN

ARTOS

9/27/1971 ar

5:45 a.m.

ON SECONDAY, LIV WOKE DONEL early with news. Two travelers were entering the Blue Spires on the path that led to the Crystal Cave. Two Fairborn …

6:20 a.m.

Donel stood with Artos and Angel on the front porch, high above the entrance to the Crystal Cave. Hidden behind the illusion given by the qulan seal, they watched the two Fairborn approach.

"Kateeri and Bachar," said Angel. "Father has sent them to bring me home. I was hoping they wouldn't come." She sighed. "But I knew they would. My father is very predictable."

"Shall we go down and invite our guests in for breakfast?" asked Donel.

*

Artos stood to one side of the cloakroom near the hall, which led to the rest of the Crystal Tower, while Angel waited near the center. Donel led the two Fairborn into the room and walked over to stand beside Angel, waiting silently.

Bachar glanced dismissively at Artos and turned his attention to Angel, but Kateeri studied him as if imprinting every detail of his being in her memory.

"Your note to your father said you were going to the Nest," said Bachar.

"My note said I was returning to the Daughters," said Angel. "When I got to the Nest, I found they had come here, so, naturally, I followed them. If I had known you were following me, I would have left you a note and saved you a trip."

"What you should have done was turn around and return to your home," said Bachar. "Get your things. We will set out at once."

"No," said Angel. "The Daughters are here to be trained by Donel. I do not choose to return to Alfhiem at this time."

"Hir Andune has directed us to return with you. I tell you again—get your things. You will come with us."

"And I tell you once again, no. I am of age, and I do not wish to return to Alfhiem at this time."

Bachar took a step closer. "Angel Andunsuruessa, your lord has ordered you to return at once. You will come with us, whether willingly or not. I do not care, but you are coming with us."

"Angel is my guest, as are the two of you," said Donel. "She is welcome to stay here as long as she desires. I warn you—do not abuse my hospitality and attempt to force your will upon anyone in my domicile."

"You do not frighten me, Magic Man. Angel comes with us, now!" Bachar took another step forward and reached out to take Angel's wrist.

"Stop!" said Donel. Bachar froze in mid-step. "Perhaps you should be frightened, Bachar. I will not allow you to lay hands upon a guest in my home. Be glad I am not an evil person. I could do far more than just freeze you in place." Donel made a gesture with his right hand, and the Fairborn was forced to catch his balance to keep from falling as Donel released the hold on him.

"Stop, Bachar," said Kateeri. "Hir Donel, do you really want to challenge Hir Andune concerning his daughter?"

"I am not challenging Lord Andune in any way. I am respecting the wishes of a guest in my home. I would extend the same courtesy to you or to any other guest of mine."

"Hir Andune will not see it in that light. You know this," replied Kateeri. "In his eyes, it will seem you extend sanctuary to his willfully disobedient daughter. He will not be pleased with her or with you."

"I know you, Angel Andunsuruessa," said Bachar. "You will not stay cooped up inside this tower. Sometime soon, you will venture outside, to hunt or just for fresh air. We will be waiting, and then you will return to your father."

"I don't think so," replied Angel. "I don't think my friend will look kindly upon an attempt to kidnap me."

Bachar's lip curled in a cruel smile. "Which friend is that? The Magic Man never leaves his domicile." He looked at Artos. "This human, perhaps?" He gave a disdainful snort. "Hnnh! I watched the other human duel in Alfhiem. He had to resort to tricks to win. Is this one so much better a warrior to champion you?"

"I wouldn't expect Artos to fight for me," said Angel levelly.

"Then who?" sneered the Fairborn scout.

A low, menacing growl answered his question. The two Fairborn both stiffened and then slowly turned to look behind them. Standing in the doorway to the cloakroom was Liv.

"I would advise you not to reach for a weapon," said Donel. "Liv is my friend. She is rather protective."

"Call her off," said Bachar. Both Fairborn held their hands where Liv could see them and remained motionless.

Angel walked around the two scouts and stood next to the large mist cat and reached out, rubbing behind Liv's left ear. "Liv and I usually go together when I go out for a walk. She and I are old friends."

"You are in no danger from Liv as long as you do not threaten her or her friends," said Donel. "I would think carefully about trying to abduct Angel outside the Crystal Tower."

"If you would ask her to stand aside, we will leave now," said Kateeri. "We will take your answer back to your father, Angel Andunsuruessa. I warn you; he will be most displeased with your decision to remain here."

"Wait," said Artos, stepping into the room. "I would ask that you do me a great favor."

"Why would we—" began Bachar.

"What would you ask of us?" cut in Kateeri.

"I have a scroll for Lord Andune." Artos held up a sealed scroll case. "I was going to send it with Angel when she returned to her father, but it would seem you will see him before Angel will. I would be very grateful if you could see it delivered to his hand."

"We are not errand boys for you, human," began Bachar, when Kateeri held up her hand, stopping her companion.

"Why do you think Hir Andune would be interested in anything you might have to say?" she asked.

"That is business between Lord Andune and myself," answered Artos. "But seeing it affects you, if indirectly, I guess it would do no harm for you to know. I am sending Lord Andune the deed to Alfhiem."

Bachar burst out laughing. "We don't need to carry nonsensical notes to Hir Andune. He doesn't find the jokes of humans to be humorous."

Kateeri's eyes narrowed. "Who are you exactly? What makes you think you could do such a thing as give Hir Andune something he already possesses?"

"Excuse me, I forget my manners," said Artos. "My name is Artos deDraconis, Crown Prince and pretender to the throne of Veda. If I am not mistaken, Alfhiem is in the Rainbow Valley, in the deHerndar demesne, not in Fairinlan, is it not?"

"Technically, you are correct," said Kateeri, giving a guarded nod.

"*Technically*, Lord Andune and everyone living in Alfhiem are squatting illegally on the lands of a Great House under my jurisdiction. In this scroll is my decree that Alfhiem is awarded to Hir Andune Naurfindl for past services as a protector of the realm. It declares that The Rainbow Valley, Alfhiem, and the land connecting it to the lands of Fairinlan are his. This frees him from any taxation that might be due to the House deHerndar and names him as a Baron of Veda."

Bachar snorted. "I think you will find you cannot buy Hir Andune's daughter, no matter what you think you can offer him."

Artos stiffened. "I had prepared this scroll before you arrived here. I am affronted you think I would feel the need to purchase one of my own subjects from anyone."

Bachar bristled, but a gesture from Kateeri kept him silent. She reached out, took the scroll, noted the wax seal, and nodded. "I will not attempt to answer for my Lord, but I agree to be your messenger for this." She turned her eyes back to Donel. "If you would remove your cat, we will take our leave."

"Liv has already stepped outside, Kateeri," said Angel.

The two Fairborn looked at where Angel was now standing alone. Smiling at them, she walked back over to stand between Artos and Donel. "Give Father my love and tell him I will return soon to discuss this matter more. Just not right now, not today. Safe journeys."

The two Fairborn exchanged looks, turned, and without another word walked back out of the cloakroom. Donel followed along to see them out. "Liv will be happy to escort you to the edge of the Spires."

Angel turned to Artos. "That wasn't necessary. They would have left."

"I didn't write the decree with this in mind, Angel. I planned on having you take this to your father when you returned to Alfhiem. Before I knew you were coming along with us. They were convenient, that's all."

She nodded. "I see. Are you sure you are not trying to buy something? Father's goodwill, perhaps?"

"I won't deny—I hope Lord Andune would look upon this as a favorable action. But I mean what I said. Through his actions, and yours with the Daughters, you have made Rainbow Valley a safer place. I brought back a piece of that raider's tunic for a reason, Angel. It is evidence. I just wish we had one of the deHerndar as well. No doubt they will demand compensation for my giving away something they think is so precious. I intend to discuss it at a Concourse in Phoenix, in person. While I am using the Truth Spell."

Chapter Thirteen:

Rite of Sacrifice

14

FINAL PREPARATIONS

ARTOS

9/28/1971 ar

9:45 a.m.

THE LAST FEW DAYS OF TRAINING flew by, at least from Artos's point of view. In the mornings, Donel drilled them on using their cryswords in unique ways—ways they had never dreamed. Bortis learned to create flames running along the blade of his sword as he swatted hunter hornets out of the air. Artos found his element was electricity, and although not as flashy as his brother's sword, it was just as deadly to the hunter hornets. Each time he connected with one of the flying menaces, there was a spark and a soft *crack,* and the hornets dropped motionless to the floor of the training hall. Artos lamented when Donel flatly refused to discuss teaching them how to fire bolts of their elements—missiles such as they had witnessed the bard Varyan do with his crysharp. After learning it had taken the Fairborn years to master the art, however, he understood and had to be satisfied with the ability to shock his foes.

The afternoons were divided between time spent having

certain uses of their regalos impressed on their minds through Donel's mysterious hypnosis sessions and the practical application of those skills.

Both brothers became more used to taking a moment to concentrate when practicing their skills, allowing them to maintain body shields while using trueseeing. They struck down hunter hornets using the newfound abilities with their cryswords.

During dinner, they usually discussed practical issues, such as the amount of dried jerky they had for the trip or what weather they could expect and how it would impact their travel.

They would end each day with one more training session, honing their newly acquired skills with their cryswords and practicing their trueseeing—battling foes that varied in size and form, from hunter hornets to giant wolves and, once, an enormous bear.

Then suddenly, the last evening was upon them.

"Instead of more practicing tonight, I suggest you spend it resting," said Donel after dinner was finished. "You are setting out first thing tomorrow morning, and I think you deserve a break. There will be time for you to practice as you make your way to Starstone Tower."

Donel did some adjusting to his table screen and brought forth a game of chess, where the pieces were controlled by the players speaking their moves aloud. Bortis and Jaek commandeered the board and played an epic match that kept the others entertained for almost two hours. Jaek won the closely matched game. Then everyone turned in for the night.

Donel was always the last to retire, and he was joined by Artos and Bortis, who waited for everyone else to make their way off to bed.

"We just wanted—" started Artos.

"I think—" said Bortis simultaneously.

Artos turned and motioned for his brother to proceed.

Bortis looked at Artos, then nodded and turned to face Donel. "I think I owe you a great many things. Not the least is an apology for my rudeness when we first arrived here."

"You were upset. I understand. I would say no apology is needed, but I will say I accept and suggest we consider it in the past. Agreed?"

Bortis nodded and turned to Artos.

Artos nodded back to his brother, then turned back to Donel. "I just want to tell you that we appreciate all you have done ... uncle." Both brothers bowed.

Part Five

Into Fairinlan

Chapter Fourteen:

Rejections and Acceptance

15

WE DON'T WANT THEIR KIND HERE

CARIMUS

9/25/1971 ar

"WE DON'T WANT THEIR KIND HERE. These are Fairborn lands." The innkeeper glared at the three humans and looked askance at Joy. "I will give you two rooms, one night only. That'll be ten silvers … each. Meals are separate, and you have to eat in your rooms. I have regular customers in the taproom, and I'll lose business if you go in there."

"That's double rate," said Joy. "My sister and I stayed here before with Rachel. You didn't make this kind of fuss last year."

"That was last year. If you don't like it, go elsewhere. There have been too many rumors of Orch and Orqui raiders up in the hills this year. People don't want Orqui here. This is a decent place."

Carimus inhaled sharply as he felt anger growing inside. Vix put a warning hand on his shoulder. If Joy hadn't told him not to speak, he would have given this arrogant innkeeper a piece of his mind. If it wasn't for the thought of finally being able to sleep on a comfortable mattress and eat a hot, home-cooked meal, he would have shouted some choice words, then walked away. He clenched his jaws as Joy paid for the rooms. Suddenly, he felt embarrassed. *I'm reacting like Bort.* This wasn't like him at all.

"We'll want the food brought up right away," said Joy. "What are our choices for dinner, and how much will it cost?"

"No choice. All we have tonight is stew. Two silver for the lot of you. No ale allowed in the rooms. No singing or boisterous behavior. You'll drink water up there, and I don't want you coming down to the taproom later." The innkeeper glared at Joy as if daring her to object.

"You said that already. Which are our rooms? We want two together, not at different ends of the hall."

"Top floor. North side. There's no one else on that floor. Yet. Dinner won't be ready for an hour. My daughter will be bringing you your stew. Can you find your way, or do you need someone to show you?" He was wearing something very near a sneer as he pointed at the stairs.

"I know the way." Joy turned and led the group up the stairs.

Carimus didn't know what to expect. He had never stayed at an inn before and was a bit surprised to find the top floor was the garret. There were only four rooms—two on the north and two on the south. Joy led the way to the first door on the north, and looked inside, and nodded her head. Carimus peeked around her and peered into the room. There wasn't much there, a small table with two chairs, a pair of more comfortable-looking chairs set facing each other near a dormered window, and two beds. Real beds with comforters and pillows. Carimus nodded, his anger at the boorish innkeeper forgotten at the sight of somewhere to sleep that wasn't just a pile of leaves.

"It's like I remembered. We had to stay up here once before when he had a few more guests. I think we are his only customers. It's late in the year; few travelers are on the road. If it were spring, there would be more. Fur trappers mostly. That's why there's only stew. If he expected more customers, they would have a fuller menu."

"You'd think he would be glad for our business then," said Vix.

"Oh, he was. He wants our silver," answered Joy.

"Then why didn't you haggle with him? With his nasty attitude, I was expecting you to tell him to go to blazes."

Joy sighed. "I could have probably gotten him to back down a bit, but we don't want to attract attention. Now he'll just remember that he cheated a Fairborn and three humans. He won't remember any details. No one overheard him, and he won't go talking about it to his customers. I heard a couple of people talking in the taproom, but I doubt any of them paid any attention to our arrival. If we had a shouting match with that jerkelf, they certainly would have."

"Jerkelf?" asked Cari.

"I was being rude, Cari. Don't you ever say that to a Fairborn unless you want a fight, because you would certainly get one."

"Oh, I wouldn't." Cari chuckled and said, "I'm not Bort. I was just wondering if he knows that word."

"I don't think you need to teach it to him if he doesn't. He can get into enough trouble on his own, I'm sure," said Vix. "If the rooms are alike, we girls will take this one, and you can take the one next door, Cari."

"The rooms are all the same, I believe," said Joy. "We can all wait here and eat dinner together. Then when Cari gets sleepy, he can go bed down next door."

"So, how far are we from Fairinhorst? Are we getting close now?" asked Carimus as he settled on one of the comfortable chairs. Vix and Rachel sat on the closer bed, and Joy sat in the other chair across from him.

"I would guess we are still about eighty miles," said Joy. "Pogue is about forty miles from Fortecitime on I Vindya Nen. That's the Blue Water, the river that runs down to Lake Tog in the lowlands. We'll start early and we can make that trip in one day. It's pretty much all downhill now for a good way. We'll find a friendlier inn there. I think we stayed at the Golden Stag with you, didn't we, Rach? When we were traveling to Aranothrond?"

"I think that was the name. I remember all the beautiful tapestries. It was very nice," said Rachel.

"We'll cross the bridge to Tarcitime and then have about forty miles to go to Haldacitime, on the far side of Hidden Vale. That's into the mountains again. It's uphill into the vale, so it will take us two days. We could push hard, but then you would be pretty worn out. Donel advised me to take the last leg of the trip at an easy pace so you will be rested when you get there. Then we'll get a room at the Oisin Inn. That's the name Kae gave me. I haven't been there."

"At Fairinhorst?" He was beginning to get excited. Soon he would have news of Duka.

"No, Cari at Haldacitime, still a few miles from Fairinhorst. We will stay at the Inn; the Gatekeeper for Fairinhorst is in the city. He is the person we must seek. No one goes to Fairinhorst unless the Gatekeeper admits them. A qulan field surrounds the entire valley where Fairinhorst is located. I hope he won't be too difficult to find. We are coming after the normal admissions.

Those are at the equinox."

At that moment, there was a knock on the door. When Vix opened it, a young Fairborn woman entered, carrying an armload of towels.

"Mára amaurea," she said with a smile. "Adar said he sent you up here without giving you fresh towels. Truth be told, we rarely use these rooms unless we have a crowd of people staying."

"Good day," answered Joy. "We don't mind. We have been on the road a few days and we want nice quiet rooms for sleeping."

"Adar said someone would bring us our dinner soon," said Carimus. "I'm guessing that would be you?"

The woman looked startled and then laughed a merry laugh. "Yes indeed. I am Vaeri Iliran, at your service, little brother. I will deliver the stew and a loaf of freshly baked bread in about fifteen minutes. I'll be fetching them directly." She placed the towels on the dresser. "I'll be back shortly."

After Vaeri had left, Joy burst out laughing and was joined by Vix and Rachel, leaving Carimus feeling bewildered.

"What's so funny?" he asked plaintively, looking at each of the daughters in turn.

"You called the innkeeper 'father.' That's what adar means. That's why she called you 'little brother.'"

Carimus shrugged. "Oh. I thought it was his name. Well, she seems to be much friendlier."

"Not all Fairborn are of the danorqui faction, but King Farnir is, and so there is little resistance to those who are. I suspect some trouble recently has turned public opinion in that direction. It wasn't prevalent the last time I came this way. Things will be better in Fortecitime. That is the only city in the

Fairborn lands that has any direct contact with humans. In fact, it is as far as humans are normally allowed to travel up the river. Any trading with the lowlands they do in Fortecitime."

"So people travel up the river to Fort-te-sit-a-me to trade goods?"

"Oh, no. The Blue Water isn't navigable to the lowlands. In fact, they should call it the White Water to the west of the city. Five or six miles to the east, it starts to descend, and it's long stretches of rapids with more than a few waterfalls. There is an airship tower in Fortecitime, and all the goods to and from the lowlands go through it. They fly above the river. The human trading company is from the city of Jacsonn on the deAnson-deHerndar border. It's mostly furs and jewelry we trade to the humans who sell us iron goods they get from the Forge-folk."

Carimus nodded excitedly. "I see. Uncle Cam never taught us about things like trade, and our other tutor, Elaer Prindar, taught us geography. I don't remember him ever talking about trade between us and the Fairborn or the Forge-folk. I wonder if he even knew about that wolfman and his ... his kingdom. Someone in the family should have known, and Uncle Cam was Loremaster. I need to learn as much as I can since I have to take his place now. Someone will have to advise Artie on trade and all those things."

"There used to be a lot more trade, but I think it has lessened of late. I don't really know why."

Soon after, Vaeri and another younger girl brought their dinner. Then the conversation was mostly about how good it was to eat food that wasn't trail rations.

9/26/1971 ar

The next evening, their welcome at the Golden Stag was less hostile, although the innkeeper's smile was less than genuine when he greeted them. He seemed happy to hear they were only staying overnight. The hostility came when they went to the bridge that led to the sister city across the river ...

9/27/1971 ar

"What do you mean, we can't cross the river?!" Carimus was stunned with disbelief.

"By order of the king. It's been that way for years. If you have business in Aranothrond, you take the boat. Only Fairborn are allowed in Tarcitime. If you are planning to stay more than the day in Aranothrond, you will need a pass from the trading guild. That's in the Civic Hall."

"We have business in Fairinhorst," said Joy. "Aranothrond would add days to our journey."

The bridge guard looked skeptical. "Humans don't go to Fairinhorst anymore. They haven't for years. Humans aren't welcome in Fairinlan."

"But the Angellar summoned me! You have to let us cross!" said Carimus heatedly. He felt his voice increase in pitch and took a deep breath.

"The Angellar!" The guard laughed. "Do I look like a total

fool? Get on with you! Go away."

"But I was!" Carimus insisted. *Don't act like Bort, Cari,* he told himself. "Ten days ago!"

"Prove it! Let's see your token. Surely you know that they always give those rare few Fairborn who are summoned a rune token?" The guard smiled unpleasantly. "Didn't know that minor fact, huh? Go away!"

"Rune token? She printed words on the screen! *Send Carimus to Fairinhorst!* Plain as day!"

Joy tried to shush Carimus, but he waved his arms wildly in frustration. Fortunately, there were no other travelers nearby, and no one besides the guard heard his outburst. The guard, however, seemed unimpressed and shook his head, pointing back the way they had come.

Cari felt the clinking of his bracelet and looked at his left wrist. He extended his arm and pointed to it with his other hand. "Runes like these?"

The guard looked disgusted, but glanced at the bracelet. His eyebrows then rose, and he looked shocked.

"Those are the tokens of Fairinhorst. A dozen of them. Where did you get them?"

"There are ten," he said, suddenly feeling more assured. "The Bard, Varyan Benoit, gave them to me. Will you let us cross now?"

The guard carefully took one of the rune bangles between his fingers and inspected it, looking at the runes on each side. Then, with a stunned look of bewilderment, waved them past.

Joy hurried them along across the bridge and into the city on the south bank.

"You never told us about your bracelet, Cari. Did Varyan really give it to you?" asked Vix.

"Yes, well, not personally, exactly. He delivered it to Castle Draconis. It was a birthday present, six years ago."

"Well, that was lucky," said Joy. "Lucky you have it, of course. Also, it confused the guard so much he never thought to say that only you could cross. He probably wouldn't have let Rach and Vix come with us. He's probably just realizing that now. But we're across now, and we will be out of the city in a little while. He won't want to admit to his captain he let some humans cross that he should have stopped."

"Yes … it's funny too. I mean wow! Maybe the Angellar was foreseeing and knew I would need it."

"Maybe. Just remember to present it to the Gatekeeper when we find him at Haldacitime."

"Oh, I will, I surely will." Carimus stared at his bracelet, regarding it in a new light.

Shortly after leaving Tarcitime, the ground rose steeply before them, climbing back into the mists for which the mountains were named. Throughout the morning, they scaled steadily through forests of larch and mountain pine, with more and more of the thousand-year varieties the higher they went. After noon, the ground leveled, moving westward in the shadows of the towering thousand-year firs, some of which had diameters of well over three hundred feet.

By midafternoon, the trail led them to the edge of the forest. To the south, the mists faded away, revealing a beautiful vista. Although it was late in the year, the meadow before their eyes was filled with golden flowers. Some were fading and drooping, but in spring and summer, the display would dazzle the eye. A mile or so away, the gold disappeared beneath a canopy of lilac and purple.

"That's beautiful!" said Carimus. "I remember Elaer's

geography lesson about Fairinlan, but I don't remember any valley like this on the maps. I know Fairinlan is full of flowers and flowering bushes. The map was full of color, but I think our maps only had mountains above the valley of Aranothrond and the twin cities."

"This valley is called Haldatumbo, the Hidden Vale. It would be more surprising if they showed it on your maps. We are a very secretive people to outsiders. It is the Fairborn nature. That is something to remember when you deal with my people. Sometimes it is merely habit, but often it is deliberate. Tonight when we make camp, we will not make a fire. I know it may be chilly, but it would be sure to offend someone were we to burn things without permission."

Carimus looked around as they followed the trail back into the mists surrounding the gigantic trees. "Offend who? The trail looks well-traveled, but I haven't even noticed a squirrel or a chipmunk, much less any people. If it wasn't for all the birds singing and calling, I would have thought nothing lived here at all."

"Just because you fail to see something doesn't mean there is nothing to see," Joy said with a slight smile.

Carimus looked around again and shrugged, and they trudged steadily onward.

A short time before dusk, Joy called for the party to break for the day. "I think this clearing to the side would be a good place to camp."

Glad for the rest, they all settled down, sitting with their backs to an enormous thousand-year-old oak tree, a rarity among the fir trees that filled the vale.

"How much further are we from Fairinhorst?" asked Vix.

"I'm not sure," said Joy. "But Donel said not to hurry. To take two days to walk from Tarcitime to Haldacitime."

"It could be walked in one day, but it is forty-two miles between the cities," a voice interrupted them from above. Startled, they jumped to their feet and looked up. A bark-covered shutter had opened in the tree, revealing a window a dozen feet above them. A Fairborn man leaned out from the opening, looking down at them. He continued, seeming unsurprised by their presence. "Most people prefer a more leisurely pace than what it would take to get there in just one. Climbing to the pass at the start makes it unlikely, though. Might I ask why you are going to Fairinhorst? You are too late for the fall testing."

"I didn't know this was a nimloth bar. Forgive us for trespassing," said Joy.

"I'm the door warden. When you leaned against the front door, I naturally looked out to see who it was. This is Tir Nah Nog, one of the seven nimloth barae of Haldatumbo. We have an inn if you are looking for a place to stay this evening. We are the only peler of the seven who can boast that."

"Three of us are human. Does that make a difference?"

"I have eyes. And ears." The Fairborn man smiled down at them. "You are speaking common, not Espro. I don't care, and my brother-in-law is the innkeeper. As long as you pay your bill, he will give you rooms. He grumbles a lot. Though he won't admit it, he'll be delighted to have guests. He rarely has many this late after the testing. The last of those who failed passed through a week ago. Those who become discouraged and leave aren't due for a few weeks. One or two usually trickle through around the next full moon. The rest of the new class will probably stay till the end of the teaching. You have silver, I trust? Orrian isn't one for charity."

"We can pay," said Carimus. *Another innkeeper to deal with. I hope he's not like the one in Pogue. Still, it would be better than sleeping on the ground again.* He looked around. "You say there's a door here? I don't see it."

"That's because I haven't opened it yet. I will forewarn you. Our peler is warded. If you try to enter with evil intentions, there will be dire results," replied the warden. A crack in the bark of the gigantic tree suddenly split wide in front of them. Steps led upward into the tree. "Welcome to Tir Nah Nog." And the window shut above them.

"It looks like we don't have to sleep on the ground tonight." Joy led the way up the steps. Carimus motioned to Vix and Rachel, then followed them inside the tree village. *I hope it's not another surly innkeeper. Remember Cari, act like Artie, not Bort,* thought Carimus. *The warden seemed friendly enough anyway.*

At the top of a short flight of stairs was a broad hall. Everlights lit the hall, and standing at the top of the stairs was the warden. He offered a small, golden ball to Joy. "I trust you know how to find your way using the man`corne?" he asked.

"I believe so. It's been years, but I should be able to follow the guide," she answered. He bowed and stepped back into a room off the hall and shut the door behind him.

"What's that?" asked Carimus. "Man cor-nay?"

Joy held out the small orb for him to examine. "When I hold it before me in the correct direction, a white spot appears. If I move it away from the correct path, the light disappears." She moved the ball so it was between her and the hall, and a white spot appeared. It vanished when she moved it to the side. "Shall we go?"

The orb led them down the hall to a side passage, up a flight of stairs to another hall, and into an open space that looked as though it might be large enough for a dance or a large gathering. Hanging on silver chains, a dozen glowing golden balls lit the spacious chamber. Around the outer edge of the vast room were many doors, some with small signs above them. A few Fairborn were sitting on a circle of benches in the center, and conversation reached their ears. Several of the Fairborn examined them curiously, but Carimus didn't see any signs of hostility. He tried to read the signs they passed, but his knowledge of Espro was insufficient for the task. After leading them a third of the way around the room, the orb pointed them to a door like all the others they had passed. Joy paused for a moment, then tried the handle and found it led into a small room with two other doors. The only furnishing was a desk with a small silver bell sitting on it. Joy took the bell, shook it, and set it down. Shortly after, a Fairborn entered the room and looked them over.

"Yes? May I help you?" he asked. Carimus examined his face, but he wore a neutral expression. He didn't seem welcoming, but not hostile either.

"The door warden sent us," said Joy, presenting the man with the golden ball. "He said you could rent us rooms. We wish to stay the night, and we'll be off to Fairinhorst in the morning."

The innkeeper pursed his lips and nodded. "I suppose I could. Do you wish meals as well?"

"If it's not too much trouble. We have traveled from Tarcitime and only had a small lunch of travel rations."

"A room for each of you, or are you planning on doubling up?"

"We can make do with two rooms. One for Cari and another for the three of us," answered Joy, waving vaguely at Vix and Rachel.

"I can do that, six silvers a room and another silver apiece per meal. That'll be sixteen silver, or I can give you a suite for twenty. Three bedrooms and a sitting room, and your meals are included."

The four travelers looked at each other. Before any of the Daughters could answer, Carimus spoke up. "I'll pay for the suite. I still have enough from what Donel gave me to do that and still have enough for meals tomorrow, too, I think."

"You shouldn't spend all your silver, Cari," said Joy. "You will need some when you leave Fairinhorst."

Carimus shrugged. "I'm not going to worry about what I may need later. Donel told me I will probably spend the winter there, and I'll hunt that pup when it's grown."

The innkeeper smirked for a moment, but remained silent, and his impassive visage returned.

"What is funny?" Vix asked him, noticing his unpleasant smile.

"Oh, nothing, nothing. I'm sure going to Fairinhorst two weeks late and demanding to be allowed to receive training will work out fine."

"I just got the message from the Angellar to go there a little more than a week ago," said Carimus. "I'm sure she won't consider me late. I was far away."

"Oh, I see … the Angellar summoned you personally, did she? You must be very special. Do you want the suite or not?"

Vix's elbow struck Carimus's ribs as he opened his mouth to protest the innkeeper's derisive challenge. "It's up to you, Cari. The suite would be nice, but it doesn't matter which we take."

What would Artie do? he thought. He nodded and then opened his coin-purse and counted out twenty silver pieces onto the desk.

The innkeeper recounted the coins, examining each one as

if he suspected Carimus might try to slip in some false ones. Carimus felt indignant, but remained silent as the innkeeper swept them up, and they vanished into his pockets.

"Kharis!" he called out, picking up the silver bell and ringing it briskly three times. "Kharis Krisnan, you lazy butterfly! I need you to show these people to their rooms."

After a few moments, a young Fairborn entered through a door in the wall behind the desk. He gave the travelers a mischievous wink and turned to the innkeeper. "Did I hear the bell tinkle, oh Master Orrian, or was I mistaken? You know I strive to give you satisfaction and I would much rather come unsummoned than miss a chance to serve."

"You know I called, you lazy tree-rat! Take these fine travelers to the green suite, then go to the kitchen and tell that good-for-nothing cook to fire up the ovens and prepare a hot meal for them. Go!" Carimus observed the way the keeper spoke to his staff. *Hmmm, I guess he treats everyone that way, not just humans.*

The young man bowed deeply to the travelers and then made a stiff salute to the innkeeper. "My feet are as wings, oh my master! I live to serve." With a friendly smile, he beckoned the group to follow him as he went to the side door and started up the stairs beyond.

"We don't get too many travelers this time of year," he said over his shoulder as he proceeded up the stairs. "And three humans, to boot. I don't recall Orrian ever having human guests before. May I ask about your business? I know it's none of mine to ask yours. If you don't want to tell me, that's fine, but my sister tells me I'm as curious as a sand cat. Whatever a sand cat is. We only have Mist Cats and a giant lynx or two here in the vale." He stopped on a landing, opened the door, and led them down a hall.

"The Angellar summoned me to Fairinhorst, and my friends here traveled with me to show me the way," said Carimus. "A sand cat is a large orange cat that lives in the desert. They sometimes have stripes and are said to be very smart. I don't know about curious, but I think all cats are inquisitive by nature."

"You don't say." Kharis stopped in front of a door with a green plaque centered upon it.

"There is a desert to the south of the mountains. I guess that's where you'd find them then." He opened the door with a flourish. "The green suite! This is the sitting room, of course. Those doors to the rear and the one to the right are the bedrooms. The doors on the left are the bath and a closet. I'll go down to the kitchen and tell the cook to start your dinner. Is there anything special you fancy? I think she told me she had both elk and moose steaks to be used up soon. She bakes bread fresh each day, and she always has a green salad. Any preferences?"

"Oh, a moose steak would be wonderful," said Vix, and the rest nodded in agreement.

"All right! I'll be back then in about an hour." He hurried off, leaving them to explore the suite.

9/28/1971 ar

The travelers arrived in Haldacitime shortly before midday and after finding the Oisin inn for the girls, they ate lunch in a local food-shop and then set out to find the Gatekeeper of Fairinhorst.

"I think we will probably need to camp in the Vale rather than stop at Tir Nah Nog on our return," said Joy. "That will leave us enough coin to stay at the Golden Stag again on the trip home. We can camp outside Pogue rather than give our coin to that jerkelf innkeeper." Vix and Rachel both nodded in agreement.

"I thought you said not to use that word?" asked Carimus.

"He makes me angry just thinking about him," replied Joy. "Besides, I said you shouldn't use that word, not me. Frankly, if I see him on our trip back, I might just use it to his face. There are enough genuine issues in the world today to think about, without his petty concerns."

"Do you think you will be safe traveling back? Not from the innkeeper. I mean, from that Kargyn?" said Carimus.

"I don't know, Cari. Not for certain, but I have traveled between Rainbow Valley and the Fairborn lands half a dozen times and never saw a single wolf, much less giant ones, until this trip. Andune sends patrols as far as Lake Deth, and we may even cross paths with one on our return trip. I think we'll be safe. We shall travel with our minds shielded and hope for the best."

"Where are we going now? Did they know at the inn where the Gatekeeper would be?" asked Carimus. He realized his palms felt sweaty. They were almost there. Soon, he would finally have some news about Duka.

"At the inn, they told me where his villa was to be found. The innkeeper didn't think there were any hunts ongoing. A hunt would be the most likely reason he was absent. That's where we are going now." She looked at the street signs at each intersection they passed until she found the one she was looking for, guiding them to a row of fine-looking chateaus separated by tall hedges. Each estate was decorated with multitudes of fruit trees and flower gardens. The residences would be magnificent in the spring and summer, Carimus thought, but were merely beautiful in the depths of autumn. Every manor house was different from the others. Each had its own theme, and the types of foliage were set to distinguish them. Tall, intricately contrived fences guarded the fronts of the separate estates, allowing passersby to see the beauty within. Carimus felt a sense of wonder at the displays. At almost the last estate on the street, Joy stopped.

"I think this is the one. The innkeeper said to look for the eagle."

A gate designed to look like an eagle with wings spread barred passage to the grounds. In the center was a circular ring composed of golden topaz. Within was a swirling design of a twisted five-pointed star of pure white translucent crystal. The inner part of the circle was composed of equal parts emerald, ruby, and sapphire.

"I think that's the sigil of Fairinhorst," said Joy. "Or of the Angellar, perhaps. The two are one and the same in so many ways."

"There's no bell," said Vix. "I wonder how we are supposed to attract anyone's attention? Shout?"

"No," said Joy. "That would be rude. There must be something …"

Carimus reached out and touched the sigil with his palm as his Uncle Cameron had shown him to open the warded door of the Hall of Mirrors at Castle Draconis, then jumped back with a hiss. "I think something just happened! I felt it."

"Did it sting you, Cari?" asked Rach.

"No, but … I can't describe it. It felt like it acknowledged I

218

was touching it."

"I wonder if you set off an alarm, or if it is the way people signal that they wish to enter?" mused Joy.

Carimus shook his hand and considered pressing the sigil again.

"Well, something happened." Vix peered through the gate towards the elegant home. "The door's open. Someone's coming."

Carimus peered through the bars. A figure had opened the door and was standing on the grand portico of the villa. The Fairborn man was tall and imposing, clad in shimmering gray. Circling his brow was a golden diadem, which sparkled in the sunlight.

"That must be the Gatekeeper himself," said Joy. "I think perhaps you touching the sigil has announced your presence to him. I would have expected a servant to come to see who was here, but that doesn't look like a servant to me."

Carimus thought so too as he gazed at the imposing figure. "I want to thank you three for guiding me here," he said, looking around at the daughters. "I would never have made it without your help. Thank you so very much."

"He's coming," said Vix.

Carimus looked back through the bars. *He doesn't look happy,* he thought. *I wonder if we interrupted something. Remember act like Artie would, not like Bort.*

Chapter Fifteen:

Gates and Gatekeepers

16

THE GATEKEEPER

CARIMUS

THE FAIRBORN WHO APPROACHED THE GATE did not look pleased to have been disturbed. He was dressed in a robe of silk, and as he walked, the grey color shifted and swirled, as if a rainbow flowed over the fine material. A cane crafted entirely of gemstones was in his left hand. He stood for a moment, gazing at them through the openings in the gate.

"You come before me wearing shields? Lower them at once," he demanded icily.

"Do as he says," said Joy. "I should have thought of that. I'm sorry."

Carimus wasn't sure if she spoke to the Gatekeeper or to them—probably both, he decided. He hurriedly dismissed the shield and waited for the Gatekeeper to open the gate.

The imposing figure studied them a few moments more, gazing at each in turn for what was surely only a few seconds, but felt like an agonizingly long time to Carimus.

The gate stayed closed. "Why are you here? I don't require servants. I am not in need of anything you might think to offer me. My time is valuable." His gaze returned to Joy as if assuming she was the spokesperson for the group.

"My name is Carimus deDraconis." Carimus held up his left wrist to display his rune-bracelet. "The Angellar sent for me."

The Gatekeeper glanced at the bracelet for a moment. Then the gates slid aside, splitting in half in the center, each side sliding in front of the ornate fence that guarded the lawn. Carimus stepped forward, but a warning gesture from the Fairborn stopped him in place, still holding his bracelet out for examination.

The Gatekeeper took hold of his wrist and examined the rune-bracelet. "Where did you get this? Did you steal it? Answer me!" His dark green eyes bore into Carimus's.

"Steal it? No! The bard Varyan gave it to me." He felt his voice rising. "He told me so himself. It was a birthday present for my tenth birthday."

"So he told you years ago the Angellar was summoning you? You finally decided it was worth your time to come?" The eyes of the gatekeeper seemed huge. They were all Carimus could see. He felt suddenly flustered, and not a little afraid of the stern figure before him. He took a deep breath and tried to center his thoughts and quell his fear.

"No ... she summoned me by writing words on the screen at the Crystal Tower. *Send Carimus to Fairinhorst.* When I asked why, she said 'Duka.'"

Suddenly, the eyes were normal again. "For all your tardiness, you bear a rune-bracelet of Fairinhorst, and by custom, you may be tested. Come back at the spring Equinox and apply then. You are too late for this year." The Gatekeeper released his arm and stepped back. The gate began to slide shut.

"I can't wait till next spring!" cried Carimus, his voice cracking again. "Don't you understand? The Angellar summoned me. You must let me speak to her."

"I see you believe the folly that you speak, but I can tell you, with certainty, the Angellar did not summon you. She does not speak to anyone. Come back with the Spring Equinox and apply for the testing with the other new applicants. Your bracelet guarantees you a place within the test, nothing more. Go now." The gate slid shut, and the Gatekeeper turned and walked back toward his residence.

"No!" screamed Carimus. "You must let me in!" He felt the frustration threatening to overcome him. He couldn't have come this far only to be sent away for months. He instinctively placed his hand on the hilt of his emerald crysword as if to draw comfort from its familiar feel. He gasped as he felt a jolt of energy travel from the sword into his body.

Joy tugged at his arm. "Cari, stop it," she hissed. He stood frozen in place.

The Gatekeeper suddenly stiffened and stood immobile for a moment. He slowly turned around and stared back at Carimus, mouthing some words the group outside the fence could not hear. He then bowed his head as if acknowledging someone not visible to the group and walked back to the gate. The gate once more slid open, and the Gatekeeper stood silently, staring at Carimus.

"This is unheard of, but you are to come with me to the gardens." His eyes flicked to Joy and the others. "Just him."

He looks as though he doesn't believe what he is saying, thought Carimus as he stepped forward with the tingly feeling of walking through a qulan field. *What just happened?* The gate slid closed behind him. He looked back and smiled at the daughters.

"Goodbye Joy, Vix, Rach. Thank you for everything. I'll see you when I return to the Spires."

He heard their goodbyes as he turned back, ready to follow the Gatekeeper, eager to learn what the Angellar knew about his lost brother. *I'm coming. It won't be much longer, Duke.*

The Gatekeeper didn't even look toward him as he turned and walked back toward the ornate domicile, so he hurried to follow.

Upon reaching the front of the home, the Gatekeeper turned, looking as though he had an unpleasant taste in his mouth. "Wait here." He then walked up the steps onto the magnificent portico and disappeared into the villa.

Carimus turned back to wave goodbye to his friends, but they had already disappeared from view, and so he turned back and studied the front of the Gatekeeper's ornate home.

While he waited impatiently, Carimus inspected the area around the front of the magnificent villa. The shrubbery was immaculately trimmed into beautiful topiary. There were several stags and a group of agile sighthounds, which he realized were sculpted to appear as if they were engaged in a hunt chasing one of the deer. He felt uncouth and out of place among the graceful designs which surrounded him. He wondered if the result was intended or if it was something only a non-Fairborn would feel.

A quarter hour later, the door opened, and the Gatekeeper returned. He walked back down the steps. "Follow me." He strode past Carimus and down the path that led back to the street.

Carimus hurried and stepped up to walk beside him, which caused the Fairborn to stop and give him a disdainful glare. *What did I do now?* he thought, inadvertently taking a step away from the haughty Fairborn.

"When I say follow, it does not mean you are to walk beside me as if you were a boon friend and companion. If you are this poor at following directions, there is no use of you going any farther. Let me be very clear with you. From now on, you are to do exactly as I say. No more and certainly no less. Speak only when you are spoken to. Answer questions as clearly and as concisely as you are able. Do not volunteer information unasked for and do not ask questions until given leave to ask." He stared at Carimus for a long moment. "Is this clear?"

"Yes, sir," Carimus answered. *Uncle Brett, on his worst day,* he thought. *Respond as you would to him.* He nodded his head and waited, staring at the ground at the Fairborn's feet.

The Gatekeeper paused again and cleared his throat. "Very well. Follow me."

The Gatekeeper turned and strode off. Carimus fell in two paces behind him, matching his steps to those of the tall Fairborn. *I wonder if he'd act this way if he knew I was the brother of the High King?* Somehow, he felt it probably wouldn't affect the attitude of the Gatekeeper in the slightest.

They proceeded out the gate, turned away from the City, and walked briskly down the grey cobblestone street.

After passing a few more palatial houses, they walked beneath an archway in a tall white wall. Abruptly they were in open country, the paved street turning to a grey gravel path that wound among the trees. Although there were no gardeners in sight, the overall feeling was of a well-tended park, not the wilderness of the Hidden Vale leading to Haldacitime. Everything grew in its proper place, with no feeling of the normal competition of nature, and yet there were no orderly rows of flowers and trees.

The Gatekeeper marched ahead of him in complete silence, never looking back at all. Carimus contented himself by admiring the scenery, so different from the grounds surrounding his home at Castle Draconis or the palace in Phoenix. After a brisk walk of a couple of miles, they came to the actual entrance to Fairinhorst. The path led between two tall, ornate white marble pillars carved with runes: three large runes on the left and seven on the right. The same runes that adorned the bracelet Carimus wore on his left wrist. Floating with no visible means of support between the two pillars was the large single rune on the back of all the charms, 'R.' The rune Varyan had told him was Raido, the rune of journeys. The Gatekeeper stopped before the entrance and turned to look back at him, so Carimus stopped too and waited.

"This is where I leave you. Enter the gate and follow the path until you reach the center. Wait there until someone comes to show you where you are to go. Do not stray from the path and do not enter the center until you are summoned." With this, the Gatekeeper turned and walked back the way they had come, leaving Carimus standing alone before the gate.

He almost asked a question, then remembered and kept still until the haughty Fairborn had disappeared from sight.

"Follow the path … Well, that's simple enough." He realized he was alone for the first time in ages. A wave of loneliness washed through him. *I wish the girls could have come with me,* he thought. *Heck, I'd even settle for Bort. I wish Duke was here. He'd think this place was beautiful too.* Thinking of his lost brother reminded him again of why he was here, and he took a deep breath and set forth. The gray gravel track they had followed from the hidden city was growing lighter, turning from gray to a much lighter shade. After a few dozen yards, it would be pure white. He walked between the pillars and felt the tingle of a qulan field as he passed through into Fairinhorst.

17

THE PARK

CARIMUS

To each side of the path, the grass was neat. Tasteful arrangements of flowers here and there bloomed as if it were the middle of spring instead of the end of autumn. The air was heavy with the scent of the flowers, and the singing of the birds filled the air with sound.

He had always liked flowers and gardens. He supposed it was his alignment with the qulans of nature. "I think I will enjoy it here," he mused aloud.

Thank you, Cari. It was a woman's voice.

He froze and looked around him. There was no one in sight. The Gatekeeper had disappeared into the trees between where he stood and the Fairborn city. The birds were still singing, and a bumblebee the size of his two hands clasped together flew across the path a few yards before him. The steady drone quickly faded away as the bee flew about its business.

"Did … did someone say something?" he asked, a distinct

waver in his voice. He cleared his throat. "Hello? Is there anyone here?"

Only the birdsong answered him. He began following the path once more—his head turning from side to side as he walked, keeping alert for anyone who might be here in the park-like expanse.

The path wove ahead, leading to the north and the west. It gently wound just enough to keep from being boring, although he could find no reason for the curving track to meander the way it did. He could see his final destination, a grove of flowering bushes about three miles away as the lark flew. Judging from the weaving of the track, he would walk at least four miles to arrive there. He was tempted to veer off the path, but the feel of the white gravel beneath his feet reminded him of the Gatekeeper's warnings, so he stayed on it. With every bird call, he glanced around nervously, his heart pounding, searching for someone in the shadows. The feeling he was being watched lingered in the air. Besides that, someone had said 'Thank you, Cari.' He was sure of that. But where was the speaker?

When the voice failed to repeat, he relaxed and began to feel sleepy. The heavy perfume was making it hard to get a deep breath of fresh air, and his eyelids slid down before his eyes. Several times he caught himself walking with his eyes closing. He yawned, stretched, and took several deep breaths. It didn't help; he found he wanted nothing more than to find a patch of soft-looking grass and curl up for a quick nap. Shaking his head vigorously, he decided he would sing to keep himself awake. He began to enthusiastically sing his family anthem.

"From the Blood of Dragons the seeds of Kings are made ...

In the darkness 'fore the dawn the pawns become afraid ...

Afraid of all the things to come in History's fiery ride ...

And as the towers tumble down, proud men will lose their pride ...

Then from the Blood of Dragons—"

As he began the chorus, he realized there were sweet voices joining in harmony. He stopped and looked wildly around. The singing stopped exactly at the same time he did, and no one was in sight—just him. He started again with the next verse. As soon as he got to the chorus, once more he was joined by the ghostly voices. It was as if he was leading a choir of invisible singers. Once more, he paused, and the accompanying singing was gone.

"This is too weird!" he exclaimed and awaited a reply. Only the birds answered him.

He walked on in silence. *At least now I'm thoroughly awake*, he thought to himself.

Being careful to stay on the path, he walked until he reached the flowering bushes. He found they were much taller than he had supposed. They were covered with blossoms of white, lilac, and dark violet, and gave a rich, sweet fragrance. At the end of the path was a circle of gravel, next to which was an ornate topiary bench made of lush green plants with red, blue, and white flowers. He examined it for a few moments before cautiously reaching out and pushing against the surface of the seat, then the back. There was no doubt it was a bench, and a very comfortable one at that. Did he dare try it? He looked all around. The path stopped at this circle. There were no breaks in the flowering bushes before him. They reached at least thirty feet into the air and made a wall before him, circling away to each side as if enclosing an area of several miles.

He thought about following the hedge wall, but the path stopped here, and the Gatekeeper had said to stay on the path and wait for someone to summon him. The flowery bench appeared very enticing, and the path ran right up to it. If he sat down upon it, his feet would still be on the path. He allowed himself a moment of hesitation before he threw caution to the winds, then sank into the floral cushion with a contented sigh. He closed his eyes and inhaled the perfume, the delicate floral aroma saturating the air.

He didn't realize he had nodded off until a soft voice broke into his consciousness.

"May I be of assistance?"

His eyes flew open, and he almost summoned his sword into his hand, stopping just in time. Standing before him was a Fairborn woman in a white tunic tied with a blue sash. She bobbed her head and smiled. "I am Alea of the seventh tier. Welcome to Fairinhorst." She gazed at him with evident curiosity.

"My name is Carimus." He offered his bracelet for her to examine.

Alea nodded but did not seem inclined to examine it, so he lowered his arm, stood up, and waited.

"Gilad túl ana i kal." She said and bowed to him.

"I am sorry. I don't know Espro. Only a few words."

"Forgive me. I have never spoken with one of your race before. I will speak in common. I said, 'welcome to the light.'"

"Oh, thank you." He bowed in return, then gazed around, wondering where she had come from.

"Your arrival here is very unusual, Carimus. You are the first human to have come in my time here. I believe the last was nearly one hundred years ago. Also, I have never heard of anyone being admitted outside the normal admittance times at the equinoxes. Pray forgive my curiosity, but may I ask you a question?"

Carimus nodded, preparing to repeat his story of being summoned by the Angellar, but Alea asked a very different question. "You are a man, are you not?"

He looked at her in confusion. "Of course. But you knew that. You just said you don't get humans here often."

Alea giggled. "No, I know you are a human. I mean, you are a male, aren't you? Not a woman."

"Of course … of course, I'm a man," he sputtered.

"Forgive me. I was sure you were, except I was led to believe that the House deSpryngdal scions were always female."

"House deSpryngdal's children are always girls. But I am not from that House. I am Carimus deDraconis. Why would you think I was from deSpryngdal?" Carimus tilted his head and gazed at the young woman with confusion.

"Ah, I see. I have been told the only Great House that ever sent their children here for enlightenment was of that Family. You are of the High King's House? Why, that is marvelous! I am so glad you have come. Are you close to the king?"

"King Aaron was my father. He is dead now. He was murdered. My brother Artos is the pretender to the throne." Sadness threatened to overwhelm him, but he remembered his purpose and pushed it aside.

"Oh, Carimus, I am so sorry for your loss. I had not heard of King Aaron's passing. But news is always slow to reach us here. At least to those of us not of the eighth tier. Those seeking enlightenment should not be distracted by unrelated matters. But I stand here nattering instead of attending to my duties. Please follow me." Alea turned and walked toward the flowering hedge. As she approached, the bushes moved aside and made an arch for her to walk through. Carimus trailed her through the opening, then stopped and gazed around in wonder.

Chapter Sixteen:

Fairinhorst

18

INTO THE GARDEN

CARIMUS

CARIMUS HAD THOUGHT THE AREA outside the center was parklike, but it was nothing compared to the heart of Fairinhorst. Perfume filled the air, along with sweet birdsong. Enormous flowers were everywhere. *This must be what it looks like to a mouse running through a flowerbed,* he thought. The daffodils and tulips were a remarkable ten feet tall, while the lilies and irises towered even higher. All the flowers were growing in patterns, he realized. Massive spirals of color drew the eye to the very center of the area, where an enormous rosebush, the size of a large tree, presided over all. Huge roses of many hues covered the massive bush. A white gravel path skirted the outside of the amazing flower garden. Branching off and winding among the flowers were paths of red, green, blue, and white gravel, all wandering among the giant flowers and leading eventually toward the center where the enormous rosebush dominated. Something inside Carimus felt at peace for the first time in ages.

I belong here, he thought. *My regalos are so in tune.*

A number of Fairborn strolled among the flowers, most wearing tunics of bright green. A few wore tunics of other colors—a handful of red and blue, and at least two in tunics of white, such as the one worn by his guide.

Alea waited a moment, smiling at his obvious sense of wonder, then motioned for him to walk with her. She turned to her left and strode down the white path that ringed the garden. He followed mutely, in awe of the harmonious beauty that surrounded him. They passed a branching path of blue gravel lined with indigo lilac and bluebells that stood at least six feet high. The next path was of red stone, and the flowers that lined it were crimson tulips and scarlet begonias, each plant standing taller than his head. Alea turned onto the third path that branched off, one of green gravel. The enormous flowers lining this path were daffodils and daisies, but the flowers were a hue he had never seen before. The daffodils were a delicate pale shade of greenish yellow instead of the bright yellow he was familiar with. The daisy blossoms varied from pale light green to deep emerald.

As they made their way toward the rosebush in the center, a soft music joined the birdsong and the humming of the insects. It was a series of notes playing in a pattern that repeated over and over. As they moved closer, the music became clearer, and he could discern voices chanting softly in accompaniment.

As they neared the center, the path became a trench dug into the earth. It led to an opening beneath the giant plant, the source of the music and chanting. They followed the green path under the huge rose bush.

Carimus paused, frozen in wonder. He wasn't sure what he had been expecting—tunnels between the roots leading somewhere, he supposed. Instead, they entered a vast open area on a green-tinted walkway, which turned to the left to hug the glossy wall of the chamber and gently sloped down. *Where are the roots?* he wondered. Other walkways were visible, some spiraling down to lower levels, with others connecting them all like an enormous spider web. Alea must have expected his reaction, for she paused and looked back at him with a knowing smile.

In the center of the vast cavern, a softly glowing white crystal pillar descended from the ceiling beneath the rosebush like a crystalline root running deep into the ground. Hanging from the ceiling were many everlight globes. Peering over the edge, he saw the walkway was suspended over a mammoth opening in the earth, which descended a great distance. No bottom was visible in the soft light. Here and there, a few walkways ran from the outer circles to encircle the gigantic central spire. His walkway went to the left, slanted slightly down, and ran around the outside of the chamber. The wall was a smooth material colored green to match the walkway. Reaching out, he ran his hand along the wall. It felt the same as the familiar grey walls of Castle Draconis. The gigantic hall was circular, and he could see the walkways spiraled down ahead of his path. After a few rows of green, the next few rings down the wall were red, then blue, and finally a series of pure white. The walkways were all connected, and the hues changed as they moved from one level to another. Here and there on walkways, he discerned Fairborn in colored robes moving about.

Alea motioned for him to follow her and continued to guide him forward.

Soon, dark openings appeared in the wall lining the circles. He looked with interest into the first one they passed, but the darkness was total, as if a black satin curtain hung within the opening a few inches back.

The music was clearer now and seemed to come from everywhere, as did the chanting. Strangely, though, it seemed no louder now than it had when he entered, only clearer. He wanted to join in, even though he couldn't quite make out the words.

"What is this place?" he blurted as he followed his guide along the walkway. They had passed rows and rows of openings. Alea seemed to know where she was going, and he had been content to follow until now. He felt his face flush with embarrassment and wished immediately he hadn't spoken. His words seemed harsh and out of place. Too late, he remembered the words of the Gatekeeper, not to speak unless spoken to.

Alea stopped and turned to face him. He mouthed the word *sorry* and shrugged his shoulders. She raised a finger to her lips and beckoned him to follow, and so he nodded, and they continued in silence. *Uncle Brett would have shouted at me for that, he thought. Oh, no, I guess he wouldn't have. But he would have given me one of his looks, the kind that makes you want to sink right through the floor.*

After a few more minutes of walking, they came upon an opening that appeared no different from all the rest they had passed, except here, the light penetrated, revealing a small room beyond. As soon as they reached it, she stopped and motioned for him to enter.

Walking through the opening, he felt the familiar tingling of a qulan field. The scent of flowers disappeared—it was as if he were breathing the cleanest, freshest air he had ever experienced. The music and chanting faded into the background. It didn't quite disappear, but became almost unnoticeable. He quickly reached the conclusion that this cubical was intended to be someone's living quarters, probably his. The walls and furnishings were the same green-colored material as the walls of the great chamber. To the left side of the chamber was a thin mattress on the floor with a green blanket folded neatly at one end and a thin pillow at the other. On the other side of the room was a mat, just big enough for a single person to sit on if they sat cross-legged. At the back of the room was a small table built against the wall with a single chair beside it. On the table was a shiny green glass goblet. In the wall behind the table was a dark opening, slightly bigger than the goblet.

The room was small, only three paces long and wide. When he turned around to look at the doorway, there was now the same black veil as all the other doors he had passed on his way here. He looked forward, examining the darkness just as Alea stepped into the room, almost bumping into him.

"Oh, I'm sorr—" he clapped his hand over his mouth, flushing with embarrassment once again.

The Fairborn woman smiled at him. "This will be your room, Carimus, while you are of the First Tier. When you entered, the room began attuning to you. This is why I gave you a moment alone. No one except you and the Enlightened Ones can now enter the doorway. When you are within this room, your needs will be met. You may come here to rest or for refreshment whenever you feel the need. An Enlightened One of the Fourth Tier will be assigned to lead you toward enlightenment. Because you did not come here with the rest of those who are now of the First Tier, this may take a few hours. Usually, one would have been your guide upon your arrival, but under the unusual circumstances, it may take a little longer. Have no fear. One will attend to you before much time has passed." She paused.

Only speak when spoken to, he thought. "I see. I thought you were my guide."

"I had no duties to attend to today, so I was asked to bring you within and show you to your room. Your guide to enlightenment will be male. Guides are always of the same gender as their students."

He nodded.

Alea walked over to a blank section of the wall, held her palm out, and a section of the panel pulled apart, revealing a small space beyond.

"This is your closet. It's empty now, but in the morning, you will find a green tunic and sash. While you are sleeping tonight, the weavers will measure you and then fabricate your garment. It will be waiting for you in the morning. They are usually very unobtrusive, but if you wake and find two or three small creatures in the room with you, do not be alarmed, for they are totally harmless. They are not truly alive, but are devices the quanti will use to measure you."

"Creatures?... Oh forgive me, I forgot again."

"This is your room, Carimus. It is true—you should always wait to be addressed by one of the Enlightened when you are anywhere in Fairinhorst. Except within the walls of this room. Here, you may speak freely."

"Oh, thank you. I understand. I shall try not to talk out of turn anymore. I am usually much better at following directions ... " he hesitated. "Well, sometimes ... usually." He glanced around at the sparsely furnished cubicle. "May I ask you a question now?"

"Yes, Carimus. Although, as far as your path to seek enlightenment, it would probably be better for you to keep most of your questions for your sensei when he joins you later."

"My sen-say?"

"Your guide, your instructor ... a teacher. They will be an Enlightened One, wearing a green sash."

"How will I know they are an Enlightened One? Will they tell me so?"

"Any seeker who reaches the fifth tier is an Enlightened One. They will have a white tunic with a colored sash. Your sensei will have a green sash because you are a first tier seeker and will wear a green tunic. He will be someone trained to help beginners on the road to enlightenment."

"I see, I think. You are an Enlightened One then?"

Alea nodded. "I have found the enlightenment of the seventh tier."

He abruptly changed the subject. "What kind of creatures?"

"Creatures?" The Fairborn woman creased her brow.

He nodded. "You said for me not to be alarmed if I woke up and found creatures in the room."

"Ah, I was speaking of the weavers. They look like insects about an inch long."

To the gist of it then, he thought. "I need to see the Angellar."

Alea raised her brow at his abrupt change of topic once again, then looked solemn. "This is not something first tier seekers ask."

Carimus took a deep breath. "When our father was murdered, my brothers and I were forced to flee for our lives. My little brother, Duka, was separated from the rest of us in a storm." He licked his lips. "We didn't know if he survived, though I believe I would have known had he died." He found himself wringing his hands and forced them to his sides. "When the Angellar summoned me with her words on the screen at the Crystal Tower, I asked why I should leave my brothers and come here. My brother's name appeared on the screen." He shrugged, holding out his hands in a beseeching manner. "That was the beginning of my journey here. I really need to ask if she knows where he is and if he is alright ... Please."

She thought for a moment, pity evident in her eyes. "I do not see any harm in your request. Your sensei will not be with you immediately, and he will not look to begin your path until tomorrow. His words today will be those of welcome and then to assist you in becoming ready to take the first steps upon the new road in your life. Very well, but remember, do not speak in the Great Hall. Even Enlightened Ones remain silent upon the walkways. The Chanters are the only ones who grace the great silence with their voices. I should warn you: it will be a tiring climb, first down a multitude of steps, several hundred, and then back up again. Are you sure you wouldn't rather rest from your journey?"

"I would rather see the Angellar first, then rest. I won't be able to rest, being so close to finally knowing. If she speaks to me, I am allowed to answer her, aren't I?"

"That will not happen, Carimus." Alea shook her head. "The Angellar does not speak. If you are sure, then you may follow me."

"I'm sure." Cari nodded emphatically. *She wouldn't have summoned me if she hadn't intended for me to know.*

"Very well." Alea walked back through the blackness of the doorway with Cari close behind. Once again, the chanting voices filled the air. The perfumed air was almost overwhelming.

The music and chanting were monotonous, yet somehow soothing and compelling. He felt the urge to join the chant, even though he could not understand the words, if they were words at all and not just soothing syllables. There was a sense of peace and calm when he concentrated on them, and he caught himself mouthing along with the voices. He clamped his jaws shut, determined not to perform another faux pas.

He walked beside Alea along the green walkway. First, they followed the wall, then turned onto one of the suspended paths that led towards the crystal pillar in the center of the vast hall. When they reached the spire in the center, the walkway changed from green to a nearly colorless, light-grey translucent path, which wound down into the depths of the hall, spiraling around the enormous crystal pillar.

He walked nearest the edge and occasionally looked over the guardrail to see if he could discern the bottom. They walked down for many minutes before the floor came into view; it must lie at least a mile below the entrance level. Alea glanced back at him occasionally, as if checking upon his desire to continue the trek downwards, but each time he gave her a single, determined nod to assure her he was resolute to make the journey to their destination, however far it might be.

After a long walk downwards, the sloping path ended at a spiral stairway. The center crystal pillar split into sections with openings between them. The white crystal took on a faint greenish hue, as did the spiral stairway they had reached. The stairs spiraled down at least another hundred feet and came to the floor of the vast chamber.

When they finally reached the bottom, Alea led him through an arched opening into the crystal spire. One of four paths to enter the center of the spire. Each opening was next to a section of the wall colored one of the four colors of the rings above. They had entered through the green arch. In the center of the room was a smaller crystal pillar about six feet in diameter that ran from the floor up to join with the spire above, a clear glassy-looking pillar with something in the center at the floor level. Alea bowed her head as they approached the center, so he followed her lead and watched her feet as they moved inwards, circling to their right, and stopping in front of the white arch.

When Alea ceased walking and turned to her left, he stepped up beside her and looked up. They were facing the clear, crystal pillar. At first, he was confused by what he saw. Then he realized he was looking at a person enclosed within it. An elderly woman, her eyes closed as if in sleep, her arms crossed across her chest. She looked very peaceful, he thought. Totally motionless. Unnervingly motionless. Her features were very pale, and she was not breathing. He realized in horror, he was looking at a corpse. Where had Alea brought him? Why were they here instead of proceeding to the Angellar?

Alea turned her head, looked at him as if reading his thoughts, and then looked back at the body enclosed in the crystal and nodded toward it. It was all he could do to keep from shouting out in dismay. He clapped a hand over his mouth and looked at Alea, who nodded at him once more, sympathy in her eyes, and then turned and walked back towards the green archway. He looked back at the corpse of the Angellar, then turned and numbly followed.

Later, he did not remember the return to his quarters. He was in shock and followed Alea back automatically. Upon entering his quarters, he stood silently for a few moments and then threw himself face down on his sleeping mat. *Duke! Where are you, Duke? How am I ever going to find you now?*

Alea had followed him into the cubicle, but sensing his distress, waited a few moments, then left quietly, without speaking.

Part Six

On the Trail

N
TEN MILES
THE MOUNTAINS OF MYST
STARSTONE TOWER
VALOR VALE
The Dancing Giants
House deDraconis
House dePenrodyn
THE BLACK Mountains
House deSpryngdal
The 'Ruins' of House deYung
HOUSE DEEAGLEDON
The KING'S VALLEY
OakWood
THE GREAT MARSH
BLASTED HEATH
TO RAINBOW VALLEY
HOUSE DEANSON
Hearnwood
HOUSE DEDARRELLYEL
DARRELLWOOD
HOUSE DEHERNDAR
THE GREY WOOD
THE HIGH FOREST
THE DARK
THE MOUNTAINS OF MYST
MAP BY INKARNATE

Chapter Seventeen:

The Journey to Starstone Tower Begins

19

A FRIEND OF SETH'S
IS A FRIEND OF MINE

ARTOS

10/1/1971 ar

THE MORNING WAS FROSTY as the group set out from the Crystal Tower. The smell of snow was in the air. Artos welcomed the frosty weather; this way, no one would think there was anything strange about a group of people wearing their hoods pulled close. They had all agreed that a group that included Fairborn would draw unwanted attention. It would be best to keep their identities hidden.

Seth and Artos led the way, with Angel and Bortis following behind. Jaek and Kae filled out the party at the rear. *We are on our way at last,* thought Artos as they left the Crystal Tower and set out on the first leg of their journey—from the Blue Spires to the Swan's Nest. *I hope Bachar and Kateeri aren't lurking in the mist, waiting to ambush Angel and force her to go back to Alfhiem and her father.*

Liv accompanied the group for the first mile or so, walking alongside Angel for the most part, stopping when they walked

247

past the thousand-year fir where she had first confronted them only a few weeks before.

Artos felt a tickling on the edge of his mind as Angel spent a moment in silent communication with the Mist Cat. She paused a moment when Liv bounded away, watching as the huge cat disappeared into the mists. "Liv tells me she doesn't scent Bachar or Kateeri. I hope they went straight back to Father, and he doesn't send them right back with a written decree for me to attend him directly."

Artos nodded. "Do you think they might be waiting at Swan's Nest?"

The half-Fairborn girl shook her head, but he thought he saw a hint of doubt on her face for just a moment. *I hope she's right.*

The next few days were uneventful. No one was waiting at Swan's Nest when they passed by, which was a relief for Artos. He had almost expected Kateeri and Bachar or even Andune himself to be there watching for Angel, but the camp was deserted.

The Giant Raven and harpy eagles were absent from the Rainbow Valley as well. The cloudy skies and the threat of snow may have been the reason, but whatever the cause, the absence of the birds and the Abomination rider should have been good news, but instead it made feel everyone uneasy, as if it might come swooping out of the clouds at any moment.

Artos felt relief when they reached the valley's northern side, joined the Heartbreak Trail, and climbed into the ever-present mists. *At least we are undercover again,* he thought. *I don't relish the thought of having to deal with that giant bird, much less the rider.*

In the afternoon of the second day of their trek, they were dusted with an occasional snowflake as they left the trail and followed Seth up a forested vale, deep into the wilds of the Mountains of Myst. When they were a few miles into the rugged wilderness, Seth called a halt, and they set up camp. Artos and Bortis shared a small tent, as did Jaek and Kae. Angel had a smaller tent of her own, and Seth … Well, Artos was never really sure exactly what Seth did for the night. The druid assured everyone there was no need to keep watch, for he enlisted the creatures of the forest to alert him if there was any danger. He was always sitting at the small fire when everyone else retired for the night, and he was always found there in the morning when they awoke.

"Do you think he just sits there all night, Art? Don't druids need to sleep like other people?" asked Bortis softly on that second night.

"I don't know. I woke up in the middle of the night last night and peeked out. The fire was banked, but he was nowhere to be seen. He may have been sleeping somewhere close by."

"Donel said his robes were sider-silk like this gear Countess Maria sent us. I didn't really think it would be better travel gear than my leathers. I have to admit, I was wrong," said Bortis.

"Yeah, they're keeping me warm enough. I guess he is comfortable. Good night, Bort."

His only answer was a soft snoring sound.

*

The next morning, the party was awakened by Seth softly calling to them.

"Everyone, wake up and come meet a friend of mine. Do not be alarmed. There is no danger."

Upon leaving the tent, Artos was glad to have been forewarned. A few yards away from the fire was an immense brown bear sitting on its haunches and looking at their camp. Sitting as it was, it was still taller than the druid. Seth stood next to the creature, smiling as he watched the party emerge from their tents, amused by their looks of alarm.

Angel was the only person who didn't appear shocked; in fact, Artos thought she looked pleased. "Is that Zeke?" she asked.

"No, but you are close, Angel. This is Zeb. He is a littermate of Zeke. They share these valleys between them and sometimes hunt together. Zeke might join us later, but probably not. It depends on his mood. He is off hunting, miles away right now. Zeb will accompany us for a few days, though."

Artos recalled the bear from his dream, but no, this wasn't that bear. That bear had been smaller, a black bear, he was sure of it. He shrugged it off. Dreams weren't necessarily accurate or foretelling. "Is there anything we should do, Seth?" he asked. *It must be seven feet tall sitting down. It's enormous.* "Does he need to get our scents or anything?"

Seth looked at the bear for a moment and then chuckled. "He says he can smell you just fine and added you all smell delicious, but wants me to tell you all not to worry. He's not hungry at the moment. It's his form of a joke. A bear's sense of humor usually involves food, one way or another."

Bortis wrinkled his nose. "I can smell him too. Please tell him I don't think he smells delicious. More like a wet dog."

Seth just chuckled.

With the rough terrain, the marching order had to adjust. Now they went single file with their cloaks and hoods pulled tight to keep out the chill wind, all except Seth, who seemed to revel in the crisp mountain temperatures. The druid led the way, followed by Artos, Bortis, Angel, and Kae, with Jaek keeping guard at the rear. Zeb came and went, sometimes walking ahead near Seth and sometimes disappearing for hours at a time. And so went the next few days.

10/5/1971 ar

"We have not made as good a time as I had hoped," said the druid on the morning of the fifth day as they ate their trail rations for breakfast.

Artos looked up from where he sat between Bortis and Angel. "Is there a problem, Seth?" *I thought things were going well.*

"It's not really a problem. I just thought we would be a day or two closer at this point. I must confess it has been over five years since I visited the deEagledon's outlying villages, and I have never come by this exact route. I judge we are still over twenty-five miles from Starstone Tower."

"The good news is we are past the roughest part of the wilderness and will soon approach Fargo, and from there to Bluffton, there are well-marked mountain trails. We shall travel much easier and make better time. The bad news is the trail will take us through both Lando and Bluffton. We could possibly skirt Fargo. Though, actually, I'm surprised we haven't been observed and met by one or another of the trappers who dwell there. Once on the trail, we will hardly be able to pass the villages without being noted by those who dwell there. Although they all farm, they are hunters, fishermen, and trappers. There are sure to be outliers around each of the villages."

"I imagine any group of hooded and cloaked strangers are sure to be of interest to the villagers," said Artos. "Do you think they will worry we are bandits?"

"I have been to all the villages in the demesne in the past and am certain to be remembered," answered the druid. "I will have to speak with the elders, and if I am needed for healing, I cannot refuse to provide aid. My vows to The Mother forbid it. If there is no pressing need, I will pass through freely and leave my promise to return soon. My best guess is that we shall arrive at Starstone Tower in three days, possibly two if we are incredibly lucky, but remember, we may need several more days."

"I thought you knew the way there," protested Bortis.

"Prince Bortis, I have never been there. Why would I know the route? Fur trappers in Bluffton trap the giant ermine in the mountains. There will be trails leading in the direction we wish to travel. I will question the elders there and ask for what directions they might provide. With any luck, some trappers may even have set traps near the tower. Getting that knowledge might pose a problem if they learn your identities, however."

"Why is that?" asked Bortis.

"Because they'd be poaching, Bort," said Artos. "The lands around Starstone are within the deDraconis demesne." *It won't be long, and we might catch sight of home,* he thought with a wrench. *Home and a monster waiting there.* His homesickness dissolved into anger. *We are coming back to avenge you, Father. Your sons will bring justice to your murderer.*

Bortis scowled, then nodded with a grim expression. "Poaching's a crime."

"That's correct," continued Seth. "But we aren't planning on revealing anyone's identity. With everyone cloaked and with your hoods all pulled tight against the weather, I don't believe any of the villagers will recognize either of you. I only use my forename when doing The Mother's work. No one in these mountains knows I hail from one of the Great Houses. It would only hinder me. I will try to question the elders alone, leaving the rest of you in the local inn while I do so."

Artos nodded. "I see the wisdom in that. We will simply be Art and Bort if asked for our names. Would it not be wiser for all of us, save you, to just stay out of the villages altogether?"

"I doubt it would be possible to go unnoticed without adding days to our trip—days and miles. A group of sulking strangers, if seen near the village, would cause alarm and attention. Then they would begin to think of bandits. People would be far more curious if you tried to pass through unnoticed. I will just introduce you as pilgrims traveling with me, and people will gawk and then quickly forget after we pass on."

Artos noticed his brother had a distracted look on his face. "What is it, Bort?"

"I was just trying to figure out the date. It's the fifth day of Tenous today, isn't it?"

"It is," said Seth. "Hopefully, we shall arrive at Starstone Tower on the eighth."

"They will have noticed our family has not arrived in

Phoenix," said Artos, thinking this was what was concerning his brother.

Bortos looked at his brother. "Yeah, and we have a date in five days. Remember?"

"What do you mean?" said Artos with confusion.

Bortis tilted his head to the side. "We planned to go horseback riding with Ellis and your fiancée. Does that ring a bell?"

"By the Sky! You're right. On your birthday! I had totally forgotten." Artos sighed. *I don't need to be thinking about that right now.* He tried to push the thought of his arranged marriage aside and contend with the business at hand. "We have more important things to worry about right now."

"Maybe we should get underway then?" said Angel, and everyone finished their jerky, reloaded their packs, and were soon ready to commence the journey.

After a few hours' walk, Seth informed them Fargo would be over the next ridge. A few minutes later, Zeb came loping back to the group, a different gait than his usual lumbering stride.

"Something's wrong!" exclaimed Seth. The huge bear stopped near the druid and rocked back and forth in agitation. "Zeb tells me there has been a fire ahead. A big one."

Soon, everyone in the party could smell the faint scent of wood smoke. At first, Artos thought it was only the normal smoke a village would produce on a frosty autumn morning, but the smell increased, and other, more unpleasant odors were added to the mix.

"Is Fargo burning?" asked Seth as they topped a ridge and started down the other side. "We should hurry. People may need aid!"

At that moment, the thick fog blew aside momentarily, and they gained their first view of Fargo ... the ruined remains of Fargo. Shells of burnt-out buildings ringed the village square—a square filled with soot and piles of ash, some of which looked suspiciously like bodies. Trickles of smoke still rose from some of the ruins. Mixed with the wood smoke was a sickening odor of burnt meat.

Artos stared down at the ruins with an uneasy feeling in his stomach. *This is where I looked down at the village and we were attacked!* He looked around, but the woods were deserted, empty, and quiet except for the distant warbling of some bird. Where were the villagers? Except for the few plumes of smoke, there was no movement to be seen. This was the deEagledon demesne, but the people were still his subjects.

Chapter Eighteen:

Fargo

20

THIS ISN'T
MY DREAM

ARTOS

10/5/1971 ar

THIS ISN'T WHAT I DREAMED, **thought Artos.** *The village wasn't burnt. But this was the spot where I stood and gazed down at it when the Beastmen attacked.* He looked around in alarm.

"I had a dream about this. Beastmen attacked us. Right here, in this very place!"

Seth looked around. "There are no Beastmen here, Art. Zeb would have discovered them and let me know. But I fear Beastmen are responsible for this. Some of those buildings look as if they are still smoldering. We must hurry down and see if there is anyone in need!"

The ever-present fog flowed back and hid the ruins of Fargo from their sight once more. Artos felt a shiver that wasn't caused by the chill mountain air. *Where are the people?* he wondered again.

"Let us proceed with caution," said Jaek. "Sometimes Beastmen burn a village, then lie in wait to ambush those who come after to give aid and succor."

Artos nodded. "I agree, we must be cautious, but Seth is right. We may be needed."

"Zeb is going to leave us shortly," said Seth. "But he's agreed to do one last scout for me. He doesn't normally go too close to a village during the daylight—but he will sniff around the outskirts. If there are any lurking Beastmen, he'll find them. I think I see a path down." The druid stood silently for a moment next to the bear, who snorted as if in protest, but then began the descent toward the valley below. He quickly faded away into the fog.

"Wait," said Jaek as he drew his longsword. "Before we follow, we need a plan, just in case there are Beastmen waiting below. We don't want to leave ourselves vulnerable."

Artos nodded and tried to think. *What would Uncle Brett do if he were here?*

"I suggest we separate slightly," said Seth. "I will go in the lead with Art and Bort just behind me. Kae and Angel stay a dozen feet behind us. Be ready with your bows. Jaek watches the rear and guards the ladies. Just because nothing was behind us as we approached doesn't mean it will stay clear. Beastmen can move in a hurry when they feel the need."

Artos looked at his brother. Bortis slowly nodded in agreement. Without a word, they each held their crysword ready in their clenched fists. Angel and Kae both notched arrows to their bows. Seth had been using his staff as a walking stick but now switched to a fighting stance and gripped it with both hands as he led the way down the steep incline.

When they reached the valley floor, the fog was not as thick as it had been above. Although it was still misty, Artos could see no immediate threat among the burnt-out shells of the houses.

As Seth led the way to the remains of the village, Zeb moved in and out of view as he prowled around the outskirts, chuffing as he walked, clearly not liking the ash and the burnt, smoky smell that filled the air.

Artos felt the hair on his neck prickle. It was too quiet; not even a bird song disturbed the tomb-like silence. The loudest sounds were the brothers' footsteps as they moved over the remains of the burnt plots, which at one time had been the villagers' vegetable patches. The druid moved as quietly as a cat and the Fairborn were as noiseless as shadows. Finally, a solitary crow cawed in the distance, and an echo faintly answered. Was it a second bird answering or a true echo? He was about to ask Seth if he knew when Seth held up an arm, gesturing for everyone to halt as he went down on one knee and studied the ash-covered ground before him closely.

"The breeze has blown the ash around and covered the ground, but underneath there are tracks. This is not the footprint of a villager." He motioned for Artos to join him.

Artos moved up and knelt to look at the track Seth had discovered, and was quickly joined by his brother. Although the ash had mostly covered it, the track was not from a human foot. It was too large. The marks made by the toes were visible and splayed widely. The foot that made the track had never worn boots. His mind flashed back to the Beastman that had burst into his room back at Castle Draconis a few weeks earlier, and he took a deep breath. "Beastmen," he said softly.

Seth stood and gazed around. "This happened a few days ago. There is still some smoke, a few things are still smoldering, but most of what we saw from above was just the ashes being eddied on the breeze. Those are bodies." He pointed at two of the charred piles. "The ruins may hold more. Wait here, and

I will look." Artos felt sick and swallowed hard as he looked around. There were a few more bodies scattered among the ruins. *This is horrible. They never had a chance.*

Jaek, Kae, and Angel stood clear of the burnt ground, scanning the area for anything that might appear. Seth moved closer to investigate the remains of the nearest cottage. He exchanged a glance with his brother as they stood up. Bortis was shaking with anger. They walked back to stand with the others. "This wasn't bandits," said Artos as he slowly shook his head, trying to collect his thoughts.

Angel's eyes met his for a moment, and she nodded, then resumed keeping watch. "It's different to see the result in person than to hear the tales told, isn't it?"

"Is this what it was like in Rainbow Valley? After the Raiders?"

"No. This is worse, far worse." The West Wind's daughter shook her head. "The raiders there set everything ablaze and then rode off. Many people in the Valley managed to put the fires out before everything was destroyed. Many of the homes escaped completely or with just minor damage, although I think they set every barn and storage shed ablaze. That didn't happen here. They destroyed everything. With winter almost upon us, there will be no time to rebuild here this year."

"I don't think there are many left to rebuild." Seth walked back to join them. The druid had a grim look on his face as he brushed the ash from his robes. "Don't look in the ruins of the buildings. From what I saw, no one escaped. They must have come in the depths of the night. By the look of it, they set the fires after they had murdered everyone here. May The Mother watch over their souls. I looked at the remains of three houses, or what's left of them, and each was the same—a pile of bodies in one room. No one trying to escape, no bodies by the doors or windows. There were fifteen homes here. To do this all at once, to murder them all at nearly the same time—there had to be at least fifty of them, probably more."

"How could they?" asked Bortis. "They would have had a watch, surely! There have been too many reports of bandits over the last year."

"All the reports of bandits and Beastmen in the Mountains of Myst have been further south, Bort." The druid leaned on his staff with his left arm and wiped some ash from his face with his right hand. "I know there have been raids by Beastmen in the Black Mountains to the east. Count Penrodyn has made several reports of them. My father and Count Herndar have made most of the reports in these mountains. Do you recall your uncle riding out to answer any complaints in the deEagledon demesne or in your own?"

Bortis shook his head. "No, but even so, I know Uncle Brett sent out warnings of bandits to all the Houses. Surely, they would have passed them along to the outlying villages."

"Probably some casual warning was given. There would undoubtedly have been a watch, even without such warnings. Those two bodies in the square were probably on guard. Most likely they were first to be struck down."

Artos saw that his brother's face was flushed and he was trembling with pent-up emotion. He felt an icy rage sweep through him. "We can't spend any more time here. We can come back later, Bort, and try to find where they came from, but we have to secure Castle Draconis before we can do anything."

Before his brother could reply, Zeb made an urgent sound on the northwesterly side of the village, drawing everyone's attention.

"He's found something!" cried Seth. Circling well outside the burnt-out husks of the buildings, he hurried towards the bear.

Artos quickly led the rest after the druid, their weapons ready in their hands. The bear stood with his head near the ground, chuffing excitedly. Seth ran up and squatted, gazing at the ground to see what had drawn the bear's attention.

"Blood." The druid's voice was hard. "This was probably where they overcame a watchman. You can see where they dragged the body back to the village. But it laid here awhile—you can tell by the amount of blood." Seth looked up at Zeb for a few moments, then nodded and turned to Artos. "Bears don't count the same way we do, but he says there are tracks of 'many' Beastmen a little way from here. Let's go look. Don't follow me too closely. I want to see the ground without our tracks to muddle the picture." The druid followed the bear a short distance to the north, then he held up his hand to let the rest know to come no further. They stopped and waited as Seth examined the ground. Zeb sat back on his haunches, chuffed a few times, sneezed, then rubbed his muzzle with his paws.

Artos scanned the surrounding area, but the ever-present mist had reduced visibility to less than twenty yards. He kept thinking figures were approaching from the fog, only to have them disperse into nothing. Fortunately, Seth didn't take long and waved them over.

Artos was no expert tracker, but even he could see that a large group had passed this way. The track of trampled grasses and pushed-aside brush led away from the ruins of Fargo off to the northwest.

"There are far too many footsteps here to get any idea of the exact number of them," said Seth. "I would say this was their path. Almost all the tracks lead away, but a few go toward the village. The returning ones mostly wiped them out." The druid shook his head, sadness heavy on his features. "Though it's not on our path, the village of Breedon is not too far out of our way, about a mile. While you continue to Lando, I will take word there and warn them. They may be next. If they are still alive, that is. They may have been wiped out by now as well."

Artos nodded. "You're right. They must be warned, but I don't think we should divide our party. If it's only a mile, we'll all go."

"They should be warned," agreed Bortis.

Seth considered and nodded. "Let's be off. One moment while I take my leave from Zeb. He didn't plan to come this far and wants to return home." Again, Artos felt a strange tickling in his mind as the druid stood close to the bear for a moment. The bear snorted, then made his way back toward the ridge they had descended earlier. Seth walked to the edge of the blackened ruins, held up his staff, and said a brief prayer to the Earth Mother, calling for a blessing on the souls of the slain villagers, allowing them to rest in peace.

Artos's thoughts were far from peaceful. *These were my subjects, murdered in their sleep. Someone needs to avenge them.*

Seth finished his prayers, turned away, and walked toward the trail that led east. Artos took one last look at the ruins, a sight to be forever etched in his memory, and followed the druid. The rest of the party trailed behind, all taking a wide route around the ruined village.

Chapter Nineteen:

The Last Few Miles

21

WHAT KILLED
THE TRAPPER?

ARTOS

10/7/1971 ar

THEY WERE BARELY THREE MILES from Fargo when Seth held up his hand and stopped the party. People were approaching down the trail, a group of fifteen grim, armed men marching to check on the situation at Fargo.

It seemed a pair of fur trappers had escaped the slaughter. They had been laying down their winter line of traps and returned to find their homes destroyed and their families murdered. They had rushed to warn the two nearest villages, one to Breedon and one to Lando. They gathered a few men from each and set out to return to Fargo. They were planning on burying the dead and then seeking the Beastmen to exact revenge.

Artos saw their numbers, how poorly armed they were, and shook his head in dismay. Fortunately, he wasn't forced to intervene. Seth was adamant, telling them how terrible their idea was under the circumstances. Most of the villagers were armed with axes better fit for chopping wood, and some were only carrying clubs. Three carried hunting bows. None looked to be warriors to Artos's eye. The trappers had not seen the tracks of the Beastmen, for they had come upon the ruins of the village at dusk and had set out to warn the other villages immediately. The men thought they would hunt a band of a few dozen Beastmen at most. They were understandably dismayed when Seth revealed the actual size of the marauding band.

After a heated discussion among themselves, they decided their best actions would be for a dozen of them to continue on to Fargo and care for the remains of the dead. They were relieved to learn Seth had blessed the remains, as they had no priest among them to do so. Although the thought of a mass grave was abhorrent to them, they agreed there would be no way to identify the charred, skeletal remains to make individual graves. The other three would return to Breedon and Lando with the news—two to Breedon when the trail divided, and one to travel with the party to Lando and explain to the people there, saving Seth from having to deliver the grim news. Only Seth's rank as a Druid of the Earth Mother kept the men from insisting he return with them to bury the dead. He explained he had pressing business and could not be delayed. Instead, he promised he would return as soon as he was able and attend to anything their villages might need from him then.

It was a grim, silent trek to Lando. Due to the chill weather, everyone wore their hoods pulled close. Artos felt none of the villagers realized that three of their group were Fairborn or had the slightest inkling of who he and Bortis were. Upon reaching the village, the party hurried on, leaving the villagers to make the explanations, and made camp a few miles up the trail toward Bluffton.

Upon reaching that village the next day shortly after noon, they confirmed the grim news had preceded them, and word had been sent ahead to Eagleroost. The village elder told them they expected a response from the castle within a few days but were pessimistic about any immediate action.

"The Beastmen waited till the deEagledons left the King's Valley for the winter," said the village elder. "I can't see the folk remaining there being able to do much till they send word to Eagleton and get word back from the Count."

Artos was forced to agree with the elder's assessment. *It will be spring before Count Stephan has enough troops here in the mountains for them to do anything.*

The party took lodgings in the village inn, and Seth went out and made queries of the local trappers to find if any of them knew a route through the mountains to Starstone Tower.

It was decided Artos and his brother would wait for the druid in the taproom while the Fairborn remained in their rooms. After waiting over an hour, Artos was beginning to grow impatient when the druid returned, accompanied by an elderly man whom he introduced as Jomac. He bid the man to sit with them and bought him a mug of ale.

"I went around and spoke with the trappers," said the druid. "No one I spoke with would admit to knowing a path through the mountains to Starstone Tower. Some pled ignorance or just refused to speak about that area at all. A few told me the area was too dangerous, and when I asked why, I was told it was haunted. I was almost ready to give up, then I met Jomac."

Artos judged the man had seen better days; his deer-skin leather coat was worn and patched, as were his breeches. If his breath was any indication, he had already imbibed a fair share of ale that day.

"Tell my friends here what you told me," said Seth after the old man had swallowed a good long pull.

Jomac sighed in obvious pleasure, wiped the foam from his mouth, and glanced at the two brothers.

"I tole yer friend here I can give ye directions to get ye to the Starstone Tower." The old man nodded at Seth.

"Tell them the rest. Tell them everything."

The man nodded again. "I'm not a popular man here in Bluffton. Most of the men here, they won't give me the time o'day. They ain't fer years. You see, I'm a hunter, leastwise I was, a few years back afore my joints got too stiff. They be mostly trappers here in Bluffton, but my family we always been hunters. An' one day I may have had a wee bit too much ale, and I told the head trapper that trapping was lazy, lazy and cowardly. I told him it took skill and nerve to find game, track it, and bring down yer quarry with a well-placed arrow. Any dang fool can set a trap. I think maybe the fool part was too much, or maybe it was calling 'em all cowardly.'" The old man grinned and shrugged. "Some people just can't stomach the dang truth." He raised his mug and took another healthy swallow. "Anyway, yer friend said ye want to get across the mountains to Starstone Tower."

"That's right," said Artos. "Can you tell us the way?"

"Ye'll not be wanting to set off over the mountains from 'ere. Ye could probably be a doin' it, but why bother when an easier way is only a few miles down the road, eh?" Jomac turned and grinned at Seth.

"Why indeed?" agreed Seth.

"Err ... yes, why?" asked Artos, feeling lost.

"If ye be goin' down towards Percy, ye'll come to The Biggins."

"That's the grove of thousand-year trees, right?" said the druid.

"Aye, that be the name of 'em. You might have anuther one, but that's what they be called here-a-bouts. Big they be and Biggins we call 'em. Now, you need to go almost to the end of the forest. Don't be setting out until ye can see they be coming to an end. That's yer sign, then." The old man took another hefty swallow of ale and wiped his mouth with his sleeve.

"Turn off the trail and head due north from there, leaning a wee bit towards the east as ye go. Ye'll find the path the trappers made. Jest about four miles and The Biggins will come to an end. Just follow the mountain pine; it'll lead ye up around Big Horn Mountain and then back to the southeast. There's good hunting in those valleys if you know where to look. Jest follow the pine trees an' purty soon ye'll be coming up on Black Peak. There be wolves around that area, so keep an eye out. There'll be a bit of a valley there going east. Jest follow that, an' purty soon ye'll be seeing the west Rune Stone. It be the north shore of the loch. From there ye can see the tower itself if the fog be willing. That valley be where ye should be watching out fer the ghost. If ye be coming in the daylight, ye should be fine. Ye couldn't pay me enough to go there at night."

Artos could see Bortis was about to ignore Seth's advice and ask questions. He kicked his brother's leg under the table, and when Bortis glared at him, he shook his head slightly.

Seth continued the conversation with the old hunter. "So what kind of ghost is it? A shrieker? Or just a floater?"

"It nay be either one. If it were just a floater, well, they don't be a hurtin' anyone other than scaring 'em out of a year's growth. An' everyone knows if ye hear a Banshee a'wailing ... git away without settin' yer eyes on it. That be a sure sign of death, ain't it? No, this be some other kind of ghost. A murderin' kind. That's why the trappers don't be a going that ways no more."

"The ghost murdered someone?" asked Bortis, unable to refrain any longer, doubt dripping from his words.

"Aye, one of the Mclurin lads. They been bringing in some fine ermine pelts from up around the tower the last few years. Then one day, Donnie he come back alone, and he ain't been the same ever after. He gets the shakes and the sweats. Sometimes he wakes half the village in the middle of the night screaming out Willie's name." Jomac shook his head sadly. "'Tis a turrabul thing."

"What did this ghost look like?" asked Bortis.

The old hunter looked each of them in the face, one after the other. "Ye ever hear tell of a hyoona? Any of ya?"

Artos shook his head. Bortis muttered something indiscernible.

"The beast?" asked the druid. "Of course. The laughing scavenger, they called it. They're extinct. They haven't been around for hundreds of years."

"Well, Donnie, he says the ghost had the head of a beast, like a wolf, but different if ye follow me. It was nigh on eight feet tall. It stood up on its hind legs like a man, but it dinna walk. It floated a ways off the ground. That's how he knew it be a ghost, you see. It floated. And it laughed, not a belly laugh, mind ye, but a laugh like a crazy man. They heard it before they seen it, you see, and they thought it be someone in trouble so theys went to give a look. They came around a big rock and they saw it. It were right beside 'em, gnawing on the body of an ermine. In one of their own traps no less, but the chain that it were a pegged down with snapped right off. Donnie say he saw some twisted, broken links a dangling from it. No man coulda snapped that chain, no giant ermine either. It be the ghost that done it." The old man took another long drink and looked at each of the three again to be sure they were paying attention.

"Well, it seen 'em there, right next to it and it slapped at Willie. With its bare hand, Donnie said. Its bare hand. An' it knocked Willie's head right off. Blood was a spouting from his neck, and his poor head went bouncing off among the rocks. Donnie, he turned and ran, like anyone wudda, and the thing chased after him, laughing like a madman. Donnie said he looked back, and the thing wasn't running after him. It were a floating a few feet off the ground! That's how we know it were a ghost. No normal creature just floats through the air!"

Artos exchanged a look with his brother. He could see the doubt on Bortis's face, and he wondered how much of the story came from Donnie and how much from Jomac, embellished with ale.

"I wonder why the village elder didn't ask me to look at Donnie?" asked Seth. "It sounds as if his mind received a horrible shock when his brother was murdered. I can ease his pain. I should attend to him."

"I kin tell ye the answer to that," said Jomac. He pointed at Bortis. "It be him."

Before Bortis could erupt with indignation, Seth cut in. "What do you mean? Why him?" Artos put a restraining hand on his brother's shoulder. Bortis looked daggers at him, but settled back in his seat.

"We've seen him afore, riding with the Duke. The elder figgured him to be a spying on us fer poachin', don't ye know? Tomm, the elder's oldest son, he's ridden with the Duke, summer afore last it were." He drained his mug and set it down on the table with a small thump and nodded at Bortis again.

"I must see to this," said Seth, rising to his feet. "There is no excuse to let Donnie suffer. Thank you for the information, Jomac." He looked to Artos. "Please buy our friend another mug of ale. I will return as soon as I see what comfort I may bring to Donnie." He nodded to the brothers, turned, and strode out of the inn.

Artos waved at the tender, and when he had his attention, pointed at the old man's glass and indicated it should be refilled.

"How long ago did the incident with the ghost happen?" he asked, turning back to the old hunter.

"It be just a few weeks back—three or four. The Mclurin lads had run their first trap line of the season, and they were making their first round to check on 'em. They be bragging how they were goin' to be making themselves rich offin' the ermine this year. But all they got was Willie deaded." The old man shook his head sadly. "They weren't bad lads fer all they was trappers. I don't know what Donnie be goin' to do now. Willie was always the leader of the two. An' Donnie, he was always the follower. When the lads got in trouble as young lads are bound to do. It were always Willie that were leadin' the way and Donnie following behind his brother like a puppy-dog."

"What's a hyoona?" asked Bortis. "And what does it have to do with the ghost?"

"They laugh, hyoonas do, like a crazy person. When I was a boy, one of the old trappers used to tell us tales `bout all kinds of creatures. One be the hyoona."

"Seth said they died out a long time ago," said Artos. "Do you think the ghost is a hyoona?"

"Not just any hyoona, lad. That be the ghost of the hyoona king, if ye follow me."

"No," said Bortis as Artos shook his head. "I don't follow

you at all. Hyoona king?"

"Surely ye know that there be a king of every kind of animal? Don't ye?" The old man took a pull from his fresh mug of ale and smacked his lips. "There be a king elk, a king bear, even a king mouse. They always be the strongest, quickest, and smartest of their kind. Well, the way I figure it, when the hyoonas died off, the king hyoona would have been the last, don't ye see? An' his ghost be what killed off Willie."

Jomac drained his glass and stood up. "I be thanking ye fer the drinks. I be much oblieeged. Be careful up in the hills there. If ye be a killin' that ghost, they'll be a bunch of people glad to stand ye fer more rounds than one."

As the elderly hunter walked out the door of the inn, Artos looked at Bortis, who shrugged, then led the way back to their rooms to discuss the old hunter's story with the Fairborn.

"I think it was the Abomination," said Artos. "Three or four weeks ago, it killed the trapper on its way to Castle Draconis."

"It could be," agreed Bortis. "The Abomination is a shapeshifter. It could look like a hyoona if it wanted to, I guess."

"I guess you could ask it, Bort," said Angel, then smiled sweetly when he glowered at her. Neither Kae nor Jaek had an opinion as to what kind of creature it could be.

After an hour, Seth returned to the inn and dashed Artos's hopes of sleeping in a real bed that night.

"I thought we were spending the night here?" said Artos from where he sat. "And then setting out for Starstone in the morning."

"I told the elder we were going to push on and try to get to

Percival by moonrise. The elder's son recognized Bort alright. He knows he's kin to Duke Bretton. The elder wouldn't admit it, but they have been poaching furs and hunting game across the boundaries on DeDraconis lands. The sooner we leave, the happier they will be."

"Is it really that big a problem?" asked Art, looking wistfully at the feather mattress.

"It is, Art," replied Bortis. "If word got to Count Eagledon that his villagers were poaching on his neighbors' lands, he would punish the village as a gesture to our House. He would expect us to do the same if we caught any of our people poaching on deEagledon lands. Uncle Brett told me so."

"I know." Artos stood up and reached for his pack. "I was just thinking how soft the bed looks."

"It's true, Art," said the Druid. "If they knew I was a son of The Darrell, they would have hidden things from me as well. Since they only knew me as Druid Seth, they would speak freely in my presence. I fear that has changed now."

"You didn't tell them who you were?"

Seth shook his head. "No, but I am traveling with retainers of the deDraconis Family. They won't be trusting of me again for a while, if ever. The sooner I take you away, the happier they will be. The innkeeper returned our silver for the rooms. Let us be on our way."

It was late afternoon when they set forth again, out of the village along a trail leading to the southeast.

This isn't right, thought Artos, as they trudged along the trail. *I don't know why the system is so unfair to everyone except a few privileged people. I'll do something when I'm king. But what?*

The smell of snow was in the air as they crossed a ridge, and their path led downhill again. The towering shapes of the thousand-year fir trees soon loomed ahead through the mountain mists.

It was dark beneath the trees. Shortly after they entered the grove of giant trees, Seth led them from the path and found a hollow between the roots of one of the enormous trees where they made their camp.

"Could you help that Donnie, Seth?" asked Artos.

"A little, I think." The druid sighed and shook his head. "Not much, I'm afraid, but I did what I could. Seeing your brother decapitated when he's standing right beside you is not something you can get over easily or quickly. I don't think he'll be waking up screaming, though. So that's something."

"What do you think they saw? I mean, what killed Willie?" asked Bortis.

"I don't know. Not a ghost. Something much worse, I imagine."

"Abomination," said Artos. "Could it be the one in Castle Draconis? Was it stalking the hills near Starstone Tower a month ago?"

"Perhaps ..." Seth sounded doubtful.

"But you don't think so?" asked Artos.

"My teachers taught me there were five great Abominations in the service of Demigoran. In the attack on Castle Draconis, there were two, and of course, the head of Tomung, that accounts for a third. I doubt the raven rider would have abandoned its steed to wander the hills. It could be any of the other three ... but something bothers me." The druid looked around the hollow where they were camped and shrugged.

"And that is?" asked Bort.

"I put Donnie in a dream state, which Donel calls hypnosis, and questioned him about the incident before I blurred it in his mind to save his sanity. He was adamant that the creature floated in the air. When it was pursuing him, it didn't walk or run. It floated. Some tales of the Abominations tell of them changing their forms to hideous giant bats, but nothing I ever heard told of them floating in beast form. So, I just don't know."

"The Abomination at Castle Draconis that first appeared as the Duke then changed to some hideous beast, climbed the wall. It didn't float—it ran up the wall like a squirrel up a tree," said Jaek. "The one that joined it later rode the back of the Raven and spoke through its mouth. We didn't see it leave the back of its steed."

"There's no sense worrying about it. We keep a careful watch. Donnie said they first heard crazed laughter. So, everyone listen sharp and speak up if you hear anything unusual," said Seth. "There's snow in the air. We've been very lucky so far. Let's hope it holds off for another few days."

10/8/1971 ar

When they awoke, a dusting of snow drifted through the giant trees, and the air was the coldest they had experienced yet on their trek. Artos was pleased the light fabric of their new outfits seemed to shield them from the worst of the cold, and no one in their company suffered from the chill. They ate their morning jerky and soon were back on their way.

When they regained the main trail, Seth frowned at the inch of new snow covering the less sheltered ground. "It can't be helped, but we shall leave a plain trail for anyone who might follow us. I had hoped to leave no sign of where we left the trail and set off into the mountains."

"Who would follow us?" asked Bortis. "Villagers from Bluffton?"

"I don't know that anyone is," answered the druid. "But I have had the feeling of being watched by unfriendly eyes ever since we left Fargo. It's probably just my guilt at leaving so many people unburied. There was no help for it, but it still bothers me. I will return there when this is behind us and say a prayer to The Mother."

Artos was about to agree that he too had felt as though they were being watched, when Angel spoke up.

"I have felt that way too, hostile eyes. You are always being watched by the creatures of the forest, but this feels different.

Artos glanced at his brother, who just shrugged. "I even felt that way when we were sitting at the inn in Bluffton. I just thought it was nerves. How about you, Bort?"

"There's a tension in the air," agreed Bortis. "I feel it too."

"We all do," added Kae. Jaek nodded silently and clasped his wife's hand.

When they set out, Seth declared the end of the forest of giant trees was nearly upon them and for everyone to look for a trail leading north. Shortly after, Kae detected signs of people leaving the path. With the fresh snow, neither brother could see any difference, but both Angel and Seth agreed she was correct. Jaek merely shrugged and said if his wife said so, it was good enough for him. The group left the trail and traveled half a mile into the forest, where Seth called a halt.

Directing everyone to take a brief rest, he cut some pine boughs and made his way back along the trail of their footsteps. After a time, he returned, using the branches as a brush to whisk away their tracks. Upon rejoining the party, he tossed them aside, declaring he had covered their tracks as best he could.

"Our tracks just stop on the trail to Percival, but it couldn't be helped. There is a slight breeze, but it's not covering our tracks. Anyone following us will know roughly where we turned off, but I think it is going to snow again soon; that should hide our trail."

The party proceeded to the north, winding through the enormous trees. In the late afternoon, when the thousand-year firs thinned and the regular mountain pine became thick, Seth called a halt in a small clearing. The snow had started falling a bit heaver; there were more drifts, and they were getting deeper. The party was tiring of the uphill trudge.

"I believe we will come to Starstone Tower before evening tomorrow," said the druid. "Let us make camp here and proceed in the morning. I don't believe we will come across a ghost, but the McLurin brothers had their fateful encounter with whatever it was that murdered Willie in the valley ahead at dusk. We need to rest. We have left an obvious track for miles, but the snow is still falling. It should cover our traces by morning."

No one argued his decision, although Artos could see his brother wanted to press on. The day's fatigue made even Bortis agree that a good night's rest was needed.

Sitting at the small fire, they heard wolves howling in the distance. It wasn't the first time during the trip they had heard such cries, but they seemed closer, more threatening than any time in the past.

"I wish Zeb was still with us," said Angel as she daintily gnawed on the stick of jerky in her hand. "Wolves don't like to cross paths with bears."

"I don't think we need worry about wolves," said Seth. "The

smoke from our fire should keep them away. Wolves have better things to do than mess with humans. If they come closer, I will wake everyone."

10/9/1971 ar

"AWAKE! ARISE! TO ARMS!!" Jaek's voice called the alarm.

Artos woke with a start, pulled out of his sleeping bag, and followed his brother from their small tent. Angel was already up, standing next to Jaek by the fire, her bow in hand. Kae was emerging from the tent she shared with her husband. There was no sign of Seth. Before he could ask the druid's whereabouts and the nature of the alarm, loud cries rang out.

Wolves howled, joining with other bellows and shrieks. His mind flashed back a few weeks to that fateful night at Castle Draconis. He had heard such cries before. Beastmen! He summoned his crysword to his hand and stood to his brother's right side. His sword dimly reflected the firelight as he swung his blade from side to side.

"Where's Seth?" he cried, but before anyone could answer, a tall Beastman with a wolf's head leaped into the small clearing, howling in triumph, waving a club over his head. A score of cries answered him as more Beastmen appeared, following the leader out of the fog with wolves howling at their sides.

Jaek swung his sword toward the neck of the creature, but it was already falling with Angel's arrow piercing its chest. The clearing erupted in chaos as the wave of Beastmen charged toward them.

The bows of Angel and Kae sang as they shot arrow after

arrow into the advancing creatures. Jaek and Bortis stood in front of them, forming a human wall between the charging foes and the archers. The blade of Bortis's sword burst into flame.

A bull-headed Beastman picked Artos as his target and swung his club at his head. He dodged to his left and plunged his crysword into the creature's chest. The beast looked down as if wondering what had happened and then collapsed. Another foe was right behind, leaping over its falling comrade, a snarl upon its wolf-like visage and two clawed hands reaching for his throat.

Before Art could swing up his sword in defense, an arrow appeared as if by magic in the creature's right eye, and it fell at Art's feet.

Bodies were piling up before Jaek and Bortis as both plied their blades with grim efficiency, but their foes had numbers and kept coming. Soon, one was bound to score an attack upon one of the defenders, and the tide would surely change! Artos looked around, trying desperately to think of a plan for their defense.

With a terrifying roar, a large black bear emerged from the forest and smashed into the Beastmen's flank. Mighty swipes of its clawed arms sent Beastmen flying left and right. *My dream,* thought Artos as he dodged again and slashed the throat of a weasel-headed Beastman wielding a pair of daggers. *That's the bear from my dream. What's it doing here?* The howls of the Beastmen changed from cries of triumph to wails of alarm as the bear roared again and swatted a pair of ratheads aside as if they were chaff. Its dagger-like teeth flashed in the firelight, adding to the Beastmen's terror.

The fight turned in their favor with the addition of the mighty bear. More of the Beastmen fell to the arrows of the archers and the blades of the men. Then suddenly, the onslaught was over. The few remaining Beastmen turned tail and ran away, howling in fear.

The black bear took a few steps after them, roaring in fury, then stopped and slowly turned to face the party.

"A friend of Seth's?" ventured Artos hopefully, still holding his crysword at the ready.

"No," said Angel shortly, shaking her head. "Not a friend ..."

"Then ..." But before Artos could frame the question forming in his mind, the bear shrank in upon itself, its form blurring and changing. The black fur morphed in form and texture into a forest-green cloak. Then Seth deDarrellyel stood before them, breathing heavily.

"Well ... now you know," he panted. "I was planning on discussing this with you, Artos," *Pant* " but somehow the time never seemed right."

"You ... you're an Abomination." Bortis's eyes opened wide, and he held his still flaming crysword before him, now directed towards the druid.

"Don't be a fool, Bort," said Angel. "Donel told you many times. Not all shapeshifters are Abominations."

The flames died away as Bortis lowered his sword. "But ... but ... how?"

"Is it a druid thing?" asked Artos. "I seem to remember Mother telling us some stories about a druid who could change his form to an otter, or maybe it was a badger. She told us that one before Father became so angry about the dragon story."

"I'd rather not discuss it right now," gasped Seth. "We need to get moving." *Pant.* "We are being watched." *Pant-pant.* "I still feel hostile eyes upon us." *Pant.* "Those Beastmen may return."

"You're right," Artos agreed, looking around and nodding.

"We need to get to the tower, but it's still the middle of the night. We're in a pine forest, and I don't think the clouds will allow any moonlight, if the moon is even in the sky and not a new moon." He felt he was babbling and stopped to think.

"One of my Regalos is Dagaz," said Seth. He held up his crystaff, which was once more wand-sized. It began to glow with a clear white light. "If we were still trying to remain unseen, I wouldn't do this, but our enemies know where we are. Speed has become more important than stealth."

Bortis nodded, held out his crysword, and again it burst into flame. "This will help a little."

Artos noted the confusion and distrust upon his brother's face, but decided there was nothing to be done about it now. "What was the rune again, Seth? Could you sketch it in the snow for me to gaze upon?"

"Dagaz." The druid took his wand and drew what looked like an hourglass on its side in the snow.

Artos studied the rune for a few moments to impress the form in his mind. He then closed his eyes and concentrated on the crysword in his hand.

There was a bright flash. It was dazzling, even with his eyes clenched shut. He staggered off balance and nearly fell. There were cries of pain all around him. He opened his eyes but quickly shut them again as his tears welled forth. The crysword in his right hand blazed brighter than the sun. There was a bright purple afterimage painfully imprinted on his sight. He almost dropped the sword as he turned his head away from the terrible light.

"Dimmer! Art, Dimmer!" he heard Seth shout as if from far away. "Make the light softer in your mind!"

He remembered Donel's lessons and began concentrating

on his crysword. He chided himself for not thinking ahead, for not taking into account the possible consequences of his actions. *Father always told me to plan ahead, to consider every action as though life were a very elaborate game of chess. I need to do better.*

"That was not well done, Artos," said Jaek from behind him. "It will take a few moments for my eyes to see again. I fear you have blinded us all temporarily."

Artos pictured the light as fading—dimming, becoming much less bright. Through his watering, tightly clenched lids, he saw the illumination fade.

"Fortunately, I was looking away from you, Art," said Seth. "My sight is almost normal again. That is much better. You can open your eyes now."

A bright purple line impaired his vision where he had looked upon the blinding light of his crysword. Tears ran from his eyes, and he wiped them away with his free hand. The line was fading, his vision slowly recovering. *I might have blinded someone. I might have blinded myself!*

"I was watching for Beastmen and wasn't looking at you either, Art. Although the light was still painfully bright. That is a fearsome weapon in itself," said Bortis.

"If you ever do that again, please warn us first," said Jaek. "My eyes are recovering, but that was most painful."

"Yes, I can almost see again. It feels as if I have sand in my eyes," said Angel as she wiped away tears. "Think what the Beastmen would have thought. They'd still be running into trees."

"I need some almas eye drops," said Kae. "I can make some easily enough. I think you scorched our eyeballs, Prince Artos, but no one is blinded, thankfully."

It only took the skilled healer a few moments to make and

then apply a balm for those whose eyes were scorched. Artos's eyes felt better as soon as Kae dropped a pale-pinkish drop into each of his eyes.

"I think we have enough light to proceed," said Seth after Kae finished giving eye drops to those in need. "Let's be off before we have any more visitors."

Part Seven

At Fairinhorst

Chapter Twenty:

To Seek Enlightenment

22

THE PATH

CARIMUS

9/30/1971 ar

WHEN CARIMUS AWOKE, he felt as if he had slept a long time. He rolled onto his back and stared at the ceiling of his cubicle as despair flooded his mind. *The Angellar is dead. How will I ever find Duke? No one here seems to know anything about him or that I was coming.* Was this just some plot of Donel's? Something to keep him away from the Crystal Tower for some dark reason? How to find his way back to Art and Bort? The Daughters are gone. Or were they? Maybe if he got up and ran back to the city, he would catch them before they left.

He jerked up into a sitting position and realized he was not alone. Sitting cross-legged on the meditation mat, quietly observing him, was a Fairborn man with brown hair and eyes, wearing a white robe with a green sash.

"Greetings, Carimus. I am Perfaren Valpho. I am a Seeker of Truth of the fifth tier. As you seek enlightenment, I will be your guide for this, the first stage of your journey, your sensei."

Carimus hurriedly climbed to his feet. "I … I am sorry. I cannot stay. I have to catch up with the Daughters. What time of day is it? How long was I asleep?"

Perfaren looked at him with sympathetic eyes. "It is nearly sunrise. As to how long you were asleep—you returned to your chamber here on the evening of Thirdday. It is now Fifthday. You seemed to be in deep shock, and a healer of the sixth tier deemed it would be best to let you awaken naturally. I have kept vigil in case you woke and needed aid or sustenance."

Carimus sank down to his knees on his sleeping mat. Too late. He could never catch the Daughters now. He placed his head in his hands, trying to keep his tears in check.

"If you are truly sure that it is your fate to leave, no one will say nay to you, but it would be strange to have spent so much of yourself to journey here, only to leave so abruptly. And I feel compelled to warn you—the Gatekeeper would not look kindly upon your petition to return should you change your mind."

Carimus looked up into the sympathetic eyes of Perfaren. "It's too late. I could never travel all the way back alone. I don't know what to do."

Perfaren tilted his head and smiled. "If I may offer a suggestion, perhaps you should fill your glass and have some manna." He nodded towards the table. "You have not taken sustenance in a very long time. It will help clear your mind as it quenches your thirst and feeds your body."

"I don't know what you mean." Carimus glanced at the table and the empty glass sitting on it. "Where would I fill my glass, and what is man-ah?"

"Manna. Did not Alea speak to you of these things?" Perfaren's eyes narrowed a bit.

"I interrupted her and insisted I be taken to see the Angellar.

She may have meant to continue when we returned, but I probably didn't give her a chance. She might even have done so, but I don't remember her saying anything. In fact, I really don't remember the trip back here from … from … down there." He felt his voice crack a little and he coughed.

"From your viewing of the Angellar?"

"Yes. I remember she showed me the closet." Carimus pointed at the wall. "And I remember her telling me about the bugs. The tailor bugs."

"The weavers."

"Yes, that's what she called them. I didn't ask her questions. I just kept telling her I wanted to see the Angellar. So she cautioned me about keeping silent and had me follow her down … there."

"This is why we delay novice seekers from visiting the cenotaph. Many feel extreme grief upon their first viewing. Alea probably should not have allowed your visitation."

"I think she felt sorry for me. And I insisted." He gazed at the floor, trying hard not to weep. *I failed you, Duke. I thought I would find you here. Or at least word of where we could find you.* He shook his head slowly, immersed in his grief.

"Take your goblet, Carimus, and hold it within the opening at the back of the table. Keep it there for about two breaths, then remove it. Grip it carefully. It will get heavier as it fills with manna."

Carimus took a deep breath and struggled back to his feet. To his dismay, his legs felt rubbery. He could never have followed the Daughters in this state. *I would have collapsed before I got out of the garden.*

Now, when it was foremost in his thoughts, he felt his stomach rumble and his throat was very dry. He took the goblet and, keeping a firm grip, held it in the space behind the table. It grew heavier, although not tremendously so. Still, he was glad Perfaren had warned him. It would have been a shame to drop the beautiful green glass goblet and perhaps shatter it or lose it down some unseen shaft.

After a few moments, he drew it forth. It was nearly full to the brim with a substance like someone had whipped milk into a froth, if milk was light green. The glass felt cooler, as if the liquid had come from some place cold. He raised it and took a cautious sniff. The color was a bit off-putting, but the scent was irresistible, though indescribable. All the good things he had ever eaten and drunk all combined into a marvelous mixture. Carefully, he took a small sip. It was so good he couldn't help himself—he drank it all down in several large swallows. His stomach exploded with a feeling of well-being, which spread rapidly throughout him. His mind felt clear, his body infused with health. The rubbery feeling in his legs disappeared, as did his hunger. His first reaction was to put the goblet back and let it refill. He was disappointed when he removed it, however. Instead of another glass of the milky manna, the glass was filled with cool, slightly cloudy water. Realizing he was still thirsty, he drank it down, although not with the same fervor as he had with the manna. The lingering taste was still delicious.

"What was that?" He realized the Fairborn man had arisen from the mat and was standing beside the table. His brown hair was cropped close to his head, and he had warm, brown eyes in a face that looked as though he smiled often.

"I told you. It is manna. It is all you will ever need to sup upon while you dwell here. Whenever you are hungry or thirsty, just hold your yulma within the opening there, and the quanti will sense your need and fill it for you. You no longer feel hunger or thirst, do you?"

Carimus realized it was true. "Do all the Fairborn eat this way?"

"Everyone here is sustained in this manner, Carimus."

"No. I mean, do all the Fairborn in Fairinlan eat, err … drink manna?"

"Ah, I understand. No, only here, within the Víre Tussa of the Angellar, do the quanti produce manna."

The Fairborn sat back down on the mat and motioned Carimus to sit upon the chair at the table. "This will be your first day as a seeker, Carimus. As such, please feel free to ask me any questions you have about the road to enlightenment. This morning is allotted to such inquiries as you may have. When your curiosity is satiated, I shall take you to see the areas open to you, and then tomorrow we shall begin your path."

Do I even want to be here? I have to find Duke. No one else has the time. Art has to get that thing out of the Castle. He will need Bort for that. But if anyone can find a way, it's Artie. He looked at Perfaren, then sat down and tried to put his thoughts in order. *What should I do?* "Will I be allowed to use the screens to speak with Donel?"

"What screens would those be, Seeker Carimus?" There was no guile on Perfaren's face; he looked genuinely puzzled by the question.

"The screens you use to far-see or communicate with people far away." *I need to ask Artie's advice. I don't know what to do.*

"I see …" The Fairborn man's eyes were filled with sympathy. "I think you will find things are done differently here than you have grown up accustomed to. There are no quanti-screens here as I have heard they use in the human Great Houses or in the Halls of the High Lords of the Fairborn. There are no screens closer than those found at the Villa of the Gatekeeper or the lord of Haldacitime. You will find, if you reach the upper tiers of enlightenment, that you will have passed beyond the need for such devices. At the lower tiers, such things would only prove distractions to your path."

"I see." Carimus shook his head. "I don't understand though." He held out his hands, frustration joining his despair. "I came here because I was told that the Angellar was a mighty seer. That she might be able to help me locate my lost brother, Duka. On the screen at Donel's tower, words formed saying to send me here. When I demanded to know why, it showed the name of my brother Duka. I never thought of coming here to seek anything except Duke."

Perfaren looked thoughtful. "Yet you wear a rune bracelet. A special rune bracelet."

"I was given the bracelet years ago, on my birthday, when I was ten years old. The Bard Varyan delivered it to me."

"Hir Varyan is an Enlightened One. Tell me, Seeker Carimus, have you observed the runes of others? Have you ever seen another bracelet such as the one you wear?"

Cari thought and then shook his head. "I haven't really looked for such things. The guard back at the bridge to Tarcitime said everyone who was summoned here had rune tokens. I think Alea had some. I see you are wearing a bracelet with some."

"Everyone who is summoned is given a rune token, usually a *single* rune token. Raido upon one side and Hagalaz on the other. This shows they are of the first tier. When they become enlightened enough to move to the second tier, they are given a second token. One with Raido on one side and Nauthiz on the other."

Perfaren held out his arm so Cari could examine the runes on his bracelet. There were five. Cari looked at his own. The bracelet he had owned for the past six years had ten rune tokens. He sighed. "I shouldn't have so many tokens, should I?"

"That is not what I am saying, Carimus. Hir Varyan was sent to deliver that bracelet to you with some particular intention. It is not for me, or anyone else, to gainsay the Angellar's will. Her vision is not the same as others. When Seeker Alea confirmed what the Gatekeeper had sent ahead, it raised some questions. The Gatekeeper's words were not in doubt. It is just a situation that had not arisen for over three hundred years. We were not sure what tier to assign you to, but upon consideration, it was acknowledged that you must begin at the beginning."

"So the Angellar was alive six years ago when she sent me the bracelet?"

"Most seekers do not ask about the Angellar so early in their journey. A seeker's sensei has the responsibility to answer those questions he deems helpful to the journey and to deflect or postpone those that he feels are not of importance or perhaps detrimental to their stage of enlightenment. It is not unknown for a seeker of the third tier to be given knowledge of the Angellar, and all who reach the fourth tier are enlightened in this way."

This is like a puzzle of some kind. But I don't know the rules for this one. "So I shouldn't inquire about the Angellar?" He realized he sounded whiny. "I don't mean to seem rebellious. I just do not know which way to turn."

Perfaren sighed. "If you have questions, you should always ask them, but just because you ask does not mean you will always receive an answer. The reward for patience is patience. You are my first Deshika, Carimus, the first whom I was chosen to lead to enlightenment. I think perhaps it will be a learning journey for us both."

"I am sorry if my curiosity troubles you." He looked down at the smooth green floor. "I don't mean to. I am just worried about finding my brother. He is the reason I am here."

"No, Seeker Carimus, you have no reason to give me an apology. I have decided that you deserve an answer. The body of the Angellar died over fifteen hundred years ago. However, her mind yet lives. Her spirit lives within the Víre Tussa. She communes with the Innermost Circle, those of the tenth level, the elders here at Fairinhorst—but few others. However, she sometimes, although rarely, chooses to speak to another. Those thus chosen are considered blessed, for she has deep and ancient wisdom that she sometimes shares."

Carimus looked up, his hope stirring once again. "So, she isn't truly dead? How can I speak with her?" Excitement rose within him.

"She chooses with whom she speaks, Seeker Carimus, not the other way around. Have patience. When she decides to communicate with you, she will do so. I would usually say *if* she decides to speak with you, but in your case, I feel there is little doubt that she will, at some time. Again, I counsel you to have patience."

Carimus nodded, feeling hope bloom within him again, instead of the soul-crushing defeat he had felt since realizing the Angellar was dead.

"Do you have other questions you would ask at this time? If not, I would ask that you allow me to retire to my own room and refresh myself. Then I shall return, and we may begin your training."

"Oh, that's right! You have been here for hours." *What would*

Artie do? "Yes, feel free to go. Do what you need to do. I beg your pardon for my thoughtlessness!"

Perfaren chuckled. "I am in no discomfort. I shall return in a short while. Change your attire, and when I return, I shall give you the tour and answer your questions concerning your seeking of enlightenment and grace." He rose smoothly, gave a slight bow, and strode gracefully from the room.

This changes everything.

When Perfaren returned, Cari was sitting at the table wearing his new green tunic and sash. He rose, placed his right fist over his heart, and nodded to the Fairborn. "Well met, Perfaren."

"Greetings, Seeker Carimus. For your first lesson, let me begin your instruction with this: when an Enlightened One approaches you, the proper form is a small bow." The Fairborn demonstrated. "If anyone in a white tunic should speak to you, the proper form of reply should include their title of 'Enlightened One.' If you are familiar with them, you may add their name afterwards. Thus, it would have been proper for you to bow and address me as 'Enlightened One Perfaren.'" He smiled as he spoke, so Carimus felt he was not being chastised, merely informed, and so he nodded, then bowed.

"Greetings, Enlightened One Perfaren."

"Greetings, Seeker Carimus," said Perfaren, bowing in return. "An exception may be made for your sensei or for a former sensei you have studied with. You may call me Sensei Perfaren, or merely Sensei."

Carimus nodded. "Thank you, Sensei."

"You are most welcome, Seeker, and thus, your journey to

grace begins. We shall not go out into the gardens today. We shall save that for tomorrow. Afterward, you may visit them any time you desire, and you may address anyone you meet in the garden who is wearing a green tunic like the one you have donned. If you desire to speak to someone wearing a different-colored tunic, you may approach them and bow. If they desire to speak with you, they will acknowledge you, and you may converse. If anyone, in any color tunic, does not desire to speak, you must allow them their silence."

"I understand. That is simple politeness."

"Perhaps, but I think it is often overlooked. The first tier seeker who proceeds to the next level of enlightenment will exchange their green cubicle for one upon the red tier and switch to a red robe. Likewise to blue and finally to the white robe of an Enlightened One. No two seekers are the same. The time spent within each level depends entirely upon the individual, their needs, and their growth. Likewise with the levels attained. Some seekers find that they reach a level of comfort and no longer desire to continue on the path to further enlightenment. This is normal and natural. In truth, few seekers pass beyond the blue tier. Many find personal completion with red. Everyone must find their own peace in their own place."

"If you are ready, Deshika, we shall begin." Perfaren bowed again and gestured toward the door.

"Before we go, I have thought of a few more questions you might address, if I might?"

"I seek to enlighten you, Deshika." Carimus was to hear those words many times in his stay at Fairinhorst.

"Well, first, what does that word ... dee-shike-ah mean?"

"A Deshika is a sensei's student. Others will address you as Seeker, but only your sensei will call you Deshika. Those who become acquainted with you will call you Seeker Carimus, or merely by your name, depending on how closely you become known to each other."

Carimus nodded. "What is this place made of? Is it all some form of crystal? Also, my tunic? I probably shouldn't have done this, but I was curious. The fabric is so light, I thought it might tear easily, but it is very strong. I found I couldn't rip it, so I thought to use my crysword to cut off a tiny snippet. But it didn't cut it! I mean, it did, but the material rejoined right behind the cut."

"I hope you didn't use your crysword to cut a sample from the wall?"

Cari hung his head, feeling his cheeks flush. "No, but I tried to shave a little from the table. I'm sorry."

"I see, and what was the result?" His sensei didn't sound angry, more amused if anything. He looked up into Perfaren's smiling face.

"The table wouldn't cut at all. After trying that, I realized I was being disrespectful. So I put the sword away with my other clothes. A guest shouldn't attempt to vandalize the property of his hosts. I looked where the table joins the wall, and there is no seam. The walls and floor join in the same manner. Then there is the closet. When it is closed, there are no joints, no seams, nothing to show it even exists, but if I reach out with my hand, an opening appears, and it slides open to each side. The walls and floor of the Winding Way at Castle Draconis are the same way ... seamless, I mean. Doors there are just ... doors." He shrugged.

"I am not familiar with Castle Draconis, but it sounds as if quanti-masters of old crafted it. The material formed with quanti is not like any other matter within the world. The same rules do not apply. The Víre Tussa of the Angellar is the same way."

Carimus nodded slowly. "Thank you, Sensei. You have given me a few things to think about."

"That is my hope, Seeker Carimus. Thought opens the road to enlightenment."

"I have always loved to learn, Sensei. If it wasn't for being so worried about Duka, I think seeking enlightenment would bring me a good deal of happiness."

"I am pleased your path may lead you to joy, Seeker. The rule for silence must be observed in the Shambe O'te Angellar, the Great Chamber, at all times, but on this, your first day, if you have a question for me in any other area of the Vire Tussa, feel free to ask and I shall do my best to enlighten you."

"I understand, Sensei."

"Excellent, let us begin." Perfaren led the way out of the cubicle into the world of Fairinhorst.

The scope of the halls beneath the earth at Fairinhorst was amazing and more than a little humbling. Carimus had always considered Castle Draconis huge, but he realized his old home could be tucked away in a corner of Fairinhorst and be easily overlooked. He had thought the very bottom of the halls was the Cenotaph of the Angellar, but a labyrinth of rooms lay deeper still within the Víre Tussa.

The sheer number of rooms alone filled Carimus with amazement. There were dozens of rooms devoted to group meditation. He was entranced by the Lire-Lin, the room where the chanters chanted. There was a gigantic library, which could have held all the books in Donel's library tucked away in a single corner. At the deepest point of his tour, he was shown another vast room lined with row upon row of benches, easily room for a thousand people to sit and not crowd each other. In the center was a large white circle on the floor with the symbol of a twisted star—the same symbol he had seen on the gate of the Gatekeeper's villa.

"This hall is huge, Sensei. Are there really enough seekers here to fill it? What is its purpose?"

"There are not enough seekers here at this time, Seeker Carimus. Though, if there were need, the call would go forth and seekers would come." Perfaren gazed around the enormous hall. "As to the purpose of the Star Chamber, that is something for another time. Let it suffice to say it is a place where seekers gather at certain times, when necessary." This was not the only question that remained unanswered that day.

Carimus noticed many small chambers were scattered throughout the labyrinth, all with the same design. In the center was a mat just big enough for a single person to sit, surrounded by nine purple candles of varying heights, each almost six inches in diameter with flames that never flickered or seemed to consume the wax or wick. Each mat held the same twisted star design he was beginning to notice in many places. Suspended above the mat from the ceiling was a bell-shaped cylinder whose edges matched the mat below—if the cylinder was lowered, its edges would align with the mat below perfectly. Once, he passed such a room and saw that the bell was sitting on the ground. Even as he watched, the wall closed and there was no sign the room even existed. He asked half-jokingly if there was a seeker sitting within the cylinder. Perfaren merely smiled without answering. He soon learned that this was indeed the case. His next thought was just how many of those rooms were there? There were many passages with no apparent reason to exist, lined with blank walls. *If all these blank walls hide those little rooms, there must be thousands of them,* he thought.

Later on the first day, he visited a few areas devoted to those whose enlightenment was of the higher tiers—areas where he should not go unless escorted by someone who had achieved that stage of enlightenment. Perfaren could walk down what appeared to be a dead-end passage, and suddenly an opening would appear before him. Several gymnasiums held seekers exercising alone or in groups, each restricted to seekers of a single tier. He saw places where they grappled in hand-to-hand combat and places where they danced. There were rooms where seekers in blue sat and engaged in mental games with no physical equipment at all. There were rooms open to seekers of any tier, with many different forms of gaming available. *If only Duke were here to share this with,* he thought. *We could have such a good time.*

There were whole rooms devoted to chess, including some where the players moved their pieces through force of will alone, others with chessboards with multiple layers, or set up for three players instead of the usual two. Carimus enjoyed chess, although he didn't like to play against Bortis, his older brother was a ruthless opponent and hated to lose. Not that Carimus beat him often. There was even a room with a board for team chess, where four players could match their skills.

He was enthralled when he discovered a pair of rooms where players sat around a small sunken area and, with their thoughts, moved small game pieces resembling real people through a miniature city. Seekers who were not engaged in playing the game could watch the action on a screen in the neighboring room.

By late afternoon, he began to feel frustrated. This was an amazing place, unlike anything he had ever imagined existed, but it wasn't helping in his cause. If only he could share these wonders with his brother. He felt he could explore for a very long time and find any number of wonders, yet nothing seemed to be of any use for discovering the whereabouts of his lost brother. Adding to his frustration, there were some areas where Perfaren merely showed him certain passages marked with symbols of red, blue, or white and told him these led to places he could not yet go at his current state of enlightenment.

10/3/1971 ar

By his fourth day, Carimus had been granted permission to venture outside his cubicle alone, though as yet he had not. His morning ritual consisted of consuming his manna, then meditating as he awaited Perfaren to come to his cubicle. Today, as he sat thinking, he had a sudden desire to look upon the Angellar again. Perfaren had advised him to have patience, but perhaps if he stood before her, she might consent to speak with him somehow. Hadn't Donel said she had used some form of mind-speak? Perhaps she was just waiting for him to go to her. *I can go stand before her and wait. What is the worst that could happen?* For the first time since his arrival, he decided to venture forth on his own.

Exiting his cubicle, he walked along the walkway until he found a bridge to the central pillar. There he followed the ramp downward. As he traveled, he realized the chanting permeating the entire Vire Tussa had become so familiar that he had forgotten it was there. He was chanting along with it in his mind without even thinking. The chant was just simple sounds repeated over and over, "Ohh... ahh... ahh... ohh... Ohh... maa... maa... ohh... Ohh... maa... ohh... ahh... ohh..." It was easy to just repeat the words rather than think about anything else, just walk and chant silently. He was careful, however, not to chant aloud, although it would have been quite easy to do so. By mindlessly chanting, he could ignore his lack of progress in finding Duke.

It was almost a shock when the ramp ended at the spiral stair, the last leg of the journey to the Angellar's cenotaph. He paused at the bottom, calming his breathing and his thoughts. Then he turned to the opening that led into the center. Did he really want to approach the crystal tomb once more? He gazed into the open space for a few long moments, still repeating the chant over and over within his mind. Then, gathering his resolve, he stepped through the arch and felt the familiar tingle of a qulan field— —

That's odd, he thought. *I didn't notice that the first time I was here. I must have been too preoccupied.* He stood still and gazed around in shock. *What happened?* Things had changed the instant he stepped through the field. The room was smaller, much smaller than it had been moments before. Nine huge purple candles had appeared, evenly spaced around the room. The floor, which had been smooth and unblemished, was now covered with the now familiar twisted star symbol. In the center, where moments before he had gazed upon a transparent crystal pillar, there was now a single large white rose being used as a throne. Sitting there with her eyes closed was a middle-aged woman.

Cari was sure she was human, for although she had slightly pointed ears, she was very normal looking, not the typical great beauty he associated with the Fairborn race. He froze in sudden recognition; it was a younger version of the woman he had seen encased within the crystal tomb, the Angellar.

Her eyes opened. She gazed at him and smiled. "Hello, Carimus." His mouth fell open in shock.

CHAPTER Twenty-One:

Breaking Free

23

THE ANGELLAR

CARIMUS

10/3/1971 ar

He realized he was sitting down, though he had no memory of doing so. Hadn't he just been standing? He was now sitting with his legs crossed in the meditative position Perfaren had shown him. The rose throne was less than six feet before him, floating a few feet above the ground with the Angellar sitting there, watching him. The smile on her face seemed bemused yet sympathetic. The scent of roses filled the air, and the chanting voices had almost vanished. Now it seemed they were very far away instead of the all-encompassing sound that had surrounded him ever since he had arrived at the Víre Tussa.

"You're not dead." He shook his head and cleared his throat. "I mean, you are. I looked at you, encased within the crystal." He looked around wildly. The walls were polished, smooth and unbroken, a uniform forest green, the color of foliage in midsummer. There was no door! The candles burned smoothly without flickering, a thin wisp of smoke rising from each dispersing into the air. Yet the only scent was that of roses, a rich and satisfying smell that added to his feeling of tranquility. Calm and peace washed over him as if he were immersed in a pool of warm, soothing serenity. "Where am I?" His voice sounded calm and didn't crack, as it was all too prone to do when he was excited or upset. *What's going on? Am I dreaming?*

"Where?" The woman tilted her head to the left and looked thoughtful. "Hmm ... That will take a little explaining, Carimus. Your mind is here with me." She smiled again. "Your body is still stepping into the viewing chamber. We are having this conversation within the Quantum realm, not the physical world you live in." She spread her hands apart and looked around the room. "Time is different here. Indeed, I'm not sure if time even exists here at all. But we humans need time to measure our existence by, and so I think we create it wherever we are. Do you understand that?" She tilted her head to the other side, a twinkle in her eye as she arched an eyebrow.

"No. How can time not exist? Is this a riddle?" He marveled at how calm he felt. He was talking with a dead woman, and he wasn't even nervous.

The Angellar chuckled. "I'm not sure I understand it either, so you are not alone. The Universe is much more complex than that which we mortals perceive, what we believe. It is much more complex than anything we can conceive. A million billion different nows all exist at once. None of them are exactly the same. Indeed, some are so different they are beyond what we can even dream."

"We are in the quanti realm?" He glanced around the room again.

"No, the Quantum realm. What you call quanti are something quite different. They are machines—tiny machines, very tiny, small beyond your imagining. They travel both within our world and here as well. At the same time, all at once."

"I don't understand. Quanti is magic ... not machines. A carriage is a machine, or a cart, or even an airship. How can tiny machines do magic?"

The Angellar sighed. "Never mind, Carimus. They considered me an expert in several quantum disciplines, and I don't think I ever totally understood either. Don't worry about it right now. We can discuss it later. One thing we have is time, as much as we need."

"But we don't!" He made waving motions with his hands. "At least, maybe I have, but Art doesn't, and I want to help him, if I can. But what I really want is to find Duke. We all do, my brothers and me. I know Art is worried about him, but he has to reclaim the Castle. If the only way I can help him is to find Duke, then I have to do that. Besides, I miss him. Didn't you send for me? Do you know where he is?"

"I told you time is different here, Carimus. You don't understand how much. When I send you back to your body, you will arrive at almost exactly the same time as when you left. No matter how long we chat here. I know you find that hard to believe, but it is the truth, and you will see shortly."

"What do you mean, send me back to my body? I am my body!" He clapped his hand to his chest. "I'm right here."

"You think you are in your body because your mind has no other way to picture yourself. Your body is still stepping into the viewing chamber. When you return there, that is what you shall be doing. Stop for a moment, close your eyes, study yourself. Are you breathing? I think you shall find that you are not, because we are not really talking. It is just that you have no other way to picture our communication, and so it seems like we are talking. Just relax and think."

"This is crazy!" He stood up and looked around wildly. There was nowhere to go. *This must be a dream. I'll wake up any minute and be in my cubicle waiting for Perfaren.*

"You are not dreaming, Carimus. Calm yourself. Relax. Look inward. The time you are outside your body today will take place in between two breaths, in between the beats of your heart. I am going to send you back in a moment. I will consider your brother's location and his well-being, so the next time we speak, I may reassure you. You have a destiny before you, Carimus, as do your brothers, all of you. Take comfort in knowing great things await you all upon the Glory Road. The trick is picking the correct path from the many which lie before you."

This is nonsense. How can I not be breathing? He sat back down, closed his eyes, and tried to take a deep, calming breath. Although he could, he felt no need. His heart should be racing. He was sitting with a woman, long dead. But he felt calm, almost numb, and he could not feel the beating of his heart. Perfaren had taught him to be aware of his breath and his heartbeat, and yet they just didn't exist. He opened his eyes and looked at the Angellar.

"You're right, I can't find my heartbeat. I don't seem to need to breathe. Am I dead too?"

"Oh, goodness no, Carimus. You are fine. I wanted to tell you a few things, which was why I summoned you. You felt a desire to see me, did you not?"

Cari nodded. "I am here speaking with you, but I don't know where here is. You say I am not in my body." He looked down at himself. "Yet I see my body sitting here in this chamber with you. I have seen your body encased in the crystal tomb, and yet you are sitting here before me. You are alive. I mean, you look as though you are alive."

The Angellar shook her head sadly. "I fear I have summoned you too quickly, yet I erred before with your great-uncle by not summoning him soon enough, and he was called away by circumstance. I had not yet spoken with Donel mind to mind to begin his training in matters of the Quantum Universe before I was forced to contact him to tell him of the death of the Keeper of the Crystal Tower and that he must return there at once. At that time, I was too slow.

But now there really is no choice. History is unfolding as we wait; the time has come for us to act. To begin, I must teach you something. When you next see Perfaren, you must tell him these words: Im anír- cin na near nin ine i pode." Carimus felt a twinge within his mind, like the ghost of a thought, appearing and then vanishing so quickly he barely had time to acknowledge its existence. "He will probably try to argue with you, but I will direct his thoughts, and he will take you to your pode and tell you how to proceed. You have seen the podes; they will do you no harm, and it will make our lessons so much easier. Will you do this?"

"I don't know what a pode is."

"You have seen them." She nodded with a smile. "You just do not realize they are podes. You will understand shortly."

He was about to ask her to repeat the phrase when he realized he already had it memorized.

"Im anír- cin na near nin ine i pode. You placed it in my mind!"

The Angellar smiled again. "Everything here is within your mind, dear boy. Now back you go!" The woman made *shooing* motions with her hands and ...

—Cari finished his step into the viewing grotto and almost stumbled. He caught himself and looked around. The chamber was as it had been before. A few yards ahead of him, the body of the Angellar lay peacefully encased within her crystal tomb. He realized he no longer felt any desire to gaze upon her corpse, turned abruptly, and retraced his steps back to his room.

When Perfaren entered the cubicle for their afternoon training session, Carimus was waiting, sitting on his mat. He rose and bowed.

"Greetings, Sensei. Im anír- cin na near nin ine i pode." He took a deep breath and watched Perfaren's face. The Fairborn paused, his eyes widening.

"What did you say, Seeker Carimus?"

Carimus repeated the words the Angellar had inscribed into his thoughts.

Perfaren gazed at him in wonder. "I have not yet even thought of instructing you in the use of a pode ... I do not understand, Deshika. I have never heard of anyone entering a pode before they had reached the third level of enlightenment. And very few before the fifth." The Fairborn froze, his eyes unfocused for a moment. He shook his head in bemusement. "You have barely set your feet upon the path of enlightenment, yet I feel you are indeed summoned. May I suggest you drink a glass of manna before we go?"

Carimus shook his head; his mind filled with wonder. *It wasn't a dream. I almost thought it had to be.*

"I supped before you arrived, Sensei. I am rested and refreshed." Carimus found himself trembling with anticipation. He looked toward the doorway and back to his sensei.

"I wonder if I will not soon find our roles have reversed," there was wonder in Perfaren's voice, "and I shall be addressing you as Sensei, Seeker Carimus. Let us proceed to the lower levels."

They proceeded to the hallway, where Cari had first observed the bell-shaped cylinders above the meditation mats and stopped at an empty chamber. Perfaren motioned for Cari to enter before him, and then stood in the doorway.

"I find myself bewildered by this series of events, but it is not my place to question. I should tell you, at the very least, most seekers spend a few weeks with the chanters and learn to accept the harmony of the Quantum throughout their being before they seek a pode. For some, it is years before they seek such, yet here we are. You have been listening to the chant without joining in, but now that changes. Relax, remember your breathing, and meditate. When you feel in harmony with the chant, join in with the chanters. Do not feel alarm when the pode lowers around you. Continue chanting and meditating. After a time, the pode will open. Then one of two things will have happened—you will either find yourself within the Quantum realm, or you will find you are still here. If that is the case, make your way back to your room and follow your normal evening routine. If you find yourself within the Quantum, you will receive guidance there. Normally this would be me, but I have not been instructed to join you there." Perfaren shrugged. "So, I am not sure what will happen thereafter as this is such a strange happenstance, but I am sure you will receive that which is required. Just as I am certain, I will receive instruction when needed. Go forth with Grace, Seeker Carimus. Follow your destiny."

Perfaren bowed and withdrew from the room.

Carimus stood and stretched, as his Uncle Brett had instructed him to do before any exercise. He then sat cross-legged, slowed his breathing, and prepared himself for meditation. *Here we go,* he thought. *I think.* By habit, he repeated the chant silently, then remembered Perfaren had given him permission to do so aloud. As he chanted, he closed his eyes and never noticed the bell-shaped cylinder slowly lowering around him.

Chapter Twenty-Two:

With Our Grace

24

THE OVERWORLD

CARIMUS

10/3/1971 ar

WHEN CARIMUS OPENED HIS EYES, he was sitting cross-legged in some kind of tent. Instead of the smooth bell shape he expected to find, green walls spiraled up as if he were sitting within a giant twisted flower bud. At first, he thought it was silent, but no, there was sound. It was not just the chanting he had grown so accustomed to; for although the chanting was there, it was very faint. There was soft music, delicate yet pervasive, a totality of sound. The familiar chanting had merged and become a small part of this grand symphony. *It's beautiful. Like an orchestra of flowers.*

As he listened, the walls split into four sections, twisted around, and then curled away from him—rolling up and melting into a smooth, round, green platform suspended in space. He looked around in wonder. He floated in a cloud of gray fog, and yet when he gazed in any direction, the fog parted, and he could see for tremendous distances. Bands of colored mist twisted and flowed. Ever moving, ever changing, in perfect accompaniment to the music. *This is amazing.* He looked around in wonder.

There was no single source of light, yet it was not dark. Surrounding him were countless shapes of every size and hue. Vast clouds of color writhed and twisted, and smaller objects too—spheres, cubes, and polygons of every shape and size. Some were above him and some were below. Some were motionless, and others moved with tremendous velocity. A wondrous dance, all keeping time with the vast symphony that engulfed him. *Where am I? What is this place?*

Surrounding him were twisted, closed tulips of many colors, mostly white or blue, but intermingled were some that were red, green, even gold and silver. All were floating with no visible support. Intermixed, he noticed some small round pads that looked exactly like the one upon which he sat. However, none seemed occupied. He was all alone in an infinite space filled with shapes, sounds, and color. *There's no one here!* Where was the guide Perfaren promised?

He leaned over and looked down. *I should be afraid, but I'm not.* Below him were more bands of color, more clouds of mist, and more of the colorful shapes. They were all around him. The bands of colored mist flowed and entwined. Some slowly changed color. *It's all too beautiful.* Some objects were flying past at tremendous speed while others pirouetted slowly by, swirling and twirling in a strange, beautiful dance. Carimus pulled back from looking down, feeling dizzy.

In front of him, a pair of regalos runes gracefully twirled past, their delicate movements mesmerizing. They were two of the runes engraved on his bracelet: Hagalaz and Raido—disruption and journeys.

The flower shapes and the pads, like the one on which he was sitting, remained motionless. At least, he thought they did. They might all be moving together in some fixed formation. He didn't detect motion, but he wasn't prepared to accept anything at face value at the moment.

A large white sphere floated up from the distance and stopped, hovering a few yards before him. A second sphere zoomed up and stopped near the first. A blue dot appeared on each sphere and expanded to take up more than half the surface. In the center of each blue circle, a black dot appeared and grew to a larger size.

Those look like eyes, he thought to himself. Then, with horror, he realized they *were* eyes. And they were staring at him!

Welcome to the Overworld, to the Quantum realm, Carimus deDraconis.

"Are you the Angellar?" he whispered, gazing at the enormous eyes.

Fading in from nowhere, a gigantic face slowly formed around the eyes. The face of the Angellar.

"Yes, Cari. It is me. What do you think of this place?"

"I don't know. Where are we? I mean, I know we are in the Quantum realm, but where is that?"

"The Overworld is everywhere, and perhaps nowhere as well. At least as far as creatures with our limits can perceive. We are in the realm that exists between all wheres and all whens. Where everything exists and everywhen and everywhat. I don't believe we are meant to understand. Our minds are not made for it."

"I'm not sure I believe it. I think I must be dreaming."

"I have often pondered that when a person dreams, he travels in this place, at least in some small way."

"It seems totally strange and yet … there is something which feels familiar too."

"The first thing you must do is connect yourself to your pode. Then I will show you how to travel. I will tell you where you may go, where you should go, and where you must never, ever go. There is danger here. There is more danger here than anywhere you could possibly imagine."

He looked around; his floating island was completely barren. "How can I tie myself? I have nothing, not even any string."

"Look in front of you, at your pode. Do you see a small silver dot?"

He was about to say no when one appeared right on the pad in front of him. "I see it. But I didn't when I first looked."

"That's because it wasn't there. It formed when you thought it into existence. This is something you must be very careful of, Cari. It is possible to hurt yourself in ways you could not imagine with careless thoughts. This is why I do not normally bring seekers here before they have developed some self-discipline." The face looked very concerned, and sad as well.

"Take the dot between your fingers and pull the cord out, then tie a loop around yourself."

"What?"

"Try."

Cari reached out with his right hand and brought his fingers together around the silver dot, lifting them and pulling out a thin silver cord. Startled, he let go, and it disappeared back into the silver dot. He tried again, and this time wrapped it around his body by raising it over his head and looping it around himself. He then tied a simple knot and looked up at the floating face. "Now what?"

"Now you may let go of the Telepse-taeth, the silver cord."

Cari obeyed. When he did, the cord tightened gently around his form and then faded away.

"It disappeared," he exclaimed.

"No, it is still there, connecting you to your pode. Look again."

He squinted his eyes and stared really hard. There it was. He could faintly see a shimmery silver thread running from his body to the dot on the pad. "Is this to keep me from falling off my pode?"

"No, Cari." There was laughter in the Angellar's voice. "How can you fall if there is no down?" The face of the Angellar slowly rotated in place until it was upside down. Cari suddenly felt as though he were hanging upside down, but before he could react, the face of the Angellar continued turning until it was right-side up to him again. "Your Telepse-taeth is your connection to your pode, your anchor. Your guide that will lead you back home when you journey far away."

"I still don't understand. Why are we surrounded by fog and yet we aren't?"

"It is the way of the Overworld. The fog is ever-present, yet it isn't. Don't try to understand the incomprehensible. Trust me on this. Now, first things first. Think of yourself standing up."

"You want me to stand?" He prepared to rise from his cross-legged sitting position.

"No. Don't do it. Think about doing it. Trust me."

Carimus shook his head. "Okay, I guess." He closed his eyes and imagined standing on the small, floating pad. He realized he was standing. The Angellar was floating in the air in front of him when he opened his eyes, right between him and the enormous face that was *also* the Angellar.

"Why are there now two of you? I mean, why is your face behind you?"

The Angellar laughed. "Look down."

Cari obeyed. He was gazing at someone sitting right where he was standing. He was standing right inside the person! With a startled yip, he jumped backward to get out of the way of the body below him and went flying off, backward through the air. He tried to stop moving backward and ended up tumbling over and over as he flew backwards through the air. "HELP!" he shrieked.

"Take my hand, Cari. It's right in front of you. Reach out."

Right in front of him, moving right along with him, was a slim, disembodied hand. He clutched at it in panic, and the universe spun around him and then slowed to a stop. He was standing right next to the Angellar, and she was clasping him with her right hand. He released his hands from hers and looked around. The ever-present fog still surrounded him, yet wherever he looked, he could see through it. Clouds of light and distant stars surrounded them. Far off, some of the many-colored shapes moved randomly in a slow dance. A bright comet streaked across the sky before him and disappeared into the distance. Some directions were blocked with gray fog eventually; others seemed clear for infinite distances, yet full of colored mist as well.

"What happened? Who was that? Where are we?"

"We are still in the Quantum realm, still in the Overworld. You jumped and flew off your pode. Don't worry. You can return there with ease. You cannot lose yourself here even if you do not know where you are."

"There was someone sitting there. My legs were right inside them."

"That someone was you. Remember, I told you to think about standing, and you did. This is your mind, Cari. You still picture yourself as a whole man, but your body is back there. Back there twice, actually. Your physical body is still sitting within your pode in the Víre Tussa back in physical Fairinhorst. Your spirit body is still sitting bonded to your pode here in the Quantum realm. Your spirit mind is here with me."

Carimus glanced down at himself, filled with doubt. What he saw surprised him again. He was no longer wearing the green tunic and sash of a novice seeker, but instead, his old, familiar clothes—the comfortable ones he wore every day at Castle Draconis when he and his brothers would jog from their rooms up to the Eyrie and back for meals. Suddenly, he felt very homesick. "My old clothes. I haven't worn these for weeks." *I left them in my room the night we ran away.*

"I suppose you think we are talking, that I am speaking words and you are hearing them?"

He nodded. "Yes, of course."

"Your mind interprets things in as familiar a way as possible. It is human nature. It is why some illusions are so insidious. People tend to see what they expect to see, or, worse, what they want to see."

"Donel trained me a little in this. He couldn't spend much time with me, though. He had to get Art ready to clear the Castle and slay the Abominations there."

The Angellar clasped his hand. "I am holding your hand. Am I not?"

"You are."

"Remember what I said a moment ago? There is no down here. Look at your feet, please."

Cari complied. There was nothing there for a very long

way—twisted bands of color, miles away. He was standing on nothing! A small moan escaped his lips, but the firm grasp on his hand assured him he was stationary. He swallowed. "Why aren't we falling?" he whispered.

"Think of standing back on your pode." Her grip tightened slightly. "Picture us standing there as we were a moment ago."

"I don't like the thought of standing half in and half out of myself like that."

"Don't think about your body there. Think of your Telepse-taeth, your silver cord, your soul tie. Look at it now, and in your mind, just follow it back to your pode. As quickly as thought, Carimus, be there."

He looked at his waist and found the shimmery cord. He could see it ran off into the distance far below him. He could follow it with his eyes. Just that quickly, his pode was drawing near, and then he was standing on it again, this time directly behind the body he knew was himself, sitting there. The Angellar released his hand and floated between him and her gigantic face, which still hovered there. Its eyes watched him just as the smaller Angellar did.

"Your physical body is still within your pode in the Vire Tussa. Your mind and spirit are here within the Taväri Ambar, the Quantum realm. Your mind is the master here. Will your spirit body to meld with your Telepse-taeth. Fill it with your spirit, your essence. Picture the seventh rune on your bracelet, Sowela: completion, wholeness. Use the regalos. Meld your spirit body into the cord. Your mind is the Master. Your mind controls your spirit, binds it."

"You dance with destiny, Carimus deDraconis. Yours is the chosen bloodline. You and your brothers must play your roles. You each have a part to play. I have foreseen so many endings, and most of them have sorrow, tears, and pain. Some paths look sunny at the start but lead to a bitter end. There are ways that appear as if there is no hope. Danger looms everywhere, with hideous ends if the wrong steps are taken. But these are the only paths which lead to the desired outcome. You and yours have the strength and the will to tweak Fate toward your desired ends as you walk the Glory Road."

As Carimus listened to her words, he watched his spirit body sitting there, cross-legged on the pode. At first, nothing changed, but as he concentrated, small bits of his seated body transformed into tiny colored blocks. They were cunningly crafted and neatly stacked to form his body. As he watched, some of the blocks went flying off one by one, piece by piece, from the motionless form of his spirit body to fuse with his silver tether. The cord was only a few feet long now, where it emerged from the silver dot on the pode to connect to his body. The tiny colored blocks were hitting the cord, shattering like drops of water and rapidly absorbing into the Vire Tussa. Faster and faster, the form sitting on the pode crumbled away and was absorbed by the silver cord. Then it was gone.

"Very good. Now we are ready to begin. Much of what I am going to tell you will probably not make any sense now. You need not be afraid to ask questions, but I fear many of the answers will be just as mysterious as the questions, and so bring you little relief."

The Angellar clapped her hands, and with a flash, everything changed. Once again, she was sitting upon her floating rose throne. Carimus was sitting in a comfortable chair facing her. It was not the same room where the throne had floated before, though there were similarities. The smooth, marble-like floor had the same twisted star inlay. The nine huge candles still circled the room, providing a bright white light. The walls were smooth and dark green. Unlike the first room, this room had a door on the wall to his left—a brown wooden door with a rounded top, looking like a door that belonged in a simple cottage.

"The Quantum realm may exist in many ways all at once, as if it is inside everything and everything is inside it, all at the same time. One form it may take is this." She spread her hands, all-encompassing. "Some call this the Spirit World or the OverWorld. I am very powerful here in the Tavári Ambar, but I only have power in a small area. The Vire Tussa is my stronghold. My mortal remains are encased within a crystal root. That is my center. My mind's kingdom is smallest here, where I am most real. My power diminishes rapidly as you move away. After a distance, I can do no more than look and talk. Farther, and I can only communicate with a very few places that have the means to receive my thoughts. However, here within the Quantum realm, I can move in different directions, other probabilities, and the farther I go from this probability, the more it changes. I have more power in distant places. I can see more of the *what may be*. Unfortunately, knowing something might happen is not knowing what will happen. Just the fact you sometimes have knowledge causes things not to happen. The farther away you are, the more 'mights' and 'maybes' exist. Do you understand?"

"Does this mean you don't know where Duka is?"

The Angellar laughed. "Oh, Cari … Oh …"

"I don't think it's funny!" He crossed his arms.

"No … It is not … Forgive me; I am not laughing at you. Just the opposite. I am laughing at a world which never fails to astound me. Your love and loyalty to your brother are so commendable, so refreshing." Her face became more somber. "There are places I have no power, places where I cannot see." She shook her head. "I look at probabilities. In many, I see your brother return to Veda. But sometimes his return is not for the world's well-being rather, it brings dire woe. This we must avoid." The Angellar gazed at him with a somber expression.

He felt his heart sink. "Return from where?"

"From across the Sea of Dragons. Duka is in Renn. More than that, I cannot see."

"Renn? How could he be there? What happened?"

"The storm that night was more than just a simple storm ... I think. I do not know for certain, but I feel it. There were more forces involved than meet the eye."

She sighed. "Renn is not an easy place to investigate. Neither farseeing nor foreseeing can accurately broach the qulan field that bounds that land."

"How can a qulan field surround an entire land?"

"It has been that way since the time of the Reckoning. I cannot explain the hows; as for the whys ... well, they are not exactly clear. Other Powers rule in that land. Tiameng is either imprisoned by the field that surrounds Renn, or perhaps she created and controls it and uses it as a shield to hide behind.

"As for Duka, I know my niece was involved with the storm somehow, but Serene no longer speaks with me." Carimus caught a momentary glimpse of sadness flitting across her face. "She cut the ties between us long ago, shortly after the Reckoning."

"But what can we do? Duke doesn't belong there! We need to rescue him! He is lost and alone." He held up his hands and looked at her imploringly.

"Duka is beyond any aid we could give at this time,

Carimus. Your brothers, Artos and Bortis, will soon face mortal danger. They need you to help them first; else, Duka will not have a home to return to. I have foreseen that possibility, but there are other futures, happier futures. You need to strive with Artos to ensure that terribly sad future never comes to pass."

Artie knows he is going into danger. Donel has told him. He has Bort to help. "But ... I thought you summoned me here to help me find Duka. Artos is far away. How can I help him?"

"I sent you that rune bracelet years ago because I foresaw you might need it to journey here someday." She gazed at him with a thoughtful expression. "At that time, I did not know why."

"You may indeed have been sent here, but it was not I who sent for you. However, I do foresee deeds that only you can perform. I see a vital role for you at this time, which is why I am teaching you these things—things you would normally not learn for months or even years as a Seeker of Enlightenment. But first, you must learn to walk before you try to run, much less fly."

What should I do? "Who sent me here, then? Was it Donel?"

"No, Donel would have said so. There are forces at play here which I cannot explain to you. I have foreseen paths that could turn to darkness. I can only ask that you trust that I wish what is best for Veda, for all Veda, and that means placing your brother Artos upon his rightful throne. Will you help me in this task?"

"Of course I'll help Art," whispered Carimus. "He should be king. He is decent and kind. What can I do?" *I'm sorry, Duke, I tried ... I really tried. You'd want me to help Artie. I know you would.*

"In a short time, Artos's party will reach the Nénarambal Tirion. Ages ago, weapons were stored in the upper armory. The Starstone itself is located there, though it has been damaged. I have foreseen that Artos will find the weapons in the armory that were forged to be used in the struggle against Demigoran's greatest servants—the Abominations. In one future, I have foreseen Artos taking the wrong weapon, and it fails against the Abomination. In another, I see him attempting to attune to more than one weapon. This he must not do! Artos is already bound to his crysword. If he tries to bind more than one other crystal weapon without the proper training, the overload of binding energy will be devastating—not only to him, but to whoever is close by at that time. In my vision, I saw Artos and Bortis both killed, along with at least one other person."

Carimus felt a cold shiver and jumped to his feet. "No! You have to warn him!"

"I told you my power is diminished away from my center. A qulan field proscribes my entrance. I can be invited to enter, but I cannot force my presence there uninvited. You, however, are blood of House deDraconis."

"How can that help? I can't get there in a few days. It's too far away."

"You are not bound within the Tavári Ambar as I am. Let me show you. Come with me."

The Angellar stood, and her rose throne silently vanished. She walked to the door, turned, and waited. Carimus looked behind him; the chair where he had been sitting had vanished as well. The Angellar gestured toward the door, and it swung open, revealing a bright, sunny day beyond. She motioned for him to venture forth. He stepped through the doorway and stopped short, looking around in wonder. *Where am I?*

For a moment, he thought he was on the branch of a thousand-year tree. There were leaves above and before him, and he stood on a smooth brown surface. The melodious chanting of Fairinhorst rang through the air. The sun was shining over his shoulder, throwing his shadow before him. Looking to his right, he was gazing down at a park with flower beds and verdant lawns surrounded by a hedgerow. He must have been sixty or seventy feet off the ground. *This is amazing. I wish Duke could see this* ... Beyond the hedge was nothing but a murky gray fog. Glancing up, he saw the stars shining down through the leaves. Wait! Stars? He looked behind him, and yes; the sun was also shining down through the branches.

The Angellar took his hand. "Birca is the regalo of healing and of growth. Hold it in your thoughts."

"Birca! Yes, Donel showed me my regalos; that was the first one." Carimus nodded and closed his eyes. As Donel taught him, he pictured the rune that resembles the letter 'B' in the forefront of his mind.

Just as he did, the Angellar took a step to the right, pulling him along after her. He gasped in a brief moment of dizziness, then he was stepping into the garden. He looked around behind him, expecting to see the enormous tree. There was only a waist-high rosebush. He was standing on a path in the center of a flowerbed in an area circled by a low hedge. Beyond the hedge, the land became more rugged, a misty area with underbrush and small bare trees scattered about in the distance. Further away was a low range of hills, which disappeared into the mist.

Cari looked up. It was broad daylight, the sun high in the sky. But the sky was a deep, dark indigo, covered in stars of all colors. The deep blue faded as it wove into the fog as it neared the hill-filled horizon. A full moon faced the sun across the sky. It was as if he stood in a clearing surrounded by fog. The air was still, nary a breeze. The only sound was the soft background music interwoven with the ever-present chanting of Fairinhorst.

He looked at the Angellar. "Where are we?"

"We are where we started. Still in the Tavári Ambar and at my center within the Víre Tussa. From here, I send myself forward to see the path of the bloodlines. I see the number and the colors needed for the cryswords for the blood of the Great Houses. I command them, and my song smiths sing them forth on the hidden forges. I send them out as birth gifts from the Fairborn to the Great Houses. Only the Houses deDarrellyel and deSpryngdal treat their crystal as if it were anything less than their due. The Houses of deAnson and deHerndar treat their crystal as if it were a wergild or a blood-tithing. The other three, including yours, Cari, just seem to consider it normal. They accept without question. Just as they accept without question that I know how many will be needed and what hue they shall be to reflect the regalos of those who are to bond with them. I have had angry deAnsons demanding more swords. Once, one family complained because I sent too many."

The Angellar suddenly started growing! She looked down at him as a giant would look at a child. Then she began to shrink. As her head came down, her feet floated up, and she shrank smaller and smaller until she was the size of a doll. She swooped around his head twice, then hovered in mid-air right before him.

"Birca is your major gift. It should be easy for you to control. You can be whatever size you want to be when you are within the Quantum realm, Cari. Make it as natural as breathing is to your physical body. Be as big or as small as you need to be. Your mind is master. Picture the reality as you want it to be. Begin." She floated closer and stared into his eyes.

"I don't know how." He looked around. "My Uncle Cameron

used screens to teach us things. So did Donel. Don't you use screens?"

"There is no need for screens here. You do know how. I told you to step out of your spirit body, but you are the one who did so. I told you to follow your cord back to your pode, but you brought yourself back. I told you to follow me here. I showed you how by doing so and pulling you along, but you are the one who changed. I didn't change you. You used your regalo. I can see your potential, Carimus deDraconis. Your brother Artos will be able to use any of the regalos in the physical realm. Here in the quantum realm, you can do the same."

The Angellar floated back a few feet away and crossed her arms as she looked at him. "On your bracelet, how many runes are there? Don't look! You have owned that bracelet for six years. You have looked at it countless times. How many runes?"

The Angellar grew back to her normal size and stood facing him. But she wasn't on the ground. She was floating at least six inches above it.

Carimus kept his left wrist down at his side and looked straight ahead, picturing his rune bracelet in his mind. There were three runes on the near side and seven more on the far side.

"Ten! There are ten bangles, ten runes."

The Angellar didn't answer but tilted her head slightly, looked back at him and arched her brow as if questioning his answer. He examined the image in his mind and realized his mistake. "Eleven runes! There is a different rune on every bangle and an eleventh rune on the back that is the same on each. Raido, the Rune of journeys. The one that looks like an 'R.'"

"Why aren't you changing size? We can talk as you practice.

Begin!"

He felt flustered. She kept changing the subject. She expected him to do every little thing she said and still listen to her every word. It was unreasonable. It was. He pictured himself growing big just so he could look down at her the way his Uncle Cameron had looked down at him when he made a mistake. And she started to grow smaller. No! He was getting bigger, just like he had thought. Feeling excited, he thought of being small, very small, and suddenly, he was shrinking rapidly. Hurriedly, he willed himself to stop and looked over at her. Eye to knee. She was now easily four times the size he was. *I did it! I changed size.*

"That's better. See how easy it is? Your mind is the master here. Remember, you don't need to keep your feet on the ground either. Nothing will pull you down. Your mind is keeping your feet on the ground, and your mind can tell them to hover in midair. Your Telepse-taeth is firmly bound to you and to your pode. Take Raido in your thoughts. Raido is the regalo of movement. With Birca controlling your body's size, you can use Raido to move from place to place. You can do this, Carimus deDraconis. I know. I have watched you do it."

Carimus pictured Raido in his mind as Donel had taught him and thought of himself flying gently up into the air—and he was. *I'm flying.* He pictured himself doing a slow backwards somersault, and he did. He went a little faster, straight up into the sky. It was exhilarating; it was wonderful. *I can fly!* He thought himself back to his normal size and went rising, wheeling, turning end over end, spinning as he did so. He swooped down, then soared upwards. He dove toward the ground and swooped up again at the last moment before crashing into the park. He flew around the Angellar in a lazy circle, lying on his side.

"I will leave you to your practice. I will not be gone long. Keep the garden here as your anchor spot. Mentally place your pode right over there. Think it so." She pointed to a spot on the ground that was completely bare, although he would have sworn it hadn't existed a moment before.

He wafted himself over and landed beside the bare spot. He thought about his pode, concentrating on the spot his cord blended into its surface. Suddenly, his pode was floating like a lily pad inches above the bare spot.

"I did it!" he crowed. He looked around proudly, but realized he was all alone. The Angellar had vanished.

"Well, she said to practice," he mused aloud. Flying was fun. If she hadn't told him to, he would have anyway. He amused himself by soaring around the edge of the hedge surrounding the park. He swooped and soared; he turned somersaults in the air and rolled over, floating on his back, exulting in the freedom of flying. He decided to see how fast he could go around and around, but the park was too small, and the circles were making him dizzy. Instead, he flew up as fast as he could while he counted to ten.

When he reached ten, he willed himself to a stop and looked back the way he had come. There was a tiny white dot a very long way away. All around were distant colored lights and shapes. He was floating alone in the night sky, surrounded by stars. He could see the faint outline of his Telepse-taeth, his silver lifeline, as he now thought of it. He imagined he was back at the end of the cord at his pode, and suddenly he was standing beside it. *This is real! I can do it. I wish Duke was here. We'd really have some fun.* Suddenly he was looking into a barn, and Duka was there, offering some hay to a small grey donkey. Then the scene was gone.

"DUKE!" he shouted, looking around wildly, but the vision had disappeared. He was floating alone within the quantum realm. Had he really seen him?

"Practice, practice, practice ..." he sighed to himself and willed himself to soar again. Quickly, he lost himself in exhilaration. Never in his imagination had he dreamed of such sensations. He shot upwards through the ether, feeling like one of the fireworks they fired from the battlements of Castle Draconis to celebrate the summer solstice. Rising, wheeling, turning, spinning, soaring up forever in the star shine. It was glorious! It was freedom! He did a series of floating cartwheels in a huge circle surrounded by distant stars.

Chapter Twenty-Three:

The Darkest Depths

25

SHUN THE DARK

CARIMUS

10/9/1971 ar

AFTER WHAT FELT LIKE A SHORT TIME, he heard a voice within his mind. "Come back, Cari."

He imagined himself swooping down and standing next to his pode. As quick as thought, he was there. The Angellar was standing a few feet away. She smiled when he appeared, and when she nodded, he thought he detected an approving glint in her eye. He bowed low before her.

"I believe you have become accustomed to traveling within the Quantum realm, Cari. Very good."

"Angellar, I saw Duke. It was just for a moment, but he was safe. He was in a barn feeding a donkey. Then he was gone, and I didn't see him anymore."

The Angellar's face took on a serious expression. "Carimus, I must warn you. The Quantum realm is filled with danger. You are safe here, but once you go beyond my borders, you will lose my protection. There are places you must avoid. There are beings which would feed upon your mind and spirit. You must learn to trust yourself and always be cautious. Your senses may deceive you. In order to make sense of the incomprehensible, your mind will sometimes reshape it into something more familiar ... something understandable. At times, this can assist you in avoiding potential dangers that could seriously harm you. At other times, it can leave you vulnerable to forces which could destroy you or drive you insane."

"Shun darkness and cold. Such places can be lairs for great evil. Beings that dwell in the Tavári Ambar cannot cross into our world unless we invite them. But those who find them seldom return. They are few and far between. One of the worst of such places is that near to Donel's Crystal Tower: the Hellesgate. In the physical realm, it is a place of colored flame, but in the Quantum realm, it is a place of impenetrable darkness and extreme cold. Demigoran cannot escape through the Tavári Ambar, but he can trap others if they venture within his grasp."

"Demigoran? Is that why Donel does not leave the Crystal Tower?"

"Yes. He is the watchman for that horrid place."

"He said his duty did not allow him to leave the tower."

"Yes. At least three times during his tenure, someone attempted to breach his qulan. He thinks all three attempts were by the Abominations. He is probably right, although he saw no sign of who made the last attempt."

As Carimus watched, a small green shoot pushed up out of the ground behind the Angellar and rapidly and enthusiastically grew into a leafy green throne on which the Angellar sat down. She gestured behind him, and he looked to find a second throne had grown up behind him. Tentatively, he also sat.

"Time grows short, Carimus. Soon you must away to warn your brother of the dangers he may unwittingly loose upon himself."

He felt a tremor of consternation. "You said we had a few days. Has something happened?"

"Time is different here. It seldom seems to match well with our expectations. Even now, Artos and his group have entered Starstone Tower. Soon they will reach the Armory. You need to warn him. I have looked at the probabilities. Mohattri is the Abomination he must arm for, and he must not try to bond to more than one of the starcrystal weapons. You must travel to Starstone Tower and warn him."

"But how will I find him in time?"

"Use your mind, Carimus deDraconis. Travel through the Tavári Ambar."

He stared at her in dismay, her words ringing in his mind. DeDraconis! How many times had he gazed through the mists across the Loch O' Wrens at Starstone Tower? Hundreds. He knew where he must go.

He nodded once, leaped to his feet, and blazed off into the star-filled sky. Art was going into danger and didn't know it. There was no time to lose.

"Carimus, I have ..." The words of the Angellar abruptly ended. He must have traveled beyond her realm. There was no time to go back. He would just have to make do.

In an instant, he was looking down out of the night sky at the fog-shrouded upper battlements of Castle Draconis, his home. He felt something tighten inside his chest as he swooped low and hovered over the Eyrie, remembering the panicked flight from their home and the monster that murdered his father and uncles. *It seems like it was years since we ran away, but it was only a few weeks ago. So much has happened, so much has changed.*

It was unnaturally quiet now. The music and familiar chanting had ceased. Or had it? He listened very carefully and realized it was still there in the background, ever so faint, but it was still there. He turned his attention across the loch.

At first, he couldn't locate Starstone Tower. The all-encompassing fog of the OverWorld surrounded him as completely as the mists shrouded the mountains encircling his home. The fog obscured anything beyond his immediate vicinity; the farther away, the thicker the fog. Just thinking of Starstone Tower didn't help. *I know it's right across the loch.* He utilized his sense of direction to find due north, then gazed in that direction, concentrating on seeing true. The fog parted like a curtain, rolling back. *There it is.* Huddled at the end of a misty tunnel stood Starstone Tower. He willed himself across the loch and was instantly floating a few yards away from a windowless gray stone wall that rose high over his head.

Whoa! Too close. He floated backward, away from the tower, and tried to think. *The Angellar said Artie was almost to the Armory. Where would the Armory be?*

Slowly, he floated to his right, moving around the tower and inspecting it from all sides. The building loomed oppressively tall through the mists, all dark gray stone unbroken by a single window. It was a many-spired castle with a huge main tower rising from the center and three smaller towers offset on three sides. *I never realized just how big this place is. It's every bit as big as Castle Draconis.* How would he ever find Art?

Carimus remembered all the times the four of them had played hide-and-seek growing up in Castle Draconis. He wasn't the worst of his brothers at that game, or the best either. Duka usually won. But he and Art had been fairly evenly matched.

All three of them were far better than Bort, who rarely found anyone and hated to play. *Now I know how Bort felt. There must be some way I can find them.*

He tried concentrating on Artos. Nothing happened; no window appeared in the fog showing him his brother. Instead, a silvery glaze covered the tower wall in front of him, then faded away.

"What was that?" he asked the surrounding fog. "I bet that's the qulan field the Angellar spoke of. They're on the other side. I'll have to go into the tower to locate them."

As quick as thought, he swooped around the castle once more, then stopped, hovering before the only way into the building he could find: the imposing double doors. He inspected them warily. He remembered Bortis getting shocked when he tried to enter the Crystal Tower uninvited. There was no doorknob. On each door was a blue crystal plate, as there had been on the Hall of Mirrors back home. For a moment, he panicked. His Uncle Cameron had keyed him to the door at the Hall of Mirrors. There was no one to key him here. Could he open these doors? He placed his right hand on the crystal plate. With a tingling feeling, white sparks burst out and harmlessly dissipated, as if trying to avoid his touch. Instead of the smooth crystal he expected, it felt as though he was pushing his hand through jelly. As he watched, it disappeared into the door.

"Whoa!" He yanked his hand back, looked at it, and then the door. Both seemed unharmed. "That's weird!" he said, then, gingerly, he reached out with his fingers spread before him. Just before he touched the surface of the door, there was the tingle of a qulan field, and again the white sparks flew, but other than a faint tingling, he felt nothing except a slight resistance.

Although he wasn't breathing, he took a deep breath. *Here*

goes nothing. Holding his left hand in front of his face, just in case, he boldly floated toward the door. For a moment, his entire body tingled as he passed through. He floated into an immense room with rows of balconies looking down from the upper floors. Each floor was lined with doors—dozens of doors on each side. Suddenly, the enormity of the task before him became crystal clear. There must be hundreds of rooms here. Hundreds! He had to find Art. And soon. Before Art destroyed himself.

He looked down. The floor was covered with nearly an inch of dust, and the dust was undisturbed. He turned around and floated back to the door, looking for tracks. There they were! They went up a set of spiral stairs on the southern side of the doorway. He floated along above the tracks, following them to the first balcony. Looking ahead, it appeared some doors had been opened, but the tracks went on. He ignored the rooms and followed the trail along the balcony. At the western end, it proceeded down another spiral stair back to the ground floor and led to the door in the center of the western wall. He paused for a moment at the door and tested for another qulan field. Finding none, he floated through into another enormous room. The tracks led across the room, skirting a grand central stairway that spiraled upwards and stopped before another door on the opposite side of the room.

He started floating across. A set of tracks left the group and proceeded to doors in the north and south, but the main body of footprints went west, so he followed them. As he reached the room's center, he came to a sudden stop. In the blink of an eye, the surrounding temperature dropped from pleasantly neutral to unbearably cold. He shivered and backed up, remembering the Angellar's words. She had said to beware cold and dark. His instincts were screaming Danger! Danger!

Hurriedly, he glanced around. Everything was quiet. Nothing except the temperature had changed. Everything was still. It all looked normal. He looked up. The stairs wound up into an impenetrable black cloud at the upper levels. *And there's the darkness.* Waves of cold descended from the gloom. There was a presence there; he could feel it. A horrible evil was lurking in the upper reaches of the main tower. *Is it the Abomination? Where is Art?*

He felt a brief flicker in his mind, and for an instant, he looked into the eyes of his brother, as if they were looking at each other through a window. Then the vision was gone in a blinding burst of white sparks.

Instinctively, Carimus threw his hands up before his eyes, momentarily blinded. Blinking rapidly, he rubbed his now-watering eyes. When he could see again, he found himself hovering above the battlements encircling the Eyrie at Castle Draconis. *That was Art! How did I get back here?*

He gazed to the north, and Starstone Tower looked back mockingly across the loch, faintly visible through a tunnel in the thick fog. *You can't get rid of me that easily.*

He pictured in his mind the room with the grand stairway and willed himself back to that spot, but instead found himself hovering before the double doors at the front of the tower.

"What if I don't want to go back in through the front door?" he protested. His voice sounded muffled, as though the ever-present fog were swallowing his words. He decided to experiment. Floating a few feet to the left side of the door, he reached out to touch the dark stone wall. He felt the tingle of the qulan field as his hand discharged some harmless white sparks, then he was pushing against unyielding stone. He moved back in front of the doors and tried again. His hand felt the familiar tingle, then it felt as though his hand was pushing through something soft but yielding.

I guess I have to use the front door. He pushed through into the entry chamber, then paused; something felt different. He gazed around the room. Everything looked the same as before, but then the room had felt empty. Now it felt as though a thousand hostile eyes were staring at him. He could see the door at the far end of the room where he wanted to go, but there was no way he was just going to float across the center of the room. It felt too exposed somehow. He turned and followed the left-hand wall, dodging around the spiral stairs and staying under the shadow of the balcony above.

When he reached the western door, he hesitated for a moment and prepared himself. He mentally chanted the canticle of Fairinhorst *Ohh... ahh... ahh... ohh... Ohh... maa... maa... ohh...* then floated through. On the other side, he came to an abrupt halt, the chant lost to his thoughts as terror gripped his heart.

Where the grand central stairway had stood only minutes before, there was now a boiling cloud of pure darkness. There was something in the darkness; he could sense it, a feeling of malicious evil wound through with hatred and mixed with fear. He remembered the terror he felt looking into the eyes of the Abomination Kargyn. This was worse, much worse. And it was looking for him!

Chapter Twenty-Four:

Carimus at Starstone

26

I HEARD YOU, LITTLE MOUSE

CARIMUS

10/9/1971 ar

Carimus shivered and nearly turned and bolted back through the door. The Angellar had told him to stay away from the cold and the dark. But Art had crossed this room, and he had to find him and warn him. He pictured the Rune Algiz and envisioned a golden helm protecting his head, his Mindshield.

He felt some of the terror melt away; his mind was hidden now from whatever was shrouded within the cloud of cold and darkness. He needed a plan. He needed to find Art.

First, I need to make myself unnoticeable. I wish I were invisible. No one has taught me that. The Angellar made me waste time changing size instead of teaching me something useful ... Wait! What if I were very small, like a mouse or, better yet, a fly? I could zoom around the room, over to the other door.

Carimus pictured himself shrinking, and the room grew larger and larger. When he reached the size of a horsefly, he stopped shrinking and swooped down within a few inches of the floor and sped off, following the wall around the room. He was not going anywhere near that dark maelstrom in the room's center.

In a few moments, he reached the far side of the room. Without hesitating, he turned and, like a mouse fleeing from a cat, he sped at the door, intending to push right through. With a flurry of white sparks, he jolted to a halt, bounced backwards and landed on the floor stunned, half buried in the deep dust.

What happened? He opened his eyes and hurriedly rolled over, peering out of the dust back at the cloud of darkness. It seemed unchanged. He was still very small, and whatever had happened didn't seem to have been noticed. He hoped.

If the white sparks were any indication, he had run afoul of a qulan field. He had passed through the one surrounding the tower with no problem. Why had this one stopped him? What was the difference? Was he going too fast? His Mindshield! Donel had told him that a Mindshield prevented him from interacting with the quanti. Could it prevent him from moving through a qulan field? Apparently, it could.

Only one way to find out. He crept close to the door and released his mental shield. He felt a surge of raw animal terror and lay huddled, gasping on the floor, his eyes clenched tightly shut. He could feel something of terrible power searching for him. He had to get away! In desperation, he bolted toward the door, his only thought to escape the horrid monster that was seeking him.

There was another flurry of white sparks, but he pushed through the yielding substance of the door and collapsed on the floor of the room on the other side. The crushing fear was gone. It disappeared as soon as he passed through the qulan.

The first thing Carimus noticed in the new room was the

lack of dust. In his tiny form, he had been nearly engulfed before he pushed through the door. Now, there was none, and the floor was spotless. The second thing he noticed was the light blue lattice of energy that spiraled up in the room's center. The lattice formed a frame encircling a flight of stone steps that spiraled into the upper reaches of the room.

Looking up, he could see the forms of three people standing on a walkway that led from the top of the stairs to a balcony. He willed himself back to his normal size and floated up to greet them. He recognized all three of them, but to his disappointment, neither of his brothers was present. It was Jaek, Tirinvo's bodyguard, and Kae, Joy's older sister, and they were conversing with Seth deDarrellyel, who was wearing the robes of a druid. He had expected to surprise them when he floated up and hovered in the air at their level, but they didn't seem to notice him. Both Fairborn looked right through him as they kept watch. They seemed to be speaking to each other, but the sound of their voices was so faint he could not make out the words. Seth was staring intently at a point over their heads. Carimus saw that although the stone steps ended at the walkway, the blue energy continued, forming stairs that led up to the room's ceiling. Seth's attention was focused on that point.

That must be where Art and Bort are. He floated up and pushed through the ceiling into another room. There they were! Art, Bort, and Angel too. As he approached, Artos placed his hand in the center of a square of blue energy positioned on the front of a cabinet. Angel and Bortis watched, standing behind him, each looking over a shoulder. He moved around Angel, and as the cabinet opened, he stopped next to his brother.

"Art ... Art!" he shouted. His brother twitched as if he had heard something and looked around. Carimus saw his brother's lips moving, but the words were faint and muddled, unintelligible. Oh no! How could he tell him which weapon to choose? *Why didn't I think to ask The Angellar how I was supposed to communicate with Art? That was probably what she was about to tell me when I rushed off. I could be back there in an instant and then come back, but there's no time.*

Artos was looking into a cabinet which held five ivory-hued cubes. Carimus marveled at the sight. The cubes were on fire! Each cube was burning with a colored flame. The one on the top shelf burned a brilliant red. The two on the bottom flickered with vibrant green flames, and on the middle shelf, one burned bright blue and the other with pure white fire. Before each cube was a label scribed with a name—the one burning with white fire had 'Mohattri' inscribed on it. That was the one the Angellar had said Art must choose. Now how to let him know?

"You want the white one, Art! The white one!" he shouted. It was no use. Art couldn't hear him anymore than he could see him. There must be a way. *Think!* The Angellar wouldn't have sent him if there wasn't.

Carimus felt his gut clench in fear as Art's hand hovered above the cube of green fire. The cube labeled 'Babich.' The other green fire cube was labeled 'Kargyn.' A wave of fear rippled over him as the Beast Man's face materialized in the fire, just as it had that night in the wilds, its wicked eyes fixed on him. Art's hand slowly moved toward the one labeled Babich before it abruptly changed direction and picked up Kargyn's green cube. Artos ignored the green fire completely, held the cube up before his face, and examined it closely. As he scrutinized it, the cube's top unfolded, revealing the source of the green flame. A bright green crystal ring blazed fiercely within the cube. Art's hand reached toward it slowly.

Carimus screamed with all his being. "No! Art ... No! ... Take the white one! The white one!"

He saw Art's hand jerk away from the green ring, and the cube's lid folded shut.

WHO IS THERE? ... WHO? clamored a voice in his mind.

Carimus's skin crawled as the words reverberated in his mind. It wasn't like the voice of the Angellar, warm and friendly when she conversed to his mind. This mind may have been human once, but any humanity it had possessed had long since been consumed by darkness.

Art set the cube with green fire down and looked at each of the cubes. Carimus nearly cheered when Art reached for the one with the white flames.

I HEARD YOU LITTLE MOUSE came the voice again. **I FELT YOU CREEPING ABOUT ... WHO ARE YOU?**

He cowered motionless and tried not to even think. He did not want the owner of this mind to find him. It searched for him in the OverWorld. He felt it, a presence that sent chills down his spine. It was as if two people in a dense fog, unable to see each other but hearing one another's voices, would know each other's general direction. The other voice had heard him but couldn't pinpoint his exact location behind the qulan field. He, however, could make a very good guess where the voice came from—the cloud of darkness and cold. He must not shout again.

Artos opened the white cube, ignoring the flames of white fire, and looked at the white crystal ring inside.

"That's it, Art," he whispered to himself, and nodded happily. "Yes ... yes."

Artos took the flaming white crystal ring and slipped it on his left hand. As Carimus watched, the ring flared brightly, and the white fire spread to engulf Artos completely. He blazed with white light, which slowly disappeared as if he were absorbing it. He stood dazed for a moment, then recovered and spoke to Bortis, who nodded and summoned his sword. Carimus sighed with relief. They were going to leave now. Art had the right weapon.

Then Artos reached out with his free hand and picked up the red cube. He was going to take another weapon!

"Art! No!" Cari shouted, forgetting his vow.

YOU THERE! ... WHO ARE YOU? shouted the voice.

Carimus could feel its attention. It knew he was here! He looked at Art. "RUN AWAY! GO! NOW!" He could feel a cloud of cold black ink spreading through the OverWorld toward him. He had to flee. Now!

Carimus jumped and found himself back above the Eyrie. He spun about and focused across the loch at Starstone Tower. The central spire of the castle was enshrouded by a writhing black cloud. With his mind's eye, he could see probes of darkness like murky tentacles darting from the cloud casting here and there through the OverWorld, trying to ensnare him. It might find Art! This was his fault. He had to distract it, till Art got away.

"I'M HERE! I'M HERE!" he shouted at the beast through the fog shrouded OverWorld. There was a crackle in his mind and he felt it become aware of him and his location. He could feel it tensing as if to spring. It was coming for him!

As quick as thought, he was racing away along his silver cord, the darkness right behind him. There was a flash of silvery light, and his pode appeared before him. He crashed into it and felt himself twirling around and around. When he opened his eyes, he was sitting in his pode as if he had been meditating, the soothing green, bell-shaped wall surrounding him. Even as he watched, it raised into the air. He was back in the meditation chamber in the Vire Tussa, in Fairinhorst. He fell over onto his side and fainted.

Part Eight

At Starstone Tower

STARSTONE TOWER
THE MOUNTAINS OF MYST
HOUSE DEDRACONIS
THE MOUNTAINS OF MYST
LOCH O' WRENS
WEST DRAGON FALLS
EAST DRAGON FALLS
ZIMMER
CASTLE DRACONIS
PERN
ENKLE
DRAGON LOCH
AMERLY

Chapter Twenty-Five:

The Tower at Last

27

TRACKS IN
THE DUST

ARTOS

10/9/1971 ar

DAWN WAS BREAKING and the pervasive fog had rolled aside when they rounded the mountain of black stone called Black Peak. Artos paused and looked south across Loch O` Wrens at Castle Draconis, four miles to the south; the first view of his home since they had taken flight almost a month before. Usually, the mists on the northern side of the loch kept the castle and tower hidden from each other, but this morning the fog had rolled aside to allow him a glimpse of his estranged home. The castle appeared deserted, with no sign of movement on the Eyrie battlements or the airships docks below. *It looks lonely,* he thought.

To their east was a large shelf of flat gray stone covered with white markings, some of which resembled the Runes of the regalos. At the far end of the shelf, small, rocky hills rose as if to protect the tower from the loch or to hide the tower's base from anyone looking from Castle Draconis. As they watched, the fog grew up around them again, hiding their home from view.

Seth led them to the northeast, and they approached the tower's base.

"I never realized how big this place is," said Bortis. "It's huge." Artos nodded in agreement.

Upon reaching the tower, Artos directed them to the north side, where the entrance awaited them. He looked for the red spires Donel had shown when they had scried here before, but they were not visible, hidden in the fog. The front doors stood closed, and a dusting of snow lay upon the ground before the doorway, unmarred by tracks of any sort.

"Here we are," said Seth, stopping a dozen feet from the entrance. "I have fulfilled my duty as your guide, Art. From here, the burden lies upon your shoulders. If you wish, I will accompany you further, but if you no longer desire my company, I understand. I would ask that none of you reveal the secret. Most people look upon shapeshifters as evil, and the Sky Sect does not encourage them to think otherwise."

"Your company is always welcome, Seth," replied Artos. "I would like to have a conversation about such matters sometime in the future, but I know you are a good man, and your secrets are yours to keep as you see fit." He looked around at the rest of the party.

"You already know my feelings on that subject," said Angel.

"And mine," added Kae.

"I have come to know you on this journey, Seth deDarrellyel," said Jaek. "Although our time together has not been excessive, I have seen nothing of you that would make me doubt your character."

All eyes turned to Bortis.

"Our Uncle Cameron taught us that Abominations were

evil before one murdered him. Donel has told us that not all shapeshifters are Abominations." Bortis shrugged. "I think I can believe both my uncles. I was surprised when I spoke before. I spoke in haste. We were friends before I knew you to be a druid. We have journeyed and fought together. We may have our work before us if Cari learns this, but Art and I can handle the Squirt." He motioned for Seth to proceed.

A light snow was falling as they approached the doors to the tower. Seth led the way, motioning for the others to stay back as he studied the ground before the doorway.

"It's no use," he sighed. "Just enough eddies in the wind cover any sign of tracks here before the doorway. I would venture that no one has entered these doors of late. But I cannot say so with surety."

"Donel told me that only those with Regalos can enter the tower," said Artos. "Once we are inside, we should be safe from the Beastmen." He stepped up towards the door. As Donel's scrying had shown, a small square of light blue crystal upon each door appeared where a handle would normally exist. *Just like the door to the Hall of Mirrors*, he thought. He reached out to place his hand against the panel.

"So you are sure Beastmen cannot be gifted, Art?" asked Seth, freezing him in place.

"Ah … Why, of course they don't. Do they? Could they?" He stared at the Druid in surprise.

"I do not know, Art. It has been a subject of debate among the Druids. Beastmen are another race, just like the Fairborn and the Forge-folk. Those races have gifted members. Why not Beastmen?"

"No," said Bortis. "They are beasts. They do not even speak."

"I know you are wrong in that, Bort. They have their own

language. There are those who feel if we did not harry them, hunt them like beasts, they would not respond in kind. Druid Aubrie has potent feelings on this, but no one from the Great Houses, except my father, has ever been willing to converse with him on this subject. At least, as far as I know."

"I don't believe it," said Bortis. "Maybe they do grunt and howl at each other. You can call that speaking if you wish. They are savage creatures whose only wish is to kill and destroy."

Artos wasn't so sure. While growing up, he had been told the same things as his brother, but Bortis had spent more time learning from their Uncle Brett, and Artos suspected Brett had been wrong in many of his beliefs. He shook his head. "It's something to think about, but not now. We need to move ahead."

Feeling the familiar tingle of the qulan field, he placed his hand firmly against it. The panel on each of the two doors glowed a brighter blue, and both doors swung inwards, although he had only touched the right-hand door. As they swung back to rest against the wall on either side of the open doorway, the tingle of the qulan field also disappeared.

Artos stepped inside. Although he had seen the room before, scrying with Donel, he expected the enormous hall to be gloomy, but the everlight strips lining the three balconies, along with the large skylights set in the arched ceiling, provided plenty of light. He carefully scanned the room. Immediately, his eyes were drawn to the floor to his left, and he froze in surprise. "Tracks," he gasped, his gut tightening.

A small area right before the doors was bare, but elsewhere, thick dust lay on the floor throughout the enormous hall, undisturbed for centuries. But a trail led from the doorway to the stairs on the left that ascended to the upper levels. The splayed, wide tracks of Beastmen.

"Hold," said Seth. "Let me look before we muddle the marks." The druid stepped past Artos and bent to examine the footprints in the thick dust.

Artos scanned the balconies above, looking for any sign of movement. Bortis stepped to his side, followed by the rest of the party, everyone staying clear of the tracks in the dust.

"You can see the doors were open for a little while," said Jaek. "This area right before the doors, the dust blew away." As he spoke, a gust of wind followed them through the door, and some of the dust before them swirled in a small cloud.

"These tracks both come and go," said Seth. "I believe we can conclude that a few Beastmen entered, went up the stairs, and then returned. I would guess only five or six, though it's hard to tell exactly. The tracks leading out are on top of those leading in."

"How could they get in?" said Bortis. "What happened to the qulan field? Has it faded away? Is it gone?"

"No," said Artos. "I felt it when I reached out to open the door, but it disappeared when I opened them."

"I think when the doors are open, the Qulan field parts," said the druid. "The masters of old probably had a reason. I can only conclude inviting people through the field must not have been practical."

Without warning, the group found themselves gently but firmly pushed a little further into the tower as if by invisible hands, and as soon as they were clear of the path, the two large doors swung shut.

The inside of the door had crystal panels identical to those on the outer side. As they watched, the bright blue of the panels faded back to the original light blue color of an inactive screen.

"That was interesting," observed Seth.

"The qulan field stopped detecting motion through the doorway and closed the doors," said Jaek. "The doors in Farnir's palace in Fairinlan are the same. They carefully remove anyone who is standing in the way so as not to squash anyone."

"I can think of ways the Beastmen gained entrance here," said Seth. "None of them reassuring."

"I agree," said Jaek.

"How?" asked Bortis.

"The first way would be that someone with regalos let them in by opening the door. The second would be that some Beastmen have regalos themselves."

Artos saw that his brother looked skeptical. He felt that way himself, but Donel had taught him not to blindly accept everything he had been taught. Could Beastmen be more than just savage beasts?

"The most uncomfortable thought is, rather than a person with regalos, an Abomination opened the door."

Artos nodded, having just come to that disturbing conclusion himself.

"What's up the stairs?" asked Bortis as he took a few steps in the direction the tracks led.

"I don't know," said Artos. "Donel's scrying came in through the doorway and proceeded directly to that door at the far end. We never looked closely at anything else. I wish we had. We were in such a hurry that last week. We didn't scry anything except these two rooms. This one and the one beyond that door."

"I think we should check on where those footsteps lead," said Bortis. "There might be something still here, and we don't want them behind us."

"Let me do that, with Seth and Kae," said Jaek. "You three keep going, Artos."

He thought for a moment and then shook his head. "We are too few to divide up. Seth, can you tell if the same number left as came in?"

"Not with certainty, Art. I think so, but I can't say for sure."

"I hate to waste time, but Bort's right. The dust will show us where they went. We can take a quick look and then proceed to the Hall of Mirrors, take a quick look in the armory, and then to Castle Draconis."

Bortis nodded grimly as the rest looked at each other and then followed suit.

"Seth, you are the best tracker here, I think. Would you lead the way?"

"I doubt I am better than either Kae or Angel, but since they are carrying their bows, I will gladly oblige."

Seth followed the tracks to the left-hand stairway and led the group up to the first balcony. The dust on the stairs continuing upward was undisturbed. Seth examined the stairs for a moment, nodded, and then followed the tracks through the dust as they went along. Stopping at the first door, he examined the floor and the tracks.

"They stood grouped here in front of the door, then went in and came back out before they proceeded along the balcony. Let us see what they wanted here. I wonder if I can open the doors?"

The door had the familiar crystal square in place of a doorknob. Carefully, Seth extended his right hand and placed it on the square. The door swung open, and they gazed into a room which, in better days, would have housed two students. The room had been demolished. Artos thought of the axes of the Beastmen he had seen and nodded grimly. A smashed personal desk and chair, along with the remains of a bed, stood against each wall. Four chairs were overturned and hacked to pieces before a wide window looking out at the Loch O' Wrens and Castle Draconis on the far side. Some dust had resettled over everything.

"I can't say how long ago this happened," said Seth. "It looks like they smashed everything and raised clouds of dust as they did it. Then they left. The dust would have settled within a few hours, at most." The druid led them back out and followed the tracks.

There were twenty rooms along the balcony, and the first fifteen had been ransacked. The tracks stopped just beyond the fifteenth door. Although there were five more rooms and the balcony circled the room to the other side of the great hall, the tracks did not continue.

"This is strange," said Seth. "Why did they rampage through all those rooms and then stop and not continue to all the rest? It is almost as if they were suddenly frightened and turned back."

"Let's go look at some rooms the beasts didn't destroy." Bortis went to the next room and opened the door. The unbroken furniture beneath the coat of dust showed the room was, as they had suspected, an obvious dormitory room for two students.

"I'd love to explore this place too," said Artis. "But not now. We have a mission. We should get on with it. We can come back later, after we've finished our task at the castle."

"You're right. I don't know what I was thinking. I guess I just hate to leave mysteries unsolved. We need to go clear the creatures from home."

"There is a mystery here," said Seth. "But I agree. It doesn't seem to be related to our immediate task. Let's proceed with our original course. There are stairs ahead, in the corner. We can go back down there."

"We're kicking up enough dust this way as it is," said Angel. "We don't need to add to it. Take the shortest route to the door."

The thick dust puffed up in clouds as they walked, but it wasn't as bad as Artos feared it would be. They followed Seth as he led the way to the stairs in the southwest corner of the hall and back to the ground floor. As they approached, the doors that led further into the tower, the druid held up his hand and motioned for the group to halt.

"Hold a moment. Something's odd here. Let me look at this." Seth took another cautious step forward and then knelt down to examine the dusty floor. A pair of large depressions marked where the dust was disturbed.

"It's almost as though something stood here to open the door, but there are no tracks leading here." Seth looked at Artos. "As if something floated through the room, then stopped and stood here to open the door."

"Like the ghost that murdered that fur trapper." Artos summoned his sword into his hand.

"A ghost with huge feet," said Seth. "These tracks show feet half again bigger than mine. A ghost that stands much taller than a normal man. Donnie said the ghost was about eight feet tall."

Kae knelt down beside the druid and examined the tracks as well. "The dust has settled in these, but I think I can make out the outlines of toes. Whatever this was, it didn't wear shoes."

"Can you say how old they are?" asked Bortis.

"Not really," answered Seth, "The dust is so thick in here it wouldn't take too long to obscure them, but if nothing stirred it up, the dust might never fill them. They could be years old, or only hours. I can't really tell."

"So there might be something waiting on the other side of the door," said Bortis. "Let me and Seth go first. Art, you stay further back."

Artos was about to object, but Jaek spoke up first. "I know you feel strongly about this, but you must remember, you are the pretender to the throne. Let others take as much risk as possible. It is not cowardice, but good sense. You can't risk yourself against every obstacle on the way. You have a crown and a throne to win. Let us do our part to get you to Castle Draconis. There will be danger and risk enough there."

"He's right, Art," said Angel. "I know you don't want to let others face danger on your behalf, but think of it this way—you will face things when you are king that the rest of us won't. Let us do our part along the way. That is all we ask."

Artos looked at Kae, standing between Angel and her husband. She smiled at him and said, "If you are expecting me to add to that, forget it. You know they're right. I don't need to tell you so."

He took a deep breath, then let it out with a long sigh. He took a step back and stood beside Angel. He nodded at his brother.

Bortis readied his crysword and flames danced along the blade. He took Artos's place next to the druid. "Shall I?"

Seth gripped his crystaff as it expanded from a wand to a six-foot staff. "I'm ready if you are."

Bortis placed his free hand on the opening crystal, and the door silently swung open.

"Nothing here," said Bortis as they entered the next room. They were now in the center-most chamber of Starstone Tower.

As they entered the enormous room, the musty smell of dust and ancient air filled their noses. Even more dust coated the floor from the centuries of abandonment, but no tracks were visible from where they stood. The entrance chamber may have been larger, but this room, at the heart of the tower, was more impressive. On the main floor, a door opened in each of the cardinal directions. They had entered from the north and could see the doors to the east and west. The southern door was hidden by the massive spiral staircase in the center of the room. Bookcases lined the lower walls between the doors, and scattered around the room were clusters of chairs and a few tables set in groups, all covered with thick dust. Seven balconies lined the outer wall, each with many doors. As with the entrance hall, everlight strips circled the walls, both above the doors on each floor and on the spire of the huge spiral stairway that dominated the center of the room. Walkways split off at each floor. The ceiling of the great hall sloped inward after the seventh level until it reached a peak high above the floor. Eight gigantic windows circled the ceiling, each with a view of a large building. It was obvious they were screens because, although they slanted up at an angle toward the center of the tower, the view they presented was as if the viewer was looking out, not up. The stairs ended at another door at the very top, probably leading to a garret at the tower's peak.

"There's Castle Draconis," said Artos, pointing up at one screen, feeling homesick. "It's like you are standing across the causeway at Brierly."

"That's Darylhelm," said Seth, pointing at a screen on the opposite side.

Bortis scanned the screens. "What are the rest of those castles, then? I don't recognize any of them."

"Demigoran destroyed them one by one. Donel told me that those are the strongholds of the original families. Only three survived the war, and Donel's brother, Caerwyn, destroyed Blachaas after Tomung's rebellion."

Seth pointed up to the one next to Darylhelm. "I think that one is Blachaas. I'm guessing it pictures them in their order around the King's Valley. Only a guess, though."

"Donel didn't say, but it could be." Artos pointed across the room. "We want the door opposite the one we came in. Only Bort or I should be able to open that one. It has a qulan field that only allows someone from the first three families to open it."

"Then I should be able to open it, too. Well, maybe," said Angel. "Unless my father's blood interferes."

"I think you're right. You are a deEagledon. We should have you open the door just to check."

The dust billowed up around their feet as they walked around the central stairway, and the air was filled with its musty smell. Seth raised his hand, the fabric of his robe rustling softly as he pointed at the floor before the door leading to the south. Another pair of huge footprints marred the dust before the exit.

"There they are again." The druid looked thoughtful. "Wait here a moment." Seth left the group and walked around the edge of the room to examine the door leading to the east. Artos watched as he bent over, as if examining something. He then turned and recrossed the room to examine the floor before the door that led to the west.

"Looks like there were tracks there, too," observed Artos.

Seth rejoined them. "Whatever it was stood before that door, too." He pointed to the eastern door. "But not the other. Curiouser and curiouser."

"That means it's probably still beyond this door," said Bortis excitedly. "It hasn't come back out to check the last one."

"Maybe," replied Angel. "Or maybe it found what it wanted beyond this door."

"More likely, it couldn't open this door and so went back to the other," answered Artos. "Remember, Donel told me only those of the blood of the first three Houses could open this one."

"Right," said Bortis. "I wasn't thinking. That means we are probably leaving it behind us. But at least it won't be able to follow us. We'll just have to be ready if we come back this way."

"Which we won't do," said Artos. "We should be on our way to the castle within the hour. I'll take a quick look in the armory at the top of this tower, but the important thing is to get to Castle Draconis and reclaim our home. Let's go."

Bortis motioned for Angel to open the door. Holding her bow in her left hand, Angel placed her right palm squarely on the panel. The door slowly swung open, and Angel stepped back and motioned for Bortis to proceed, but before he could take a step, Seth stopped him.

"Wait."

Bortis stopped and looked back around the room. "Did you hear something?"

"No," replied Seth. "Step back, away from the door a moment,"

They all stood back, and, in a moment, the door closed.

Seth looked at the group. "Did anyone else notice something strange in there?" He nodded his head towards the now closed door.

"I did. At least if you mean what I think you do," said Angel.

"I didn't see anything. I was looking for the ghost, but it looked empty to me. What did you see?" said Bortis.

Seth and Angel exchanged glances. "Exactly," said the druid. "It was empty, very empty."

"There was no dust on the floor," added Angel.

Seth nodded, stepped forward, and placed his hand against the crystal plate. Nothing happened. "It would seem my dePenrodyn blood is not pure enough for the door quanti." He motioned for Bortis to approach the door.

Bortis placed his hand on the crystal, and, once again, the door swung open. Artos's attention went first to the floor. The dust that settled throughout the tower was nowhere to be found in this room.

"You're right," said Artos, "the floor is clean. Why is that?"

No one had any answers, so they cautiously entered the new chamber, allowing the door to close behind them.

Slowly, Artos surveyed the octagonal room, searching for some reason for the unnatural cleanliness. The air seemed fresher here, with no trace of the mustiness he had noticed in the outer chambers. The three walls facing the cardinal directions each held a door. The rest of the walls were lined with empty bookcases, which were also free of dust. Unlike all the other doors they had seen throughout the tower, these were not made of wood but the same dark stone as the walls of the tower. Each door bore the Mark of one of the Great Houses: House deEagledon straight ahead to the west, deDraconis to the south, and dePenrodyn to the north. Each door had a crystal-opening plate.

What really captured his attention, however, was in the center of the room. Spiraling up clockwise were steps made of the same light-blue crystal as the screens, each step two inches thick. Just wide enough for a single person, each step glowed softly. Amazingly, nothing supported the individual steps.

Each step floated all alone in space. Looking up to the next floor, Artos saw the room grow larger, and a balcony circled the room with everlights spaced above the doors. A walkway extended from the landing to the stairs. The stairs continued their upward climb. Far above, there was a small balcony on the western wall, with the steps abruptly ending at that level.

The hair prickled on Artos's neck. "I feel like we're being watched, as if we are not alone here." He looked around the room again.

Bortis shook his head. "Who could have opened the door? You don't think the ghost is of our House, do you? Don't be silly, Art." He noticed the stairs. "By the Sky. What's holding up the steps?"

"Donel said they're safer than they look. The quanti holds them together, I guess. He said you can't fall off the sides. He forgot to mention there was nothing holding them up, though. It must be the same magic. But what happened to the dust? Why is it so clean in here? The air feels fresher too." Artos walked over to the door with the dragon of House Draconis and placed his hand on the crystal plate. The door swung open to reveal a long narrow room with shelving on each side. A single everlight was mounted on the far wall, lighting the empty shelves, not so much as a speck of dust anywhere.

Bortis walked over to the door with the old dePenrodyn symbol, not the Griffin, which was the House symbol now, but four intertwined circles. The door stayed firmly shut.

"I guess having Count Penrodyn for my grandfather isn't enough," he said.

Angel placed her hand upon the panel of the door marked with the deEagledon eagle. The door swung open to reveal another empty room, just like the one Artos had opened.

"I wonder what they stored here?" she mused. "Whatever it was, it's gone now."

"Donel said they would be empty," said Artos as he walked over to the floating steps, which were being examined by Seth.

"I have never heard of anything like these steps, Art. Look, try this." The druid stood to the side and waved his hand above the nearest step. His hand passed freely over it. Artos waved his left hand over the step and felt just the faintest tingle of a qulan field. "Now move to the front as if you were about to climb the steps and try it."

Artos positioned himself in front of the steps and waved his hand above the first step.

"Now, move your hand over the side."

Artos moved his hand to the right side of the step. Resistance, like a solid but invisible wall, appeared. He pulled his hand back, so it was no longer over the step, moved it to the side, and waved it above the step. His hand moved freely over the step, but when he moved it back, the invisible barrier stopped it.

"A one-way wall. Donel didn't tell me that. He only said you couldn't fall off." Artos shook his head in wonder.

"I take it this is our route onward?" asked the druid.

"Yes, the Hall of Mirrors should be up there." Artos pointed toward the higher balcony. "The Armory above that. He told me only those who have the regalo of Ansuz can access it." Artos nervously placed his foot on the first step. It felt solid, as if it were firmly part of a structure, not floating unattached in space. He put out his hand and pressed against the invisible wall. Just feeling the glassy smooth wall helped to calm his nerves, even if it looked as though there was nothing there.

As Artos started up the stairs, he again felt as though he

were being watched. The tower was so quiet it was almost as if he could hear the stillness itself. Not even an echo of their footsteps marred the silence. He progressed cautiously up the stairs, slowly taking one step at a time, constantly looking around the room. Waiting for ... he wasn't sure what, but something.

The first landing was a balcony which encircled the room. When he reached that level, the stair step was double the size. There was only the smallest gap between it and the stone walkway which led across to the balcony. Each of the eight walls had a door in their center—wooden doors, not stone like the three below. Artos stopped for a moment to examine the balconied walkway. Like the stonework at Castle Draconis, there was no seam between the side walls and the floor. It was as if they were carved from a single piece of stone.

"Any reason we should check behind those doors?" Bortis asked.

Artos cleared his throat, his skin tingling in the oppressive silence. "I'm sure they are empty, but I don't feel right leaving them unchecked."

He led them across the walkway to the nearest door. Using the opening screen revealed another dormitory room, except there was only one bed, and the furniture was more luxurious. And no dust.

"Living quarters for some instructors, I would guess," said Seth. "Do we need to examine the rest?"

"Probably not," said Artos, "but I have felt like there was someone watching us ever since we entered this tower. Let's take a quick look in each room. It won't take us that long."

All the rooms were identical, and all were empty. Artos then led the way up the stairs until he reached the apparent end, another double-sized step. The invisible sidewall of the stairs felt unbroken beneath his hand. It surrounded the top step on three sides. The only opening was to the walkway, which ran across to the small balcony where a door stood, flanked by a pair of ever-lights, the door Artos knew led to the tower's Hall of Mirrors. There was no opening where Donel had said the route to the armory should have been.

He stepped off the crystal step and strode across the walkway to the single door that faced him. It appeared no different from the doors on the first landing, an unmarked wooden door with the light blue crystal panel in place of a doorknob.

The balcony was double the size of the walkway, wide enough for two people to stand side by side without crowding. Artos stood to the side and allowed the group to reach the landing with him. "Bort, why don't you take everyone into the Hall of Mirrors and wait for me there? I'll go on up to the armory and then join you in a few minutes."

"Nope, no, uh-uh," Bortis shook his head. "The rest can wait here while you and I go up there, or we can all go into the Hall of Mirrors. Then you and I can come back, but no way are you going up there by yourself." Artos knew from his expression he would not change his mind. And he felt some relief that he wouldn't be going up into the armory all alone.

"I suggest Bortis is correct," said Jaek. "Perhaps we should divide into two groups of three. Since Kae and I do not have the needed regalo, we and another will wait here, and the three of you proceed onward and see if there is anything of use above. Then we all can proceed on to Castle Draconis."

"We know it's safe," said Artos halfheartedly. "I'm the only one Donel has given training to use what might be up there.

There is no need for anyone to go but me."

"Not only is Bort right," said Angel, "but you shouldn't even be the first to go up. Let Bort and me go first, and you follow us. We think it is safe and nothing is waiting up there, but we don't know it as fact."

"But I'm the one he taught. Not Bort."

"I guess we'll just have to see, won't we?" Bortis stepped around his brother and walked back to the last crystal step. "Ansuz is that rune that looks like an 'F.'" He switched his crysword to his right hand, closed his eyes, and placed his left hand before him against the unseen wall. His hand stayed motionless for a moment and then moved forward. He flashed a triumphant grin and then looked back, the grin dissolving quickly away. "Where are the stairs?"

"They're invisible, Bort. Just like the wall. Donel said they lead up to the top floor, and you can't see anything until you get there. Do you want me to go first?"

But Bortis was already feeling for the stair with his left foot. He stepped up and forward and stood there as if he were standing on the air itself. He took another step, his left hand on the invisible wall, climbing on the invisible stair.

Before Artos could react, Angel moved around him and followed Bortis, only pausing a moment before stepping onto the invisible stairway.

"I guess that settles who goes with you," said Seth. "Donel and I discussed it before we left the Crystal Tower, and he advised me not to go up there. I agreed. My regalos are mostly of the nature quans."

Artos moved to follow Angel and his brother. He placed his left hand against the invisible wall and concentrated on the rune Ansuz. He felt the wall dissolve before him and tentatively placed his right foot out, feeling for the invisible stair. It was there. He placed his hand against the side wall, and he stepped up and forward, then looked up just in time to see Bortis's legs vanish into thin air as he walked upward into the unseen room. Angel's head, then shoulders, also disappeared. Not to be left behind, he quickly pursued.

Chapter Twenty-Six:

Artos in the Armory

28

WAS THAT CARI?

ARTOS

10/9/1971 ar

As Artos neared the top of the invisible stairs, he moved through a qulan field stronger than any he had experienced before. Instead of a momentary tingly feeling of stepping through a thin barrier, it was as though he pushed through a thick wall of static electricity. Then it was gone. He stepped into a large, well-lit octagonal room.

Four large windows took up the front half of the wall space, the rest filled with four large cabinets—two on his left and two on his right—each with the familiar light blue panel in place of a knob or handle. Glancing behind him, he saw he had entered the room through a door-shaped field of bluish energy.

What drew his immediate attention was the strange object occupying the center of the room made of crystal of varying colors. There was a frame of four circular hoops. The largest, looking as though it were made of diamond, was a foot thick and a dozen feet in diameter. It stood vertically on the room's floor, looking as though a push could start it rolling like a huge barrel hoop. A smaller circle of ruby floated inside, horizontal to the floor, with a sapphire circle hovering vertically inside it. Inside the other three was the smallest, a circle of emerald, floating at a forty-five-degree angle to the other rings.

Suspended in the middle of the rings was an eight-foot-diameter sphere of ruby. At first glance, it appeared sprinkled with diamonds, emeralds, rubies, and sapphires. The gem-like spheres scattered over the surface in no pattern he could discern. An opening gaped on one side, and within could be seen a padded chair with a bank of various gems before it. Except for the largest hoop, balanced on the room's floor, neither the sphere nor any of the hoops were attached to anything. They just hovered within the diamond-crystal hoop.

"What in the sky's name is that thing?" asked Bortis, a few feet ahead of where he had appeared. Angel turned away from the strange device and looked back at Artos as if she, too, was awaiting an explanation.

"It must be the Starstone, the weapon that Donel told me about. The weapon the tower was named for. Except, he said Caerwyn destroyed it." Artos stepped closer. "Some of the smaller spheres are scorched, though. Well, some of the green ones are. The rest aren't." Sure enough, most of the green spheres had blackened spots on them, although none looked truly damaged. "It's the weapon Caerwyn used to destroy Blachaas."

Angel slowly turned around, looking at the windows. "I don't think these are windows. I looked at the whole tower pretty carefully, and I didn't see a single one anywhere. You couldn't have missed these from the ground. They are too big."

Artos looked out across the loch towards Castle Draconis.

"It resembles clear glass. But I think you must be right. It has to be a screen. For one thing, it's too clean." He carefully reached out and touched the surface with his left hand. "It is. You can feel the energy."

"Not only that," said Bortis. "Where is the fog? There's no mist."

"You're right," said Artos. "There's none anywhere you look."

"Look at the view," said Angel. "Look carefully at the first window and then at each in turn. Then look back at the first one. The screens are all on one side of the tower, but the view is all around, in every direction."

Artos nodded. "You're right. You can face one way and be looking all around you. That's even better than the screens in the Eyrie. Let me see ..." Remembering his lessons, he reached out with his thoughts and let his mind bond with the screen. He stared hard at the castle across the loch. It was as if he were rushing across the surface of the water to peer close up at the battlements that overlooked the loch from the castle. Suddenly, his vision blurred. For an instant, he saw the face of Carimus looking back at him, eyes wide in surprise. Then his brother's face was gone, and he was once more looking at Castle Draconis from across the Loch O Wrens.

"Did you see that?" he said, stunned.

"See what?" answered Bortis. "You touching the screen? Yeah, I saw it. Cammy would have cracked your knuckles and given you the 'never touch the viewing screens' talk."

"No! It was Cari! He was staring back at me through the screen."

"I'm sorry," said Angel. "I was looking at this cabinet. Where did you see Cari? What was he doing?"

Artos pointed at the "window" in front of him. "I bonded my mind to the screen to farsee across the loch. Suddenly, the screen changed, and Cari was looking back at me. He seemed surprised to see me."

Bortis was facing the screen with his eyes closed. "I can farsee the castle, but I don't see the squirt there, Art."

"No! He wasn't at the castle … I don't think. I don't remember what was behind him. It was dark. I don't know. I was so surprised to see his face that I didn't notice anything else."

Angel shook her head. "It just looks like a window to me, even though I know it's not. Donel never taught me to farsee with the screens. We were concerned with other matters. I wish I had asked him. If we get a chance later, maybe you can show me how." She turned her attention back to the screen, a look of concentration on her face.

"We're wasting time," said Bortis. "Just what are you searching for here? I mean, a weapon, but what is it? What does it look like? Shouldn't we be searching these cabinets?"

"Donel didn't know. We want a weapon to use against the Abominations."

"There are four cabinets. Let's look inside." Artos walked up to the first cabinet, reached out, and placed his palm against the crystal plate. The door swung open, revealing ten empty shelves. "Nothing here." He pushed the doors closed.

"Yeah, I bet Great Grandfather Alexavier had the place stripped," said Bortis.

"I don't think anyone besides Caerwyn knew exactly how to get in here. At least that's how Donel described it."

"Then let's get back on track. See if there's anything here, and let's go. We should be hunting Beastmen by now."

"And some Abominations," agreed Artos.

"Art ..." Angel's voice sounded strange. Both brothers turned to look and found she was staring at a tall black tower on the screens. Artos recognized it at once. It was the castle Seth had pointed out as Blachaas, the stronghold of House deYung, the castle Caerwyn destroyed.

"That's the castle Donel's brother destroyed," he said. "How did you call it up on the screens?"

"I was wondering what the deEagledon keep looked like, and suddenly I was looking at Eagleroost," she said. "I recognized the banner with the family crest. I decided to look at the Anson and Herndar castles and then Daryelhaas." She pointed at the screen. "Next, I decided to look at the ruins of Blachaas ..."

"And somehow you got the view of the castle from before it was destroyed," continued Artos.

"When I first moved the view from the deDarrellyel castle to this one, it went across a place where everything was black and dead."

"The Blasted Heath," said Bortis.

Angel nodded. "When I first looked, it was just ruins, but then the image wavered, and then it ... it rippled, and suddenly that was the image."

"We were just looking at those castles a little while ago out in the other room," said Bortis. "You just called up the same image."

"Maybe ... " said Angel. The image on the screen disappeared, and once more the screen looked as though it were a window looking at the lands around the tower.

Artos turned back to the cabinets and stepped over to the second cabinet. He placed his hand on the crystal plate and looked into another empty cabinet. "Nothing here." He started to swing the doors shut.

"Wait," Bortis was pointing at the bottom shelf. "There's something."

Artos looked back at the bottom shelf and saw a small piece of paper lying there. He went to pick it up, only to have the corner crumble away. He bent over to look closely. "It's too old. It's falling apart. Looks like somebody left a note when they cleaned out these shelves."

"What's it say?" asked Bortis, moving in closer.

"The ink has mostly faded away. I can make out a few words. Something-ields, something, black ceram-something fails. Something -her shows prom-something. It fades away for a while, then something neither ceramic lasted but surprising leather, something, something. That's all."

"This isn't what we came here for, Art. Check the other cabinets and let's go." Artos could tell from his brother's tone he was getting impatient.

He gave his brother a tense grin, then stepped over to the third cabinet. "I think this is the one." He moved his hand back and forth a few inches from the crystal plate. "It's tingly. I feel something. Energy."

Art!... Art!

"Did you hear that?" Artos looked around.

"Hear what?" said Angel and Bortis in almost perfect unison.

"Cari. I swear I heard him call my name."

"Cari is miles away from here, Art," said Bortis. "He's at Fairinhorst now. Probably showing off at school, like always."

"Yes, you're probably right. I hope he found where Duke is."

"Yeah, for both their sakes. For all our sakes." Bortis looked over at the final cabinet, shrugged, and stepped over to open it.

Artos placed his hand on the plate, and the doors swung open. This cabinet wasn't empty. There were five cubes, each made of the same light blue crystal as the screens. Each had a name inscribed in bright color on the front: Tomung in red. Mohattri in white. Anndr in dark blue. Babich and Kargyn in green.

"Here they are! Okay, I have to think for a minute. I'm not sure which one to take—maybe more than one? Donel said for me to look at them and trust my gut."

"Don't take all day, Bro," said Bortis. Before Artos or Angel could protest, he added, "But take as long as you need. You want to get it right the first time."

Angel placed her hand on Artos's shoulder. "Donel is a knowledgeable man. If his best advice was to trust your gut, then do so. Follow your instincts. Just think about it for a minute or two." She nodded, then turned away and walked back to look out the screen window.

Artos turned his attention to the five boxes. The names of the five Abominations. This was like waking up and finding yourself in the middle of a myth, a folktale. Four different colors, just like the colors associated with the quans, the regalos. He thought back to what Donel had told him about the monsters. He didn't really say anything about Tomung other than he was the leader of the Five. He didn't know anything about Mohattri. Anndr was strong in the regalos of the mind. His name was in blue, and that was the color of the regalos of the mind. *That would fit, I think. That puts Tomung with the body and Mohattri with the spirit. Donel said he thought the other two were the most bestial. Green is the nature quans. That makes sense too, I guess.*

Now, which weapon should I take? I believe Tomung's head will be freed from the restraints that kept it a trophy, but how dangerous could that be? If Donel is right and the thing can grow back a body, the question is 'How quickly?' It has been three weeks. I don't think that could be enough time, but what if I'm wrong?

We know one of the other Abominations killed Father and the others. That's the one I need a weapon against. I don't think I need to worry about Anndr. Donel thought he was on the giant bird. No, it was one of the other three, but which one? Two of them are green. I wonder if that means the weapon inside might be good against either of them, or maybe not?

He sheathed his sword and reached for the cube with Babich inscribed. At the last second, his dream of running with the wolves and slaying the deer flashed through his mind. His hands moved of their own accord to the other green cube, with the name Kargyn. Carefully, with both hands, he picked up the cube to examine it more closely. As he did, the front of the cube quietly, smoothly folded back along with the top, exposing the interior. On a black velvet lining lay a ring made of brilliantly polished green jade. It begged to be touched. He set the open cube back on the shelf and slowly reached inside to take out the ring.

Noo! ART! … Nooo!

He jerked his hand away from the cube and watched as it closed as silently as it had opened.

Cari? He looked around. That was Cari; he was sure of it. Angel was staring at the screens, and Bortis was examining a small wooden box. The last cabinet was open beside him.

Hmmm ... My gifts are of the spirit, the white gifts. He felt drawn to the cube labeled in white ... Mohattri. *Donel said trust my gut. My gut says take the white one.*

He reached out and carefully put his hand on the cube labeled Mohattri. At his touch, the top folded back just as the first had done. Inside was an exquisitely crafted ring of polished pearl. He reached for it slowly, expecting to hear the disembodied voice of Cari raised in protest once again. Instead of warning and alarm, what he felt as he touched the ring was excitement and joy.

"I think this is what I want, Bort," he said, looking over at his brother.

Bortis set down the wooden box and stepped over next to him, holding a pair of black leather gloves. "A ring? How does it work?"

"I'm not sure. I'm going to try it on. It's crystal, and I think I have to bond with it."

"Be careful." Artos could see the worry in his brother's eyes.

He took the ring and slid it on his left ring finger, away from the hand he normally carried his crysword. It slipped on easily over his knuckle and onto his finger. He felt it adjust and tighten slightly around his finger, with no danger of it sliding off. When he bonded with his crysword, he was entranced for over an hour; he hoped this wouldn't take as long. Duke bonded with his sword in an instant. He hoped for a similar experience.

It was not the same as bonding to his sword.

Artos knew he was standing still, but for an instant that either lasted for many years or for less than a second, Artos fell through a swirling vortex of many colors. He felt as though the light was first holding him up, then throwing him down, then twisting him inside out. For one brief instant, there was a hideous face before him—a spotted, bestial face with two white cloudy eyes above a snarling muzzle full of nasty-looking teeth, and a huge, bright green third eye directly in the middle of its forehead. Then it was gone. *What was that?*

"You okay, Art? You looked pale for a second there," said Bortis.

Artos grimaced and shook his head. "That wasn't so bad. It was like bonding with my sword, but it was over a lot quicker." Artos summoned his sword to his hand, something he had done many times every day for the last five years. It was as normal as drawing a breath. Except he always summoned it to his right hand. Why had he just used his left? He switched hands. That was strange. Uncle Brett had made him practice summoning it to either hand, of course, and he could do either with no effort whatsoever. His brother was one of the few left-handed people he knew, but Artos was right-handed.

Artos replaced his sword in its sheath, then looked at the four remaining cubes. What if Anndr were at the castle now? Then there was always the possibility Tomung could grow a new body in a week or two. Maybe he should carry the rest of the cubes with him, too, just in case. He reached out to pick up the first cube.

Art! Nooo! He jerked his hand back. It was Cari again. A wave of terror swamped him, so palpable his knees felt shaky. *Run away! Go! Now!*

Before he could consider what it meant, Angel called out, her voice filled with alarm. "Are you ready, Art? We should go. Now."

The brothers looked as Angel hurried back from the front of the room to join them. Her face was pale, and Artos thought she looked more upset than he had ever seen—worse than when she looked upon the ruins of Fargo. He abruptly closed the cabinet doors. *It can't have grown a new body back. Not yet.*

"What is it? Did you see something outside?" asked Bortis.

"Is something wrong?" asked Artos.

"I was trying to use the screen again. Just to see if I could. I was trying to look at the main tower. I felt something's thoughts.

Something bad … I think it noticed me. We need to leave!"

"What did you see?" asked Bortis as all three looked at the screens. The keep's central tower loomed above them. Artos thought it seemed threatening somehow, more ominous than before.

"I didn't see anything. I felt it. Like I can feel Liv's thoughts. Only Liv's thoughts are clean and natural. This felt completely horrible, evil, unclean."

"I have the weapon." Artos held up his left hand, showing the shiny, pearlescent band. *If only I knew what to do with it,* he thought. "Let's go!"

Artos turned and stepped over to the spot where he had entered the room. A door-sized bluish haze hovered in the air. As he approached, he could see Seth on the walkway leading to the Starstone Hall of Mirrors. It was as though the gateway had just opened up right at the top step of the quanti-stairway, bypassing the invisible stairs completely. He waved to Seth, but the druid looked away with no reaction.

"It looks like the steps were one-way only. Hey, Seth," he waved at the druid, who remained oblivious to his presence. "Come on. Let's go." Artos cautiously stepped through the gateway, with Angel and Bortis right behind him.

Chapter Twenty-Seven:

On to the Castle

29

WE HAVE TO LEAVE

ARTOS

10/9/1971 ar

ARTOS'S SUDDEN PRESENCE made Seth jump in surprise, and he instinctively tightened his grip on his crystaff, bracing for battle. He immediately relaxed upon realizing it was Artos, followed by Bortis and Angel.

"That was a shock. I expected you to come back down the stairs," said the druid.

"I'm sorry, Seth. I could see you, but until I stepped through, you couldn't hear me. I tried to call to you."

"You gave me a fright," said Seth. "Appearing like a ghost out of thin air. I've been feeling uneasy, anyway. I thought I heard my name called a little while back, but there was no one there. It feels like we're being watched."

"I feel it too," said Angel. "I think there is something here in Starstone with us, something evil. It could be an Abomination. I felt its thoughts. It knows we're here now."

At that moment, a distant wailing cry shattered the silence

that had enveloped the tower since they had first entered.

"What was that?" Bortis turned to face the door below, through which they had entered, his crysword flaming in his hand.

"It knows we are here," repeated Angel.

"Nothing can get through the qulan field," said Artos. *But they did at home.*

The wailing cry sounded again and then disintegrated into hideous laughter.

"Did you find what you sought?" asked Jaek.

"Yes … I think … I hope. I have something anyway. Come on." Artos hurried toward the door at the end of the walkway. "I'm not sure what it is, but it had the name of one of the Abominations. It's a weapon ... of some sort." He held his hand to the screen, and the door swung open. The room was almost identical to the Hall of Mirrors at Castle Draconis. No screens were painted black, and there was no trophy stand like the one that had held Donel's crysharp. His eyes first went to the screen with the double dragons, but Donel's screen was inert, as were all the rest. No matter. He had hoped Donel might be looking in, but he knew how to open the gate to Castle Draconis. There was no time to waste.

He stepped up to the table. Bringing the R rune Raido to the forefront of his mind, he placed his hand on the screen set into the surface. "This is what we've come for," he said, concentrating on the regalo.

In the center of the wall to his left, a light blue rectangle of light, the size of a large door, appeared.

Artos looked at his brother. "This is it."

Bortis took charge. "Okay, Jaek and I go first. You and Seth behind us, brother. Kae, you and Angel follow, arrows notched.

Be ready to shoot. Let's go." He stepped up to the doorway, crysword in hand. Jaek drew his longsword and stepped up beside him. They gave each other a quick nod, glanced back to see that all were ready, then stepped through the gate together.

Seth held his crystaff at the ready, and he and Artos walked through next.

The Hall of Mirrors in Castle Draconis appeared exactly the same as the last time he and Donel had scried into the room. As Artos stepped into the room, he could smell a faint, sweet aroma of peaches, but it was tinged with the distinct smell of woodsmoke mixed with decay. Jaek and Bortis were flanking the door that led into the castle, swords at the ready. After Angel and Kae entered, Artos turned to the oaken table in the room's center and placed his hand on the screen there. The blue rectangle of the gate disappeared. Just as they had been at Starstone, all the screens were inert. *I was hoping Donel would be watching for us. We can't wait. I have no idea if they know we are here. Hopefully, we can surprise them, but that means we go now!*

"I was going to leave the gate open as a retreat, but right now, that idea doesn't make me happy. I don't like thinking something could follow us here. It may be a bad idea, but …" he shook his head and looked at the rest.

"Leave it closed. We won't need a retreat," said Bortis.

Artos and his brother locked eyes for a long moment, and then Artos nodded. He didn't need words to know what his brother meant. Bortis meant they would succeed, or they would die trying. There would be no retreating. He nodded again.

"We're ready," said Angel. Kae simply nodded.

"Okay," said Artos, "I know we discussed our strategy a lot; the closing off of our retreat doesn't change a thing. We'll make our way to the bottom and then start back up and clear every level as we go. We'll stay in the same order. Put your shields in place, mind and body. Let's go."

Bortis opened the door, and a stronger smell of decay wafted into the room. In the distance was a faint, bellowing roar. Artos steeled himself. The battle for the castle was underway.

Part Nine

The Battle for Castle Draconis

Chapter Twenty-Eight:

Castle Draconis

30

THE BATTLE BEGINS

ARTOS

10/9/1971 ar

THEY LEFT THE HALL OF MIRRORS in their planned formation. Artos and Seth stood in the doorway as Jaek stepped into the corridor, which led to the Great Hall, turned left, and paused. Bortis slipped across to the far side. When he was in position, Jaek gave a nod, and they began their cautious advance, Jaek on the left, Bortis to the right. Seth and Artos followed, walking down the hall's center. Kae and Angel trailed behind.

Artos thought the stench of death and decay would become more intense as they left the Hall of Mirrors, but instead, he noticed the scent getting weaker, or he was becoming desensitized to it. What stood out more than the smell was the chill in the air. Castle Draconis was usually kept at a moderate temperature, but a chill hung in the air, much colder than usual. Occasionally, the sound of coarse laughter or a hoarse shout echoed through the silence, making the stillness seem more pronounced. *I don't know what's worse,* he thought. *The silence of a tomb or the sounds of those beasts.*

There was only one opening in the hallway between the Hall of Mirrors and the Great Hall, that of the stairway leading up to the Royal Quarters. Before they reached the opening, Jaek paused and pointed at the floor in front of the passage. The carpet had a large, dark area. Jaek motioned for everyone to stand fast, then slowly approached and kneeled down to inspect the discoloration. He tapped it with his sword, making a wet splat. There was a puddle in front of the stairs.

Jaek peered around the corner to look up the stairs. He waved his hand in the air, signaling that the way was clear. He stood up and moved around the wet area of the floor as he and Bortis continued down the hall toward the Royal entrance to the Great Hall.

Artos paused as he passed the opening. A cold draft crept down the stairs and then toward the Great Hall. His gaze drawn to the carpet on the stairway; it was soaked through. Water was leaking down the stairs from the levels above. *Where is that coming from? Why is the air so cold?* He shook his head. *No time for that now.*

Just then, came a rattling clatter from somewhere ahead, and once again, loud bellowing laughter shattered the air. Jaek and Bortis reached the entrance to the hall, and each looked into the well-lit Great Hall. Jaek waved for the rest to come forward.

"No one here," said Jaek softly. "Unless they are hiding on one of the balconies."

Bortis's voice trembled. "Art ... Look ... look at the trophies." Artos could hear his brother's breathing becoming heavier with rage, the back of his neck turning red.

Artos stepped up behind his brother and looked into the Great Hall. The stench of death was stronger here. There was his father's throne, and above it, the row of trophies. His stomach clenched as he tried to process the sight before him. Rage and sorrow battled for control of his emotions. Where the bald, sneering face of Tomung once hung on the wall, a new board was sloppily hung in its place. Spiked to the bloody board were two grotesque heads. The bloated yet familiar faces of his father and Uncle Cameron leered down at him.

Bortis growled, "Revenge." The ferocity of his voice matched the rage building within Artos. He took a deep breath, grabbed his brother's shoulder, and whispered a shushing noise. Bortis's eyes were filled with rage, but he clenched his teeth and gave a slight nod.

"We need to find the thing that did this, Art!" Bortis uttered a quiet, menacing whisper through tightly clenched teeth. "Find it and kill it!" He shrugged off Artos's restraining hand and snorted, striding with purpose into the silent Great Hall, where only weeks earlier they had shared in the joy of Duka's birthday. He slowly turned, his eyes sweeping the balconies that overlooked the grand central room. Artos could just make out his brother's words as he muttered to himself, "Where are you hiding?"

Artos started to follow his brother, but found his way blocked by the arm of Jaek, who was shaking his head. "You and Seth wait here with Angel until Kae or I say it's clear." Artos nodded reluctantly.

The Fairborn warrior slid his long sword back into its sheath, looked to his wife, and nodded. He pulled his short bow from his shoulder and readied an arrow. The two Fairborn walked together into the Great Hall, all the while scanning the balconies as they joined Bortis in the room's center.

Artos nervously transferred his crysword from hand to

hand as the two Fairborn archers bracketed his brother. His father's eyes seemed to bore right through him.

"Is something wrong, Art?" asked Angel, stepping up beside him. "Sorry, that was a stupid way to put it. Of course, something's wrong. I'm so sorry you have to see their heads hanging there ... like that ..." she trailed off for a moment.

"Why do you keep changing hands with your sword? I have come to know your habits. You always carry your sword in your right hand. Bort always favors his left. You two just naturally stand so your swords are always away from each other. Defending each other."

"Uncle Brett used to have us pair that way." Artos looked down at his hands, glad to think about something besides his father's head, and took the sword back into his right hand. "It's the ring, I think. My sword wants to be in the hand that's wearing the ring."

"Maybe that's the way it's supposed to work. Have you thought about switching the ring to your other hand?"

"I don't know. They're both crystal. Uncle Cameron always told us not to touch crystal to crystal. We never sparred with our cryswords. So I felt I should keep them apart."

Just then, Jaek beckoned for them to join him in the Great Hall. As they moved into the hall, a distant crashing sound came from beyond the doors which led to the Winding Way, accompanied by a faint bestial roar.

Bortis whirled around to face the source of the sudden sound. "Filthy beasts. Let's go."

"Back in formation," said Artos, and they started toward the Winding Way. His skin prickled, and once more he had the feeling of being watched.

When they reached the Winding Way, a burst of raucous

laughter made it obvious the commotion was coming from the lower levels. The air in the castle was stale and acrid; the normal quanti air fresheners were being overwhelmed by the stench of sweat, decay, and wood smoke. Bortis took his place on the right-hand side of the descending passage, with Jaek back on the left.

The inner wall of the way, solid and unbroken from the Great Hall all the way to the Eyrie, was lined with huge archways down to the ground floor of the keep, one level below. Jaek cautiously looked down at the floor below with his readied bow. Seeing no targets, he slung the bow over his left shoulder and drew his longsword. He nodded to Bortis, and they began the trek to the lower floor.

After two complete revolutions, they reached the inner courtyard. Artos was shocked by its condition. It was littered with trash. Two shattered oaken beams lay in front of the main gates, as if the Beastmen had tried unsuccessfully to batter the gate open. But the large iron-bound gate was closed, and the bars were in place. The doors to the storerooms and offices were a different story. All stood open, some torn from their hinges. Broken furniture lay scattered all around. Artos felt cold anger building up inside as he surveyed his ransacked home.

Jaek waved for the party to stop and stood listening. Howls and bellows rang up the way from below, but the courtyard area seemed empty. Jaek looked to Bortis, pointed at his eyes, and then gestured to him again. Bortis nodded and then took a long, slow look at everything. Artos knew his brother had lowered his Mindshield and was using his trueseeing spell. After a long moment, he signed all clear. Jaek nodded and then indicated they would proceed further down the Winding Way.

The inner wall of the Winding Way was solid again between

the ground floor and the River Level below. They had only made half a revolution down toward the bottom level of the castle, the river level, when a Beastman with the snout and tusks of a boar came walking up the way. Artos barely had time to raise his sword before the Beastman grunted in surprise, then slumped to the floor. Kae's arrow jutted from its chest.

Jaek quickly examined the body, and when assured the creature was dead, resumed leading the group down the Winding Way.

Artos realized his sword was gripped in his left hand again. He replaced it in his right hand. *I'd like to ask Donel about this. Why does my sword go to my off hand?*

The sounds of the Beastmen grew louder as they neared the bottom of the way. The lower courtyard at the foot of the Winding Way had always been kept clear between the various storerooms and the outer dockyard. Artos had imagined they would find the creatures in the barracks of the guards or the cottages in the cavern behind the docking area, where the servants and families of the guard lived. This was not the case.

When they reached the bottom of the ramp, they found the courtyard occupied. A few dozen of the Beastmen were engaged in various activities in the open space, grunts and growls echoing from the dark stone walls. The air was thick with the smell of smoke and rank sweat, as some of the creatures cooked over the fires made from smashed furniture. A pair grunted and strained, wrestling with each other. More were lying on the ground snoring.

A wolf-headed man saw Bortis as he neared the end of the ramp, pointed, and howled loudly. A dozen replies echoed around the courtyard.

"DRACOOONIIISSS!" yelled Bortis. As he shouted the

deDraconis battle cry, the blade of his short sword transformed into a three-foot blade of baleful red flame.

Artos had planned to use the rune Laguz to transform his crysword into a storm-blade, infusing it with the power of lightning in his strikes. In his mind, he instead formed Dagaz, the rune of Light, and he stopped himself just in time to avoid dazzling everyone, friend and enemy alike. He realized his sword was in his left hand again. *What's going on? I'm losing control.*

As he froze, the rest of his party went into action. Jaek engaged with a wolf-headed Beastman brandishing a huge club. Kae and Angel fired their bows rapidly, the twang of the strings reverberating through the air. Seth stepped up between Jaek and Bortis, his crystaff crackling with electrical energy. The Beastmen died in a chorus of rage-filled howls echoing throughout the courtyard.

Bortis charged into the disorganized enemy and mowed them down with his flaming blade. A mound of bodies formed before the staff of the druid and at the feet of the Fairborn bladesman. More fell to the arrows of the Daughters.

Artos's grip on his sword tightened; in his mind, he pictured Laguz, and his blade crackled with energy, blue sparks roaming up and down the length of the sword. He followed Seth and Jaek into the center of the courtyard to join Bortis. The air was heavy with the rank odor of the Beastmen's sweat, wood smoke, and the smell of water from the cavern beyond, where the cottages of the castle staff resided alongside the barracks of the guards.

Bortis glanced around, his face a picture of unrestrained fury, as if dismayed to realize he had no more opponents left in the Inner Court. Just as he opened his mouth to speak, an arrow struck him in the center of his back, shattering against his shield. Bortis was nearly knocked over by the force. Through the archway's open gate flew more arrows. Jaek dodged one as another struck Seth and bounced off. Artos ducked as one flew past his left ear. The rest failed to find targets.

Regaining his balance, Bortis surged forward, the rest following closely behind. As Artos passed through the archway into the Outer Court, his eyes began to sting; the smoke was thicker here. A half dozen Beastmen archers dropped their bows and took up their weapons as more charged from behind them. The two groups collided with a cacophony of clashing metal.

This time, Artos was not left out of the action. He and Seth stayed in front of the two archers as Jaek and Bortis forged ahead into the center of the group of Beastmen. Artos would never forget the blind fury on the faces of his foes that day, the unrelenting hate. In what seemed like hours but was actually mere minutes, the last of the Beastmen fell to Jaek's sword and Kae's arrow simultaneously.

It was only after the foe fell that Artos could begin to digest the total destruction the Beastmen had wrought. The Outer Court was an enormous cavern where, beside the warehouses that held the House's goods, both the castle staff and the majority of the Castle Guard made their homes.

Had made their homes. The thirty cottages were nothing more than piles of charred timbers in a morass of ash. The barracks and dormitories were unburned, but not a door or window remained intact; the doors had been ripped from their hinges, and the windows smashed. The warehouse doors gaped open as well and ransacked goods lay scattered around the cavern floor.

At the docks, three ships all looked intact to Artos's eye,

but everything else within the cavern appeared to be burned, ransacked, or smashed.

Jaek had suffered a few minor cuts or bruises from the skirmish, but everyone else was unharmed. Kae gave her husband first-aid in the form of almas, and Angel stood guard at the base of the Winding Way.

"Forty-three," said Seth. "I wonder if there are any more large groups of them camped anywhere else?"

"That's about the same as we accounted for in their attacks on the Eyrie," said Jaek, from where Kae was ministering to his needs. "Before we retreated. I don't think there can be many more, Art."

"We've searched the docks, the barracks, the storerooms, and the cottages," said Seth. The druid closed his eyes and shook his head. "I mean the ashes where the cottages were." He made the diamond pattern of the Church of the Four. "May Mother Veda have mercy on their souls." His voice echoed in the cavern as he said a blessing over the room in general. The druid faced Artos. "At least they burned the bodies. We will have a ceremony and bury what bones there are when we finish clearing the castle, Art. It's all we can do."

Artos surveyed the area and exclaimed, "It's just as it was at Fargo. They murdered them in their beds and then burned the cottages around them."

Bortis murmured, "Donel was right. There's a ship at the docks that doesn't belong. Two of those ships have our House markings, but not the third. Somehow, they tricked the guards into opening the gate. The House markings were removed, so I couldn't tell whose it is, but doesn't belong to House deDraconis."

"There is something strange going on," said Jaek. "With

the Beastmen, I mean. I have battled them once or twice before, years ago on the northern borders of Fairinlan." The Fairborn shook his head. "It was not like this; usually, they show more emotion than just hate and bloodlust."

Bortis snorted, obviously unconvinced. "Yeah? Like what? What emotions do the beasts show?"

"Fear," said the Fairborn warrior. "It was rare for a group of Beastmen not to turn tail and run after a few of their number were slain. It was as if these didn't care if they lived or died as long as they could harm us."

"I agree," said Seth, looking grim. "I think the abomination bewitched them, may even be controlling their actions. If so ... it knows we're here."

"We have to hope we still have some element of surprise on our side," said Artos, then he sighed. "But that's probably too much to ask. We need to find the Abominations." He wiped his face with his free hand and tried to think. *What would Uncle Brett do? What are our best tactics?*

"It's a big castle. Maybe you should go to Brierly, Bort, and bring some guards from the gatehouse. That way, we could station some to watch our backs as we make our way up through the castle."

Bortis lifted his sword with a determined look in his eyes, his voice unwavering. "I'm not going to leave you. I mean, I know you wouldn't be alone, but I'm not going."

"It has to be one of us. If we send anyone else, they will just get bogged down with questions, you know that." He realized his sword was in his left hand again, and what's more, he had no idea when he had switched hands.

His brother shook his head. "You're stuck with me. The quicker we find those Abominations, the sooner we can worry about other things."

"Blast!" Artos sheathed his crysword. "This may take a minute. My sword wants to be in the hand that's wearing the ring. I'm going to switch hands. I'll have to get it over the knuckle." He was expecting a struggle to take the ring off his left hand. He had large knuckles, and the ring was fitting snugly on his finger. Grasping the ring with his right hand, he gave a strong tug. The ring moved past his knuckle so effortlessly he almost dropped it in shock. When he slid the ring onto the third finger of his right hand, he felt it tighten again.

"Gee ... that took forever, Art," said Bortis with a sardonic smile.

Artos decided to ignore him. "Let's see if this makes any difference." He held out his hand and summoned his sword. The diamond-white blade appeared in his hand. Before he could say a word, the blade changed hue. The white shifted—sapphire-blue, then ruby-red, then emerald-green, and finally jet black. Artos gasped as thousands of needles prickled all over him, then he stiffened for an instant, then slowly relaxed. At the base of the blade, the black faded back to white diamond, and the entire blade followed suit. All except the last inch of the point, which stayed jet black.

Again, energy swept through his body. His eyes closed, and he swayed slightly.

He was floating, looking down at himself, surrounded by a stunning white aura. Bort was standing beside him, radiating a vivid red glow. Angel and Seth also had glowing auras. Seth had a luminescent, jade-like glow. Angel and Kae were a softer, lighter green and Jaek was

surrounded by a very faint reddish glow; his aura was much more delicate, like a whisper in the wind.

He could feel the power of the castle around him, and he could see every detail of its structure. The walls seemed to be made of glass, as if they weren't really there. A lattice of pale blue energy coursed through everything. He could see right through it all. He was swirled around like a leaf on the wind, aware of everything around him in the castle, everything within the lattice of energy.

A flare of bright light caught his attention somewhere above him. It was in the Royal Quarters. It was a white light, but it was not the pure white of his aura; gray shadows twisted and flowed throughout. As sure as if the name was in bright lights above it, he knew this was Mohattri, the foe he was destined to destroy. He felt an overpowering urge to run toward it. It took all of his self-control to stand there and not charge off. Something was wrong with the Royal Quarters, everything was blurry there. Everything close to Mohattri.

He tried to concentrate on Tomung—where was the other Abomination? He could see the remaining Beastmen with faint reddish auras similar to Jaek's; they were spread out across the castle. A few had stronger auras of red. The ones closest to the Abomination. So it was true—some Beastmen did have regalos.

There was no trace of Tomung. Was the trophy dead then? Or had it been taken somewhere else? Somewhere outside the Castle?

Suddenly, he was gazing down at the castle as if from a great height. His head was spinning. No, his entire being was spinning, and he was falling, falling back at the castle. Swirling like an autumn leaf tossed in the breeze. Back through the castle ...

*

Artos took a staggering step and found Bortis's hand on his shoulder, holding him steady, a worried look on his face.

"I'm sorry that took so long," said Artos as he shook his head to clear the cobwebs. "I'm back."

"Back? What are you talking about?" Bortis narrowed his eyes. "You stood there with your eyes closed for about two seconds, then you swayed a little bit, and I grabbed your shoulder. You didn't go anywhere."

Artos pointed his sword up towards the center of the keep. "Mohattri is there. The king's rooms, I think."

"That's my best guess too," nodded Bortis. "That's up five floors. Won't take us long to sweep the rooms up to there."

"No! Bort, that's where it is. I saw it in my mind. There are a half dozen others there too. Beastmen, I mean. It's the King's suite, I think." Artos closed his eyes and tilted his head back, trying to see it all again. "It's gone now, but for a moment, I could see the entire castle and everyone inside it. There are about a half dozen Beastmen up by the Eyrie and a few other pairs scattered around. Guarding the other entrances, I think. I could see everything—the entire castle in my mind … everything. There are less than twenty Beastmen left and Mohattri. I didn't sense Tomung at all. I don't think he's still in the castle. It's the ring—it detected Mohattri. It wants me to run to it, to destroy it. That's what it was made to do. I have to fight to keep from charging toward it." He opened his eyes and shook his head.

Bortis turned his head slowly and looked at the rest of the group. "This is your call, Art. I mean … you're in charge. I don't know … We have a plan … but … if you are sure …"

Jaek looked Artos in the eye. "You are sure?"

Art nodded. "What's worse, I ... I think it was aware of me. I felt something was looking back at me, just for a moment."

"Can we go straight up the Way to that floor?"

"No," said Bortis. "The Winding Way only connects with the orchestra balcony on that level. The Royal Quarters isn't open to it. It's really the only area that you can't enter directly from the Winding Way. There is a passage that connects them, but it only opens from the royal side. The quickest way is back through the Great Hall and up those first stairs we passed. Or, we can go up to the floor above—that's the Noble Level—and down to the Royal Level. The same stairs."

"I think there's a Beastman watching the Great Hall," said Artos. "He must be hidden in the shadows since we didn't see him when we passed through, but I think there was one alone there."

The Fairborn warrior thought for a moment. "Perhaps we can use this information to our advantage. Let me think." Jaek reached into his belt-pouch, produced a piece of chalk, and offered it to Bortis as he brushed a place free of debris on the floor. "Sketch me a map of the Royal Quarters. Art, show me where you think the Beastmen and the Abomination are."

Artos nodded, then shook his head from side to side again to clear his thoughts, then nodded once more.

"Are you okay, Art?" asked Seth. "You look a little woozy."

"I'm fine. I just have to adjust to only seeing this room instead of the complete castle. For a moment, I could see every living thing, us standing here too. It was ... disorienting."

Bortis knelt and drew a hasty map of the king's rooms, and when he was finished, Artos took the chalk and marked the rooms where he thought the current occupants were.

Jaek regarded the map for a long moment, then nodded. "Alright, let's consider our strategy as we head back up. We'll make our final plan when we reach the Great Hall. Art, try to keep your attention on the here and now while we are moving. Seth, keep an eye on Art. If he goes into another daze or something else happens which we should know about, give two quick whistles." The Fairborn demonstrated. "Got it?"

The druid repeated the signal, then nodded he was ready. They resumed their formation and started back up the Winding Way. The castle seemed eerily silent now, as if it were holding its breath, waiting for some calamity to strike. *Like a tomb*, Artos thought again.

There was a short hallway connecting the Great Hall and the Winding Way. They huddled together just inside and took stock. The double doors to the hall stood open just as they had left them when they passed through before.

Jaek ghosted forward, keeping tight to the left-hand wall, paused when he reached the doors, and cautiously peered in, his eyes sweeping the room. After a moment, he slipped back to the side and returned to the group.

"I couldn't see anything. The room's still empty, but the balcony up top at the far end was totally in the shadows. There could easily be a watcher there." The Fairborn warrior looked at Artos. "Can you detect anything now?"

Artos closed his eyes and turned his awareness to the ring and his crysword. For an instant, everything blurred, the castle shooting up all around him. He saw himself standing in the hallway, his friends near him. He perceived Mohattri's aura shimmering above and ahead of him. Then everything exploded in a burst of whirling colors. His consciousness shifted back into his body, and he almost lost his balance to the overwhelming vertigo. Then he felt Bort's hand, a comforting weight on his shoulder, and he inhaled deeply. "It's still up there." He pointed up and ahead and swallowed. There was a lump in his stomach, and he could feel a malevolent presence.

Jaek thought for a moment. "Kae, come up to the door with me and take a look. See if there is anything you can target." The party all moved closer as the two Fairborn hugged the wall back to the entrance of the Great Hall.

Jaek eased his head into the doorway first and looked into the hall again. After a moment, he pulled back and whispered, "No light strip in the hallway up there. It was made so people up there could look down into the hall unseen. It's too far from here to spot him in the shadows."

Kae nodded, took his place, and peered around the edge of the door, then stepped back, shaking her head. "There might be someone there," she whispered. "But nothing to target. It's too dark."

The two Fairborn rejoined the others. Jaek rubbed his chin. "We can't remove the sentry; we can't even be sure there is one."

"Alright, I have an idea," said Bortis. "We march through like we don't know we're being watched. So don't everyone look up at it. Just act normally, like when we came through before. Keeping our guard up, so if it shows itself, Kae will see it and kill it. Angel, you still watch our back. Here's my idea: When we get into the middle of the hall, I'll complain angrily that I don't think we should retreat. I won't shout or anything, but I'll speak out. Art, then you reply that we're going to send for reinforcements. Then, reluctantly, I'll pretend to go along with the idea. We'll act like we are going to the Hall of Mirrors. Then instead, we go right up the stairs."

He looked at everyone with an arched brow. When no one

disagreed, he continued. "The stairway isn't wide enough for Jaek and me to go side by side and have room enough to swing our swords, so we'll stagger. I'll lead the way since I'm shielded. I'll hug the right wall. Jaek stays three steps behind and on the left wall. Then Seth, then Art." He looked at Angel and then at Kae. "Your bows won't be of much use on the winding stairway, but keep them ready for the halls above when we reach the top."

Artos nodded. "When we get close, I'll move up and join Bort," he held up his hand with the crystal ring and his crysword. "This weapon was forged to slay Mohattri."

Jaek nodded. "When we reach the King's chambers, Seth and I will back you two."

"If you think I won't use my crysbow against that monster, you better think again," said Angel. "Kae's arrows aren't quanti like the ones I'll be shooting, but I bet she still can hurt it."

"I guess we'll find out," said Kae, her usually cheerful face grim.

"It sounds like a plan," said Jaek and looked at Artos, who nodded.

When everyone was ready, Jaek and Bortis led the way into the Great Hall. Artos was careful not to stare at the passage leading from the King's balcony. The passage where he just knew unfriendly eyes looked down at them.

When they were almost to the entrance of the hallway that led back to the Hall of Mirrors, Bortis stopped and looked back at his brother. "We don't need to get more men. We can handle them!" Artos knew the anger in his brother's voice was real.

"Bort, we were only here to scout—now we know their numbers, where they are. Once we give the word, the troops will be here in less than an hour. We'll open the gate, let them in, and we'll finish this."

"Alright … but I still think we should attack."

They passed through the doorway out of the Great Hall without incident. As they walked down the hall towards the stairs that led up to the Royal Quarters, Jaek remarked, "We may have fooled no one, but good job, Bort." Bortis just shrugged.

Artos shivered in the chill of the breeze coming down the passage. *Why is it so cold?* It felt even colder than before. He felt the dampness in the air as they approached the large puddle before the stairs.

Jaek bent down and carefully examined the puddle, feeling the water with his fingertips. He waved for the others to approach.

"The water trickling down the stairs is icy," he whispered and looked at the brothers. "Any idea where it would come from?"

"There are places where you could block the drains and turn on cold water," Artos replied softly. "Why would you, though?"

"The stairs will be slippery, and it will be harder to walk silently," said Jaek. "That's most likely the intention. What will we find at the top of the stairs?"

"The first landing we'll come to will be the Royal Quarters," Artos nodded grimly. "That's where I think it's waiting. The stairs continue up to the noble level and then the prince's level, our old rooms, but I think those are all empty. There is a hall off the landing. If there's a watcher stationed to look over the Great Hall, that's down the hallway to the right. To the left, the hall runs down to the Royal Sitting room and bedchambers beyond. There are four connected rooms across the hall which also lead to the royal suite. Remember, there are a few Beastmen around up there too, as well as Mohattri."

"That was how I remembered it from when we ran up the

stairs on our way to your rooms that night. Are the rooms all connected to the hall and each other?"

"Yes. I think all the doors are usually shut, but there was something funny about the hall. I'm not sure what. It was all blurry somehow."

"Very well. Let's move up to the landing and evaluate the situation there. Everyone, be careful. Watch the wet steps." The Fairborn motioned to Bortis, who nodded grimly, then led the way up the stairs.

Chapter Twenty-Nine:

The Royal Quarters

31

IT'S ICE

ARTOS

10/9/1971 ar

Artos mentally praised the thermal qualities of the House deSpryngdal garments as they moved up the stairs. The air grew more frigid with every step. The reason for the chill became apparent when they arrived at the Royal Level. The walls, floor, and even the ceiling were encased in thick, glistening layers of ice.

The doorway to the room across the foyer was unblocked, and the door stood open, but to the east, the door to the next room was covered by ice, and the hallway continuing that way was almost completely filled. Only a short, narrow opening was left. To traverse the hall, a person would have to stoop low as they walked on the treacherous surface. To the right, the ice was thinner and only coated the floor.

How did the creature do this? And why? Artos looked around, appalled. The air was cold and heavy, there was an oppressive underlying feeling of terror, as if evil was lurking, waiting to devour his soul. *The footing will be treacherous, but not unfamiliar. Mohattri didn't have an uncle who trained her on frozen ponds in the wintertime. Thanks again, Uncle Brett.*

After a quick appraisal of the hall, Bortis retreated a few feet down the stairs and motioned for everyone to join him. "I don't know how that creature froze everything so thoroughly," he whispered. "But I think I understand why. We have a choice of how we approach it. We can go one at a time down that narrow stretch of the hall or we go through the rooms with the Beastmen. With a floor of ice either way."

"We should head through the rooms so we can stay together," said Artos. "But we should check if there's a watcher first and remove it. Otherwise, he'll come up behind us as soon as we make any noise."

"That will be hard to do silently," said Jaek. "We don't want to alert the enemy until we attack. Hopefully, by surprise."

"Leave the watcher to us," said Kae, and Angel nodded in agreement. "We'll wait here on the stairs. If one appears, it will die. The hall leads right to it, I hope?"

"Yes," said Artos. "The hall leads to the balcony. It runs down about forty feet to a corner. Then it's about twenty more to the arch that opens onto the Great Hall."

"I smell a trap," said Seth. "It's pretty obvious, really. We are to be channeled into going through the four rooms with the Beastmen. The Abomination swoops down the hall and falls on us from behind. Don't you think?"

"The ice will slow it down too," said Bortis. "By the time it gets behind us, the Beastmen will be dead. Not much of a plan."

Jaek shook his head. "After the beast murdered your father, it ran up the wall as easily as it ran across the floor. That's probably why it made the floors all ice."

"It won't know we know that. Can we use that plan against it somehow?" Artos looked around at the group. "Any suggestions?"

"I have a thought," said Jaek. "It depends on where the Beastmen are, though. We didn't see any through the open door across the hall. That is room one. They might be waiting there in ambush, or they might be deeper in. We have to plan for either contingency. My gut feeling is the next room to the west, room two, will be empty as well, and they'll be waiting to jump us in room three."

"It would be nice to know where they are, but ..." Bortis shrugged.

"I can try to scry again," said Artos. "Give me one second." He closed his eyes and concentrated.

It was easier to slip into the state every time he did so. He experienced a brief sensation of vertigo, and for a moment, the lattice of energy surrounded him once more. There was a watcher near the Great Hall and two groups of Beastmen in the last two rooms to the west before the Royal Sitting room.

The Abomination was a cloudy shape of writhing blackness waiting in the sitting room. The instant he saw it, he became aware of two glowing red eyes burning back into his. It knew he was there!

The shape gestured. Suddenly, he was tossed into a swirling maelstrom of twisted color and energy, and he fell from a long distance...

*

Artos found himself leaning against the wall, held in place by his brother.

"What happened?" they said simultaneously.

"You first," said Artos as he shook himself, then bent over and picked up his crysword from where he had dropped it in the icy water that soaked the stairway's carpet.

"You stood there for about two seconds, maybe three, and then your head slumped to the side, and I caught you and kept you from collapsing."

"It felt longer than that." He shook his head, trying to clear the cobwebs. "It looked at me. It knows we're here."

"Are you sure?" asked Seth.

Artos nodded grimly. "I saw everything, just for a minute. There is a watcher out by the balcony. The other four or five Beastmen are in the rooms further down. Like your hunch, Jaek."

"No sense in waiting then," said Jaek." Let's do this. I'll go first, with Seth following me. I'll engage the Beastmen. I won't have any problem, even with half a dozen of them, but Seth will be my backup, just in case. The commotion will draw the Abomination out to attack us from behind. By the time it gets to you, the Beastmen will be dead or soon to be. Seth's actual job will be to turn and face the Abomination. Art, you and Bort will each wait to the side of the doorway of the second room. When the Abomination enters the room, Seth will use his magic to distract the creature. Then you two attack from its flanks, and Art can use the weapon forged to destroy it."

Artos nodded. "I'm not sure exactly what they intended

the weapon to do, but I'm sure it does more than just locate the beast. When my sword touches the creature, it will be something spectacular; I'm betting on it. I can feel the weapon thirsting for its life."

"I'll be ready to cover my eyes," said Seth, flashing Artos a quick smile.

"We'll wait for the watcher," said Angel. "It won't join the Abomination against you. We'll turn it into a pincushion."

"We're guessing the Abomination will be much faster than the watcher because of the icy floor," said Jaek. "If the watcher gets there first, let it go by, wait for the Abomination to go into the room, then follow and shoot at whatever target presents itself. Don't face the Abomination alone."

"He's right," said Artos. "Your job is the watcher, first off. Don't attack the Abomination until after the watcher is dispatched."

Angel smiled. "We won't steal your glory, Art." He smiled tightly in return.

When he was sure all were ready, Jaek led the way. With soft, sure steps, the Fairborn moved across the ice-covered floor of the foyer into the first of the four rooms that led to the king's sitting room. Seth followed close behind him, then Bortis, and finally Artos.

The floor of the room was still ice-covered. Jaek stayed near the wall as he led the way to the open doorway and to the next room. Looking in, he motioned for the others to follow.

When Artos followed his brother into the second room, Jaek was nearing the closed door to the next room, with Seth close behind. He and Bortis each moved off to the sides, Artos to the left, Bortis to the right. Each turned so their backs were to the wall with their cryswords nearest the doorway, positioning themselves to ambush the Abomination when it followed them out of the first room.

Once Jaek reached the far door, he looked back to see if everyone was ready. Seth was a step behind him. Artos and Bortis were in place at the sides of the door they had come through. When he saw he had their attention, he nodded, smiled a tight smile, and gave them a thumbs-up with his left hand. Artos gave him a small wave. He watched as the Fairborn took a deep breath, turned around, flung open the door, and jumped into the room with a slide and a loud shout.

Chapter Thirty:

First Blood

32

NOT QUITE WHAT
THEY EXPECTED

JAEK

SETH

WHEN JAEK LANDED AT THE READY, he expected to be facing some surprised Beastmen. Instead, it looked as though they were expected. All three were holding weapons, but no large clubs or huge axes awaited him here. To his consternation, he saw the two wolf-heads and the Beastman with the head of a bull were holding longswords—black longswords that gleamed like polished jet—black-bladed cryswords! At that instant, he realized he was in much more danger than he had anticipated.

Behind the wolf-heads, the door to the next room stood open. Inside, he could see two Beastmen with the heads of wild boars, also bearing black cryswords. They were standing next to a brass gong. Upon seeing him, one of the boar-heads slapped his crysword against the face of the gong, which rang forth with a loud crash. Then they charged forward, their wide splayed, clawed feet gripping the icy floor better than his moccasins.

"Seth!" he shouted and slide-stepped to his right, thrusting at the wolf-head coming at him on that side. His longsword met the blade of the black crysword, and the black blade sheared through his fine steel blade as though it were a twig. The pointed third of his blade fell to the ice with a clatter. Pulling the remaining blade back in desperation, he tried to formulate a plan. The next thrust by the Beastman was soon to follow, and his sword would be useless in attempting to parry.

Seth didn't see the damage to Jaek's sword as he took another step onto the icy floor. He did see the black cryswords and two more Beastmen entering the room. *We're in trouble,* he thought as he realized their plan had gone awry. *I can't turn my back on this.* Jaek could handle three Beastmen, without a doubt. Five Beastmen with cryswords was another matter. Jaek would be at a serious disadvantage without a crystal weapon of his own. *Art will see I haven't turned back. He and Bort will have to do without me for a minute.*

The druid shouted at the second wolf-head as he stepped to the left, swung his staff around and pointed the blunt staff at the bull-headed Beastman as if it were a spear. The Beastman gave a mocking shout and swung his crysword to knock the staff aside. Seth raised the tip nimbly out of the weapon's path, dropped it back down, and pressed it against the chest of his foe. The Beastman's sword slammed into the open door and drove it back into the wall. It bounced back in the opposite direction and swung closed with a bang. The bull-head sneered, then looked shocked as Seth mentally extended a six-inch-long razor-sharp point to burst from the blunt end of the crystaff into the surprised creature's chest. It collapsed with a choking cry, drawing the attention of the second wolf-head.

Seth quickly retracted the blade and swung his staff to block the slash from the charging wolf-head. He executed a low counter-swing as a follow-up, hoping to take out a leg and cause the Beastman to fall on the slippery, ice-covered floor. The wolf-head growled as the staff smashed against his leg and spun around, taking a half step back while flailing wildly with his sword.

Meanwhile, Jaek had dodged the first thrust of the now-growling wolf-head and then lost half of his remaining blade, knocking aside the riposte. He heard the grunting breath of an excited, boar-tusked Beastmen behind him. He had only a moment until he was attacked from behind. He kicked out with his left foot into the right knee of his wolf-head attacker and nimbly used it to spin on the ice to face the new threat. A painful yelp came from the wolf-head as its knee cracked. Jaek used his spinning motion to throw the remaining few inches of his sword at the face of the furthest away boar-head. He continued the spin, pushing his body to his left to narrowly avoid the thrust of the closer boar-head. As he continued, he grasped the boar-head's sword arm and directed his thrust into the midsection of the wolf-head behind him, who was fighting to stand erect with his injured knee. It howled as his companion ran him through and collapsed to the icy floor in a pool of blood.

Releasing the arm, he continued to spin, pushing off the boar-head, who was staring dumbfounded at the ally he had just skewered, to face the other boar-head who had dodged the hilt of Jaek's broken sword. It swung its crysword in a murderous cut at the Fairborn's neck. Jaek threw himself backward out of the sword's path, crashing into the boar-head, who was pulling its sword from the body of the now dead wolf-head. Jaek drove his elbow hard into the kidneys of the boar-head and twisted to his right to put both boar-heads in front of him. As he spun, the boar-head who was attacking him thrust at him again.

Once more, the Fairborn warrior twisted. At first, Jaek thought he had evaded the blade, but the whisper of pressure touched his left arm. As he spun away, he felt blood running down his wrist. With his right hand, he pulled his dagger from its thigh sheath.

Seth swung his crystaff around over his head, letting the staff slide through his hands to grasp it by the end just as it lined up with the remaining wolf-head. He lunged once more. The wolf-head tried to pull back, but before he could gain traction, the razor-sharp spear point impaled him. He collapsed. The druid quickly glanced over at Jaek.

Jaek was backing up with a pair of boar-heads moving up to flank him and come at him from opposite directions. Seth pulled back the spearheaded crystaff, and shouted, "By The Mother!" Then he threw it across the room at the boar-head on his left.

At the sound, the boar-head turned and swatted the spear out of the air with its black crysword, contempt apparent on its tusked face.

The creature charged at the unarmed druid, as Seth hoped it would. His splayed feet clawed for traction on the icy floor. Seth summoned his crystaff back into his hands, knocked the black crystal sword aside, and smoothly continued the swing with the butt end of the staff up under the chin of the boar-head, knocking its head back. As the Beastman fell backward to the floor, he spun the staff around once more, slamming the spear point through the creature's heart.

When Seth yelled and the boar-heads turned to look, Jaek made a diving attack at the distracted Beastman to his left. His dagger passed beneath the lunging blade of the boar-head and lodged deep within its side. The beast looked down incredulously just in time for its chin to meet the hard fist of the Fairborn warrior, knocking its head back. Before it could recover, Jaek's dagger slashed the boar-head's throat, dropping the last Beastman. The Fairborn dropped his dagger and clutched his wounded arm with his other hand.

Seth saw the blood gushing down Jaek's left arm and made his way across the icy floor. Jaek tried to wave him off and pointed at the closed door. "The Abomination … Seth!"

Seth ignored Jaek's words. Jaek was spurting blood. An artery must have been slashed; Jaek would bleed to death in minutes if left untreated. Seth clamped his hands around the wounded arm and concentrated on bonding the severed blood vessel. He invoked the regalo of healing, of growth. The flesh merged under his hands as he chanted a healing prayer to Mother Veda. From behind the closed door, he heard a shout and then a loud scream. With a loud thump, the door burst open behind him.

Chapter Thirty-One:

Mohattri

33

TO THE DEATH

ARTOS

From across the room, Artos heard Jaek's cry of "Seth!" Then the door to the third room slammed shut, separating the brothers from the Fairborn and the druid. He had time to look at his brother in dismay, but before either could speak, a scrabbling sound came from the room behind them. *Could it move that fast?* thought Artos. He heard the ice screech outside the door and tensed to attack. But no Abomination came through the door.

"Foolish little boys," came a deep, rough voice. "I know you're standing there ready to jump out at me. I can smell your dragon blood. Come out and let's talk. Don't be afraid. You don't have to sulk around corners."

Even through his Mindshield, Artos could feel the attention of the monster. He could feel its monstrous mental force attacking him, hammering on his Mindshield, looking for an opening to enter his mind. Artos looked at Bortis, and they each shook their heads at the same time. Bortis lifted his crysword, and flames adorned the blade once again. Artos raised his sword in an answering salute to his brother, then directed his attention to the crysword. No regalo confronted him. He again felt an eagerness from the weapon, and then nothing. Panic filled him. The ring and the sword. They were meant to destroy Mohattri. Why wasn't anything happening?

At that moment, a squealing shriek split the air from beyond the Abomination. The watcher must have arrived from the balcony, and Angel and Kae must have shot it. He felt the Abomination's attention shift away from him. It was going to go kill Angel! Artos didn't question how he knew this. He had to act now!

"Mohattri!" he shouted as he stepped in front of the open door and looked back into the first room.

Even though Veryan had shown him the creature in its bestial form, he was not fully prepared. He stepped back, feeling a chill of revulsion. Muscles rippled under its matted black fur as it stood before him. The creature was seven feet tall, gaunt, and bestial, with the fanged jaws of a monster and muscular arms and legs. A putrid smell entered his nostrils. His stomach churning, he clenched his teeth to keep from gagging in revulsion.

With a menacing hiss, the large, red eyes glared at him with hate. He could feel its malice battering futilely at his Mindshield. It clenched its fists, and from each hand, a glistening foot-long black blade extended. It smiled at him with barred fangs, hissed again, and took a step forward.

Mohattri's mouth opened wide and emitted a screech. A beam of pure sonic force struck him in the chest like a battering ram. He slid backward across the ice on the seat of his pants, a horrid ringing in his ears.

The Abomination burst through the doorway and immediately turned to the right, swinging its right arm up. It caught the descending fiery blade of Bortis's crysword and pinned it to the wall with its black blade. Its left arm swung in an arc designed to slash open Bortis's throat, or maybe remove his entire head.

Artos watched in horror as Bortis reacted with pure instinct. His sword and left arm were pinned against the wall. He grabbed at the blade with his right hand, wearing the glove he had found in the cabinet in the armory. The thin and supple leather of the glove should have been sliced through by the razor-sharp crystal blade, along with Bortis's flesh. Instead, there was a flash and a crunching sound. The Abomination hissed with dismay as the black crystal blade failed to do any harm. The creature jumped back, releasing Bortis's pinned arm and causing him to stagger to his right before he regained his balance.

Artos rose to his feet and shouted a wordless cry of rage. The creature turned and looked back and forth between the brothers.

"I have to admit you make a better showing than any of your pitiful relatives." The creature made a hissing chuckle. "Someone's been teaching you. Still, do you think you stand a chance against me? Such arrogance." The monster feinted toward Bortis, who retreated back another step. In an instant, the blade from the creature's left hand changed from a rapier-like blade to a twelve-inch black needle that flew like a dart straight at Artos's chest.

Artos reacted without thinking, and his sword flicked up and struck the missile. The black needle shattered in a bright flash, and with a loud *crack!* was no more.

Mohattri hissed at the noise, but its attention quickly shifted back to Bortis as he leaped forward and thrust at the creature's neck. Mohattri parried the blow with its right-hand blade and then quickly riposted. Bortis slipped on the ice and clumsily knocked the counter-thrust partially aside, so the blade only slashed his shoulder instead of piercing his chest. Bortis went pale instantly and gave a hoarse cry. Artos saw a change flash across his brother's face. He suddenly looked drained, as if the blade had sucked the vitality from his body. He gave a weak moan as he fell onto his back and tried to roll away.

"BORT!" cried Artos as the creature gave a triumphant shout, a new blade sprouting from its left fist. It turned back to face Artos, its face contorted with hate.

Artos realized he had been expecting something spectacular to happen when he confronted the Abomination with the weapon designed to defeat it, but other than a brief feeling of eager awareness, there was no reaction from the weapon. It was up to him, after all. Staring into the blazing red eyes so filled with hate gave him an idea. He held up his sword with the blade pointed at the ceiling.

"DAGAZ!" he shouted, clamping his eyes tightly shut and trying to call forth the brightest light possible.

Mohattri's red eyes were open wide when the light of a hundred suns flashed blindingly in the room.

Mohattri screamed, and the sonic blast knocked Artos off his feet backwards into the door that led to room three, knocking it open and leaving him sitting on the ice in front of the doorway.

ANGEL
KAE

Crouched with Kae on the stairs, waiting for the watcher Beastman to come charging from the balcony, Angel heard faint shouts and knew the fight had begun. Then she heard the scraping of claws and had a brief glimpse of a large, black, furry something as it moved out of the ice tunnel and into the room across the hall, disappearing from sight. The two archers barely had time to look at each other in shock at the speed of the monster when their attention was drawn to the scratching sound of splayed, clawed feet scrabbling on the ice.

The watcher came down the hallway from the overlook, slipping and sliding on the icy floor. Shouts came from the room across the hall. With smooth grace, the two archers stood up and drew back their arrows for the shot.

A boar-headed Beastman burst into view, and the two bowstrings twanged as one. Two arrows plunked into the chest of the monstrous warrior. The boar-head gave a loud squealing roar.

To Angel's dismay, the creature didn't instantly fall dead, but instead turned to charge, a large mace with a black crystal head clutched in its monstrous hand. Even as Kae was drawing a second arrow from her quiver, Angel was pulling back the string of her crysbow. On the string, an arrow of white light materialized out of nowhere. Gently, she released the string, and the arrow of light flew with precision to strike between the Beastman's eyes. The creature's head snapped back abruptly and it collapsed, twitching.

As the archers started across the foyer to follow the Abomination, there was a bright flash of light and a scream of such magnitude that both girls dropped their bows and covered their ears.

ARTOS

The force of Mohattri's scream deafened Artos. His head threatened to explode. His eyes flew open. He dropped his sword and clapped his hands to his ears. The Abomination frantically rubbed its eyes, then dropped its hands down, swinging its arms wildly, a blade extended from each fist. *YES! It's blind!* he exalted. He pushed himself to his feet and summoned his crysword to his hand.

As soon as he grasped the hilt of his blade, the sword began to change. The blade grew till it was double in length. Coruscating bands of color swept down the blade from the hilt to the point where they dissipated in a flurry of colored sparks. A golden aura of light surrounded his body as if encasing him in golden armor.

It's my turn now! he thought, lunging at the creature. His gleaming sword cut through the air to intercept one of Mohattri's sharp black blades. The Abomination's blade shattered in a cascade of purple sparks. A faint, far-away crackling sound reached his ears, as if his hearing was distorted. The black tip of his crysword abruptly extended a further six inches, and the black color spread further back toward the hilt, leaving the sword's blade half jet black and half diamond white, covered with flowing bands of color and dripping colored sparks. Artos gripped the now enlarged hilt with his other hand and swung the blade around to connect with the monster's remaining blade with the same shattering results.

Artos could see Mohattri was screaming. Its mouth was open wide, but the sound was faint, as if it were not standing right in front of him, but far away. His golden armor was absorbing the sonic attack, nullifying it. As he watched, its body begin to change, to shrink.

In an instant, all the thick black fur was gone, replaced with a plain gray robe. She was small, pale, and hairless with gray skin and huge, blind-looking white eyes. There was a blue tattoo of the rune Hagalaz etched on each cheek. Her appearance was even more disturbing than her monstrous shape. It was twisted and deformed. The creature flailed away blindly, her fists striking him, abruptly dissolving the golden armor. He felt his energy being sucked up by her blows as she battered away. *I need to end this quickly,* he thought.

Artos suddenly felt as if everything was in slow motion. The sword in his hand shrank back into a short sword. He thrust, the blade stabbing the creature through her heart. The ring on his hand blazed with hot white light. There was a painful burning of his ring finger, and his crysword blazed to match it. One last wave of color washed down the length of the blade, taking the black color away as it went, leaving him holding his pure white short sword again.

The body of Mohattri turned to dust before his eyes. Then dust fell from where the ring had been on his finger. His eyes closed, and he slumped to the floor.

Chapter Thirty-Two:

Fairinhorst Again

34

DID WE WIN?

CARIMUS

10/9/1971 ar

CARIMUS OPENED HIS EYES. "Artie!" he shouted and sat up with a start.

He looked around. He was in his cubicle, on his sleeping mat. Perfaren was with him in the room, leaning over the table. After a moment, he turned and offered him a manna-filled goblet.

Carimus realized how weak and thirsty he felt. He gladly took the offered cup and drained it in one long drink. He handed back the now-empty goblet to his mentor, who set it back on the table, then leaned back to recline upon his elbows.

"Your pode will nourish your body while you are in the Overworld, seeker. It will keep your body fresh and rested, but there is one thing it cannot do. Something that every seeker must do for themselves."

"What is that, Sensei?"

"Sleep, Seeker Carimus." The Fairborn looked grave. "Sleep

and dreams are a very necessary thing for every person. You went far too long without either. This is one reason I thought you were not yet ready to make your first excursion into the Tavári Ambar. Without proper instruction, such voyages are extremely unwise. Yet here we are." Perfaren shook his head and sighed.

"The healers have examined you, and you seem none the worse for wear. When the Angellar informed me that you were unconscious at your pode, I hurried there, found you, and had you brought here. The healers examined your body, but the chief danger was to your mind. Tell me, how do you feel? Is there any dizziness or numbness? Do you have a headache?"

"I'm okay, but I have to know—what happened to Art? Did they get to Castle Draconis, or did that thing get him?" He tried to sit up again, but a wave of exhaustion forced him to remain prone. He laughed. "Okay, I'm probably not fine, but I'm just weak, no headache. If I tried to stand up, I would probably feel dizzy. My head is alright, but I'm worried. There was a monster ..." He trailed off, going over the events in his mind. "I think it followed me back. The Angellar needs to know!" He made to sit up again, but Perfaren placed a restraining hand on his shoulder.

"The defenses of Fairinhorst are still in place. Be assured, the Angellar knows if anything tries to intrude upon her stronghold. If anything followed you, it failed to breach her defenses."

"I need to talk with her." Waves of exhaustion swept over him. "I just need to rest a few minutes." He lay his head back down on the mat as his eyes closed ...

*

He was standing before the rose throne, with the Angellar regarding him with an amused smile.

I felt it was best to put you to sleep, Cari, so we could have this conversation. My healers have decided you need rest, and I concur.

"What happened to Artie? There was a monster at Starstone Tower! It was there in the cold and the dark, just like you told me. I had to warn Art, so I tried to sneak past it. It heard me though. I thought it was going to get Art, so I yelled at it. Then it came after me and I ran away. I think it followed me back!" He looked around the interior of the chamber, half expecting the monster to appear.

Nothing tried to follow you into Fairinhorst, Cari. Whatever followed you didn't try to enter here.

"I'm glad. I was worried. I shouldn't have run off so quickly." He hung his head and studied the floor before the rose throne. "I think I got Art to take the right ring, but then he was going to take another one too. I tried to stop him. That's when the thing heard me, and I ran. Is Art safe?"

Yes, Cari, your brother is safe. Sleep now. We will speak again soon.

The scene dissolved around him, and he sank into a deep and dreamless sleep.

Chapter Thirty-Three:

We Won

35

WHAT WAS THE COST?

ARTOS

WHEN ARTOS OPENED HIS EYES, everything was blurry. Two worried faces stared down at him in a blur. Feebly, he rubbed his eyes, and the faces resolved into Angel and Kae. His head was spinning. He felt dazed and confused as they helped him sit upright. Looking around, he felt a chill run down his spine.

Seth was carrying the limp form of his brother. *Is Bort dead?* He tried to shout his brother's name, but his voice failed him. Struggling, he tried to get to his feet, but he felt so weak he nearly fell back to his knees.

Leaning heavily on the shoulder of Angel, he managed to stand upright. At her direction, they moved together, one step at a time, slowly across a vast expanse of ice to the stairs. Seth led the way, carrying the motionless form of his brother. He and Angel were last, trailing Kae and Jaek, who were also leaning on one another. One of Jaek's arms was heavily bandaged and worn in a sling. The stairway down seemed endless. He concentrated on putting one foot ahead of the other, going down the slick, wet stairway. Finally, they reached the bottom, and after another seemingly endless trek, he was standing in front of a door with a crystal screen. As he stood staring at the door, he realized Angel was pleading with him to please open it. He focused on the task. *I can do this.* He placed his hand against the screen and bid the door to open, then watched as it swung open. He was so tired.

Several people were trying to talk to him. He could hear them in the distance. Was that Donel speaking? Was he here? He was trying to decide who to ask about Bort when he sat down on the cushioned oak bench with a thump. The room was spinning round and round. Just a short nap …

Chapter Thirty-Four:

Aftermath

36

AND NOW
IT BEGINS

ARTOS

10/10/1971 ar

11:15 a.m.

ARTOS SLEPT THE EVENING and then the night away. His first thought upon awakening was of Bortis. He was relieved to see his brother snoring softly on another bench nearby.

Jaek and Kae were sitting near his brother, but when he stirred, Kae rose and moved closer.

"How are you feeling, Art?" She reached over, took his wrist, and examined his right hand. "How does your hand feel?"

He remembered the ring blazing brightly with burning light. He flexed his fingers, and his hand felt pain-free. "I feel okay. My hand feels good. I thought I burned it, but ..." He flexed his fingers again.

"Oh, you did. It was bright red, scalded. You had some cracked ribs as well. Nothing almas and some rest can't deal with. You will feel weak for a few days. That creature was stealing your life-energy, your essence, like she had with Bort.

447

Only time can heal that kind of injury, but you will both be fine. My husband as well. Seth helped with his wound. He was cut with a black crystal weapon. The black crystal feeds on life energy."

"Black crystal weapons?" Artos shook his head.

"The Beastmen had black cryswords," said Jaek.

"The watcher we dealt with had a black-crystal mace," said Kae.

"Where is Angel?" Artos looked around the Hall of Mirrors. "And Seth? Are they alright?"

"Hunting," said Jaek. "I tried to get them to wait till I could join them." The Fairborn warrior tried to lift his arm, grimaced in pain, and lowered it. "They didn't want to wait. They left about four hours ago. Seth said they'd report back around noon. Another hour or so."

"They should have waited." He tried to remember his vision of the castle and the number of the foes remaining. "I don't think there were very many left." He rubbed the side of his head. "I don't really remember. It's like I was dreaming."

"That's what you said." Kea nodded. "Angel remembered, and she and Seth decided to go find them while they were still separated. She said if we waited, they might join together and be harder to overcome."

"Was Donel here? On the screens, I mean."

"Yes, he was waiting for us when we returned here last night," she glanced at the timekeeper above the room's door. "He will be back soon."

"I'm here now," came the voice of his mentor as the screen with the double-dragon icon above it changed from inert to active. The concerned face of Donel deDraconis gazed back at him. "Well done, Artos. Well done indeed." The magic man smiled. The smile changed back to concern. "How is Bortis?"

"He's fine," said Bortis, sitting up and running a hand through his hair. Artos thought his brother looked extremely pale, no matter what he said.

"The weapon I found in Starstone destroyed her." Artos looked at Donel. "It's all fuzzy now. I think there might be another Abomination hiding there."

"In the Armory?" asked Donel.

"No, it couldn't get in there, but there was something there somewhere. Angel and I both sensed it. And just before we left, we all heard ... something. It howled, and then it made a horrible laughing sound." Artos shrugged. "We didn't see anything."

"I'll scry. Other than the Hall of Mirrors, I can't look into the Armory Tower, but I should be able to search the rest of the building."

"It may hide with illusions," said Artos, remembering his lessons. "You can't truesee through the screens."

Donel smiled. "You never know what you might find if you look hard enough. The Darrell will be checking in on you at noon. I expect Maria will join as well. I'm going to take a quick scry at Starstone, but I'll be back to join the conversation." With that, the screen from the Crystal Tower went inert.

At Kae's insistence, the brothers each breakfasted on a stick of jerky while they waited for the upcoming meetings. As they were finishing, the door to the chamber pushed open, and Angel and Seth entered the Hall of Mirrors, to everyone's relief.

Angel gave Artos a smile and a thumbs-up when she saw he was sitting up and eating.

Seth sat down on an empty bench and stretched. "There were ten of them left," the druid reported. "They had a barricade across the top of the Winding Way with six of them on guard there. There were two at the doors to the airship docks and two more at a watch post on the west side. I'm happy to say that none of them were armed with cryswords. I believe it is safe to say that Castle Draconis is free of Beastmen."

"The bad news," said Angel, "is there was no trace of the missing head of Tomung."

"I was afraid of that," said Artos. "I tried to locate him, but all I saw were Beastmen and Mohattri."

"You destroyed one Abomination," said Angel. "You recovered your castle, and that's the important thing."

Artos nodded. "I just hate knowing he's out there somewhere. It feels like the job's not finished." He took a deep breath and then sighed.

"It's just beginning," said Bortis. "Your job, I mean. No one will be able to say you aren't worthy to be king."

Shortly after noon, Donel rejoined them via the screens, along with The Darrell and Countess Marie.

"I have viewed everywhere I can within Starstone," said Donel. "I found no sign of anything there now." Artos thought Donel didn't look convinced, a thought shared by Bortis.

"Now?" asked Bortis. "Nothing now?"

"In the uppermost rooms of the central tower, there were some signs that someone had been there not long ago. The dust had been disturbed in several rooms, but I didn't scry anyone there now."

"That is something we will have to keep an eye on," said Artos. "I will open the school there again. But first things first. We need to get the castle back in order, and then we need to make the announcement to the other Houses."

Plans were made for Artos to journey to Phoenix with The Darrell on his airship in two days. Both House deDarrellyel and

House deSpryngdal would send troops to help secure his castle while he was away in the lowlands.

Donel speculated that the head of Tomung had been placed into the care of Anndr, who, upon his giant crow, had taken it back to whatever stronghold the Abominations maintained in the wastelands to the east, far beyond the Black Mountains. Everyone agreed the troubles with the Abominations were far from settled.

Then there was the matter of the traitors in the Houses deAnson and deHerndar. They discussed the matter well into the afternoon until Kae insisted that Artos and Bortis needed to eat and rest.

The next morning, Artos began the immense clean-up needed to bring Castle Draconis back to a respectable condition.

First, he directed his brother to take Seth and see what the situation was across the moat at the gatehouse. Sargeant McArn was among the first of the troops that Bortis found across the Loch in Brierly. They left a skeleton guard at the gatehouse across the loch and moved the rest of the men from there into the castle.

Bortis and Jarid also gathered what servants there were, and with a few volunteers from the people of Brierly, they brought a group to begin the enormous undertaking of restoring the castle.

Once they returned, Artos removed the grisly remains of his father and great-uncle from the wall of trophies and prepared to entomb their remains in the family crypt. That afternoon, Seth held the ceremony, also sanctifying the ashes in the cavern, the only vestiges of the Beastmen's massacre of the staff and guards.

Artos quickly promoted McArn to be captain of his personal

guard and Corporal Shawn Dorime to Captain of the Eyrie. Captain Jarid derDraconis was promoted from Captain of the gatehouse to Marshal of Castle Draconis, replacing his father in the role. All in all, it was a very busy day.

There was a hint of snow in the evening air as Artos stood on the Eyrie battlements. Tomorrow he would be down on the airship dock awaiting The Darrell's airship, but this evening was his. He gazed at the King's Valley from the highest point of the castle—his castle. That seemed so strange to consider, but it was true. His father and his uncles were gone. *It's just me and Bort now. At least until Cari comes back. I wonder if he found news of Duke?*

As he waited, he tried practicing his farseeing without a screen to aid him. Donel had told him that he didn't need a screen to farsee, something Uncle Cameron had never even suggested was possible.

He placed his newly healed right hand against the hilt of his sheathed crysword. Donel had told him it wasn't necessary, but he felt that maybe using it as a crutch might make it feel easier, more natural. When Cameron had taught him to use the quanti, he had taught him it was a needed accessory. Uncle Cameron was probably wrong, but old habits were the hardest to break.

He focused his concentration, forming the runes Ansuz and Ehwaz in his thoughts. He looked to the southeast, toward the demesne of The Darrell. His vision went fuzzy, then suddenly, the green and black banner of the House was flapping in the wind in his view. He was gazing at the manse of Darrelhaas. Sitting on the expansive rooftop was a small airship, the big green lift-balloon swaying in the breeze, the sails as yet unfurled. Men in the deDarrellyel livery marched up and down the gangway, preparing the ship for tomorrow's journey. It wouldn't be long now. He would climb aboard that ship with his brother and a handful of the surviving House guards, and they would fly to the capital.

He didn't look forward to Phoenix, but the Solstice was just over sixty days away. Before the Concourse of the Great Houses, there was so much to do. He had to convince his grandfather, Count Estel, and his future father-in-law, Count Eagledon, to stand with him. Then, with a majority of the council behind him, he would be crowned King of Veda. Afterwards, they could explore the rot within the Houses. House deAnson and House deHerndar must be examined and proved loyal to the crown. There would be new guards to train and servants to hire. Some of the palace servants would have to be relocated next spring to make Castle Draconis his summer home. He projected a great deal of turbulence in the upcoming months.

How different from the plans of a few short weeks ago. Instead of the double birthday party for him and Duka, along with the announcement of his betrothal to Elaine, now there would be a betrothal announcement and a coronation. *I wonder if Cari has found any trace of Duke?* he thought again. He felt a pang of guilt. He never even discussed either of his absent brothers with Donel and the rest.

Artos sighed; so much needed to be done. He pulled back his vision, scanning the road that led from the deDarrellyel demesne to Castle Draconis. Yes, there they were, a few miles along the way. The Darrell had dispatched another hundred troops to secure Castle Draconis while he was away. They were marching along the road, throwing up dust as they passed through the drought-stricken land that lay before the desolated heath extending to the ruins of Blachaas. Count Glendon had assured him they would arrive sometime tomorrow morning.

Remembering the unusual sight of Blachaas Angel had seen on the Starstone screens, Art moved his vision away from the marching troops and scanned the Blasted Heath, which lay before the mountains and the entrance to the deYung lands with his newfound farseeing. The heath was a nightmarish vision of scorched earth and ashes. Three hundred years and still no new plant growth disturbed the ruined ground. Artos shook his head and marveled at the destruction caused by the ancient weapon.

He looked further up the heath until he gazed at the burnt-out shell of the deYung stronghold. As he gazed at the ruins, he added the regalos for trueseeing. His vision shivered, and suddenly, as if a bubble burst, he was staring at the stronghold as he had seen it in the memorial screens at Starstone—whole and undestroyed. The building looked deserted, abandoned. *What is going on?* he thought. *Is it destroyed, or isn't it?* As he watched, he saw a bat fly out of an open window at the peak of one of the castle's towers and flit off on its nightly feeding flight.

With another shiver, the scene changed, and once again he was staring at ruins. Though he tried to evoke trueseeing again, the effort was futile. The vision of the unbroken castle did not return. Artos shook his head, then rubbed his eyes. The ruins mocked him; what was real?

Artos felt his knees grow rubbery, and he leaned against the battlements to keep from falling. As if in a dream, he stood alone on a vast plain facing another monster, like another Mohattri, but he knew somehow this was a different foe, and he had no special weapon for this monster. He summoned his crysword to his hand and readied himself for battle, but suddenly the creature began to ripple, to twist and change, to grow ... to grow enormously. Giant batlike wings sprang from its back; it opened its huge, fanged maw and roared. It was a dragon!

Then the vision was gone. He was standing on the battlements, staring at the distant Black Mountains. Somewhere beyond those mountains would be the remaining Abominations. Mohattri might be destroyed, but Tomung remained, as did Anndr of the monstrous Raven, and the rest. His conflict with the Abominations wasn't over. It was more likely to have only just begun.

APPENDIXES

THE CALENDAR OF VEDA

The calendar of Renn and Veda consists of three hundred and sixty-four days in twelve months. Eight months of thirty days and four of thirty-one. The months with the equinox and solstice are the longer months. There are six holidays: New Year Day, Spring Equinox, Summer Solstice, Autumnal Equinox, Winter Solstice, and Year End Day (also called Old Year Day). The equinoxes are especially Holy for the Earth Mother Veda. The Solstices are dedicated to the Sky Father Quai. New Year Day is dedicated to The Unknown, and Old Year Day to Time.

Janus	30 days	New Year Day on the 1st
Febrous	30 days	
Marcous	31 days	Spring Equinox on the 15th
Aprilous	30 days	
Maymont	30 days	
Junmont	31 days	Summer Solstice on the 15th
Julous	30 days	
Augous	30 days	
Ninmont	31 days	Autumnal Equinox on the 15th
Tenous	30 days	
Minquos	30 days	
Rastous	31 days	Winter Solstice on the 15th and Old Year Day on the 31st

The days of the week are known by number names:

Firstday - Monday

Seconday - Tuesday

Thirday - Wednesday

Fourthday - Thursday

Fifthday - Friday

Sixthday – Saturday

Sevenday - Sunday

The First Age of Man ended with the First Quantum War. There followed a period of time when the world was in chaos, which ended with the Second Quantum War and the Reckoning. This was followed by the rise of the Great Houses in Veda. The calendar starts after the Reckoning. The years are labeled as xxxx ar, which stands for After the Reckoning. The Glory Road begins in 1971 ar. This is roughly two thousand years after the end of the First Age.

DRAMATIS PERSONAE
THE GREAT HOUSES

<u>DEDRACONIS</u>

Aaron Draconis
High King of Veda

Evelyn Draconis ne`dePenrodyn (*deceased*)
Queen of Veda

Cameron deDraconis (uncle of Aaron)
Archduke Archbishop of Veda

Bretton deDraconis (brother of Aaron)
Duke Grand Marshal of the Armies of Veda

Artos deDraconis (son of Aaron)
Crown Prince of Veda

Bortis deDraconis(son of Aaron)
Prince of Veda

Carimus deDraconis (son of Aaron)
Prince of Veda

Duka deDraconis (son of Aaron)
Prince of Veda

Donel deDraconis - the Magic Man
Earl High Wizard of Veda

DEEAGLEDON

Stephan Eagledon
Count Eagledon

Stephanie Naurfindl ne'deEagledon (*deceased*)
Viscountess deEagledon
(elder twin sister to Stephan by 13 minutes)

Renee Eagledon ne'deHerndar (wife of Stephan)
Countess Eagledon

Jon deEagledon (brother of Stephan)
Baron deEagledon

Alan deEagledon (son of Stephan)
Viscount deEagledon

Elaine deEagledon (twin sister to Ellis)
Viscountess deEagledon

Samuel deEagledon (son of Stephan)
Viscount deEagledon

Juneau deEagledon (daughter of Stephan)
Viscountess deEagledon

DEPENRODYN

Estel Penrodyn
Count Penrodyn

Ravena Penrodyn ne'deHerndar (*deceased*)
Countess Penrodyn

Walter dePenrodyn (son of Estel)
Viscount dePenrodyn

Ruth Diana dePenrodyn ne'deDarrellyel
Viscountess dePenrodyn (wife of Walter)

Johan dePenrodyn (son of Estel)
Viscount dePenrodyn

Katlyn dePenrodyn (daughter of Walter)
Viscountess dePenrodyn

Marx dePenrodyn (son of Walter)
Viscount dePenrodyn

Violeot dePenrodyn (daughter of Walter)
Viscountess dePenrodyn

Roberta dePenrodyn (daughter of Walter)
Viscountess dePenrodyn

DEANSON

Boris Anson
Count Anson

Yanet Anson ne'deHerndar
Countess Anson

Kramer deAnson (son of Boris)
Viscount deAnson

Floyd deAnson (son of Winston)
Viscount deAnson

Viki deAnson (daughter of Winston)
Viscountess deAnson

DeHerndar

Charlton Herndar
Count Herndar

Annis Herndar ne'deAnson (wife of Charlton) (*deceased*)
Countess Herndar

Fredrick deHerndar (son of Charlton)
Viscount deHerndar

Jaccque deHerndar (son of Charlton)
Viscount deHerndar

Pitor deHerndar (son of Charlton)
Viscount deHerndar

Liza deHerndar (daughter of Charlton)
Viscountess deHerndar

DeDarrellyel

Glendon Darrellyel
Count Darrellyel

Yasbeth Darrellyel ne'deSpryngdal (wife of Glendon)
Countess Darrellyel

Tenna Fey deDarrellyel (sister of Glendon) (Druid)
Priestess of the Green Bough

Yoshua deDarrellyel (son of Glendon)
Viscount deDarrellyel

Seth deDarrellyel (son of Glendon)(Druid)
Priest of the Green Bough

Brandigim deDarrellyel (daughter of Darrell) (Druid)
Priestess of the Green Bough

DESPRYNGDAL

Maria Spryngdal
Countess Spryngdal

Rubyia deSpryngdal (daughter of Maria)
Viscountess deSpryngdal

Cassia deSpryngdal (daughter of Rubyia)
Viscountess deSpryngdal

Persons of Interest

Castle Draconis Guards, Staffs, Etc.

Guards

Captain General Daneel derDraconis
Marshal of Castle Draconis

Captain Jarid derDraconis
Captain of the Gatehouse Guards

Sargent Ian McArn
Captain of the Eyrie Guards

Corporal Shawn Dorime
Corporal of the Eyrie Guards

Staff

Elaer Prindar (half Fairborn)
Tutor to the Princes

Agnes Dorime (Widowed mother of Shawn)
Cook (pastry chief)

The Church of the Four

Pietro Neubre (Grand Bishop of Quai)
Canon of the Sect of the Sky

Stanley Aubrie (Great Druid of Veda)
Cantor of the Sect of the Earth

The Fairborn

Farnir Naurfindl
King of the Fairborn

Claudian Naurfindl
Queen of the Fairborn

Meldien Naurfindl (younger brother of Farnir)
Prince

Andune Naurfindl (eldest son of Farnir)
Fairborn Prince (removed from the royal line)

Tirinvo Naurfindl (second son of Farnir)
Fairborn Crown Prince

Jaek Ka'Naurf (liegeman of Tirinvo)
cousin to the royal house

Varyan Beiniot` (Bard to the royal house)
cousin to the royal house

Angela Andunsuruessa (daughter of Andune)
not recognized by the royal house

Kaerin Arastina
senior Daughter of the Wind

Joycel Arastina (Kearin's younger sister)
a Daughter of the Wind

THE DAUGHTERS OF THE WIND

Angela Andunsuruessa
Leader of the Daughters of the Wind

Kaerin Arastina

Joycel Arastina (Kearin's younger sister)

Catlyn Petrie

Susi Petrie (Catlyn's younger sister)

Vixen Fauntaneer (Sarah)

Ava Fauntaneer (Vixen's younger sister)

Rachel Symtth

Sherri Lucarn

ARCHDEMONS

Demigoran
Imprisoned in the Hellesgate

Tiameng
In exile in Renn

Yeenaghou
Whereabouts unknown (presumed deceased)

THE FIVE ABOMINATIONS

Tomung
Leader of the Five - Lt. to Demigoran

Mohattri
Lt. to Tomung

Anndr

Babich

Kargyn

ESPRO
THE FAIRBORN LANGUAGE

Short sword - *Sinta ecet*

Pain-stick - *Naeg-nast*

Why are you here - *Whime arae tye símen?*

Who are you - *Man arae tye?*

I am - *Ni ame*

And - *ar (or) a*

I challenge you - *Ni challarge tye*

Honor has been questioned, who will answer? - *Nohor ncas brin quintarè, man indóme ocerato?*

I stand for my honor; I pay homage to you, Lord Andune - *Ni termáre an mime nohor, Ni paime nohmage ana tye, héru Andune*

Poison-Sumac - *Sae-Sangwa*

Human - *Orqui*

Beastmen - *Orch*

Bodyguard - *rúatan hrondo tíri*

Stop - *Dar*

Sun rise - *amrún anor*

Awaken - *echuiv*

Sun - *anor*

Dagger - *Sicil*

Starstone Tower - *Nénarambal Tirion*

Abomination - *Sauraonna*

Duel of Honor - *Dala Ath Emar*

Dueling ring - *corin dala rind*

Man wolf - *Rúatan ráca*

In the name of my sister - *esse i esse -o mime seler*

In the name of The Mother - *esse i esse -o i amil*

My - *mime*

The - *I*

Name - *esse*

Stone - *ambal*

Blue Water - *Vindya nen*

Good Day - *Mára amaurea*

Tree home - *Nimloth bar*

Come to the light - *Tul ana i kal*

Welcome - *galad*

Seeker/student at Fairinhorst - *Deshika*

Cup - *Yulma*

Please place me within the pod - *Im anír- cin na near nin ine i pode*

Silver tie - *Telepse taeth*

Spirit World (Quantum Realm) - *Tavári Ambar*

THE RUNES OF REGALOS

THE QULANS:

White — Spirit, Blue — Mind, Red — Body, Green — Nature

1. Mannaz	White (Red/Blue)	Self	Shape change
2. Gebo		Partnership	
3. Ansuz	Blue	Communication	Mindspeak/ Farsee
4. Othila		Separation	
5. Uruz	Red (White/Blue)	Strength	Strength
6. Perth			
7. Nauthiz	Blue (White/Red)	Constraint	
8. Inguz			
9. Eihwaz	Red (White/Blue)	Defense	Shield
10. Algiz	White (Blue/Red)	Protection	Mindshield
11. Fehu			
12. Wunjo			
13. Jera	Green	Harvest	
14. Kano	Red (White/Blue)	Clarity	Flame/Truth Sense
15. Tiewaz	Red (White/Blue)	Warrior	

16. Birca	Green (White/Blue/Red)	Growth	Healing
17. Ehwaz	Blue (White)	Movement	Farseeing
18. Laguz	Green (White/Blue)		
19. Hagaluz	Green (White/Blue/Red)	Disruption	Destruction
20. Raido	Blue (Red)	Journey	Swift Travel
21. Thurisaz			
22. Dagaz	White (Green)	Breakthrough	Light
23. Isa	Green	Standstill	Ice
24. Sowela	White (Blue/Red/Green)	Completeness	Wholeness
25. Skjebne	White (Red/Blue)	Destiny	

THE TIERS OF ENLIGHTENMENT AT FAIRINHORST

1st tier seeker – green tunic with a green sash

2nd tier seeker – red tunic with a red sash

3rd tier seeker – blue tunic with a blue sash

4th tier seeker – white tunic with a white sash

5th tier enlightened one – white tunic with a green sash

6th tier enlightened one – white tunic with a red sash

7th tier enlightened one – white tunic with a blue sash

8th tier enlightened one – white tunic with a rainbow sash

ACKNOWLEDGMENTS

The team at diyMFA:

Gabriela Pereira - My first mentor, who has guided me from the beginning.
Jeanette Smith - Who first lessons added so much to the starting of my book.
Jenn Walton - early readings and advice.
Laura Highcove - early readings and advice.
AK Nevermore - pure spunk

The team at The Book Incubator:

Mary Adkins
Liz Pickart
Harrison Gale
Gayle Brown
Ashley Strosnider
Lucas Schaefer

The Team at Paper Raven Books:

Morgan Gist Macdonald
Megan Buttaro
Brianna Shaffery
Rachel Yoldi

Christine Roberts

Charlotte Zang

M.A. Hinkle (my *Fantastic* developmental editor)

Brian Dooley

Colleen Tomlinson

My Beta readers:

Theresa Cross - my alpha beta

Mitch Howard - also my first line editor.

Pam Warren

Ed Daniel

C. William (Bill) Heinowski

Darrell Hopper

The Glory Road
Book Three:

Song
of the
Owl

PRELUDE

HOPE

9/14/1971 ar

PRINCESS HOPE CRACKED OPEN THE DOOR to her quarters and peeked down the hallway. The coast was clear, not a soul in sight. Not that she expected there to be anyone there, but her mother, Queen Serene, had left the palace along with her newest consort, and she was known to have extra-protective notions sometimes. Hope wouldn't have been overly surprised to see a pair of royal guards patrolling the hall where the suites for the two princesses were located. It wouldn't have foiled her plans by any means, but it would have been a slight nuisance.

She slipped out of her rooms and started walking softly down the hall.

"Where do you think you are going, Princess Hope?" came a voice behind her, causing her to jump and look around quickly.

"Destiny! Don't do that. You startled me out of a year's growth." It was her sister, watching from the door to her suite with a knowing grin on her face.

"Mother says you're growing up too fast anyway, so it's all good."

"Serene wants us to stay her little girls forever. She doesn't like to admit we are both in our twenties now, even though it's obvious that you are an old crone. I, however, am still young and beautiful. Everyone always says so."

"Yes, I'm the smart one. You're my beautiful but dumb stepsister."

"I'm just as smart as you are." She gave her head a quick shake, tumbling her dark hair around her shoulders. "I just don't keep my nose buried in a book every minute, that's all."

"Well, if I'm an old crone, then you are, too. I'm only a few months older than you are, after all."

Hope stamped her foot. "I am not!"

Destiny crossed her arms and frowned. "You are too!"

The two girls burst out laughing. The adopted daughters of Queen Serene were both lovely young ladies and close friends, although Destiny thought Hope was too rash and often acted blindly without thinking things through. Hope, on the other hand, thought Destiny was far too cautious and thus lost out on a great many opportunities for fun.

"You never answered my question, Hope. Where are you going, and what mischief are you about to get into?"

"I thought you went with Mother and Panther this morning," said Hope, deflecting the question yet again. "Why aren't you up at Vampieer?"

"I'm not bloodthirsty like you, Hope. You know I don't like the Games. They're bloody and boring. I'm surprised you're here and not there. Wasn't Seth fighting today?"

"So what? He'll win his fights; he always does. And besides, I have an experiment to try. Something I read about in a book. So there, Miss Smarty-Bookworm."

"Uh-oh, and you waited till Serene wasn't here. That's not good."

"Serene knows I practice magic. So do you. She knows we both do."

"Of course she does. She taught us. She set boundaries too, which makes me think you are going to do something she wouldn't allow if she were here. Now the question is, should I come and try to keep you out of trouble, or should I get the heck out of the palace before you bring it down around our ears?"

"That earthquake wasn't my fault; I just sneezed at a bad time. Besides, it was just a little tremor. Serene thought it was funny."

"She isn't here if you sneeze today."

"She wouldn't want me to try this spell … not because it's too dangerous," she added quickly, seeing her sister was about to object. "But because she thinks we should stay little girls forever."

"What kind of spell are you thinking of?" Destiny crossed her arms. "Are you going to summon an elemental or something?"

"No. Of course not," Hope shook her head. "Elementals are dangerous. I wouldn't try that unless Mother were here. I had a vision … well, it was a dream. But I'm sure it was true. I was with this handsome young man. Now I'm going to use one of Mother's circles to locate him."

"Just to locate him?" Destiny looked extremely skeptical. "Nothing more than that? Are you sure?"

"Maybe … probably. I'm just curious. Mostly."

"Hmmm." Destiny looked doubtful. "So we're just going to look at some handsome man. You are just going to scry, then?"

Hope turned away and continued down the hall. "That's all … probably."

Destiny sighed and joined her sister.

Hope led the way to the main hallway and then walked past

the master stairwell to a small, nondescript door that looked as though it led to a servants' pathway, but was in reality the door to the spiral stairway that wound upwards to the short hall that led to Serene's hidden magatory, the place where she worked her secret spells. Some magic Serene cast while sitting upon her gilded throne in the center of her grand hall, but there were some spells that even a queen did not care to reveal to just anyone. Her magatory was where she worked those spells. A pair of marble gargoyles sat at the end of the hallway, their heads turning to watch the two princesses as they approached down the short hall that ran from the stairs to the blank wall at the far end.

"Your mother isn't here, Princess Hope," said the gargoyle on the left.

"You know you are not allowed to play here," said the one on the right.

"Oh, pooh," said Hope. "We aren't children anymore, Ferdinand. Destiny and I have our own Barony's now. Queen Serene is away at Vampieer, and I need to gather a few things she forgot. Now open the door."

The two door guardians exchanged glances and shrugged, and each reached out an arm and touched their palms together. The wall behind them shivered, and an archway with double doors appeared.

Hope pushed open the doors, and the two sisters walked through the opening into Queen Serene's magatory. The smell of mystic incense filled the air, and candles of black wax, which never grew shorter, burned in sconces around the room, filling it with a dim flickering light.

Hope walked around the runic circle inscribed upon the floor in the room's center and approached a door on the far side of the room, a door of black iron with a dull crimson square set in the center.

"Hope," said Destiny. "What are you doing? You know you can't go in there. That's where Serene's time scrying orb is. That's where she views all those creepy visions of the past. She keeps that door locked."

Hope pulled some thin black leather gloves from the pouch at her waist and put them on her hands. Smiling at her sister with a spiteful twinkle in her eye, she pulled a small silken bag from the pouch, reached in, and pulled out a key formed of crimson crystal.

"Hope!" cried Destiny. "No! You stole Mother's key. She'll be furious."

"I borrowed it," replied Hope. "I'll put it back in her room before she returns tonight. She'll never know it was gone. Unless, of course, my own sister were to snitch." Hope smiled sweetly. "Then I would have to deny it and never speak to her ever again."

"Horsefeathers," said Destiny. "You know I won't say a word. But Gustaf and Ferdinand will tell her we were here. You know they will."

"I have a little spell that will make those two forget we ever entered here," replied Hope as she took the crystal key and pushed it into the crimson square set upon the black iron door. "They'll report we came and spoke with them and then left." She grinned mischievously. "Unless you'd like for them to say you went into her room by yourself?"

The door creaked as it slowly swung open. Destiny sighed, shook her head, and followed her sister into the room beyond. A short time later, there was a distant rumble of thunder.